HOMICIDE
for the
HOLIDAYS

CHERYL HONIGFORD

sourcebooks
landmark

Published by Sourcebooks Landmark, an imprint of Sourcebooks, Inc.
P.O. Box 4410, Naperville, Illinois 60567–4410
(630) 961–3900
Fax: (630) 961–2168
www.sourcebooks.com

Library of Congress Cataloging-in-Publication Data
Names: Honigford, Cheryl, author.
Title: Homicide for the holidays / Cheryl Honigford.
Description: Naperville : Sourcebooks Landmark, [2017] | Series: [A Viv and Charlie mystery]
Identifiers: LCCN 2017014664 | (trade pbk. : alk. paper)
Subjects: LCSH: Radio actors and actresses--Fiction. | Radio serials--Fiction. | Murder--Investigation--Fiction. | GSAFD: Mystery fiction. | Historical fiction.
Classification: LCC PS3608.O4945 H66 2017 | DDC 813/.6--dc23 LC record available at https://lccn.loc.gov/2017014664

Printed and bound in the United States of America.
VP 10 9 8 7 6 5 4 3 2 1

Also by Cheryl Honigford

The Darkness Knows

For
Mom—who took me to the library on Wednesday nights
(and any other time I asked)
and
Dad—who lugged the old Underwood typewriter out to the
dining room table so I could hunt and peck out my first stories

CHAPTER ONE

---◆---

December 23, 1938

Joy to the world and all that rot, Vivian thought. She tossed a handful of tinsel on the towering spruce in the corner of the den and sighed. The last thing she wanted to do was put on a happy face for her mother's Christmas party, but that was precisely what she was expected to do this evening.

"You missed a spot."

"Hmm?"

"Right there." Vivian's younger brother, Everett, nodded his auburn head toward a gaping swath of green near right front center. It was the only spot on the eight-foot tree that Vivian hadn't managed to cover in gaudy silver tinsel. She dipped her hand in the box, grabbed a handful of the shiny strands, and tossed them haphazardly at the void.

Everett glanced sidelong at her, one eyebrow raised.

"Say, Mrs. Claus. Who curdled your cream?"

Vivian sighed and dropped the box of tinsel to the floor.

"I don't know about you, but this party is the last thing I want to be doing tonight. Especially when Mother's invited her new…her new…" She flapped her hand as she searched her mind for an appropriate word for her mother's new companion, Oskar Heigel. Stray bits of tinsel floated lazily from her fingers to the Oriental rug.

Everett watched her with a frown. "Boyfriend?" he supplied.

Vivian wrinkled her nose.

"I know," he said. "It's absurd."

Vivian knew he meant both the idea and the term. Everett, five years younger than Vivian, was a sophomore at Northwestern. She didn't see him often, but Vivian was glad he was home now. He was the only one that could possibly understand how uncomfortable this situation made her. Their mother expressing romantic interest in a man other than their father was awkward, and it seemed sudden, somehow, even nearly eight years after their father's death.

Everett shrugged, then leaned down to fit the plug into the socket. The blue, green, and red lights strung around the tree blinked to life. Everett swept his arm out in a *ta-da* motion. Then he stood back and eyed their handiwork with a critical air. "Well, what do you think?"

Vivian blew air out over her protruding bottom lip, ruffling her bangs.

"I think it's a garish spectacle," she said.

"Well, you know Mother's motto. The Bigger the Better."

Vivian laughed in spite of her mood. That was true. When it came to Christmas trees, their mother favored the grand. But this year's specimen was frankly ridiculous. It had been delivered that morning by two burly men who'd dragged it through the house, trailing needles everywhere. They'd had to saw off the bottom two feet to make it fit, and it still brushed the plaster ceiling.

She leaned forward and inhaled deeply. It did smell heavenly though: pine and sap and the earthy dampness of thawing mud. That smell brought every Christmas of her childhood to the surface of her memory in an instant.

"It was Father's fault," Everett said. "Indulging her like that with her very first tree. Set a bad precedent."

Vivian followed her brother's eyes to their mother, who was fussing at the refreshment table on the other side of the room. If Vivian wanted any indication of how she would look in twenty-odd years, she need look no further than Julia Witchell. Vivian had inherited her mother's petite stature, her strawberry-blond hair, and her soft brown eyes. It wasn't a terrible prospect, honestly.

People often said they looked more like sisters than mother and daughter—much to Julia's pleasure and Vivian's chagrin. But her mother's outwardly pleasant face belied a fierceness of character and a tendency toward perfectionism that was most often aimed squarely at Vivian—though others often found themselves in the crosshairs. Vivian watched as her mother pointed an accusing finger at the tray of hors d'oeuvres. The target of her mother's displeasure at the moment appeared to be the housekeeper, Mrs. Graves.

"The Christmas Tree Ship," Vivian said, turning back to the tree. Their father had loved to tell that story. He'd taken their mother down to the docks on the Chicago River the first year they were married to pick out their tree from the decks of the famous ship itself. That old-fashioned schooner had trolled the waters of Lake Michigan every fall to make its way to northern Wisconsin and fill itself to bursting with Christmas pines. According to the oft-told story, their mother had roamed the deck for a solid hour before picking a giant tree that proved almost impossible to get home to the small apartment they were renting at the time. But their father couldn't refuse her. He said he could never refuse their mother anything.

Vivian blinked away the tears that sprang suddenly to her eyes. She missed her father, never more than at this time of year. She reached out and brushed her fingers against one of the glass icicles hanging on the tip of the branch closest to her. It swayed under her fingertips, sparkling in the lights. She realized too late that her touch had been too forceful. The icicle rocked dangerously, then slid from the branch and fell to the floor with a crash. She flinched, waiting for a sharp rebuke from her mother.

None came. Vivian slowly opened her eyes and unclenched her fists. She glanced over her shoulder, but her mother was no longer fussing with the canapés. She'd left the room before the crash. Vivian and Everett looked at each other in relief.

"Don't worry about it, Viv. You know the saying: 'You have to break a few ornaments to make a Christmas,'" Everett said.

She rolled her eyes at his lame attempt at a joke. "I believe that's eggs and omelets."

"I'll get the broom," he said.

"No, I'll get it. It's my mess."

She strode across the room before Everett could dissuade her. Cleaning up would keep her mind off the party. But as she drew closer to the kitchen, she could hear her mother's voice raised in irritation. Her mother was prickly at the best of times, but preparing for her parties always brought out the worst in her. And her mother's worst was something Vivian didn't want to touch with a ten-foot pole. *Best to avoid the situation entirely*, Vivian thought.

She doubled back to the front staircase and hopped up to the second floor. She'd just grab a broom from the second-floor utility closet, she thought. But she paused on the landing, her eyes falling on the closed door of her father's study at the top of the stairs. Her heart clenched suddenly, and before she could think too deeply about what she was doing or why, she opened the study door and stepped inside, closing the door behind her with a soft click.

The study was dark and quiet. It smelled male, of tobacco

and leather bindings. Vivian stood there for a moment, leaning against the door in the dark and intending just to pause long enough to gather her strength before the party began in earnest.

The only light in the room came from the distant streetlamp outside. It was faint, but her eyes followed it to what it illuminated: a picture frame sitting on the top of the bookcase. Her spirit lifted immediately at the sight of it, and she crossed the room to fetch the frame from the shelf. She smiled down on the contents: a tattered paper Saint Nicholas ornament she'd made as a child. Despite its homeliness, her father had loved it so much he'd had it framed and placed where he could see it all year round.

She touched her fingertips to the glass, remembering the day she had given him the ornament. The Christmas of 1918 when she was almost five, her father had nearly died from the Spanish flu, though she hadn't known that at the time. She remembered handing her father the Saint Nicholas shyly, afraid of looking straight at him. She hadn't seen him since he'd fallen ill two weeks earlier, and the wasted man lost in the bedclothes looked very little like the large, strapping father she'd always known. But then he'd smiled weakly at that ornament, at her—and Vivian's heart broke a little recalling it even now, almost twenty years later.

She wanted this reminder of him, of what they'd shared as father and daughter, back on the Christmas tree where it belonged. She turned the frame over, removed the pins, and pulled off the backing. As she did, something flashed in the dim light and fell to the floor with a clatter. Vivian crouched and squinted into the darkness. She saw nothing with the first few sweeps of her eyes, but then there it was—just the tip sticking out from underneath the radiator. A tiny silver key.

CHAPTER TWO

---◆---

Vivian had kept all manner of secrets from her father, but she'd never suspected he'd kept any from her—until now. She stared at the tiny key in her palm and then glanced around the study. It had to open something in here, but what? She switched on the desk lamp to see better, moved to the filing cabinet, and pressed the tip of the key to the lock at the top. She expected it to slide in easily. When it didn't, she wiggled it, turned it upside down, and tried again. No, it definitely didn't fit. Her eyes scanned the room again and finally fell upon the large mahogany desk in front of her. Of course.

She sat in the desk chair and slipped the key into the drawer lock. She turned it, and with an audible click, it opened. Her palms grew sweaty, her stomach sour. It was ridiculous, she told herself. Her father had had nothing to hide. But if he'd had nothing to hide, why had he locked this drawer and hidden the key so well that no one was able to find it until now, so long after his death? She swallowed and pulled the drawer open before she lost her nerve.

It was empty. She tugged again on the pull, tipping the drawer down slightly.

No, not quite empty.

The large white envelope that had been wedged in the back appeared with a soft ripping noise. A tear had opened down the side, and the distinctive green of currency peeked through. Vivian leaned in closer to discern what was scrawled in pencil near the bottom right corner. *A. W. Racquet.* She glanced toward the doorway, the sounds of laughter and music becoming louder as guests arrived at the Christmas party downstairs. Her eyes swept the room, then caught on the framed photo of her mother on the desk. Vivian's heart pounded as she pulled the envelope out and lifted the unsealed flap. Inside lay a thick wad of neatly stacked bills. She passed a thumb over them, listening to the muted whir of more cash than she'd ever held in her hands at one time before.

Then her thumb caught on the very last bit of paper. It was thicker than the bills and a cream color that, at first glance, blended in with the back of the envelope. Vivian slid it out halfway, and her eyes darted over the sentence scrawled on it in pencil: *Talk and you lose everything.*

Terror trailed icy fingers down her spine—a visceral memory of reading similar words directed at her only a few months ago. Her hands started to shake, the envelope rattling. But Vivian couldn't tear her eyes away from those words. The note was not addressed, and it was unsigned. She flipped the paper over, but it was blank on the opposite side. The edges were torn, as if it had been written in haste and ripped from a larger piece of paper. She read the sentence twice, a third time, but it still made little sense. It was obviously a threat. But had her father been threatening someone else, or had someone been threatening him?

A floorboard squeaked in the hallway outside. Vivian shoved the cash and the note back into the envelope, dropping it back into the drawer before locking it. Her fingers slid down the dark-green velvet of her gown and over the smooth surface of her matching bolero jacket. *Dash it all, no pockets.* The doorknob rattled and began to turn. Vivian pulled the bodice of her dress away from her chest and deftly tucked the key under the edge of her brassiere. A split second later, the study door opened and Everett's head poked into the room.

"There you are," he said. His eyes flicked over the desk and the disassembled picture frame upon it. "What are you doing in here?"

Vivian forced a smile, her heart hammering in her chest. She scanned Everett's face, but she could read nothing among the freckles except mild curiosity. Her instinct had always been to keep everything close to the vest with him. He wasn't a scabby-kneed kid anymore, but he had a long history of being indiscreet, as younger brothers often do. Her head was spinning, running through the many possible meanings of what she had found. She couldn't have him announcing in the middle of the family Christmas party that she'd managed to open her father's long-locked drawer and had found a stack of cash and an ominous note.

"I came to get this," she said. She snatched the old paper ornament from the disassembled frame and held it up.

Everett's brow wrinkled. "And what exactly is that?"

Vivian looked down at the treasured ornament. Old Saint Nick had seen better days—but not much better. She'd never been much of an artist, even at five years old. He was sun-faded and tattered, the red of his suit bleached a dusky pink, the tinsel on the end of his cap ragged and sparse. Still, her father had thought so much of the ornament that he'd had it framed shortly before his death. *And then he hid the key to his desk drawer in the frame's backing*, she thought. Her stomach twisted.

"It's Saint Nicholas, of course," she said.

Everett raised his eyebrows.

"You made me think of it with all your reminiscing about Father and Christmas past," Vivian went on, touching the scrap of remaining tinsel with her fingertip. "I thought I should free him from his frame and put him back on the tree where he belongs."

Everett shrugged, frowning at her childish handiwork. "That thing hardly seems worth the trouble."

Vivian grabbed a pencil from the cup that sat on the blotter and chucked it at him. He laughed as it glanced harmlessly off his shoulder.

"Anyway," he said as he straightened up, his face mock

serious. "I came to inform you, Miss Witchell, that guests have started to arrive and your absence downstairs has been noted by management."

Vivian rolled her eyes. The annual Christmas party was their mother's crowning achievement. The entire family should be present and accounted for at all times. They must put on a united front.

"Come on," Everett said, cocking his head toward the stairway with a smirk. He waggled his bronze eyebrows at her. "Mrs. Graves has whipped up a new batch of eggnog, and she's been pretty heavy-handed with the bourbon."

Vivian coughed as the liquor burned her throat. Heavy-handed was right, she thought, eyeing the elderly housekeeper across the crowded living room. Mrs. Graves was chatting with Oskar, her mother's…well, her mother's new friend. Oskar was on the far side of middle age, with a steel-gray handlebar mustache and a noticeable paunch. Her mother had spoken of him before, but this was the first time Vivian had been introduced. She hadn't had a chance to exchange more than two words with him, but she knew he was some sort of financier from Switzerland.

Mrs. Witchell beamed from her place at Oskar's side, and Vivian felt a twinge of guilt at begrudging her mother a little happiness. Her mother hadn't seen anyone romantically since her husband's death, and almost eight years was a long time for anyone to go without a little companionship.

Vivian gazed at the Saint Nicholas ornament now hanging on the towering, tinseled fir and frowned. She could feel the weight of the little key pressed firmly against the skin of her breast, the jagged edge making indentations in her soft flesh with every inhale of breath. This key, the money, the secrecy. What could it mean?

"Uh-oh. I know that look."

Vivian turned to her best friend, Imogene, who had sidled up to her. Vivian forced a smile. "What look?"

"The *something's in my way* look." Imogene stared at her, the corners of her mouth turned down.

Vivian smiled and held her hands out to the crackling fire, even though the air in the crowded room was stifling. She glanced sidelong at Imogene and found her staring in expectation. Vivian sighed. Imogene was right. There *was* something in her way—a locked drawer full of cash and the sudden niggling suspicion that her father had been up to no good.

"I can't go into it here," she whispered. "But I just found something strange in my father's study."

"Stranger than this?" Imogene reached out and tugged on Saint Nicholas's paper boot, releasing the pungent scent of the north woods from the branches of the tree. Vivian glanced around to make sure no one else was within earshot.

"Like a locked drawer full of cash strange."

"Locked?"

"Eight years locked. We all thought the key had been lost." They'd searched for weeks for that key, turning the house upside down. They'd finally given up, and Vivian had forgotten all about that locked desk drawer—until tonight.

"And it's full of cash?"

Vivian nodded.

Imogene narrowed her eyes. "Hmm… Sounds like the beginning of a *Darkness Knows* episode."

"It does, doesn't it?"

"Maybe you should call Harvey Diamond."

Vivian glanced over her shoulder at Graham Yarborough, who stood on the opposite side of the room chatting with one of her mother's society friends. Harvey Diamond was Graham's fictional alter ego on the radio program *The Darkness Knows*. He and Vivian starred in the popular program together—though Vivian's character got to do little more than fall into trouble and scream for Harvey to save her.

"Not *that* Harvey Diamond," Imogene said. "The real one."

The real one, Vivian thought. Charlie Haverman's smirking, angular face sprang to mind, and Viv's stomach flip-flopped. Charlie's real capers as a private detective had been the inspiration for Graham's fictional ones. He'd even been a consultant to *The Darkness Knows* for a time. True, Charlie could help her get to the bottom of this—if it was anything at all. The problem was that she hadn't heard from Charlie in almost two months, not since they had investigated Marjorie Fox's murder at the station, not since they… Vivian flushed thinking about the night she and Charlie had spent together.

"What are you two whispering about?"

Vivian turned to find Graham smiling down at her, his deep-brown eyes twinkling.

"Oh, nothing," Imogene said, shooting a glance at Vivian. "Christmas memories."

Vivian cleared her throat. "Speaking of Christmas past, isn't the *Carol* on?" Listening to the dramatization of *A Christmas Carol* starring Lionel Barrymore had become a tradition for people all over the country during the past few years.

Graham said, "Yes, but they have Reginald Owen doing it this year instead of Barrymore. Your mother's got some choir from Lincoln Center on anyway." He jerked a thumb toward the tall radio cabinet standing on the far side of the den and mimed a yawn.

Imogene's eyes fell onto the mantel clock and widened. "Oh shoot, that *is* the time, isn't it? I have to go. I'm headed to a late dinner with George's family, and I have to change my dress…fix my hair… Oof." She patted the perfectly set dark wave over her ear. "Sorry, Viv." She leaned over and gave Vivian a hug and a kiss on the cheek. "How about you meet me for some last-minute shopping tomorrow?" she said sotto voce. "You can fill me in on everything then, and tell me about any detectives you may or may not have contacted."

Vivian rolled her eyes and turned to watch Imogene go. *A whirlwind in a skirt*, she thought with a smirk.

Graham cocked his head to one side. "Say, you play the piano, don't you? We could get some caroling started—liven this place up a little."

"Oh no." Vivian shook her head. "I never got past the scales. I have horrible memories of having my knuckles rapped by old Mrs. Crenshaw when I deigned to hit the wrong key."

"Poor girl." Graham's dark eyes sparkled as his face lit with a grin. A lock of his thick, black hair fell over his forehead, and Vivian resisted the sudden impulse to brush it back with her fingers. He was matinee-idol handsome, the chiseled planes of his face dark perfection. *Graham Yarborough is any woman's dream*, Vivian thought absently. *Any woman but me.* Even so, when he teased her in that husky baritone as he just did, Vivian felt an echo of the attraction she'd once felt for him, and she almost forgot they were only playing at being sweethearts.

"Maybe we can persuade Everett," she said. "He was always so much better with his lessons. Longer fingers…" she said, holding her own hands out and wiggling her small digits.

They both looked toward the divan where Everett was cozying up to his new girlfriend. He'd mentioned her, but Vivian couldn't recall the girl's name. She was another student at Northwestern, and likely the reason Everett had been so busy and away from home so often since the term started.

"Actually, I don't think we're going to be able to pry him away from that warm embrace anytime soon," Vivian said, sighing. "How about I put on a record?"

"And how about I bring you a refill?"

She'd drained the glass of eggnog without realizing it. So it wasn't only the questions about her father that had her head spinning, she thought. But Graham seemed not to notice. He winked, took her empty glass, and headed in the direction of the punch bowl.

Vivian turned to the extensive record collection housed in a glass-enclosed bookcase. Her mother's taste in music was decidedly more staid than her own. Vivian flipped through various renditions of chorale ensembles, searching for something, anything, recorded in the past ten years. She'd nearly given up hope when she spied Guy Lombardo's version of "Walking in a Winter Wonderland." That would do for a start.

She pulled the shellac disc from its paper sleeve, held the edges with the tips of her fingers, and blew any dust off the platter before placing it atop the spindle on the record player. She dropped the needle and smiled with satisfaction as the jaunty sounds of Guy Lombardo and His Royal Canadians poured through the horn-shaped speaker.

She crossed her arms and listened, letting her eyes range over the Christmas cards displayed on the mantel above the crackling fire. She opened one idyllic country snow scene to find *Freddy and Pauline* scrawled inside in a tight, neat hand—most likely bought, signed, and sent by Freddy's loyal secretary, Della. Uncle Freddy, as Vivian had called him almost her entire life, had shared an office with her father in the Rookery downtown for nearly fifteen years. She wrinkled her brow as she placed the card back on the mantel. Surely Freddy Endicott had been invited to the party tonight. He was always invited, but she hadn't yet heard his booming laugh ring out from the crowd.

"I'm a big fan."

Vivian jumped and turned to find Everett's girlfriend hovering near the phonograph. Someone had broken that warm embrace after all.

The girl continued in a breathless undertone. "I know Everett wouldn't want me to say anything like that. It would embarrass him no end to have me fawning all over you, but I wanted to tell you that…I truly admire your work." The girl stuttered to a stop and looked at Vivian with wide blue eyes.

"Well, thank you," Vivian said, searching her memory desperately for the girl's name. She lowered her chin and added, "And don't worry. I won't tell Everett."

The girl laughed and touched her fingertips to the hollow below her throat. Vivian took in the delicate orchid charm dangling from a dainty gold chain a few inches above the neckline of the girl's dress. "Everett's Christmas gift," the girl said before Vivian could ask. "Isn't it lovely?"

Vivian nodded. "Lovely," she agreed. Where had Everett found the money...and the taste? He'd never had much of either, in her experience.

"You know, he told me he had an older sister named Vivian, but I guess I didn't make the connection to *The Darkness Knows* before tonight, when I heard your voice. Isn't that silly?"

"Mmm-hmm...silly." Vivian glanced over the girl's head. Where was Everett?

"Everett *also* didn't tell me Graham Yarborough would be here," the girl continued. "I'd read you two were an item, of course. Who hasn't? But I guess I hadn't expected it to be real, you know."

Vivian bristled at the word *real*. She narrowed her eyes at the girl and her open, guileless face. Then she glanced at Graham and found him engaged in animated conversation with Everett next to the punch bowl, waving her fresh glass of eggnog around enthusiastically as he spoke.

The truth, known by very few, was that Vivian and Graham's high-profile romance was most definitely not real. It had been cooked up by the station's publicity department when Vivian had started on the show two months ago, and the fans had gone gaga for the idea of the stars of their favorite detective serial becoming a couple in real life. Oh, Vivian had been attracted to Graham at first, but that was before she really knew him, before Marjorie Fox was murdered, and before Vivian suspected Graham of killing her.

Graham hadn't killed Marjorie, of course. But there was something about the way he'd reacted to the woman's murder and its aftermath that still bothered Vivian. He hadn't told her the whole truth about his relationship with Marjorie—Vivian was sure of that. Plus, Graham had shown Vivian a side of himself that he hadn't shown the rest of the world, especially his fawning, mostly female fans. He'd been cold, calculating, and shrewd—all of that lurking just under the ever-affable veneer. Vivian was always on her guard with Graham now. He still had secrets, and now she found herself perpetually waiting for the other shoe to drop—whatever that other shoe might be.

As if he had been summoned by her thoughts, Graham appeared at Vivian's side. He handed her the glass of eggnog and allowed a rakish smile to creep over his face.

"I don't believe we've been introduced," he said, extending a hand to Everett's girlfriend. "I'm Graham Yarborough."

Her cheeks bloomed a dainty rose as she shook his hand. "I know. I'm Gloria Mendel, Everett's…" She glanced at Vivian's brother, who had joined the group, glass of eggnog in hand. "Well, Everett's girl, I suppose."

Vivian almost saw Everett's chest puff with pride at the acknowledgment.

"You haven't been peppering Viv with questions about the radio business, have you?" Everett asked, putting an arm around Gloria's shoulders.

She blushed further. "It's just so exciting to a nobody like me."

"You're interested in the radio biz?" Graham asked.

"Oh, I think it's fascinating."

"Maybe you can come down to the station one of these days then, Gloria," Graham said. "Watch a show in person."

Her blue eyes widened. "Really?" she said, looking to Vivian. "That would be wonderful."

Vivian smiled. "Of course," she said. "We'd love to have you." She lifted her drink and took a long sip.

"Say," Graham said. "Speaking of the show, have you heard from Chick?"

Vivian coughed on her eggnog. "Charlie? No. Why do you ask?"

The truth was, she'd hoped to hear from Charlie. But in the last two months there'd been nothing: no calls, no visits to the radio station, no contact whatsoever. She thought of Charlie the last time she'd seen him, lying in a hospital bed, hurt, vulnerable. She thought of what he'd told her before she left. "Call me when you need me," he'd said. And she *had* called him, as soon as she'd realized what getting her job back at the station would mean—the continuation of a very public romantic relationship with Graham.

She'd been willing to chuck it all, including her fledgling career, if Charlie didn't approve. But she didn't know if Charlie approved, because he hadn't answered. When she'd called a second time, Vivian had left a message with his answering service. He hadn't returned that call either. Then Vivian had gone to his office on the south side of the Loop and found it empty. No forwarding address. Nothing. Charlie Haverman had disappeared from her life almost as if he'd never been there.

After a while, Vivian had stopped looking for him to appear in the control booth during the live broadcast of *The Darkness Knows*, stopped expecting the phone to ring. Maybe their connection had been too tenuous, forged too delicately in a time of stress. They'd only had a few days together, and once Marjorie's murder was solved, there was nothing to bind them anymore. They had nothing in common except an attraction—but for her, that attraction had been like a magnet to true north. She'd never told Graham what had happened between her and Charlie, because the detective's disappearing act had rendered that conversation moot.

"Have *you* heard from him?" She tried to sound casual and was surprised to find she'd succeeded, at least to her own ears.

Graham shook his head, and then his expression clouded. "I wish all that business hadn't happened to make him quit as our consultant. Things on the show aren't the same without him."

All that business. A funny way to refer to a murder and an attempted murder, Vivian thought. It had been the scandal of the year—if not the decade—in Chicago. Marjorie Fox, the reigning star of WCHI, had been murdered in the actors' lounge right before Halloween, and Vivian had had the misfortune of finding her body. After Vivian discovered a note that indicated she might be next on the murderer's hit list, things had gotten decidedly more complicated.

With Charlie's help, Vivian had uncovered the murderer and the fact that Marjorie Fox and Mr. Hart, the head of the station, had been Charlie's birth parents. The killer, the station head's daughter, Peggy, had not only wanted Marjorie out of the way, but also her half brother, Charlie. Vivian had saved his life in the nick of time, and now Peggy sat behind the bars of the Cook County Jail awaiting her trial for murder. In the end, Vivian couldn't blame Charlie for wanting to keep his distance from anything having to do with the station or any reminders of that time, including her.

She shook her head. What this conversation needed was a change of subject—especially since Gloria's eyes had widened with interest at the mention of "all that business at the station." Graham's clever euphemism wasn't fooling anyone.

"How's the *Pimpernel* coming?" Vivian asked Graham.

Graham's heavy brows drew together. "It's getting there, but I'm still not pleased with act 2."

Vivian turned to Gloria and Everett. "Graham's writing, directing, and starring in his own radio play of *The Scarlet Pimpernel* next Sunday evening on WCHI."

The girl's eyes widened in admiration. "Gosh, that's great."

"*The Scarlet Pimpernel…*" Everett said, forehead wrinkling. "I had to read that in school, I think. Spies and the French Revolution, or something like that?"

"Something like that," Graham said. "And Viv's starring with me. It's only a local show, but it's something," he added with a shrug.

"And who knows what it may lead to?" Vivian said, smiling up at Graham's handsome face. For *both* of them.

An insistent dinging noise made them all turn their heads toward the opposite side of the room, where Oskar stood next to the towering Christmas tree, tapping the side of his wineglass with a silver spoon. Mrs. Witchell stood at Oskar's side, her arm looped through his.

"I would like to propose a toast," he announced, his clipped Swiss German accent slight but noticeable only in that his leading Ws became Vs. "If you will indulge me, it is something of a custom where I come from to get serious and rather melancholy at a time like this…" He smiled and raised his half-full glass. "To wonderful times spent with friends and family, and to the possibilities of a new year."

They all raised their own glasses. Vivian's eyes flitted over Graham, Everett, and Gloria as she repeated, "To the possibilities of a new year." She clinked her glass against each of theirs, but Everett and Gloria now only had eyes for each other. Vivian watched as Everett took the girl's hand and pulled her off toward a secluded corner. The idea that her little brother had a girlfriend still made Vivian uncomfortable, and she turned her eyes away to find Graham studying her, a frown on his handsome face, as if she were a difficult algebra equation.

"I'm afraid I've got to be going," he said. He shrugged and smiled the blinding Graham Yarborough special that could charm the skin off a snake.

"Going? So soon?"

"I promised I'd have a fresh draft of act 2 by tomorrow morning. There's a lot of work to be done and precious little time to do it."

She followed him to the entry hall and watched as he plucked his overcoat and fedora from the overloaded coat-tree. Then he held his hat to his heart and lifted his chin. "It is with a heavy heart that I leave you, my darling," Graham announced in his foppish Percy Blakeney voice, the true identity of the Scarlet Pimpernel.

Vivian clasped hands to her heart and batted her eyelashes. "I long for your return, dearest one," she said.

He donned his coat and gloves and turned at the threshold to say, "I shall count the minutes until we are reunited at rehearsal the day after the morrow!" Then he reached for Vivian's hand and kissed the back of it before turning on his heel and springing down the snow-covered steps.

Vivian smiled and watched him stride down the sidewalk. She pulled the bolero jacket tighter around her to ward off the chill, and the smile faded as her hand again brushed against the little silver desk key tucked into her brassiere.

CHAPTER THREE

E very one of the three million residents of the city of Chicago seemed to be bustling down State Street—all elbows and sharp heels. No surprise, really; it was the eleventh hour on Christmas Eve. Well, four forty-five to be precise, and most of the department stores closed in forty-five minutes. Not an ideal time to go shopping, Vivian thought, but there was nothing for it now. She and Imogene were in the thick of the rush. In the past few hours, they had fought their way through the crush of humanity down the string of department stores: Marshall Field's southward to Mandel Brothers, Carson Pirie Scott, and The Fair, then back up again. Vivian's head throbbed and her feet ached. But there would be no rest for the weary.

Last on the shopping list was a gift for Imogene's eight-year-old nephew, so they had coasted through the revolving door of Marshall Field's and stepped off the escalator into the fourth-floor toy department. And now Vivian was pressed into a candy cane–topped display case as last-minute shoppers jostled her and Imogene dithered.

"Chemistry set," Vivian said decisively. "All little boys want chemistry sets."

But Imogene's brow only furrowed in response as her brown eyes darted between the chemistry set and a board game called Camelot.

Vivian sighed and glanced down at her feet. She should have worn more sensible shoes. Her toes were pinched, and the three-inch heels were doing her arches no favors. All she wanted to do was sit down—at least for a few moments. She glanced around, wincing at the sharp pain in the balls of her feet as she forced herself up on tiptoes to see over the crowd. There had to be a place to sit somewhere in this melee.

She poked Imogene's shoulder.

"I'm off to find a chair before I collapse from exhaustion," Vivian said. "Come get me when you're finished."

Imogene waved a hand in acknowledgment without looking up and worried her lower lip with her teeth.

Vivian wove in and out of the curving glass display cases, her eyes flicking from dolls to stuffed animals to board games. *Toys, toys as far as the eye could see, but not a chair in sight.* As she walked, Vivian found herself following a line of children and parents as she wound through the aisles. The line ended at an elaborate stage set with Santa's Village proclaimed on the sign hanging above.

Santa himself stood on a raised platform along with his sleigh. There were no chairs here either, but there was a railing to lean against, and that was better than nothing. Vivian placed her packages on the floor at her feet and leaned on the barrier separating the platform from the excited children. It was nearing closing time now, and the sense of anticipation was palpable. Childish whispers and giggles filled the air. Santa's voice boomed as he greeted a new group.

"Merry Christmas, children!"

A boy of about three with intensely serious dark eyes and a little girl no more than six, who could only be his sister, took their places in the sleigh next to the store's Santa Claus. They were still bundled in their matching red-plaid winter coats and scarves. They'd apparently been marched right from the street to the fourth floor by their harried mother, who stood ten feet away, a Brownie camera clutched to her midriff as she peered through the viewfinder on the top of the case. The children stood stiffly, their eyes carefully averted as if looking directly at Santa might make him disappear like a distant star in the night sky. Smiles were plastered to their wind-chapped faces.

Vivian couldn't help but smile herself as her eyes ranged over the tableau. Marshall Field's spared no expense. Santa's suit was a plush red velvet; the cuffs, real fur. His long, white beard wasn't real, but it was lush and full and snowy white. His sleigh was an ornately carved wooden affair, a large bag overflowing with wrapped gifts resting in the back. The coursers reined to Santa's sleigh were real taxidermied reindeer, complete with jingle-belled harnesses, she realized.

They were posed with one front hoof raised as if they were about to leap into the sky at any moment.

Vivian's eyes strayed to those still in line, tiny bright-eyed boys and girls hopping from foot to foot in breathless anticipation. Their eyes sparkled with wonder. And why wouldn't they? This place was wondrous, and these kids had well-heeled parents able to whisk them to the Loop to visit this fantastical wonderland. These kids were certain to find what they'd asked for under the tree tomorrow morning, with or without Santa's intervention.

Then Vivian's thoughts turned to children on the opposite end of the spectrum. She'd thought of the Chicago Foundlings Home often since she'd visited with Charlie a few months back—especially after she'd learned that Charlie had been one of those children left long ago on the home's doorstep. Though he hadn't been wanted by his birth parents, he had been wanted. He'd been adopted as an infant and raised in a loving, stable home. That alone made him luckier than most. Not all the children found a home—especially those with sickness or a deformity. Vivian had found her mind straying to thoughts of those little forgotten ones at this time of year. They had no parents, no families at all. Who would make sure they got something under the tree?

Her mind had stuck fast to that question over the past few weeks. She couldn't shake it or the sick feeling in her stomach. So she'd taken matters into her own hands and brought Santa

Claus to see the home's children the week before. She'd
arranged it with Sister Bernadine beforehand, of course, and
roped Joe McGreevey from the radio station into playing the
part of Santa. He was the only man she knew with suitable
enough roundness to his belly to truly fill out the rented suit.

Vivian had paid for it all herself and told no one. She'd
sworn Joe to secrecy. She knew she could've gotten publicity
for it, kudos for her generosity in the papers, but the idea felt
hollow to her. The Christmas party was for the children and
not to further her career. She'd only had enough money to
buy one small gift for each child, but the memory of all those
little faces so ecstatically happy at receiving that one paltry gift
had made her heart clench in equal parts sadness and joy.

"Adorable little ankle biters."

Vivian blinked out of her reverie and looked to Imogene,
who'd sidled up to her. Vivian glanced toward the box in
Imogene's hands.

"So what did you end up with?"

Imogene held the box up so that Vivian could see the
picture of a cabin on the front. "Lincoln Logs," she said
with a note of triumph in her voice. "Sure to be scattered
under every piece of furniture in my sister's home by New
Year's Eve."

Vivian laughed. She'd attached the silver desk key to a string
and had been wearing it around her neck all day. And now
as she bent down to pick up the packages she'd rested on

the floor at her feet, the key swung out from underneath her sweater on that string and flashed in the electric lights.

"What's that?" Imogene said.

Vivian caught the key between her thumb and index finger and regarded it for a moment before tucking it back under her sweater. In the hustle and bustle, she'd somehow managed to forget about its existence. She straightened again.

"It's the key I told you about last night—the one I found that opens the drawer of my father's desk."

Imogene's dark eyebrows rose. "Makes for an interesting accessory."

Vivian shrugged. "It's just so small I'm afraid I might misplace it." Silly, perhaps, to carry the key around with her, she thought. But that key felt important even if she didn't know exactly why.

"You said you found money in the drawer?"

Vivian glanced around before speaking, as if anyone shopping for Tinkertoys might care to overhear. "Money," she whispered. "And a threatening note."

Imogene's eyes widened. "Not another threatening note," she said. Vivian knew her best friend's thoughts had immediately gone to the Marjorie Fox affair and the two threatening notes Vivian had received.

"This one was directed at my father, I assume."

"What did it say?"

"'Talk and you lose everything,'" Vivian whispered.

"What does that mean?"

"I have no idea."

Imogene was silent for a moment as she tapped her fingers on the railing. "What are you going to do about it?" she asked.

Vivian shrugged again.

Imogene's attention was drawn to a new group of children posing stiffly with Santa. She watched them for a few moments in silence, eyebrows drawn together over her nose. Then she turned back to Vivian. "Actually, I'm not sure what you *could* do. I don't mean to sound crass, but your father's been dead for years. Anything to do with him would be ancient history by now. Wouldn't it?"

Vivian frowned. She knew Imogene was right. Nothing she found in that drawer could possibly have any bearing on the present day. Still, something pricked at her conscience. Something about that envelope of money was wrong. The note was wrong. The fact that her father had hidden the key to his own desk drawer was wrong.

"It's just so odd," Vivian said more to herself than Imogene.

"It is that," Imogene agreed. "But on the other hand, everyone has secrets, Viv. And most of those secrets aren't half as interesting as you'd imagine them to be. There's probably a perfectly mundane and reasonable explanation for all of it. But the fact that your father isn't around to fill you in on any of it has got you in a tizzy. So your overactive imagination has started to cook up a conspiracy where none exists."

Imogene had a point, Vivian thought. The voice of reason—that's one of the myriad reasons Vivian liked her.

"You're probably right," Vivian said, tracing the outline of the key with her fingertips under the fabric of her sweater.

"I know I'm right. You forget how well I know you, Vivian Witchell."

Vivian rolled her eyes, and then she elbowed her friend lightly in the ribs. "So what are your secrets, Miss Crook?"

Imogene smiled enigmatically at her, placing a splayed hand on her chest. "Me? I have no secrets, interesting or otherwise."

"Right. Would you spill for a hot chocolate in the Walnut Room?"

"And a scone?"

"And a scone," Vivian said. "You drive a hard bargain. Let's hurry before they close."

She looped one arm through Imogene's, and they headed toward the up escalator.

The Walnut Room on the seventh floor of Marshall Field's had been dazzling. The forty-foot tree had been covered in every glittering bauble imaginable, and the scent of pine wafted gently over the room. The scone and hot chocolate had been delicious. But none of that holiday perfection had stopped Vivian's mind from returning to the key and her father's desk. As if of its own accord, her mind arranged and rearranged the facts of the hidden key, the money, and the note into something nefarious. If Imogene had actually let any secrets slip during their conversation, Vivian was sure she hadn't noticed.

Then Vivian had returned home and thought about the mystery all through Christmas Eve dinner. She'd been a terrible conversationalist, responding to all inquiries with monosyllables. She'd hardly touched her roast goose and had only a few spoonfuls of the fragrantly steaming plum pudding. The only thing for it, she decided, was to have another look in that drawer and see if she couldn't set things to rights herself. After all, she'd been interrupted by Everett and hadn't gotten a proper look at anything in the drawer the evening before. Perhaps there was something she'd overlooked.

So after everyone had gone to sleep, she snuck back into her father's study. She sat down at his desk. Vivian put the key in the lock and pulled the drawer open, taking the bills from the envelope and counting them: $3,750 in cash. None of the bills were dated past 1930. Now that she was thinking more clearly it was obvious to her: the *AW* scrawled at the bottom of the envelope was her father's initials—Arthur Witchell. *Racquet*, however, was still a mystery.

And that note. She read it again, looking for any clues she might have missed, but the message remained vaguely menacing and equally cryptic. Vivian's initial terror had faded, but seeing a threatening note like this still made her uneasy, bringing back memories of the notes she had received just a few months ago—fakes, of course, meant to throw everyone off the scent of the killer's real motive, but frightening nonetheless.

She had a feeling, however, that the threat she was looking at right now had been quite real. *Talk and you lose everything.* She stared at the note until the letters blurred together and then shoved it back into the envelope. She dropped the envelope back into the drawer, then closed and locked it again. No, this idea hadn't worked at all, she thought. Her unease wasn't lessening. It was growing.

CHAPTER FOUR

❖

Vivian's eyes passed over the photos pinned to the wall next to her bedroom vanity mirror in the early morning light. They were cut from the November issue of *Radio Stars* magazine—a Halloween-themed photo shoot she and Graham had posed for the day following Marjorie Fox's murder. She smiled at the one of her sitting on the table pretending to carve the teeth of a jack-o'-lantern while Graham looked on adoringly. The caption read: "Vivian and Graham partake in a little pumpkin fun." It wasn't quite the cover of *Radio Stars*, but it was a good start. It would be bad form to admit it, but Marjorie's murder and the resulting publicity had been a real boon for Vivian's career. The ratings of *The Darkness Knows* had spiked in the two months since, and Vivian and Graham had never been so popular—especially as a couple.

She'd hooked the key and string over the spindle of her vanity before going to bed, and now she plucked the little silver key from its resting place and wound the string around her hand a few times before making her way downstairs. Vivian had moved from her childhood bedroom to the coach house shortly after that edition of *Radio Stars* had hit the newsstands. She was supposed to be on her way up, and living in her mother's house didn't quit fit the bill for an up-and-coming starlet's abode. The coach house wasn't *technically* out from under her mother's roof, since her mother still owned it, but at least it was Vivian's own space. Besides, rent in Chicago was costly.

Vivian was actually doing her mother a favor by keeping the place livable. The Graveses had lived here before Vivian's father and Mr. Graves had passed away in short succession. After her husband's death, Mrs. Graves had moved into the main house. It was easier that way, with the two widows under the same roof. Plus, Vivian thought her mother secretly liked the company. But as a result, the coach house had been uninhabited for almost eight years. Things had started to fall apart without someone around to keep an eye on them.

Shivering against the chill, Vivian hurried across the backyard, opened the back door, and stepped into the kitchen. The heavenly aroma of cinnamon and cloves wafted from the oven, and her stomach rumbled in response. The warm room was empty, and Vivian slipped on tiptoe through the kitchen to the servant stairs at the back of the house.

She avoided the creakiest of steps and made her way silently up to the second floor. She'd had a lot of practice sneaking up these back stairs over the years. She smiled as the most recent time sprang to mind, and heat rose to her face at the memory.

Charlie had carried her up these stairs that night. *Charlie*. She had Charlie on the brain. She'd dreamed of him last night. The dream itself was now gauzy and faint, but the feeling of it was still with her. The thrill, the excitement in the pit of her stomach at being near him. She felt a twinge of sadness. What had happened to him? Had he been unable to return her call? Had he been hurt on a case? She shook the thought away. As painful as the idea was, she'd rather believe he'd chosen not to call than that something had happened to him.

Vivian made her way down the hall to her father's study, pausing near the landing of the main staircase to gauge any activity in the house. There was no danger of her mother or Everett waking at this hour, but she knew Mrs. Graves was somewhere around—and even though the housekeeper was getting on in years, she still had hearing like a bat.

Vivian slipped into the study and slid into the soft leather chair behind her father's enormous, carved oak desk. The disassembled picture frame still lay on the blotter. She rested her palms on the desktop for a moment and took a few deep breaths. The room smelled of leather bindings and faintly of Johnson's Paste Wax, not unpleasant but slightly stale. Her eyes flickered over the rows of law journals sitting on the floor-to-ceiling bookshelves opposite. Arthur Witchell had been gone for almost eight years, yet everything in this room was exactly as he'd left it. Imogene was right. Eight years was a long time, and what was in this drawer and whatever it might mean was ancient history. Vivian decided to look this one last time, and then she'd put that key right back where she'd found it. She'd forget she'd ever seen that money, that threatening note, and move on.

Vivian fit the key in the lock, turned it, and pulled the drawer toward her.

It was empty.

She ran one hand along the bottom and sides. It was well and truly empty. The money was gone. The note was gone. It had disappeared from a locked drawer that Vivian had the only key to, as far as she knew. She blinked for a minute, eyes trained on the empty expanse of the desk drawer, thinking that if she stared long enough, the envelope might rematerialize in front of her. Then she entertained the idea that she'd imagined all of it. There had never been an envelope full of money, never a threatening note. But no, it had been there last night. She'd counted that money. She'd stared at that note until her vision blurred. What on earth was going on? The implication was plain. Someone else had known about the money and the note all along. And now that someone else knew that she knew.

Vivian felt along the insides of the drawer, along the outsides, and above the top edge, finally pulling the drawer out in frustration. There had to be something else. Something that explained this money and this note—why her father had locked them away so securely and why someone had taken them now. Something that would clear everything up in one fell swoop and allow her to have a happy Christmas without these niggling questions invading her thoughts.

There was no false bottom to the drawer, but as she ran her fingers along the back wall, they caught on a large piece of tape. She upended the drawer and pulled the heavy tape off with a loud ripping noise. There was nothing plastered to the wood underneath it, but something was stuck to the tape itself. She blinked. Another key. This one was slightly larger than the first and made of brass.

Vivian pried the key from the tape and held it up to the morning light. A number was stamped on one side—*242*. She sat motionless, staring at the key and hoping it would speak to her, that it would magically give her a clue to the secrets it had been keeping. But all Vivian heard was the ticking of the clock in the corner and the pounding of blood in her ears as her pulse began to race. One hidden key was odd. Two hidden keys was a conspiracy.

Vivian thought back to the night her father had died— February 12, 1931. She had turned seventeen the month before and, even by her own admission, had been a holy terror to her parents. But by February of that year she'd been attempting to make amends and to not be so brazen in her disrespect for her parent's rules, especially her father's. When she'd delivered his nightly Bloody Mary in the den that evening, he'd had the *Chicago Daily Tribune* unfolded on his lap and was staring at the

front page. The headline at the top screamed CAPONE CITY
HALL BOSS, pronouncing Al Capone the de facto leader of
the city of Chicago. It had been more or less true at the time,
although it wouldn't be for much longer.

Arthur Witchell had been a bear of a man, standing over six
feet tall and wide of shoulder. He'd been nearly bald, and the
hair that remained had turned from mahogany to stone gray
in the past few years. His eyes had been pale blue, and he'd
worn half-glasses to read. They'd been perched on the very
end of his nose. Vivian might have looked like her mother,
but she shared her curious nature with her father. Her father,
for better or worse, had indulged that curiosity.

He had been so absorbed in his thoughts as he gazed down
at the newspaper that night that Vivian had had to hold the
drink directly in front of his nose before he even noticed that
she was standing there.

His head had jerked up, and he'd blinked, startled. "Oh,
Vivian." His eyes landed on the glass she held. "Mrs. Graves
too busy with dinner?" He took the glass from her and set it on
the side table, folding the newspaper and setting it down as well.

Vivian shrugged. "I asked if I could bring you your drink
tonight."

"Well, this is a nice surprise. May I inquire as to why?"

Viv sat on the ottoman at his feet and clasped her hands
between her knees.

"No reason," she said. Her stomach flipped at the lie. The

truth was that she was trying to get back into her father's good graces. There was a Valentine's dance coming up at school, and she desperately wanted to go. The way things stood between them now, she would have to wait until hell froze over to leave the house for anything beyond school. It was her own fault though, and she knew that. She'd tested her father's patience, and even though Arthur Witchell doted on his only daughter, his patience had its limits.

She remembered the look of white-hot fury on his face when he'd caught her sneaking back into her own bedroom the night after the Green Mill. She'd reeked of liquor and tobacco, and he'd been so angry that it had frightened her. That had been just before Christmas, and she'd been careful during the six weeks since. She hadn't snuck out, hadn't smoked one cigarette, but the fragile trust she'd built with her father had been broken that night. Perhaps irrevocably.

He looked terrible—drawn, pale, thinner—and if she wasn't mistaken, she'd smelled alcohol already on his breath, although he normally only had one drink in the evening.

"Working on a big case?" she asked. He filled her in on big cases from time to time. But they hadn't talked much in the past few months. Things were strained between them, but Vivian thought maybe he'd cooled down sufficiently for her to start mending fences. Not only to get permission to go to the dance, but also because she missed talking with him. He used to share his work with her, but now she didn't know what he was working on. He glanced over at the paper, paused as if he was considering whether to say something, and then nodded.

"Yes, but it's coming to a close, I think."

"Good. You need to take care of yourself, you know."

He smiled, his eyes flicking over to the fireplace. "Oh, sweetheart, you know I've never been much for that."

"I think you should take a nice long rest—go somewhere tropical. Put your feet up in the sun. And take me with you." Vivian grinned, and they both glanced toward the frosted-over window, the February wind howling against the pane.

"That sounds like an excellent idea," he'd said. But there hadn't been much enthusiasm behind his words. He put his palm on his chest and winced.

"Maybe you shouldn't drink that. It'll exasperate your indigestion," Vivian said.

Her father glanced down at the drink.

"Ah, it's never stopped me before. Constitution of an ox."

They'd smiled at each other just as the telephone trilled in the hall. Vivian turned, her heart hammering. She'd been expecting a call from a boy she liked. There was always a boy in those days. But her father had clasped her hand, pulling her attention back to him.

"Everything I do is for your mother, your brother, and you. You know that, don't you?"

She'd smiled and squeezed his hand, glancing toward the front hall again, distracted by the boy at the other end of that telephone.

"Of course, Father."

She thought he was being sentimental. Except that her father was rarely sentimental. She wished she'd realized it then. Maybe she could have changed things somehow if he'd stayed. Maybe she could have saved him. But then Mrs. Graves called to tell Vivian the telephone was for her, and she'd run off and left him.

Vernon Banks, her crush du jour at Waller High, had wanted to give her an early Valentine's Day present, and she'd had a few minutes to sneak out before dinner. Because of that, Vivian hadn't been there when her father had the heart attack, and the boy she'd been so keen on hadn't even stuck around long enough to see his chintzy token of affection turn her finger green.

Vivian heard the telltale creak of the tricky floorboard in the hall and broke from her reverie. She shut the drawer, locked it again, and slipped the silver key into her pocket, clasping the other key in her left hand. She was already leaning forward, resting her chin on one hand and staring off into space, when Mrs. Graves stuck her gray head through the open doorway.

"Oh, Viv," the older woman said, placing one palm over her heart. "I thought I heard someone up here. You're up and about early today."

Vivian glanced at her, sighed, and leaned back in the heavy leather desk chair, which rolled backward under her weight. The housekeeper walked across the room to stand at the window. Mrs. Graves was somewhere in her seventies. Vivian suddenly felt a twinge of guilt. She should know exactly how old Mrs. Graves was. She was a member of the family, and she and her husband had been around for Vivian's entire life. Her husband, Herbert, had been something of her father's man Friday—chauffeur, valet, companion, and confidante. Mrs. Graves was small, wiry, but tough as nails. She kept a baseball bat under her bed for protection, and Vivian had no doubt that if it ever came to that, she would use it. Mrs. Graves's thinning gray hair sprang out from her head, and in the backlight from the window, Vivian thought the housekeeper rather resembled a dandelion gone to seed.

"I wanted to sit in here for a few minutes. You know, this is where I feel Father the most." Vivian reached over and opened the small wooden cigar box on the corner of the desk. The heady scent of Cuban tobacco wafted toward her, so pungent even after all this time. Tears sprang to her eyes. That smell was her father. It was almost as if he were standing right beside her. She touched the gold band around one cigar with the tips of her fingers: Epoca, the label said. An expensive brand, no doubt.

"We all miss him," Mrs. Graves said, smiling sadly.

Vivian looked toward the window to give herself a few seconds to compose herself. A feeble pink glow was starting to come into the sky, the dark study lightening bit by bit. "I can't believe this is the eighth Christmas without him. The eighth Christmas without his horrid rendition of 'God Rest Ye Merry Gentlemen.'"

Mrs. Graves smiled at the joke. Arthur Witchell had had a terrible singing voice.

He hadn't lived to see Vivian's success as a radio actress. When he died, the idea of being an actress hadn't been even a glimmer in her eye, a thought in her head. She'd been a boy-crazy teenager out to have a good time—and out to do anything her mother would disapprove of. She was still doing that though, wasn't she? Vivian turned to smile at Mrs. Graves again, and then she noticed the older woman's tears.

"Oh God, I'm sorry. I'm being thoughtless. This is a rough time of year for you too, isn't it?"

Mrs. Graves had lost her husband a month after Vivian's father. His car, the Witchell family car, had hit a patch of ice on Ogden Avenue early one March morning and skidded into a lamppost, killing him instantly and maiming her father's intern, Martin Gilfoy, who'd been in the back seat. It had been a terrible blow for everyone already reeling from Mr. Witchell's death.

Mr. Graves had been like a member of the family. So had Martin, come to think of it, and now they hadn't seen him in years. He'd taken such a long time to convalesce, and then he'd just drifted out of their lives. The way people did when the person holding them together was suddenly gone. Arthur Witchell had held so much together, and so much had changed in the blink of an eye when he'd died.

"Christmas is hard, but I think it's worse in the fall. That's when your father and Herbert used to go up to the cabin on

Cranberry Lake for their annual duck-hunting trip. I miss them both then for some reason." Mrs. Graves wiped the tears from her lined face.

"That's right," Vivian said. She'd forgotten all about her father's fondness for hunting. And forgotten what good friends her father had been with Mr. Graves, so good that they'd gone on trips together and stayed at the family cabin in Wisconsin every year. Mr. Graves had spent more time at that cabin than Vivian ever had. She wasn't a cabin sort of girl.

"They never did come back with much of anything," Mrs. Graves said with a wistful smile. "But I don't think the trip was really about hunting—except, perhaps, hunting for whiskey and a poker game."

Vivian smiled. "I'm glad my father had a friend like your husband."

Mrs. Graves pursed her lips together and nodded. She looked off toward the frosted window. She was silent for a moment, and the next words out of her mouth seemed to be meant only for herself.

"It was just so sudden, you know. I hadn't expected it to happen that way."

Vivian waited for Mrs. Graves to continue.

"I'm sorry?"

Mrs. Graves remained staring out the window. Vivian wasn't sure the housekeeper had heard her question, but then she spoke again without turning.

"Your father. Herbert. All of it. So sudden. So…" She grappled for a moment with the word before she found it. "Unnecessary."

Vivian narrowed her eyes at the housekeeper, trying to decipher her cryptic remarks. She hadn't expected it to happen that way? And all of what? Was she saying that her father's and Herbert Graves's deaths were somehow connected? Certainly almost all death that hadn't come from prolonged sickness could be considered sudden. But *unnecessary* was an odd choice of words. When was the death of a loved one ever *necessary*? Vivian opened her mouth but shut it again as she searched for an appropriate response. The older woman was noticeably agitated. She clutched the sides of her apron and stared, unblinking, out the window at the snowy back lawn and the coach house beyond.

"Gone before their time," Vivian said. She felt stupid as soon as she said it, but nothing else remotely soothing came to mind. It was on the tip of her tongue to ask Mrs. Graves about the money, but surely she would have said something by now if she'd known. If anyone knew the inner workings of this household, it was her.

Mrs. Graves turned her head and looked at Vivian for a long moment, her eyes searching Vivian's face. Then she blinked, and the fog that had come over her features cleared. "Yes," she said. She shook her head. "I have to see to the buffet." Her hands came together in front of her ample bosom as if in prayer. "Come down when you're ready. I've made those cinnamon scones that you love."

Vivian's stomach rumbled, but she had some thinking to do. "I'll be down in a minute," she said, and waited until she heard Mrs. Graves return to the first floor before relaxing her fingers to expose the brass key once again. She'd been clutching it so hard that it had left a perfect red imprint in her palm.

If Vivian had any lingering doubts over whether the envelope of cash and note were suspicious, their disappearance and the discovery of this key taped to the back of the drawer dispelled them. Envelopes of money didn't just vanish from locked drawers. And taping keys to the back of those locked drawers was not normal behavior. Her father had had something to hide, and Vivian wasn't the only one who knew it. She sat at his desk for another few minutes, soaking up his presence but feeling uneasy. She put the picture frame back together and set it on its perch atop the filing cabinet. She slipped the brass key into her pocket, along with the silver drawer key, and went down to breakfast, conspiracy theories beginning to swirl in her head.

Vivian's fingertips brushed the aged tinsel on the edge of Saint Nicholas's cap. The Sistine Chapel Choir piped softly from the Vatican from the floor-model Philco radio against the far wall.

Someone had taken the money. That meant one of two things had happened: someone had known the money was there all along and took it when they found out she knew, or someone found out about the money because of her. That first option could be any number of people. The second option left only the person who had come upon her just after she'd opened the drawer—Everett. She glanced over her shoulder at him. He sat on the sofa on the side nearest the fireplace, looking through a book of Greek myths that Gloria had given him.

Then her mind returned to the earlier conversation with the housekeeper. Mrs. Graves said she *hadn't expected it to happen that way*. If she had indeed been referring to Vivian's father's death, what way *had* she been expecting? And then there was that note threatening that her father would lose everything. All Vivian could think about was how her father had lost everything after all. He'd died so suddenly. Unexpectedly. *Unnecessarily*, Mrs. Graves had said. Vivian turned back to Everett, suddenly unable to bear the thoughts swirling in her head.

"You helped Father at his office, right?"

Everett looked up from his book and studied her a few seconds before answering. "Well, that depends what you mean by helped… I saw a lot of the insides of his filing cabinets. I was a kid—barely out of short pants. I wasn't old enough then to do much but make a nuisance of myself. Why do you ask?"

She touched the brass key through the fabric of her pocket. Could it be the key to a filing cabinet? Then she sighed. She doubted Everett knew anything. He'd been twelve when Father had passed—hardly the age at which a father would confide in his son about serious things. Still, Everett had been around Arthur Witchell's law office more than Vivian had and might have seen something—even if he didn't understand what it had meant at the time. After all, their father had been grooming Everett to follow in his footsteps. He was only an undergraduate at Northwestern, but he was already focused on law school. It had been his only dream since their father's death.

"I've been thinking about him today…and I wondered how much you'd seen of his practice. I never got to see that part of his life."

"I don't think I can tell you much except that I alphabetized until my eyes crossed."

Vivian walked over to the fireplace and picked up the Christmas card from Uncle Freddy.

"Do you think there was a part of his life, his work, that we didn't know about?"

"I think there's a lot about Father we didn't know," Everett answered.

Vivian turned to face him. "What do you mean by that?"

Everett shrugged. "Well, he died before we could know what he was all about…as a person, I mean."

"Yes." Vivian sighed. "I miss him."

"Me too," Everett said.

Vivian turned the Christmas card over in her hands. "Do

you think he was a good person?" She glanced up to find Everett studying her.

"Of course," he said. "What kind of a question is that?"

It had been a ridiculous question to ask. How else would Everett have answered?

"I mean…he was a lawyer, Ev. You've heard all the jokes about lawyers—out for themselves, liars, thieves, ambulance chasers…"

"Hey! You're addressing one of those future ambulance chasers."

Vivian smiled.

"What's all this about?" her brother asked. He put the book aside and leaned forward, elbows on his knees.

She could just ask Everett if he'd taken the money, she supposed. That would be the easiest thing to do. But if he hadn't taken it, then the question itself would open up a whole new can of worms. She would have to explain everything, and she wasn't sure she was ready to do that. Because although Everett might be a future man of the law, he could never keep a secret. He'd run to their mother and told on Vivian when he'd caught her smoking cigarettes behind the garage with the neighbor boy, Jimmy Durden. Vivian had been thirteen at the time, Everett only eight, but her mother's lecture about what proper young women did and didn't do still rang in Vivian's ears—and probably would for eternity. And although she didn't have proof, she'd always suspected Everett of even greater indiscretion.

She was certain that he had told their father, just a few months before he died, that Vivian was sneaking out of the house to meet boys. Everett was the one who'd gotten her into such hot water that night after the Green Mill. He might be older now, but not that much had changed. If she told him any of her suspicions about their father, she had little doubt that he'd go straight to their mother with the information. He couldn't help himself. It was his nature. Honest to a fault. Law was a poor choice of profession for Everett, in Vivian's opinion. He wasn't crafty enough.

He also wasn't crafty enough to steal thousands of dollars and a threatening note from his dead father's locked desk drawer and then calmly converse with her as if nothing had happened, she thought. Everything Everett thought or felt was always written all over his face. And right now she could see that all he felt was bewildered at her choice of conversation.

"Nothing," she said. "I'm feeling sentimental, I suppose. Being cooped up in the house for the past few days...too much time to think. And Oskar the other night, making toasts and playing lord of the manor. What do you make of him?"

Everett frowned. "He's nice enough. I haven't had much of a chance to talk to him."

Vivian nodded.

"Mother seems to like him," Everett went on. "And she hasn't had anyone since Father." His voice trailed off. "There's something about Oskar that's familiar though. I can't place it. Like I've seen him before somewhere."

"He's a big-shot something or other," Vivian said. "I'm sure his picture has been in the papers. What did Mother say he did?"

"She said he's a financier." Everett shrugged. "Whatever that means. Certainly not my crowd. Anyway, I'm glad she's happy. Maybe he'll loosen her up a little."

Vivian smiled at the absurdity of the idea of Mrs. Witchell "loosening up" at any time. "My thoughts exactly. Speaking of happiness…" She plopped down onto the sofa next to him, jostling the book in his hands. "What's with this Gloria?"

He closed the book with a thump and glanced away, his cheeks pink. "What do you mean?"

"I don't know anything about the girl. Where did she come from? Who are her parents?" She asked the last question in a perfect imitation of their mother's affected finishing-school diction.

Everett laughed. "There's not much to tell. I met her at a football game. She's a Kappa Kappa Gamma. She's pretty and funny and smart." He shook his head in amazement. "Boy, is she ever smart."

"And her parents?" Vivian prodded, still imitating their mother's voice.

"Average, everyday people as far as I know."

Vivian widened her eyes in pretend shock. Then she smiled, dropping the snooty act. "So it's serious?"

"I think so. We've been seeing each other for two whole months. I'm thinking of pinning her."

Vivian whistled in genuine surprise. "Well, well, that *is* serious. I know a Lambda Chi Alpha boy doesn't give his pin to just anyone."

Everett's blush deepened under the sprinkling of freckles on his cheeks. "What did you think of her? Be honest."

"She seemed swell, Ev." Vivian reached behind her to pluck a pomander from the bowl on the sofa table, bringing it up under her nose to breathe in the heady scent of orange and cloves.

Everett beamed. "I think so too," he said.

"And that was a lovely necklace you gave her for Christmas," she said, picturing the orchid charm and the way it glinted in the light. "Where did you get the money for something like that?"

Everett ducked his head. "Oh, that. It's nothing."

It seemed quite a bit more than nothing. "No, really," Vivian said, poking him in the arm with the scented orange in her hand. "How did my dopey little brother manage to buy such a nice present for his girlfriend?" Everett had no money of his own. Their mother paid his tuition and room and board, and Everett was too busy studying to have any type of job.

He looked away from her. "I have my sources," he said. He picked up the copy of the *Tribune* that had been left open on the arm of the sofa and began leafing through it.

She looked at the swirling auburn cowlick at the crown of

his head. Then it hit her. Mother had given him the money. Having to accept money from your mother to buy a Christmas present for your girlfriend wasn't the most adult thing in the world. No wonder he was so embarrassed and evasive.

Vivian wanted to apologize, but she knew that would embarrass her brother further. She cleared her throat, dropping the orange back into its bowl, but Everett spoke before she did.

"Hey," he said, his finger planted on a picture in the sports section. "Gloria and I are going to the opening night of Sonja Henie's ice review this evening. It's sold out, but I have connections. I could find two more tickets if you and Graham would like to tag along."

Vivian glanced down at the photo underneath the headline SEABISCUIT IS 1938 TURF KING, which showed a smiling young woman in a short, white skating costume, a large glittery bow in her braided blond hair.

"You and your connections," Vivian teased. "Thanks for the offer, but Graham's busy getting *The Scarlet Pimpernel* together. I'm sure he'll be working all evening."

Everett raised his coppery eyebrows. "On Christmas?"

"He's a hard worker."

"I'll say." Everett looked up from his book, his brown eyes—the exact shade as her own—locked with hers. "Viv, can I ask you something?"

"Sure."

"You and Graham. You aren't really together, are you?"

"Of course we are." Vivian glanced away. She should have told her family that the relationship wasn't real, but she just hadn't been able to. She hadn't realized it herself until a few weeks after Halloween and Marjorie Fox's death. After all, she and Graham had already discussed the unromantic fact that their publicity relationship was mutually beneficial for their careers. There should have been no doubt that was all he wanted from her—a show for the cameras. But he had also kissed her, really kissed her, that night a few days after Marjorie's murder when he'd taken her to Chez Paree.

Now she suspected that had been more for Charlie's benefit than his own. Graham didn't want her, but that didn't mean he wanted Charlie to have her either. They'd been like two dogs marking their territory, she thought. And that kiss had been staged for Charlie to see so he would know to back off. Happily, it hadn't worked.

But then Charlie had slipped from Vivian's life, and Vivian and Graham's staged publicity dates had continued just as before. Graham had never shown any interest in taking it further than that chaste peck on the lips. Vivian's ego had taken a hit, but she had also been relieved. She hadn't been interested in Graham anymore either. So they continued pretending, and not discussing why they were pretending.

It was cowardly on Vivian's part not to confront the issue

head on, but things at the station were going so well that she didn't want to rock the boat. And besides, a real friendship had grown between her and Graham through all of that pretending. Vivian found she liked him even if she didn't think of him romantically, and she liked the sense of purpose and camaraderie they shared.

However, a sham *was* a sham, and she felt terrible about keeping the truth from her brother, but Vivian knew she had to be careful in her confidences. Her family wasn't in show business, and they wouldn't understand that she and Graham needed to keep up the pretense at all times. Everett was likely to let the truth slip to one of his friends, and soon it would be in the papers that she and Graham were faking for publicity. That would be beyond embarrassing for them both.

"I have eyes, Viv."

"What does that mean?" Her stomach dropped. Could he tell by looking at them that it was all an act? Boy, she was some actress.

He leaned over and nudged her. "I guess now I know what it's supposed to look like when a boy admires a girl. And when Graham looks at you, and you look at Graham…it looks like it should on the surface, but well, there's nothing behind it, is there?"

"Is it that obvious?"

He shook his head. "I can only see it because I know you. Graham doesn't make you light up inside."

Vivian couldn't help but laugh at her brother's uncharacteristic sincerity. She met his eyes, serious and appraising, and her laugh faded. Boy, he was in deep with this Gloria girl. She'd never seen him like this before.

"My kid brother, love doctor," she said, chucking him on the shoulder. "You're really learning something at that expensive school, aren't you?"

He blushed, opening his book again. He gazed at a painting of Medusa and her writhing snake hair. "So why are you pretending?"

Viv tapped an index finger against her lips. "It's sort of a condition of my employment," she answered, wondering how far she would let this condition go to boost her career. Marriage? Children? She shook her head. No, most definitely not. The sham would have to end, and the sooner the better. Perhaps after all the fuss with *The Pimpernel* was over. After the holidays when Graham was in better humor. Funny how the idea of a lifetime on Graham Yarborough's arm would have thrilled her a few months ago. But that was before she'd seen his true character. And before she'd met Charlie.

Vivian sat in the chair across from her mother's desk, feeling like she was at an interview with a bank examiner. She fidgeted as her mother finished some correspondence, her fountain pen scratching across the stationery. Vivian twisted an emerald ring around her finger—she'd been surprised to find the ring in her stocking this morning—and glanced out the window.

Vivian was reminded of another "chat" in this room, years ago. It hadn't been winter, but the end of summer—the cicadas humming in the trees outside. Vivian had returned to the city after spending the summer at her aunt and uncle's house in Lake Geneva. She and her mother had never had a good relationship, but that summer it had been especially tense—to the point of snapping. She'd been back in the house two days when her mother found the copy of *Lady Chatterley's Lover* that Vivian had hidden under her mattress. More likely, Mrs. Graves had found it while making the bed. The idea of the prim housekeeper opening that book and discovering the scandalous things inside made Vivian smile.

Her mother had demanded to know where Vivian had gotten such "filth" and then attempted to give her a lecture on sexual education that tangentially bordered the sexual and didn't come within spitting distance of the education. Meanwhile, Vivian bit the inside of her cheek to stop herself from laughing. She'd wanted to tell her mother that she hadn't learned anything from that book that she hadn't already known—mostly from her own experience. But she was wise enough, even at seventeen, to know that while the revelation would have been satisfyingly shocking, it would have not have helped her case.

She'd been confined to the house until school started again—two long weeks. Vivian wondered what had ever happened to that book. Maybe she should check under her mother's mattress, she thought and stifled a giggle. She tamped down her smile, and when she turned from the window, she found her mother looking at her, a serious expression on her face.

She gazed at Vivian, fingers threaded over the blotter on her desk. Then she launched right into the subject at hand without preamble—as was her mother's custom. An unnerving quality, Vivian thought.

"I have what I suppose is a combination Christmas and birthday present for you," her mother said.

"You've already given me a Christmas present," Vivian said, looking down at the beautiful emerald ring.

Her mother waved one hand dismissively at her. "That was from Saint Nicholas."

Vivian waited while her mother gazed off toward the window, lost in thought. Then her focus returned, and she trained her brown eyes on Vivian's.

"This gift is from your father."

"From Father?"

"I'll set up a meeting with the lawyer, a Mr. Henrick, in a few weeks to get the details, but the thing is, Vivian, you'll be coming into quite a bit of money on your twenty-fifth birthday."

Vivian narrowed her eyes at her mother in disbelief. The

only conversation they'd had about her twenty-fifth birthday previous to this was her mother letting Vivian know that she was getting a bit "long in the tooth."

"Your father left this money in trust for you."

Vivian blinked at her mother. Money? For her?

"How much are we talking about?"

"I don't know exact sums, but I do know that it is a substantial amount."

Substantial, Vivian thought. *What constitutes substantial?* Her mother thought talking about money in specific terms was gauche, so Vivian knew better than to press the topic. She'd get specifics from the lawyer in a few weeks, but *substantial* sounded like enough to move out of her mother's house. *Substantial* sounded like enough to make her own life. She felt like laughing, or crying. Her father was saving her once again—stepping from beyond the grave to make a shield between Vivian and her overbearing mother.

"Of course, you'll also get your share of my inheritance when I pass on," her mother said, pursing her lips into a thin white line.

Vivian glanced back down, setting her eyes on her mother's uncomfortable expression. Her mother had always had the real wealth in the family. It came from the vast reserves of her father's meatpacking fortune left in trust, as far as Vivian could piece together. Julia shared the fortune with her two older sisters—all of them distancing themselves from the source of their wealth. Huge sums of money made by butchering animals at the Union Stock Yard. *Talk about gauche.*

Her mother was silent for a long time, but Vivian knew the conversation wasn't over. There was that particular vertical line between her mother's brows. Vivian's surprise inheritance was just the beginning of what her mother had called her in to discuss. Her mother's dark eyes flicked to the window, and she spoke without looking at her daughter.

"There are men out there who prey on young women in your position, Vivian." She paused and then fixed her eyes on her daughter. "Look at what's happened to that poor Barbara Hutton."

Vivian's eyes flicked to the ceiling. It was difficult not to roll her eyes in front of her mother, but she was trying her damnedest. Vivian was nothing like Barbara Hutton, the Poor Little Rich Girl and heiress to the Woolworth fortune. Hutton had inherited a vast fortune at twenty-one and had seen nothing but trouble since. She'd been in the papers a few months ago over her nasty second divorce. First, she'd married a sham playboy who spent her money like water, then a man who'd beaten her so terribly he'd put her in the hospital. Two awful marriages already behind her, and she was only a few years older than Vivian.

"Ah," Vivian said, her eyes moving down to meet her mother's. "So the hordes will set upon me once they realize I have more than two nickels to rub together, and you think I'll fall for the first oily huckster to pay me a compliment."

Julia pressed her lips together again. She had a particular set
of wrinkles forming around her mouth from repeating that
movement over and over. Vivian liked to think of them as her
mother's "disappointment lines." Vivian's glance strayed to the
mantel and the framed photograph of her mother in a glittering
white gown with cap sleeves and tiny embroidered flowers—a
genuine Worth, her mother had told her often with pride.
Her mother was so young in that photo, her cheeks blooming
roses and full of baby fat. That had been 1907, the tail end of
the Gilded Age, when coming out was de rigueur for families
of means. But then again, her mother's family had had quite a
bit of panache. Vivian's father's meager origins had diluted the
family bloodline, and Vivian was grateful for that.

Her father had had the paper opened to the article about Barbara
Hutton's lavish coming-out ball in New York City when he'd
called her into his study that evening in late November of
1930, his index finger resting on the photo on the society page.
Barbara Hutton had looked beautiful; she wore a sparkling
beaded dress and a pointed, starlike crown on her head. But she
also looked horribly sad, as if the photographer had caught her
as she was about to burst into tears.

Vivian had read the article. Barbara's ball had been
extravagant. Hundreds of guests had attended—among them,

Hollywood stars like Rudy Vallee and Maurice Chevalier. And the papers had skewered her. So much money spent on a party when the world had fallen into the bleakest of depressions and most people were struggling to eat.

"Your mother would like you to come out, you know," her father had said.

Vivian sighed. She'd be seventeen in a little over a month. A year was plenty of time to whip her into shape and plan a ridiculous party for her eighteenth birthday, but she had no interest in a debutante ball. No interest in being paraded around in front of marriageable young men. She looked down at that photo in the newspaper. It seemed to Vivian like a hellish existence—beholden to money and the family name. Vivian had stayed silent. She hadn't known what to say. She would have protested, but her father already knew her position on the matter, and protesting would be like preaching to the choir.

"I took your side about boarding school, if you recall," he'd said, fixing his light-blue eyes on her.

He had. Her mother had wanted to send her to Rosemary Hall, her own alma mater, the moment Vivian had turned fifteen. Her father had stood his ground. Vivian had not been sent to Connecticut to learn which fork with which to eat shrimp; she'd attended a public high school right there in Lincoln Park. *The horror.*

Vivian had no doubt that was why her mother had pressed so hard for a coming-out party. There was little chance of

Vivian making a good match while rubbing elbows with the common folk. And perhaps that was why her father had been thinking of taking her mother's side. He was a smart man, and he knew which battles to pick and which to concede. He wasn't a snob, but he was also no fool.

"Are you saying I have no choice in the matter?" Vivian asked.

"I'm saying you should think about it."

Vivian sighed again, louder, so there would be no misunderstanding how she felt. "I don't want to think about it."

"It's important to your mother."

"A lot of things are important to Mother."

Her father sighed then. Vivian noticed how tired he looked. He took his spectacles off and rubbed them with the handkerchief he'd pulled from his front pocket. He was gathering his thoughts, stalling. She knew his closing argument was coming, and she knew she wouldn't win.

"I know times have changed since your mother was your age, Vivian. But she is your mother, and she wants what's best for you. You're becoming a young lady now, and soon it's going to matter very much how you act and who you associate with— whether you like it or not." He'd stared at her. She'd squirmed and looked away, mistakenly thinking that he couldn't know what she'd been up to—about her sneaking out and occasionally drinking. About the questionable young men (and some not-so-young men) she'd been seeing behind her parents' backs.

In hindsight, he had to have known, of course. How could he not? She wasn't as slick as she'd thought, and shimmying down drainpipes was a risky endeavor at any time of the year, but especially after the frost came. Not to mention that Everett had seen her the last time she'd done it. She'd caught his eye as she'd lowered herself over the sill and onto the ledge outside her bedroom window. Little sneak. He'd told Father on her; she was sure of it.

But her father had said nothing more on the subject that day. He'd merely tapped that photo and stared into the fire. Letting the idea simmer in her head. A coming-out party. The last thing she wanted. But then he'd died, and all thoughts of her daughter's future connections had left her mother's mind—at least for a time. The coming-out had never happened. And she had Father to thank for that too, in a manner of speaking.

"Vivian…"

Viv blinked herself back into the present, returning her attention from the photo of her mother at eighteen to the real-life woman in front of her. "I would appreciate your attention. This is an important matter."

"Of course."

"I was saying that it's customary to receive any inheritance at twenty-one, you realize. There's a reason your father delayed yours. I'm sure you understand why."

Vivian swallowed. Her father hadn't trusted her to make good decisions at that age. Twenty-one wasn't far enough removed from the reckless seventeen-year-old he'd known. Even Vivian had to admit she would have wasted it, would have fallen for some gold digger, some good-for-nothing, alcoholic gambler. She couldn't blame Father for thinking that. She hadn't been trustworthy then. Perhaps he'd wanted her to marry before she came into money. That way, her husband would be sure to love her for herself rather than her bank account. But could her father have believed she'd be married by now? Maybe so. He'd been her champion, but even he hadn't been progressive enough to imagine his daughter unwed at nearly twenty-five— practically an old maid.

Her mother studied Vivian, her mouth turned down at the corners.

"Is it serious with this Graham fellow?"

Vivian opened her mouth to produce the requisite flippant answer, but then shut it again. "No," she said.

Her mother nodded. "I'm all for a bit of fun, but I think it's time you started thinking about your future, Vivian."

Vivian bit her tongue. Since when was her mother all for a bit of fun?

And her future? All she did was think about her future. But she knew what Julia had meant—her mother's idea of a future, not hers. Her mother's future was a man to take care of her, to set her up in a fine house with a few well-behaved children. Membership on some not-too-demanding but high-profile charity committees. In other words, a carbon copy of Julia Witchell. Vivian's idea of a future did not involve marrying and being beholden to any man. She considered telling her mother that, but she didn't want to suffer a lecture today. She already had a headache.

Instead, she nodded, trying to look as though she were taking the suggestion seriously.

"My future," she said. "Yes. I think so too, Mother."

Joe McGreevey, one of the directors at WCHI, phoned Vivian's house in midafternoon. They were a female supporting character shy on some half-baked Sherlock Holmes–style mystery on late that afternoon. *Who in the world wanted to listen to murder and detection on Christmas Day? Grisly to say the least*, Vivian thought. She agreed to do it only because she knew she could not refuse.

She thought again of the conditions of her employment. Things were going well for her, but that didn't mean she could afford to play the diva. And she certainly wanted to stay in Mr. Langley's good graces. Graham had gone to bat for her with the new head of the station after all that mess with the press and her suspension during the investigation of Marjorie's murder. But Vivian still felt like she was on thin ice, and one wrong move could send her whole career back into a tailspin.

Vivian hopped aboard the red-and-cream streetcar as the leaden sky began to melt into dusk. The conductor on the back platform nodded without speaking as he took her dime. He spit three pennies out of the coin changer strapped to his waist and handed them to her. The back of the car was open to the air, and even though he was well bundled against the chill, the tips of his nose and ears were painted a painful cherry red. Vivian headed into the enclosed passenger section and slid into a wicker seat. The inside of the car was marginally warmer and almost empty save a snoring older man near the front.

She watched the well-appointed homes of the Gold Coast quickly turn into the motley mix of the shopping and financial district as they neared the Loop. The conductor at the front had stuffed a wad of newspaper between the clapper and the gong so that the insistent *ding, ding* of the bell situated directly above his head had been rendered a muted *thwack, thwack.* She was grateful for that. The dull ache between her eyes was beginning to worsen.

Vivian considered everything that had happened today, not least of which was her mother informing her that she was coming into a substantial amount of money. Substantial. She wanted to be giddy about that, she *should* be giddy about that, but her mind just wouldn't latch on to the idea. Instead her thoughts were running round and round.

She hopped out again at State and Madison, marveling at how empty a teeming metropolis could look when everyone but her had reason to stay in their warm homes. She frowned and pulled her hat lower over her ears. The icy wind worked itself into a veritable frenzy as it rent through the metal and limestone canyons of the Loop. She ducked her chin into her upturned collar and negotiated the empty sidewalks the two blocks west on Madison to the Grayson-Cole Building that housed the studios of WCHI on the eleventh and twelfth floors.

The station itself was a ghost town. The only activity centered around small Studio G on the eleventh floor. It was two minutes to air when Vivian hustled into the room. Someone shoved a script into her hands, pointed to her part, and they were off.

She hadn't had time to rehearse, so Vivian had to read cold. That was a terrifying prospect on live radio, and her nerves were still on edge after she said her lines, even though she'd finished without a hiccup. The show was nearing its end, and things had gone as well as could be expected considering the actors for this performance were all brand-new to the station and generally inexperienced. They were so young and keen to make a name for themselves that they'd volunteer to work on Christmas Day if it meant a starring role in a show—any show. She'd been of a similar mind-set not so long ago.

Vivian's role had been a chintzy one—a minor character with only a handful of lines. She was sure that they hadn't truly needed her to come in, but she was also sure that Langley wanted to make sure she knew who was boss. She glanced at him in the control room. He was a squat, jowly, red-faced man who wore a perpetual scowl. There was no need for the man to be here today of all days, but there he was just the same.

Before he'd been promoted to interim station head, Mr. Langley had held the lessor role of program director at the station. He'd backed Frances Barrow for the role of Lorna Lafferty on *The Darkness Knows*, and the former head of the station, Mr. Hart, had backed Vivian. Vivian had won the role, of course, but Mr. Hart had left the station shortly thereafter. Mr. Langley was not one of Vivian's biggest fans, and Graham had practically had to beg the man to keep her in the role after Mr. Hart's departure. Vivian knew that if she placed just one foot wrong, Langley would replace her with Frances. It was simple, really. He had her jumping through hoops. And jump she would, she thought, until she could use this job to catapult herself into something better.

Mr. Langley seemed pleased enough about the performance. He smiled at Vivian, a tight little closed-mouth smile. She returned it and then gave her full attention to the action at the center of the room. The episode had reached its crescendo. Having solved the crime, the brilliant sleuth would now confront the murderer with the error of her ways.

"Arsenic," the actor playing the sleuth said, his voice dripping with condescension.

The "murderess" gasped into the microphone. "You can't mean…poison?"

"You know as well as I do, Wilhelmina. Arsenic—they call it the inheritance powder in the newspapers. Put a dash in Aunt Lillian's soup, and the fortune is yours."

"You can't be serious. Where on earth would I get arsenic?"

"Why, from your own cellar, of course."

The organ thrummed ominously in the corner of the room, the hands of the young man playing it dancing wildly on the keys.

"You fooled the doctor. I admit, you almost had me too, but I was too keen for you. I found this open container of Rough on Rats downstairs. That's right, Wilhelmina. A few spoonfuls in her nightly tea induced a sudden, devastating fit of apoplexy in someone with no history of the malady."

Vivian turned her head to hide the roll of her eyes. This was low-rent stuff. It didn't really matter though. No one was listening anyway.

Her mind returned to her father and the locked drawer. She thought over and over about the cash, the second key, but most of all, the threatening note: *Talk and you lose everything.* What did *everything* mean—his career, his fortune, his home, his family…his life? She frowned. She didn't have any of the answers, and she wouldn't stumble upon them by wading through the jumble of thoughts in her head. She needed help. But she certainly couldn't bring any of this up to her mother or Everett, at least not yet. Maybe not ever, her sick stomach told her. No, it was clear to her now. There was only one person she could talk to about any of this, one person who could help her get to the bottom of this without her mother finding out.

Charlie.

CHAPTER FIVE

❖

Vivian checked her reflection in the window of the Tip Top Café. The gray fox fur of her new wool winter coat framed her face beautifully, she thought, and her blue Robin Hood–style hat set off her strawberry-blond curls to good effect. She freshened her lipstick and pressed her hand to her stomach to settle it, then walked over and pulled open the door.

She'd tried Charlie's office number last night in desperation, expecting the answering service or, worse yet, the operator informing her in nasal tones, "I'm sorry. This line has been disconnected." She'd stood shivering, staring out the window at the wind-swirled snow sparkling in the light of the back porch from the front house. The money and note were gone, and now she had yet another key. And someone knew she knew about all of it. The only one who might be able to help her was Charlie. He wouldn't answer, she'd told herself listening to the faint burring ring of the telephone. But then he had.

The small diner was crowded with post-holiday bargain

shoppers. The din of dozens of voices met her ears, and she sniffed at the tang of frying onions thick in the air. Her eyes passed over the crowd and landed on the booth nearest the counter.

Charlie's head had snapped up at the jingle of the bells hanging from the front door, a lock of dark-blond hair falling over his forehead. He brushed it away as his eyes caught hers, and he smiled. Vivian's insides turned to goo at that smile, despite her every resolve to remain detached. Part of her had hoped she would feel nothing upon seeing him again, that maybe she would have a professional discussion with him about her father and come away somehow relieved that Charlie had rejected her. But the twinge in her stomach told her that was not to be.

He stood as she reached the booth and took her coat and gloves. His fingertips brushed her wrist, then across the top of her hand where they lingered just a little longer than necessary, and his blue-green eyes flashed down and then up again.

"You look…well," he said.

She flicked her eyes down and up in a perfect imitation of him, and watched his slow smirk of recognition. "You don't look too bad yourself," she said, sliding into the booth. He sat on the opposite bench, and they looked at each other in silence, expectation and longing pulling like a visible strand between them. Vivian glanced away, afraid that if she held his gaze any longer she'd burst into flame.

She cleared her throat. She hadn't actually thought about what she'd say when he was in front of her—in the flesh.

Where have you been? The question floated to the front of her mind, but she pushed it away. She didn't want to start him on the defensive. He'd disappeared for a reason, and it was probably one she didn't want to hear. Better not to know the details.

"How have you been doing since…well, since everything?" She winced at the inanity of the question. Charlie had been through things she couldn't imagine. He'd found his birth parents, only to see his mother murdered and his father shun him. And he'd almost been killed by his half sister. It was a plot as convoluted as one of the sappy melodramas Vivian appeared in at WCHI.

Charlie shrugged, shifting his weight. "I've been all right, I suppose."

"I'm glad," she said.

Vivian's eyes were drawn to Charlie's right temple, where that horrible purple bruise had been when she'd last seen him. There was still a tiny knot there, but he was otherwise unblemished. She wanted to reach over the table to touch it, to let her fingertips run down his cheek and rub her thumb along the stinging stubble at his jawline. She sucked a deep breath in through her nose. *Focus, Vivian, focus.*

The waitress came over and filled their coffee cups without a word, dropping a couple of tattered menus on the table.

Charlie stirred a dollop of cream into his coffee. Then he

glanced up at Vivian, one eyebrow arched. "So what's the professional opinion you need?"

"Right," she said. *She'd* called *him* after all. She looked down at the table. Lifted her spoon. Set it down again.

"You did ask me here for my opinion on something, didn't you?" He took a sip of coffee, regarding her seriously over the rim of the ceramic mug. "Let me guess. You've gotten yourself into trouble again."

"It's not me," she said. She dropped two sugar cubes into her cup and stirred vigorously. "It's my father."

Charlie paused. His brow furrowed, and he sat back in his seat again. "I thought your father was dead."

"He is."

Vivian leaned toward the detective and pitched her voice low. "When my father died almost eight years ago, we couldn't find the key to the top drawer of his desk. We all assumed it had been lost. Well, I found that key on Christmas Eve, and I opened the drawer…"

"And?"

"I found cash. A big, fat envelope full of bills. And another mysterious key taped to the back of the drawer. And there was a note. It said, 'Talk and you lose everything.'" She locked eyes with him and paused to let the import of the words sink in.

Charlie took another sip of his coffee.

"Well," Vivian said. "What do you think?"

"What do *you* think, Viv?"

Vivian looked down at the table. "I think it's fishy," she said. She wrinkled her nose, then added in a rush of words before she could lose her nerve, "I think he might have been involved in something illegal."

She lifted her head to gauge Charlie's reaction, but his face was impassive. He took another sip of his coffee, then returned the mug to the table, glancing around before speaking.

"Well, Viv, I can think of one reason a man would have a secret locked drawer full of cash, mysterious keys in secret hiding spots, and threatening notes," he said, leveling a cool aqua gaze on her. "That man was doing something he shouldn't."

Vivian opened her mouth to protest, but the denial rose and died in her throat in an instant. It was exactly what she'd suspected and feared. She tapped her fingernails against the ceramic coffee mug.

"I guess I was hoping that you might have some other explanation. I can't...I can't see my father..."

"Did he play the ponies?"

She shook her head.

"Then he had a bit on the side?"

Vivian looked up and narrowed her eyes. "Another woman? Of course not," she snapped. "He loved Mother."

Charlie threw up his hands. "Look, Viv, I'm asking you the questions I would ask any client in your situation. Don't take it personally. There's always some concrete reason that an otherwise respectable citizen would take up with the wrong element."

"I'm sorry," she said and stirred the coffee she now couldn't bring herself drink. She watched the swirling vortex, unsure how to continue.

"What did your father do for a living again?" Charlie asked.

"He was a defense attorney."

Charlie whistled through his teeth. Then he leaned in toward her and lowered his voice. "That's easy. He gambled, laundered money, threw cases…" His expression softened as he looked at her, and he added, "I know it's hard to hear, but it's what you expected, isn't it? You can't swing a dead cat without hitting a crooked lawyer in this city. Without hitting a crooked *anything*…"

Vivian shook her head, still in shock at the idea of her staid, respectable father doing something like fixing cases or laundering money.

Charlie rapped the knuckles of one hand on the table and flicked his fingers toward the waitress to signal for the check. "I say stay out of it," he said. "Pretend you never found that money. Let your father, and his memory, rest in peace."

"Maybe you're right," Vivian said, her voice flat. But it would be hard to forget that the money and the note had existed—especially now that they were gone. Should she tell him that they had gone missing? Maybe that wasn't important after all. And it wouldn't be important at all if she dropped all of this like Charlie wanted her to.

But then the waitress returned with their check, and Vivian's mind switched to the more urgent matter at hand.

The check? Charlie was leaving? Already?

"I know I'm right. I don't want you messing around with any gangsters." He glowered at her for a moment before his expression softened, one corner of his mouth quirking up.

Vivian forced a smile in return, but it quickly faltered. She looked down again. *Gangsters*, she thought. Could her father really have been involved with gangsters?

When she looked back up, Charlie was still gazing at her, his smile faded into something softer, more intimate. The air between them was charged, thick with possibility. *Just ask him*, she thought. Ask him why he never called you back. And then tell him that it doesn't matter. Tell him that whatever the reason that you don't care. Forget it. You can start from scratch. *Tell him*. Her lips parted.

"Excuse me."

Vivian blinked. A young girl had come up to the booth. She was clutching a napkin to her chest and looked as though she were about to hyperventilate. The girl glanced from Vivian to Charlie, considered him for a moment, and turned back to Vivian.

"Do you think I could I have an autograph, Miss Witchell?" She thrust the napkin toward Vivian, flushing purple with embarrassment.

"Oh, of course," Vivian answered. She turned to Charlie. "Do you have a pen, by any chance?"

Charlie reached into his inside breast pocket and handed the fountain pen to Vivian with a smirk.

"What's your name, dear?" Vivian asked, pen poised above the napkin.

"Norma."

Vivian scrawled, *To Norma. Always reach for the stars. Vivian Witchell.* She began to hand the napkin back when the girl interjected, "Oh, could you date it as well?"

"Sure," Vivian said. She wrote *December 26, 1938* underneath her message. "Might I ask why?"

The girl answered in a rapid clip. "Oh, it's so that if this turns out to be a pivotal moment in your career, the autograph will end up being worth more than if there wasn't a date on it. Everyone's doing it these days."

"Very sensible," Charlie said.

Vivian smiled and handed the napkin over. The girl's eyes flicked toward Charlie again. "You're… Well, you're not anybody, are you, mister?"

"Nobody worth knowing," he said with a wink.

The girl nodded at him, her cheeks fiery all over again. Then she turned on her heel without another word and scurried back to her own booth.

"Looks like you've hit the big time," Charlie said.

Vivian smiled and glanced after the girl. She usually loved being asked for her autograph, but something about having it happen in front of Charlie made her feel superficial. She knew

Charlie thought the entertainment business was shallow in general and that he thought Vivian shallow in particular. But the validation *did* matter to her. She was good at her job, and she took pride in hearing it.

"That happens every so often now. I have to admit it's nice. Let's hope for her sake that today is a pivotal moment in my career," she said with a laugh. She turned to Charlie again, but his smile was gone, and his eyes were cold. The window of opportunity for heartfelt confession had passed.

"You know, I listen to the show when I can," he said. "It's good. *You're* good."

"Thank you." It was a kind thing to say.

"And I've seen you in the papers, of course," he said. "How *is* Yarborough?"

Vivian swallowed. So that was it, then. Graham. Graham was the reason he hadn't returned her call. Charlie believed that after everything that had happened, she'd chosen Graham over him. She almost laughed with relief. It was a misunderstanding that could easily be remedied. She had to admit that it pleased her a little to see the jealousy evident under Charlie's polite facade. He'd never liked Graham, and he hadn't liked seeing her *with* Graham.

Her eyes caught on the girl and her friends huddled in the nearby booth, and she realized that she couldn't tell Charlie the truth. Not here. Though they weren't looking at her, she knew the girls were listening, leaning toward her to catch snippets of her and Charlie's conversation—as they surely had been since the moment Vivian walked into the coffee shop.

Vivian clenched her hands into fists under the tabletop. She'd learned her lesson about keeping her mouth shut. The last time she'd blabbed something she shouldn't have, it had ended up in the newspaper. She'd been temporarily fired from *The Darkness Knows*, and her career had almost ended before it had begun. She couldn't risk that happening again—not when everything was going so well.

"Graham's fine," she said finally, her voice tight. She forced a smile. "He misses you though."

"Misses *me*? Why?"

"Because you're Harvey Diamond, of course. The *real* Harvey Diamond. Graham needs your stories, your insight, to base the character on, you know. Without you around, he's just guessing."

"I think we're all just guessing."

"That's a very Harvey Diamond thing to say."

Charlie smirked as the waitress returned, bearing the check for their two coffees. Both Vivian and Charlie reached for it, and their hands brushed. Vivian snatched the strip of paper toward her, feeling a thrum where his fingers had brushed hers.

"I'll pay," she said, clutching the check to her bosom as if Charlie might try to steal it from her. "I'm the one who asked you for the consultation."

Charlie leaned back in the booth. "Suit yourself," he said.

Vivian fished some change out of her handbag and made a show of looking at her wristwatch. "Oh," she said, not even registering the time. "I must be going. I have rehearsal…"

"Sure," Charlie said, a smile curling at one corner of his mouth. "It was nice to see you, Viv."

"You too," she said, meeting his gaze again for an instant before looking toward the door. She stood up, and he helped her on with her coat. His hands didn't linger this time. She was close enough to smell the citrusy aroma of his aftershave, and she closed her eyes against the memory of what it had been like to press her nose against his neck. What it had been like to breathe him in, to touch him. She turned back to face him, and she thought she saw frustration flit across his face for an instant. Had he thought this meeting would go differently as well?

"Thanks again for your help," she said.

"Anytime."

She turned her back and felt the stab of regret in her chest. She closed her eyes and fought the urge to turn back and explain everything—the gaggle of listening girls be damned. Instead, Vivian hitched in her breath as she pushed the front door open with a jangle of bells and stepped out into the biting December wind.

CHAPTER SIX

———◆———

Vivian crossed Madison to the Grayson-Cole Building. She
hopped over a puddle of slush near the curb and turned
back toward the coffee shop, pretending to brush the dirty
water off her plastic shoe covers. She fought the urge to look
back, but now she couldn't help herself. Charlie was visible
through the large plate-glass window, sitting back down in the
booth. As Vivian made eye contact, he turned away. He'd been
watching her, she thought. Hope fluttered in her chest, and she
raised her hand to wave at him, but a streetcar clanged past,
blocking her view, and she let the hand fall back to her side.

The doorman nodded at her as he swung the door wide. She
nodded to the new security guard, who looked bored standing
his post in the lobby. The old guard, Del, had lost his job not
long after Marjorie's murder because he'd been leaking information to the *Chicago Patriot* about the murder investigation.
Del had roped Angelo, the elevator operator, into the scheme
as well, but thank goodness, Angelo hadn't been canned.
Vivian had always had a soft spot for Angelo, and he'd actually

helped her career with all the publicity he'd generated through his leaked gossip. Now, he stood at attention beside the elevator labeled *Express to 11*.

"Miss Witchell," Angelo said, beaming. "You're looking well today. You had a nice Christmas?"

"Yes," she said. "You?"

"Wonderful. My daughter came down from Waukegan with her family. You spend the holiday with Mr. Yarborough?"

Vivian nodded, careful to keep her expression neutral. For all she knew, Angelo could still be leaking gossip to whoever would pay him. "Graham gave me this," she said, tapping the little enamel-and-gold bird brooch pinned to the lapel of her wool coat.

The older man whistled in appreciation. "He sure is sweet on you."

She held her smile, pretending to be happy about Graham's attention. She tried not to think of the man she'd just left, but that was impossible. She closed her eyes, and Charlie's easy smile appeared on the back of her eyelids. She opened her eyes and sighed in frustration. The flutter he'd started in her stomach at the diner hadn't subsided with the distance she'd put between them. There was nothing for it then, she decided. She had to see Charlie again.

WCHI had sprung back quite well from the tumult of Marjorie Fox's murder. Mr. Hart was gone, of course, having had such a large role in the entire scandalous affair. His daughter, a fixture around the station, had killed WCHI's biggest star and had tried to kill his son. Though Mr. Hart wasn't directly involved in either incident, he couldn't stay as head of the station. The scandal was too much to overcome.

Mr. Langley was the interim head of the station now, and things were much as they had been before all of that sordid business happened. In fact, in many ways, things were even better now. The station had never produced more nationally sponsored shows, including Vivian's own *The Darkness Knows*, which had been steadily climbing in the ratings since Vivian joined the cast in October. She was sure what had spiked the rise in listeners had been her intimate role in Marjorie's murder, her appearance in so many newspapers, and her accompanying "romance" with Graham—but she wasn't complaining.

Vivian stepped off the elevator onto the eleventh floor and made her way past the large, auditorium-style studios where the shows with orchestras or live audiences were held—*Quiz Time* or *The Carlton Coffee Hour*, before the latter moved to Hollywood. Things were still quiet today, the day after Christmas, the halls almost empty. So it was not difficult to spot her best friend and the acting head of the station's secretary, Imogene, barreling toward her, her dimpled face alight.

"You'll never guess what George gave me for Christmas!" Imogene cried. There was no preamble. Vivian stopped and waited for her friend to reach her.

"A vacuum cleaner?" Vivian teased.

Imogene rolled her eyes. "Be serious."

"I am being serious. George is a practical guy."

Imogene thrust her left hand under Vivian's nose. A tiny sapphire winked at her in the hallway lights from Genie's ring finger.

"No!"

"Yes!"

Vivian embraced her best friend, her smile faltering for a split second when she was sure Imogene couldn't see. She pulled back and searched her friend's face. Imogene was beside herself with excitement. She'd been living on pins and needles for over a year, expecting a proposal at any moment. And Vivian had been on vicarious pins and needles as well.

"How did he propose?" she asked. "Details, please."

"On Christmas," Imogene said, her eyes gone dreamy. "He took me ice skating on the pond at his parents' farm after dinner. And right there in the middle of the ice, he got down on one knee and popped the question. I said yes, of course."

"That's wonderful, Genie," Vivian said, clasping the other girl's hands. "Really."

"Really?" Imogene's brow wrinkled as she searched Vivian's face. There was no hiding anything from Imogene. "What's with you?"

"Oh, it's nothing," Vivian said, suppressing a smile. "I had coffee with Charlie is all." She tried to keep her voice light, but she could tell by Imogene's expression that she hadn't been successful.

Imogene's brown eyes widened. "So you *did* call him."

"I did."

"Good for you," Imogene said. "How did it go?"

"Well." Vivian frowned. "Not great."

"Meaning?"

She sighed. "I don't know. He was…aloof."

"Aloof." Imogene crossed her arms.

Vivian bit her lower lip in thought. Her statement wasn't entirely true. Charlie hadn't been aloof until the subject of Graham had come up. Until she had missed her opportunity to tell Charlie that what he had been seeing in the papers about them was untrue.

"Did he explain why he never called you back?"

Vivian shook her head.

"Did you even ask him?"

Vivian shook her head again.

"Well, that's the first thing I would have asked."

"That's not why I called him this time," Vivian said. She picked at the fur on her lapel. She wanted to tell Genie everything about what had happened. She had to tell *someone*, but this was not the place. The walls had ears at WCHI.

"You told him about the locked drawer full of cash?"

Vivian narrowed her eyes and peered down the deserted hallway. "He thinks my father was up to no good."

"No good like what?"

Vivian shook her head. "It's too horrible to discuss. And Charlie said I should let sleeping dogs lie."

"Will you?"

Vivian shrugged.

"Hmmm. To me, this mystery sounds like a terrific excuse to stay in touch with a handsome detective," Imogene said.

Vivian said nothing. Her friend was right. It was a terrific excuse, and although things hadn't gone as planned at the diner, Vivian was not ready to admit defeat. Not just yet.

Imogene glanced around to make sure the coast was clear before leaning in and whispering, "You told him about you and Graham, of course."

Vivian sighed. "You know I can't do that."

"How can you not? That's vital information! And Charlie's a detective. If anyone can keep a secret, he can."

"I can't risk it after what happened the last time." Vivian glanced back over her shoulder toward the elevator. Angelo was gone.

Imogene narrowed her eyes. "I'd risk it if I were you."

Vivian exhaled. That's exactly what she wanted to do. That's what she *would* do if she got another chance.

"Anyway, congratulations on the engagement, Genie. I'm ecstatic for you and George."

"Thanks, Viv. And keep your calendar clear. You're my maid of honor."

Hugging Imogene one last time, Vivian pushed the idea of Charlie and her father's dirty dealings out of her mind. She had a rehearsal to get to in Studio C.

Despite his best efforts, Graham hadn't made any progress in convincing the writers to round out the character of Harvey Diamond. He was still entirely one-dimensional: a hard-nosed, tough-talking gumshoe who led Vivian's character, his long-suffering sidekick Lorna Lafferty, on romantically while leading her out of danger. Unfortunately for Graham, the listeners didn't want character growth. They wanted action.

Today was their first read-through of the latest script. This week found the intrepid duo wading through the opium dens of Chinatown in search of a missing heiress. Vivian's character, Lorna, had more dialogue than ever, and she carried much of the story, having been kidnapped by white slavers and forced to try to talk her way out of the sticky situation. It ended well, of course. Harvey Diamond always saved the day, but this was an edgy episode, much more daring than anything else they'd tried to date. Vivian could see the shift in direction the station had taken since Mr. Hart's departure. Mr. Langley had more modern ideas about what constituted entertainment, and he was willing to take chances.

However, it looked like the sponsor might be getting a little nervous about all the chances being taken with their expensive baby. An unfamiliar man stood in the control room next to Mr. Langley. He was in his midforties and attractive, with dark wavy hair. He was dressed to the nines in a perfectly tailored pin-striped suit. He surveyed the room through narrowed eyes and puffed away at a Sultan's Gold cigarette, tapping the ashes into a glass tray perched on a tiny pedestal at his right elbow. He had *ad man* written all over him. His look was carefully crafted to impress, and Vivian didn't know anyone who smoked Sultan's Gold cigarettes if they weren't under contractual obligation to do so.

As Vivian watched, the man looked at her and then leaned in to say something to Mr. Langley. They both smiled at her, and Vivian felt her insides unclench. She returned the smile and watched the Sultan's Gold man's smile soften from one of calculation to one of flirtation. Whatever this official-looking man was here for, it clearly wasn't about her. She followed their eyes to Graham on the opposite end of the room. He too was puffing away. A hazy cloud of cigarette smoke hung about his head.

Vivian hoped he'd at least had the presence of mind to

smoke an actual Sultan's Gold under the watchful gaze of the sponsor's representative. Graham tended to sneak his own preferred brand of cigarettes into the studio. She spotted the telltale gold stripe around the cigarette between Graham's lips and sighed with the relief.

"Afternoon, everybody." The director, Joe McGreevey, shouted to be heard over the raucous din of the rehearsal space.

All heads in the studio snapped to the control booth.

"You may have noticed a new face in the booth today. This is the Sultan's Gold radio account representative, Stuart Marshfield."

Vivian shifted her attention to Mr. Marshfield and offered him a brilliant smile. He exhaled a cloud of smoke as he regarded the group and gave them a nod.

"Okay," Joe continued after a beat. "Let's take it from the top, everybody!"

The room hushed. Bill Purdy, the show's announcer, stepped forward, one hand cupping his right ear, the other hand clutching this week's script. The microphone wasn't live, but Bill played his part as though it were.

"And now it's time for another edition of that tantalizing tale of detective muscle, *The Darkness Knows*," he said. "Sponsored by Sultan's Gold, the cigarette that's truly mellow. Today, we open on Harvey Diamond's downtown office. Diamond is at his desk when a well-dressed man of middle age bursts in, followed by Diamond's right-hand gal,

Lorna Lafferty." Bill shot a nervous glance into the control room, but the ad man's gaze was focused on Graham.

Dave Chapman, utility actor on the show, stepped forward. He specialized in playing the heavy, the goon, any number of assorted bad guys, as well as any other minor male character that popped up in the script and needed a voice. Though in this episode, he was playing the wronged instead of the accused.

"Diamond, you've got to help me," Dave said, a pleading look on his face.

"I tried to stop him, Harvey," Vivian said. "He doesn't have an appointment."

Graham stubbed out his cigarette and stepped toward the dead mic.

"That's okay, doll," he said. "Help you with what...uh, Mr....?"

"Gold."

"Mr. Gold. Have a seat and fill me in."

"It's my daughter, Diamond. She's been kidnapped."

"Kidnapped? Oh, Harvey!" Vivian rolled her eyes and shot a look at Merle Glassman, this episode's writer, who hovered behind Graham, eyes riveted to the script before him, pencil poised to make notes. Lorna Lafferty said "Oh, Harvey" at least five times an episode. Harvey Diamond wasn't the only character remaining one-dimensional. Vivian flipped through the script searching for the signature Lorna Lafferty scream. There it was, on the top of page 3 when Lorna was grabbed by the kidnappers. *Well, if it ain't broke, don't fix it*, Vivian thought.

"Did you get a ransom note?" Graham asked, looking at Dave.

"No, but I got this letter in today's mail," Dave said.

"May I see it?" Graham furrowed his brow in concentration as he feigned reading the note. "'They're holding me against my will. Please, help me. I'm at the Golden Lion. Myra.'"

"The Golden Lion? That's in Chinatown," Vivian announced.

"Pause for organ tease and then sponsor jingle," Joe said. During the real show, there would be an organist and a trio of women singers who belted out the tune that began, "Sultan's Gold. You'll be sold on the cigarette that's truly mellow." But today was only a read-through. The actors were there to iron out the script, to catch any holes in the plot or inconsistencies that dedicated listeners would surely notice. "Announcer..." Joe beckoned to Bill, and he stepped up to the microphone again, one hand to his ear.

"And now back to our story. A mysterious Mr. Gold has asked for Detective Diamond's help in locating his missing daughter."

"Chinatown, you say?" Graham asked.

"Yes, I went there last week," Vivian said. "Donald Fryman took me out for some chop suey, and I noticed the sign for the Golden Lion down the street. You can't miss it."

"Donald Fryman?"

Vivian and Graham raised their eyebrows at each other. Then they both looked toward Merle Glassman, the writer. Was he adding a love interest for Vivian into the mix? Perhaps things would get interesting for Vivian at least. Perhaps her character would be allowed to grow into something beyond second banana. Or maybe they were thinking of adding this allusive suitor for Lorna in order to make Harvey jealous and act on his true feelings for his girl Friday. There were so many ways this story line could play out, and Vivian was pleasantly surprised at the turn of events.

"Yes," she said with a smile in her voice. "Donald Fryman. You know him—the big, beefy-looking fellow who hauls the mail sacks off the truck."

"I know him all right," Graham answered gruffly.

"Hold it," Joe announced. They all turned to him and waited while he held a brief hushed conversation with the sponsor's representative. He turned to Merle, still hovering behind the actors with his pad of paper and pencil at the ready. "I've changed my mind. I don't like the direction this is going."

"Don't like the direction?" Vivian asked.

"I don't like the jealous angle for Harvey," he replied, looking off into space as he considered it. He shook his head. "No, I don't like it."

Vivian's stomach sank, and she caught Graham's eye. He shrugged, as if it was exactly what he'd expected to happen.

"Harvey is a tough guy," Joe explained. "He shouldn't be jealous of anyone."

"But I think it's a subtle way to show that Harvey's human," Graham interjected. "I like that we get to see some movement on the attraction between the two of them. It's been simmering under the surface for months." He looked at Vivian, and she glanced quickly away.

Joe nodded and placed one stubby finger to his chin, pointing to Merle as he said, "Cut it. It slows down the story."

Merle nodded and wiped out the extra lines of dialogue with a few strikes of his pencil.

"Good job, everyone," Joe said. "But I'd like to move on to the section about the business partner. That dialogue seems a little choppy to me. Bottom of page 14."

Vivian flipped back through her script. She wasn't in this scene between Harvey and Mr. Gold, where they realize that Mr. Gold's business partner knows more about the daughter's kidnapping than he's been letting on and that he's involved in the whole nefarious scheme.

The business partner mentioned in the script made Vivian's mind wander to her father's business partner, Uncle Freddy, as she watched the rehearsal proceed. Of course, she'd agreed to drop the issue of her father's mysterious drawer. She'd promised Charlie as much, but there was still something fluttering at the back of her mind, and she couldn't let it go without talking to Freddy. He had to know something about that money in her father's desk, and if he didn't, well, there was no harm in asking. But if he did know, he might be able to settle this niggling ache in her stomach and put the whole matter to rest. She'd go see him as soon as rehearsal ended.

Vivian glanced at Mr. Marshfield in the control room. She watched him watch Graham and wondered what all of this could be about.

When she walked over to Graham, he was lost in his own world, staring down at a script—not for *The Darkness Knows*, but for *The Scarlet Pimpernel*. She watched his lips move, working through a bit of dialogue. She touched his arm, and he glanced up.

"Oh, hi there, Viv," he said. He raked a hand through his thick black hair and sighed.

She sidled up to him so that both of their backs were turned to the control room.

"What's with the ad man?" she asked out of the side of her mouth.

Graham glanced over at the man talking with Mr. Langley and smiled. "Oh yeah, I was going to tell you about that. Mr. Marshfield wants me to pose for some magazine advertisements for Sultan's Gold."

"Magazine advertisements? That's fantastic!"

Graham nodded, eyes narrowed, and took another drag on his cigarette. He turned his back to the control room and made a face at the taste of the Sultan's Gold, then exhaled. "It's a big step," he said.

She could picture the ad already: Graham's face in three-quarter profile, a self-assured half smile on his lips, his dark-brown eyes trained on the reader, a Sultan's Gold cigarette balanced in fingers held below his chin. The text appearing in a balloon above him would read:

Graham Yarborough, radio's Harvey Diamond, says, "I smoke nothing but Sultan's Gold. The mellow taste and smooth flavor of Sultan's Gold cigarettes calm my throat and assure me of a confident vocal delivery every time."

"Just you?"

"For now, but I'm working on getting Lorna into the picture. That Sultan's Gold man was watching you awfully closely during rehearsal. I don't think it'll take much convincing."

Vivian's heart thumped in her chest. "A magazine advertisement… Wouldn't that be something?"

He nodded. "Ratings are through the roof, and I think they have big things in store for us, Viv. I've heard whispers of moving the show to Hollywood."

Hollywood? That was the big time. All the most popular radio shows had moved to Hollywood: *Amos 'n' Andy*, *Fibber McGee and Molly*, even *The Carlton Coffee Hour* from their own station. She had so many questions, but Graham had already

turned his attention back to *The Pimpernel* script in his hands.
She took in his uncharacteristically disheveled appearance.
There was a day's growth of stubble on his cheeks and dark
smudges under both eyes.

"How are things going?" she asked.

"I'm beat," he said. "And it's only Monday. *The Pimpernel*'s
wearing me out. I was up almost all night working on it."

"Poor boy," she said. "Can I do something to help?" He
was taking this side project much more seriously than Vivian
had ever imagined he would.

Graham smiled down at her and then glanced off toward the
other side of the room. He shook his head at someone over
her shoulder and brushed her hand from his arm. "I'm afraid
not," he said, his eyes still trained on the far side of the room.
"I'm the captain of this ship, and I'll go down with it."

"Well, isn't that dramatic?" she said with a laugh.

Graham opened his mouth to reply but was cut off by his
writing partner, Paul, who'd charged up to them, wedging
his thin frame in front of Vivian. "Say, Graham, let's get some
lunch, huh? We need to work on this dialogue."

Vivian stepped away, rubbing her arm where Paul had
brushed up against her. She didn't know Paul well enough
to dislike him. It was his general presence that she objected
to. He seemed to always be around these days. He'd been
nothing more than a peripheral character at the station, a
writer who worked on the comedy shows, until Graham had

taken him on as his partner in this *Pimpernel* gambit. Now the man was always hovering, buzzing like a mosquito.

"Hello, Paul," Vivian said.

A perfunctory smile flashed across his narrow face. "Oh, hello, Viv," he said. His attention returned to Graham, his finger tapping a staccato rhythm on the papers he held.

"Yes, let's do that. I think the end of act 1 could use some going over," Graham said finally.

"Right."

"Sorry, Viv, I've got to run." Graham glanced back at the control room before leaning down to give her a peck on the cheek.

Vivian watched the men leave, and then her eyes strayed to the control room again. Langley was gone, but Mr. Marshfield was still standing there in a haze of blue-gray smoke. He'd seen everything between Vivian and Graham just now. Hopefully, he hadn't heard everything as well. And hopefully, he'd found their chemistry undeniable enough to include her in the ad and several more to come. She smiled at him and resolved to start smoking Sultan's Golds if that's what it took to merit Mr. Marshfield's regard. As she watched, he stubbed out his cigarette with a flick of his wrist. His eyes caught hers through the cloud of smoke, and he winked.

CHAPTER SEVEN

❖

Vivian approached Freddy's office slowly, as if sneaking up on it would somehow make the past less vivid. The Rookery was down the street from WCHI, but she generally avoided it, averting her gaze when she had to pass the revered piece of Chicago architectural history. She could never see or think of that building without encountering memories of her father.

Sometimes, she'd accompany her father on Saturday trips downtown to his office. She'd usually sit in the corner and read until he was finished with his business. Then they'd go out to lunch and take in a movie. She remembered one particular Saturday when she was about twelve and he'd taken her against her mother's admonitions to Valentino's last film, *The Son of the Sheik*, at the old Castle Theater on State and Madison. It had been released a few weeks after Valentino died so tragically of appendicitis.

Oh, how she'd swooned in that movie theater over his smoldering, soulful expressions and his utter devotion to the heroine, Yasmin. She'd imagined herself as Yasmin for months afterward, starring in lavish daydreams during tedious mathematics classes. Her father took her to that film, as well as the rereleased original, *The Sheik*, several more times without her mother's knowledge that September.

Vivian tried to keep her swirling emotions at bay, but as she entered the vestibule of the venerated Rookery building, her stomach knotted of its own accord. She hurried past the bank of elevators into the miraculous airy light court in the center of the building. It had always taken her breath away to enter that space, all blinding white marble and gold Moroccan trim. She stood in the middle of the floor, eyes raised to the wonderful, vaulted greenhouse-style ceiling, so unexpected in the middle of an office building, and stood with the weak winter light falling onto her upturned face. After a moment, she hopped up the marble main staircase, fingertips trailing along the brass railing, to take the spiral stairs to the third floor.

Vivian pressed the door buzzer to suite 310 and sucked in her breath, smoothing the fur lapels on her coat and straightening her hat. The door opened and Della, Freddy's secretary, stood regarding her. The wide smile on her face faltered, and confusion flashed across her pretty features for the briefest of instances before her smile brightened again.

"Vivian!" she said. "What a surprise. How long has it been?"

Vivian smiled at Della. She looked just as Vivian had last seen her—pretty and efficiently put together. Della had joined the firm a few months before Arthur Witchell's death, and Vivian hadn't seen much of the woman since. Back then, she'd been fresh out of secretarial school and eager to please. Now, she was dressed quite well in a long-sleeved gray wool frock, with a mauve enamel flower brooch pinned over her heart, her hair pulled back into a knot at the nape of her neck. She looked like a woman in charge.

"Della," Vivian said. "It's been too long. You look wonderful."

Della blushed and raised one alabaster hand to her hair. "Thank you," she said. "You're here to see Mr. Endicott, I presume?"

"I am. Is he in?"

Della nodded. "Come right in. He'll be pleased as Punch to see you." She motioned into the interior of the office.

The reception area hadn't changed one bit since Vivian last walked through the door seven years ago. The dark wooden paneling glowed in the dim light from the large window facing Quincy Street, the wide sill crowded with a veritable jungle of plants somehow managing to thrive in the gray winter light. A piece of stationery curled from the top of the typewriter on Della's desk. The one thing that had changed, that Vivian could see with any certainty, was that the gold plate on her father's office door had been removed, leaving a dark rectangle of wood. Vivian felt her heart thump once and wondered why the absence of something so innocuous could make her feel her grief so keenly.

The door buzzed again and Della rushed off to answer it, disappearing into the tiny vestibule.

"Della, my girl!" a male voice boomed from the hallway.

The voice was a familiar one, but before Vivian could place it, Martin Gilfoy strode into the room. He kicked his stiff right leg out in front of him as he walked, making him appear to be goose-stepping like those German troops in the newsreels. Then his eyes fell on Vivian and he stopped. His bad leg almost gave out under his weight, but he grabbed hold of the coatrack to steady himself.

Ah, so that's who Della had expected me to be, Vivian thought. She'd be disappointed in finding herself too, if she'd been expecting someone like Martin at her door.

"Well, if it isn't little Viv Witchell," Martin said, a smile lighting his face. His dark-blue eyes flicked over her. "Not so little anymore I see."

"And Martin Gilfoy," she replied. "Still an incurable flirt."

He laughed, flashing perfect white teeth. Martin's boyish handsomeness had matured, she noted. He was still tall and thin, but there was a weightiness to his frame that hadn't been there before. His dark hair was combed back, and mischief sparkled in his blue eyes. His smile highlighted that dimple in his right cheek that she'd found so irresistible at sixteen. She'd found everything about Martin irresistible at sixteen, come to think of it.

He'd been in his last year of law school the last time she'd seen him, working as a clerk for her father. He'd been an older man, a college man: smart, handsome, charming, and terribly flirtatious—a dangerous combination for the likes of Vivian then as now. She'd flirted with him, but nothing had happened between them despite her valiant attempts to get his attention. But she had been a girl then, and Martin had rightly seen her as such.

She glanced down at his right leg. His hand was splayed across the thigh, but if he felt any lingering pain there, it didn't show on his face. She hadn't seen him since his accident—the accident that had killed Mr. Graves and gifted Martin with that permanent limp. She'd avoided the Rookery and its memories, and Martin hadn't stayed on as Freddy's partner as everyone had assumed he would. After he'd recovered from the accident, he'd moved on to greener pastures. He was now a highly regarded assistant state's attorney for Cook County. Though his and Vivian's paths hadn't crossed personally, her mother liked to keep abreast of his activities and inform Vivian whenever she got the chance. In her mother's opinion—in anyone's opinion—Martin Gilfoy was a catch.

He held Vivian's gaze and his easy smile but addressed the secretary now seated behind her typewriter again. "It *is* the fourth Monday of the month, isn't it, Della?"

"Yes, that's right."

"What's the fourth Monday of the month?" Vivian asked, glancing at the WPA calendar pinned over Della's desk and featuring an artistic blue, red, black, and brown lithographic rendering of a rocking horse in front of a Christmas tree and hearth.

"My standing lunch date with one Frederick Endicott, Esquire," Martin said. He nodded toward Freddy's closed office door. "But I'm afraid I may have been stood up for a pretty lady this time."

"Oh no." Vivian blushed as her eyes flicked to the floor and back up again. "I was passing by and realized I hadn't seen Freddy in ages, so I dropped in. I'll go. You two have plans."

"No, stay," Martin said. "I insist." He continued to hold his smile and her gaze.

Della cleared her throat. "You know, Mr. Endicott's alone, and I'm sure he wouldn't mind if you went in. I think it would a nice surprise for him." Della smiled at her and nodded toward the closed door of Freddy's office. Vivian appraised the tilt of Della's head and her wide-eyed interest, and understood that she was cramping the secretary's style. Vivian wasn't the only one taken with Martin's ample charms. Then the door marked *Mr. Frederick Endicott* jerked open.

"Well, well, Viv!" Freddy stood framed in the doorway, beaming. He was tall and still quite fit for a man nearing fifty, handsome with twinkling blue eyes. He walked out to greet her with arms stretched wide. "What's the occasion?"

"It's just been too long," Vivian said, clasping his arms and leaning in to give him a light peck on the cheek.

"Ahem," Martin said. "What am I? Chopped liver?"

Freddy shifted his attention to Martin, who was tapping his wristwatch in mock annoyance, and said, "You know you can't hold a candle to our Viv here, Gilfoy. You wouldn't mind pushing back our lunch half an hour, would you, old pal?"

"Of course not," Martin said. "Ladies first." He perched on the corner of Della's desk, leaning in to give the secretary his full attention.

Freddy ushered Vivian inside his office and closed the door behind them.

"So just in the neighborhood?"

"Unfortunately, no," she answered. She removed her coat and handed it to him to hang on the coatrack in the corner.

"What's wrong? Nothing serious, I hope."

"I hope so too," she said with a heavy sigh.

"Well, come in, come in," Freddy said, gesturing her into his office.

She sat in the comfortable chair opposite his desk, hands pressed together in her lap as she waited for him to close the door. Her eyes ranged over the scant decoration—a few framed photos, all business related. He moved a large pile of paper from his desktop to the safe behind him with a grunt and turned back to her, fixing her with an intent stare.

"Now what's the problem?" he asked.

"I found something in Father's desk the other evening, and I was hoping you could help me figure out what it means."

Freddy's thick blond eyebrows lowered to meet over the bridge of his nose. "That depends on what you found," he said.

Vivian cleared her throat. "I don't know if you remember, but there was a drawer that was locked and we couldn't find the key after his death…"

Freddy's frown deepened, but his expression didn't change to one of recognition.

"Well, it *was* locked…" she continued. "For almost eight years until I found that key, quite by accident, the night of the Christmas party."

"Really? Where?"

"It was hidden behind a picture frame in his office."

Freddy nodded, looking unsurprised. "And what was in the drawer?"

"Money," she said. "A large envelope stuffed full of cash— almost four thousand dollars' worth."

She held off on mentioning the note until she could gauge his reaction to the money.

Freddy focused at something over her shoulder, his finger-tips tapping against his chin. He relaxed. "Oh, Viv," he said, leaning back in his chair, a smile spreading across his face. "Is that all?"

"Is that all?" she asked, confused. "What was my father doing with all that cash? Doesn't that seem odd to you?"

"Not with your father, no," he said. He laced his fingers over his midsection and smiled at her. "You were a bit young to know about any of this, and he kept it from you, from your mother as well. But your father had been burned…in the crash. Not irrevocably, of course. But it left its mark on him. He held tight to his cash after that—I guess literally, in this case. He had a great fear of becoming destitute, you know. Of losing everything. I suppose because of where he'd come from. He didn't want to find himself back there."

A crease appeared between his brows as his expression grew more serious. "He had a rough go of it for a while there. I was so worried about his safety that I loaned him the money to pull him out. Not that it was that great of an amount, but he was too proud to dip into your mother's family money."

"Worried for his safety?" Vivian's mind immediately went to that threatening note. Someone had been after him after all.

Freddy nodded, deep in thought. "He was so despondent for a few weeks in November of that year that I was afraid he'd do harm to himself."

Vivian's mouth dropped open. "He would never have done something like that," she said.

Freddy shrugged and glanced out the window. "Maybe not. Frankly, I'm sorry you had to know anything about it."

Vivian swallowed. She was sorry too. Her unbreakable bear of a father had been so despondent over something that he'd considered ending his own life? He had certainly bounced back. Shortly after losing almost everything, he'd been able to buy his family a luxurious home in one of the city's most prestigious neighborhoods. How on earth had he pulled that off?

"Well, then where did the money in the drawer come from?"

"Where do you think it came from?" Freddy smiled at her.

"I don't know," she said. "Gambling?"

"Gambling?" Freddy's smile faded. "I'm afraid you've got the wrong end of the stick there."

Vivian thought of the other things Charlie had suggested: another woman, laundering money…but she couldn't bring herself to mention them. Those ideas seemed so ridiculous, so sordid, here in the fine, upstanding solidness of the building in which her father had practiced law for more than twenty years, and in the presence of Uncle Freddy, who was looking at her with such kindness and bafflement and fatherly concern. She glanced out the window and was afforded a view of gray December sky. It had started snowing again.

"What about enemies?" she asked.

"Enemies?"

"Yes, did my father have any? Anyone that might want to hurt him?"

Freddy leaned forward, lips pinched into a thin white line. "Vivian, I'm not sure where you're going with all of this."

She sighed. Freddy seemed so genuinely baffled, and she suddenly couldn't bring herself to tell him about the note. And now that it was gone, she had no proof that it had ever existed. She was starting to doubt whether she'd actually seen it.

She shrugged, defeated.

Freddy must have read the worry on her face, because he leaned toward her, his fingers intertwined over the open ledger on his desk. "Your father and I were partners...friends... He was good in the stock market, believe it or not. Made some savvy real-estate investments. All perfectly aboveboard. If he'd been doing anything illegal, I would have known about it. And if he had made any enemies, I would have known about that too," Freddy said, his voice strong and authoritative.

Freddy's expression turned serious. He lowered his chin and made purposeful eye contact with Vivian across the desk. "You know, a few months back, I thought I was going to have to represent you in court," he said.

"Oh, that," she said with a sigh. Vivian was tired of having to discuss Marjorie Fox and her untimely demise. "I was never a suspect," she added. She'd been taken aback by the change in subject, especially to that particular subject. Marjorie Fox's murder wasn't something Vivian liked to think about if she could help it. The image of the dead woman's vacant gray eyes flashed into her mind, and Vivian willed it away with a shiver.

"Was your life in danger? I heard there were threats."

Vivian smiled ruefully. "Not really," she admitted. "You can't believe everything you read in the papers." Even though she had seemed to be the next intended murder victim, it had all been a ruse to draw attention away from the real plot. Charlie's life had been in danger the entire time.

"Speaking of the papers, it seems I can't open one these days without reading about what you did last Saturday night. In fact…" He smiled and held up one finger. He swiveled in his chair, plucked something from the top of the small safe on the credenza behind him, and then returned to face her, his handsome face alight. He slid a copy of this week's *Radio Guide* over the polished surface of the desk. "Page 28," he said.

Vivian flipped through the magazine, even though she already knew what she would find—she'd looked at it a million times—and was greeted with a photo of herself smiling for the camera as she presented a wrapped present to Frances Barrow. The caption underneath said, "Fast Friends at Chicago's WCHI. Vivian Witchell presents an early Christmas gift to Frances Barrow at the station's yuletide party." Vivian smiled, her lips pressed together. The photo had been staged, the beautifully wrapped box empty.

Fast friends indeed, she thought. Although Vivian and Frances's relationship had moved into a sort of détente in the past few months, calling them fast friends was quite a stretch. She and Frances had called an informal cease-fire on battling for roles and boyfriends. At least, Vivian thought they had. Frankly, she had been too busy working since Marjorie's death to worry much about station politics and maneuvering.

"I'm proud of you, Viv," Freddy said, bringing her back to the present. "And your father would have been proud of you too."

Vivian swallowed and managed a nod. She closed the *Radio Guide* and folded her hands in her lap.

"I'm sorry I haven't been in touch," Freddy continued. "I should've phoned you when I heard about that affair at the radio station."

"Don't worry about it, Uncle Freddy," Vivian said, then coughed to clear her throat of the emotion harboring there. "There was nothing you could have done."

"Still, I feel responsible for you, even though you're a grown woman now. I feel as though your father would expect me to look out for you."

"Well, I know who to call if I ever find myself in legal trouble," Vivian said, attempting a joke.

A hint of a smile touched Freddy's lips. "Let's hope you never do, my girl."

Vivian bent her head and studied her nails. She felt stupid for having come here. She knew Freddy didn't intend to make her feel that way, but she felt like a petulant child in his presence.

"How's your mother?" he asked.

Vivian looked up at him, grateful for the change of subject.

"Busy, but you know Mother."

"I used to have dinner at your house at least once a month, didn't I? I miss those dinners."

"That settles it then. Come tonight. We'd all love to have you."

Freddy raised his eyebrows as he considered the invitation. "You're sure?"

"Bring Pauline," Vivian added.

Vivian saw his eyebrows fall and come together over the bridge of his nose in an unconscious scowl.

"Ah, well…" His voice faltered.

He didn't have to say it. He and Pauline were on the outs. Vivian had seen that coming long ago. She reached out and placed her hand atop Freddy's on the desk. He squeezed hers quickly before letting go.

Vivian hadn't liked Pauline. She was too young for Freddy and clearly had no designs on being a proper wife. She was not much older than Vivian, in fact, and more concerned with dancing and having a good time than being what Freddy needed her to be. He was a successful attorney with designs on public office. He needed someone strong, smart, and supportive, someone like Vivian's mother. She'd always thought that, and in the years since her father's death, she'd often wondered why nothing had ever brought Uncle Freddy and her mother together. They'd make a handsome couple. They had a shared history. But maybe that was the problem. That shared history included the ghost of her father lingering between them.

CHAPTER EIGHT

❖

A snippet of conversation floated up to Vivian as she made her way down the front stairs.

"…show your face here again."

Vivian paused on the landing, cocking an ear to hear what followed. It had sounded like Mrs. Graves's voice, and there was anger in it. Nothing followed, and Vivian realized that whoever was standing in the front hall below could plainly see her feet on the landing. So Vivian stepped down the remaining flight of stairs, intending to pretend she'd heard nothing at all.

The housekeeper stood with her back to the front door, and when she looked up at Vivian, there was a scowl on her face. Uncle Freddy and Martin had their backs to Vivian, but Martin was looking off to the side, and Vivian could see a spot of color high on his cheekbone. Was he embarrassed or angry, or both? What had she interrupted? Then Martin turned and caught sight of Vivian on the stairs.

"Ah, Viv, there you are," he said.

"Am I late?"

"Yes, but quite fashionably, I see." He grinned at her, and the tense air between the three of them dissipated. Mrs. Graves met Vivian's eyes for the briefest of instances before she rushed off, carrying the men's hats and overcoats.

"Flatterer," Vivian said, reaching out to clasp Martin's hand in greeting.

He brought her hand up and brushed his lips against the back of it. She turned to Freddy and smiled.

"Freddy, so glad you could come."

He nodded at her, and she noted the flush on his cheeks. She suspected it wasn't entirely from the cold. She arched an eyebrow at Martin, and he frowned at her.

"I'm glad both of you could make it," she said. "Mother will be delighted. She won't be down for a few minutes though. Can I interest either of you in a drink?"

"A lady after my own heart," Martin said. "Lead the way."

Vivian turned with a smile and headed into the den just off the foyer.

"I must confess that I'm a bit nervous to be in the company of a bona fide radio star," Martin said, following close behind.

She smiled and glanced toward Freddy, who'd walked off to the opposite side of the room to stand in front of the fireplace.

"Well, 'star' might be overstating it a little."

"Oh, don't be so modest. Freddy showed me your photo in that magazine."

"Did he? It's just the *Radio Guide*." She smiled at Martin and glanced down at the rug.

"Unfortunately, I must also confess that I haven't actually heard the program in question. A detective show, is it?"

"For shame," she chided, tapping his arm playfully. "Don't you have a radio in that office of yours?"

Martin hung his head and then glanced up at her, the picture of contrite remorse.

"I do not, but I'll get one right away tomorrow. And I promise not to miss another episode." He studied her for a moment, long enough for her to feel the heat bloom on her chest. "With your pluck and steely reserve, I can only assume you play the detective."

Vivian shook her head. "I'm the sidekick who gets into trouble and screams for help a lot."

"Sounds delightful," he said with a laugh. "When's it on? I'll have to tune in."

"Thursday evenings, eight o'clock."

Vivian turned and raised her voice so that it carried across the room. "So about that drink. What'll you have, Freddy?"

"Scotch," Freddy answered without turning from the fire.

Vivian turned back to Martin and raised her eyebrows in silent question.

"Scotch is fine. Thank you."

She made her way to the bar and poured two drinks from the decanter. She delivered one to Freddy and then returned to Martin. "How's life in the state's attorney's office?"

"Busy. Always busy. But it keeps me on my toes, and it's something new all the time. Speaking of, I thought about contacting you a few months back after that murder at the station."

"Yes, that was a horrible business."

"Is that why you came to see Freddy today?"

She shook her head, reluctant to let even someone like Martin in on the real reason. "Are you prosecuting the case against Peggy Hart?" she asked.

He shook his head. "I had to recuse myself—personal connection to a witness."

"Oh, right." She took a sip of her drink and noted his emphasis on *personal connection*. The man was always flirting, she thought, even when talking about a murder case.

"I don't think it'll go to trial though," he continued. "Not if Miss Hart pleads guilty, and from all indications, it looks like she will."

"I'm glad," Vivian said, sighing. She hadn't been looking forward to having to testify at Peggy's trial. She was glad for herself and glad for Charlie. He shouldn't have to relive any of that nightmare either.

Vivian followed Martin's gaze to Freddy, standing looking morosely into the fire.

"What's going on with him?" she whispered.

Martin shrugged. "He was drunk when I picked him up. I think it might be Pauline… There's trouble there."

There had always been trouble there, Vivian thought. "He told me. What happened between them?"

Martin shrugged. "Pauline was never one for social standing and things like joining the ladies' auxiliary. Now that Freddy's up for a judgeship, that's the kind of wife he needs her to be."

"A judgeship? He didn't mention anything about that earlier. That's wonderful."

Vivian saw the question in Martin's eyes. She knew he was wondering about the content of their earlier conversation. She glanced away as if she hadn't noticed.

"Freddy, dear, it's been too long!" They all turned to find that Julia Witchell had swept into the room like a queen, Oskar trailing half a step behind her. She walked up to Freddy and took both of his hands in hers. "We missed you at the Christmas party."

Freddy's blue eyes flicked from Julia to Oskar and back again. His mouth turned down under his pencil mustache at the sight of the other man. "Yes, well, it couldn't be avoided. I'm sorry to have missed it. I'm sure it was a wonderful time. Your parties are always the event of the season."

"Well, I'm glad you could make it tonight." Julia stood on tiptoe and pecked him on the cheek. Freddy flushed and glanced quickly away toward the fireplace, clinking the ice in his glass.

Vivian saw her mother's nose wrinkle at the alcohol on Freddy's breath.

Freddy stuck a hand out to Oskar. "Frederick Endicott," he said. Oskar shook his hand and introduced himself.

Julia's eyes drifted over to Martin.

"And Martin! I was delighted when Vivian told me earlier that she'd run into you and invited you to dinner. It's been far too long." She rushed over and clasped Martin's hand. He bent down slightly so she could press a kiss to his cheek. "Where on earth have you been keeping yourself?"

Vivian turned her head and rolled her eyes. Like her mother hadn't been keeping tabs on the eligible lawyer all along.

"I'm still with the state's attorney's office," he said.

"Ah, is that so?" She looked meaningfully at Vivian. "Such an important job."

"I like to think so."

Martin smiled at Mrs. Witchell, and Vivian saw the blush bloom on her mother's cheeks. They moved toward the dining room, and Vivian followed Martin's glance from Oskar to Freddy. Martin's and Oskar's eyes locked for a second, and Vivian saw something pass between them.

Everett and Gloria joined the group as they moved from drinks in the den to the dining room. Gloria was seated to

Vivian's right, Martin to her left. Everett and Freddy sat across the table, and her mother was at one end of the table, Oskar at the other. The dinner was a last-minute affair, sparked by Vivian's spur-of-the-moment invitation to Freddy and then Martin. Once they were coming, her mother had decided to invite Oskar and Gloria as well and make it a true party. It was still the holiday season after all.

"I hate to be a nuisance, Viv," Gloria began, leaning in toward her from the right. "But do you think I could come down to the station to watch this week's performance of *The Darkness Knows*? Graham said I was welcome anytime…"

Vivian bristled at Gloria's familiar way of addressing Graham. She smiled at the girl anyway and forced a politeness she didn't feel. "Of course," she said. "You and Everett can both come. You've never seen the show done, have you?" She looked at her brother.

Everett shook his head. "I'm afraid I can't. Thursday nights are when the fraternity's officers meet."

"Surely not during Christmas break?"

"We take our obligations seriously," he said, chewing on a mouthful of mashed potatoes. "We have the spring fund-raiser to plan. But you can go ahead without me, Gloria."

Gloria didn't seem the slightest bit put out. "It's going to be so exciting!" she exclaimed, clapping her hands together in glee. "I've seen *Quiz Time*, but that doesn't count. Nothing like *The Darkness Knows*…"

"We don't usually invite an audience to watch, you see," Vivian said. "*The Darkness Knows* doesn't broadcast from an auditorium like *Quiz Time*. I'm afraid you'll have to stand in the control room with the production staff and be quiet as a mouse."

Gloria shrugged. "No bother. What's this week's episode about?"

"I'm afraid I'm sworn to secrecy on the plot," Vivian said. She mimed locking her lips and then tossing away the key. "You'll have to wait until Thursday evening like everyone else."

"Where is Graham tonight, by the way?" Gloria asked.

"He's holed up working on the script for this Sunday's performance of *The Scarlet Pimpernel*. He's having terrible trouble getting act 2 the way he wants it."

"Ah," Gloria said, bringing a forkful of glazed carrots to her lips. "I imagine it's quite something to adapt a novel like that as a radio play. A lot of long hours…"

"He's been working so hard on this program," Vivian said. "He's the director and the coauthor. He's been working day and night rewriting act 2 with his coauthor, Paul."

Gloria nodded in sympathy.

"Yes, very hard," Vivian repeated. She pressed her fork into her pile of mashed potatoes with a little more force than necessary. "Mr. Heigel," she said, turning to the older man at her right. "Mother hasn't told me where you two met."

Oskar rested his knife and fork on the edges of the china

plate and glanced toward the end of the table at Julia, smiling. "Please, call me Oskar. We met at a charity event for the European Aid Society," he said. "She was so dazzling. I was asking everyone at the party who she was, hoping they would introduce me to her. In the end, I decided to introduce myself. So I worked up the courage to ask her to dance, and she turned me down."

Everyone at the table laughed, except for Freddy. Vivian couldn't help but notice that he hadn't looked at Oskar during the anecdote. In fact, he seemed to carefully avoid meeting the man's eye, though they were seated around the corner from each other. What he did do, however, was drink. As she watched, he finished yet another scotch and held it up to be refilled.

"Oh posh!" Julia tittered and threw her hands out in front of her face to push away such a ludicrous idea. "I turned you down because I had worn brand-new shoes, and my feet hurt so terribly."

"Yes, yes, that may be true. But I like to tell it my way. It's a better story. It gets me sympathy, although I clearly deserve none with someone as lovely as you on my arm."

The women at the table sighed audibly. Vivian caught her brother glaring at Oskar. He was obviously setting the bar too high, in Everett's estimation. Vivian bit her lip to choke down a laugh.

"What exactly is your profession, Mr. Heigel?" Freddy asked.

"Please, it's Oskar," the older man answered, locking eyes with Freddy across the table.

"Well then, what's your profession, Oskar?" Freddy's voice hardened slightly.

Vivian and Everett exchanged glances.

"I was a banker for some years. Now I do charity work."

"A charity case is more like it," Vivian heard Freddy say under his breath. Thankfully, no one else at the table caught it, and Freddy was at least sober enough not to repeat it. She glared at him. He was drunk and not suitable for polite dinner conversation.

"Say, where's Pauline tonight?" Everett asked, shooting a nervous smile in Vivian's direction. She grimaced and shook her head. Nice try, but poor choice of subject.

"Your guess is as good as mine, kid," Freddy said and drained his glass. "Say," he said, turning back to Oskar. "What's that accent? A bit of the Deutsch?"

"I was raised in Germany, but I lived in Switzerland most of my adult life. Until I came here, that is," Oskar responded. His mouth twitched. With Hitler threatening to overrun Europe, being German wasn't the most desirable of nationalities.

"Then you fought with the Huns?" Freddy asked. He smiled as if he were joking, but his voice was hard.

The table was deathly silent except for the nervous scratching of forks on plates. Why on earth would Freddy bring up something as awful as the Great War at dinner—especially with another war looming on the horizon? Vivian glanced around the table, silently urging someone to do something, say something to swing the conversation in a better direction. No one did.

"Regrettably," Oskar answered finally with a small smile of apology. "And I wish I could say I was too young to know better. I had no choice in the matter. Drafted, you see."

Silence again. Vivian scanned her mind for a suitable topic, anything other than wars and drafts and rising animosity. Her eyes darted about the table. Everett looked at her helplessly. Martin cleared his throat to her left as if he might wade into the fray, but then he must have changed his mind because nothing followed. Vivian shifted uncomfortably in her chair.

"And you?" Oskar continued, turning to Freddy. "I assume you did your part for Uncle Sam? Perhaps we could have met across the trenches?"

Freddy blanched and looked down at his untouched pheasant. "I'm afraid not. Ruptured eardrum."

"I see." Oskar said, a slight smile visible under his voluminous mustache.

Fifteen-love, Oskar, thought Vivian. She glanced at Everett across the table. Was it possible that these two men were sparring over her mother? She glanced at Julia Witchell, sitting regally at the head of the table. Vivian had to admit that her mother had aged well. She was plump, but it suited her. It kept a healthy hue in her cheeks. Not to mention that she was a wonderful schmoozer. She knew everybody who was anybody, and she was also a member of one of the wealthiest families in Chicagoland. Vivian knew that her mother was something of a catch, despite her old-fashioned rigidity and stubbornness to move entirely into the twentieth century. But Vivian supposed the two middle-aged men at the table weren't interested in a woman with progressive social ideas.

Someone cleared their throat, and then the tension passed over like a summer storm. Martin asked Freddy something in low tones. Vivian couldn't hear their conversation, but at least Martin had gotten Freddy off topic.

Vivian turned back to Gloria. "What are you studying at Northwestern?"

"Journalism."

Vivian sniffed. She wasn't fond of journalists after what Mack Rippert had done to her at that rag the *Patriot*. What she'd done to herself, she amended. But he had tricked her… and she had fallen for it and almost lost her job as a result. He'd begged that dance from her at Chez Paree and fed her a cheap line. She'd been so naive that she'd given him a couple of plum quotes about the murder before he revealed himself to be a reporter.

When she'd turned down his request for a full interview, he'd used those quotes to write a story about her that, though mostly true, painted her as flippant and casual about a woman's death. All of that after she'd promised Mr. Hart she wouldn't speak to the papers about Marjorie's murder. She'd been burned and had nearly killed her burgeoning career in the process. It had taken Graham's intervention to get her job back as Lorna Lafferty on *The Darkness Knows*. She'd learned her lesson about reporters all right. She'd grown to be more careful about sharing her confidences, period.

"What sort of journalism do you intend to do?"

"Investigative," Gloria said.

"Real hard-nosed pieces," Everett chimed in. "Digging up the dirt."

"Like politics and unionizing…things like that?" Vivian's voice trailed off. She couldn't think of any other serious topics one might investigate in a hard-nosed way.

"Maybe," Gloria said, a slight smile on her perfectly penciled red lips.

"Gloria's terrific," Everett interjected, jabbing his butter knife in her direction. "She's written some interesting stuff."

Gloria looked down. "Below the fold, pieces on things like our sorority fund-raiser. Small potatoes."

"No it's not," Everett said. "It's a stepping-stone. Gloria wants to be a career girl like you, Viv." He beamed at the girl, and Vivian forced a smile.

"How was the show last night?" she asked him.

"Not half bad. That Sonja Henie can cut some ice."

Vivian mmm'd in agreement. She had no idea if Sonja Henie could do any such thing. She glanced at Uncle Freddy across the table. He was pushing the potatoes around his plate with his fork, staring at the table. The he looked up and caught her eye. He looked alarmingly green about the gills.

"If you'll all excuse me for a moment," he said, already standing. He dashed out of the dining room before anyone could speak.

Vivian exchanged glances with her mother, the older woman's eyebrows drawn together in disapproval. Freddy never could hold his liquor.

"I hear you're headed for law school, Everett," Martin said, breaking the awkward silence.

"That I am."

"Let me know when you're ready for some real-world experience. I can fit you into the state's attorney's office—if you'd like, of course."

Everett's eyebrows shot up. "You mean it? That would be aces. Thank you."

"It's the least I can do after all your father taught me."

"I hear there may be a city council seat in your near future, Martin," Vivian's mother said.

"If everything goes to plan."

Vivian glanced sidelong at him and saw the smile flash on his face. A smart, ambitious, undeniably handsome young man could go far in this town, she thought. Then her eyes shifted to her mother. Julia's ruddy eyebrows rose a fraction as if to say *Are you making note of all this youthful vigor, Vivian?*

"Then perhaps you'll set your sights on mayor? Governor?" her mother asked, a lightly teasing note to her voice.

"Let's not get ahead of ourselves," Martin said. Then he turned to Vivian and winked. Her breath caught, and her mind refused to work for a moment. And just like that, she felt sixteen again, her stomach fluttery over the attentions of worldly Martin Gilfoy.

"Arthur would be so proud," Julia continued.

"Well, he taught me everything I know, and I'm grateful for that." Then Martin leaned in toward Vivian, his voice pitched low. "Then again, I'm glad those days are over. Your father was a wonderful teacher, but he also worked me like a rented mule."

Vivian laughed and nudged Martin's arm with her elbow. "You know Father loved you like a son. And he *would* be proud of you."

She watched Martin's playful smile falter, but then it rebounded as brilliantly as ever.

"Thank you," he said simply.

Vivian glanced over in time to see her mother's satisfied smile. Martin may have his sights set on an elected position, but Mother Witchell seemed to have Martin in mind for a potential son-in-law.

Martin turned from the fire as Vivian handed him the glass of after-dinner port.

Ah now, she thought, as she caught his handsome profile by the light of the fire. Here was a suitable match—prescreened by her dead father and an assistant state's attorney with designs on public office. Frankly, Vivian was surprised that she'd had to be the one to invite Martin to dinner. A likely candidate right under her nose this whole time. She glanced over her shoulder at the uncomfortable scene across the room. Oskar and Freddy sat on opposite sides of Mother on the divan, glaring at each other like two dogs fighting over a bone.

"She won't be so gauche as to ask herself, but Mother is dying to know if there's a *Mrs.* Gilfoy on the horizon."

"Why? Is she interested in the position?"

Vivian laughed.

"I could do far worse than your mother, you know. Though I'd say she has her hands full at the moment."

Vivian snorted. "You're right not to throw your hat into that ring. *Is* there a lucky lady in the picture?"

He shook his head. "No one in particular."

"That's too bad."

Martin's eyes shifted to her. "And why's that?"

"Don't family men do better at the polls?"

"Ah, that's true. But my wifelessness is not for lack of trying, you see. I haven't found the right woman yet."

"Perhaps your standards are too high."

"I don't think so." He held out one hand, ticking off the

qualities as he named them on his fingers. "She'd have to be charming, smart, beautiful, witty, quick with a joke, light on her feet…"

"I'm afraid you've run out of fingers."

"Then let me continue on the other hand. Did I mention witty?"

"And you think you'll find all of that in one woman?"

"I know she exists somewhere out there." He nodded solemnly and locked eyes with her. "Maybe closer than I thought. But in my head, I kept thinking of her as perpetually a child of sixteen—when that is clearly no longer the case."

Vivian swallowed and glanced away. She was amused to find that her heart beat a little quicker under his gaze. There'd always been a spark inside her for Martin Gilfoy, and she knew if she allowed herself to fan the flames a little, it would turn into a full-out bonfire.

"Say, what are you doing for New Year's?" he asked.

Charlie's face automatically appeared in her mind. They'd left things unsettled. She had no doubt she would see him again. She had to. Despite what he'd said, what was between them wasn't over.

"There's this party at the mayor's house, you see…sure to be a bore. You don't have to come if you don't want to… I'm afraid I can't offer you much in the way of dancing…" Martin motioned to his lame leg.

"Only the mayor? Call me when you've got an invitation to the White House." She smiled at him. She did wish she could say yes. "The truth is that I'd love to, but I can't. I'm in rehearsals all week for a special production on New Year's Day, and we have dress rehearsal all day and probably all night on Saturday. I can't guarantee I'll make it out before midnight." *Not entirely true*, she thought. If Charlie had been the one asking, she'd have found some way to go.

"I see," Martin said, returning her smile and exposing that irresistible dimple in his right cheek. "After this production is over then?"

"Maybe," she answered. She saw no reason to turn him down flat. Best to keep her options open. She could do far worse than Martin Gilfoy, even if he was precisely who her mother wanted for her.

She turned toward the fireplace, the logs crackling and popping. They watched the flames dance for a few moments in companionable silence.

"Why on earth did you stay away from us so long?" she asked finally.

"Did you miss me?"

Vivian glanced at him. "We *all* missed you," she answered after a pause.

His face clouded, and his eyes returned to the fire. "Mrs. Graves didn't."

So her anger *had* been directed at Martin in that scene

Vivian had interrupted earlier. She suspected that Martin knew she had overheard part of the conversation, although she wasn't willing to admit it. Martin cleared his throat.

"It was all so sudden…everything that happened. I had a long period of recuperation after the accident, and then, well, it was awkward. Arthur was gone, and I didn't want it to seem like I was ingratiating myself."

"Never. You were part of the family. You still are."

Martin's smile faded as his eyes swept over the room.

"It's…odd…to be here after so long. And it's uncomfortable knowing that Mrs. Graves still blames me for what happened."

"Blames you? But it wasn't your fault," Vivian said.

Martin shrugged and gazed into the fire. "I'm here, and her husband isn't."

Vivian sighed. "What happened was an accident, Martin. We all know that." She reached out and placed a hand on his arm. He placed his own hand over hers and squeezed.

"How is your leg?" she asked.

Martin shrugged, kicked his right leg stiffly out in front of him, and smacked it with his palm.

"It's useable most days. Stiff as a board, others. The doctors say it was a miracle I was able to walk again. I have nightmares about it sometimes still. That car cutting it too close on the curve, pushing us onto that patch of ice, seeing that lamppost come closer and closer. Knowing there was nothing I could do to stop it." He shivered.

Vivian swallowed, the hairs on her arms standing on end. "The car was forced off the road? I didn't know that."

Martin shrugged. "I don't think it was on purpose. Ogden was a solid sheet of ice that night. But in my dreams, it all seems so ominous…and I wake with this terrible feeling of dread."

"I'm sorry."

"Don't be." He glanced at his wristwatch. "*I'm* sorry for turning this wonderful evening so morbid. I'm afraid I need to say good night. I have court early tomorrow morning."

"It's nice to see you again, Martin." She pushed herself up on tiptoes and brushed his cheek with her lips. "Try not to be such a stranger, would you?"

He looked down at her and winked.

"You couldn't keep me away now if you tried."

CHAPTER NINE

V ivian couldn't sleep. She lay awake in her bed, staring at the ceiling and thinking about the evening. Martin. Mrs. Graves. Freddy. Gloria. So much unexpected tension. And then there was Charlie hovering in the back of her mind. Seeing him again had sparked the ember within her. She had to see him again, but how? Her thoughts swirled and tangled. No, sleep was impossible. So she dressed and went back to the front house.

The money and note may be gone, but maybe there was something in her father's study that might help her make sense of things. She let herself in the kitchen door and started up the back stairs, then stopped. She heard a man's voice. She stood still, held her breath, listened. It had to be coming from the radio in the den—the muffled voice of a male announcer. She retreated down the stairs and tiptoed down the hall to the den doorway.

Someone was sitting in Father's chair in front of the radio. With the light from the streetlamp hitting him at just the right angle, Vivian thought for a split second that it was her father. Her heart jigged in her chest. She stepped backward and bumped into the hall table, jostling the vase that sat on top of it. The man in the chair turned. It wasn't her father, she saw. It was Oskar.

"I'm sorry," she said. "I didn't realize anyone was in here."

"No, no, come in," he said with a noticeable crack in his own voice. He had his head cocked toward the speaker, and his face was a mask of unguarded concern.

"Has something happened?" Vivian asked, her stomach sinking. She eyed the radio with trepidation. A lot of bad news seemed to be coming out of it these days.

Oskar stared at her for a moment before snapping out of his reverie. "Oh no, nothing specific," he said. "That whole situation in Europe has me so worried." He smiled feebly at her as he passed a handkerchief over his mouth.

"Yes," she answered. "It has us all worried. But I can imagine what it's like for you."

Oskar glanced up at her, eyes narrowed. "Can you?" he asked.

"Well, yes, you being from…the area… I can imagine…" Everything coming to her mind was trite and inadequate. She couldn't imagine what it was like for him, and she had no idea why she'd said it.

Oskar's expression softened. "I apologize," he said. "It seems I always expect the worst of people."

Vivian stared him, confused.

"You don't know then?" he asked.

"Know what?"

"Your mother hasn't told you." He looked at her expectantly. When she shook her head, confused, he added. "I'm Jewish, Vivian."

Vivian blinked. Her mother hadn't said a word. In fact, she'd told Vivian virtually nothing about Oskar. Perhaps now she understood why. "No," she managed to say. "She hasn't mentioned it."

"Good," he answered. "I'm not ashamed of it, of course. But it's nobody's business. Especially not these days."

They sat in silence for a minute, listening to the tinny sounds of the news reporter mumbling through the speakers.

"You have family over there," she said.

He nodded. "Two sisters and their families near Munich. I've been begging them for years to leave, but they insist that things can't get any worse. But they are. They're getting worse every day." He cocked his head toward the speaker. "Now I hear they're deporting all Polish Jews from Germany, and Poland won't take them. All those people in limbo, lives in chaos. Where do they go? They're running out of time."

They. Not merely Oskar's immediate family, but all Jews in Europe. Vivian knew that's what he meant, but she couldn't reconcile the idea in her head. It was too large, too terrible. Running out of time—out of time before what? Vivian shook her head.

"My family has been trying to leave since they destroyed the synagogues about six weeks ago, but they haven't managed to secure the right papers yet."

"But I thought Chamberlain made peace with Hitler," Vivian said. Doubt clouded her voice. She suddenly felt so ill-informed. She hadn't been paying much attention to the news lately. She never had—unless it involved her.

"Peace." Oskar snorted and then sat upright and snapped the radio off with a decisive flick of the wrist. He turned to her, a kind smile on his face. "I'm sorry," he said. "I get carried away."

"It's all right," she answered. She swallowed and tapped her fingers against her hip, desperate to change the subject. "You know, it's nice to see a man in Father's chair."

Oskar glanced up at her, the light glinting off his spectacles. He smiled slightly, opened his mouth to speak, but hesitated and closed it again.

Vivian started backing toward the door. She felt bumbling, uncomfortable, incapable of saying the right thing, or anything close to the right thing. Was there a right thing? She'd already turned to leave when he finally spoke up.

"Your father was a good man," he said, his voice so low she almost hadn't heard him.

Vivian turned back to face him. "You knew him?"

He nodded. "He was my attorney."

"Your attorney?" Her father had been Oskar's attorney?

Vivian's heart began to race. If she'd learned anything in her time investigating with Charlie, it was that little in life, in *her* life anyway, was mere coincidence.

"He did some immigration paperwork for me," he said. "It was long ago and far away." He said with a wistful smile. "They haven't kicked me out of the country yet, so he knew what he was about."

Vivian laughed, and then she bit her lip. She wanted to ask if Mother knew that Oskar had known her father, but she didn't. Of course she had to know.

"Then you'd met Uncle Freddy before," Vivian said, the idea dawning on her. The two men hadn't behaved as if they'd known anything about each other before this evening, but how could they not have if Oskar had been a client of her father's? That might explain the obvious animosity between them—animosity on Freddy's part, anyway. Perhaps his foul mood wasn't only freshly stirred jealousy over her mother.

Oskar shook his head. "In passing, perhaps. I dealt strictly with your father." His stern expression softened. "I wish he were here to help now. He was a good man."

"He was," Vivian said, surprised to find a lump in her throat yet again. After she'd made her excuses and was climbing the back stairs to her father's study, she realized that perhaps by stressing that her father was a good man, Oskar was also somehow implying that Freddy was not. But how might

Oskar know such a thing? Maybe all of this was just bad blood over her mother. *Her mother.* Who would've guessed?

Vivian had poked silently around the dim study, looking for anything that might help her understand her father and his reasons for a locked drawer of cash. She found nothing, of course. She knew she was kidding herself. What could she find that would possibly explain any of it after eight years? She slumped into the chair at his desk, staring into the darkness.

After a few moments, she found herself putting the little silver key into the lock as if her hands were working independently of her mind. She watched, fascinated, as her fingers pulled the drawer open. Empty, of course. She was almost relieved. She started to slide it closed again, and then something caught her eye. A smudge? No, not a smudge. And the drawer was not entirely empty.

Vivian leaned down. It was difficult to see in the ambient light from the streetlamp outside. But scrawled in pencil across the bottom of the empty drawer in a hand Vivian didn't recognize was *Stop before you hurt everyone you love.*

Vivian sucked in her breath. This message hadn't been there the day before when she upended the drawer and searched every inch of it. She was sure of it. It was delivered in the same tone as the note in the envelope of money, but this message hadn't been meant for her father. No, someone had written that message especially for her, and they'd written it today. Her pulse pounded in her ears. But it wasn't precisely fear she felt. It was more like excitement. Because that niggling feeling in her gut hadn't been wrong after all. She was on to something.

CHAPTER TEN

C harlie's office was on the second floor of a three-story walk-up on the south side of the Loop. The facade of the brick building had once been a creamy yellow color, but the soot of forty-odd years of city life had turned it the color of tobacco-stained fingers. Vivian stood looking at it from the bus stop across the street. She hadn't called to schedule an appointment, and she was surprised to find herself having to work up the nerve to approach. The neighborhood wasn't downtrodden exactly, but it was shabby, the buildings leaning a bit, crumbling around the edges in disrepair.

This wasn't the office Peggy Hart had lured Charlie to with the promise of reconciliation with his father, their father, two months before. There, Peggy had knocked Charlie out and opened the gas lines, intending for him to suffocate and be out of her life forever. Vivian had been to that office once after she'd tried to call him without success. She'd found it empty. He'd moved without telling her where. But, as it turned out, he hadn't moved far—one block over and one block down. If she'd only known that at the time, she thought. Vivian rubbed her arms, chilled through.

She gathered her nerve and crossed the street. Gray-brown snow clogged the gutter, and she picked her way through the slush that had yet to be cleared from the street. Then she hopped up the wide stone steps to the front door. A panel by the door listed Charlie's name and that of one other, Marshall Lisky, bookkeeping. They shared the second floor. The other four slots were either blank or crossed out with the thick, black strokes. There was no buzzer, so Vivian walked up the flight of stairs to the second-floor landing.

His name was stenciled on the frosted glass of the door: *Charles Haverman Jr.—Private Inquiries*. She didn't knock, but instead turned the knob with trepidation. Her guts churned, because she had to see Charlie again in the flesh *and* she had to ask for his help.

A young woman sat at the desk in the almost-empty room, wearing a wool coat around her shoulders like Red Riding Hood. She looked up from her *True Romances* magazine, marking her spot on the page with a manicured forefinger. "Can I help you?" she asked. She tossed her luscious brown hair over her shoulder as she inspected Vivian.

"Is Mr. Haverman in?"

The woman glanced toward the closed door to her right. "Mr. Haverman is in conference and not to be disturbed. I can take a message for you, if you like."

Vivian glanced toward the door. She didn't hear any voices.

She didn't hear anything except the tapping of the secretary's fingernail on the open magazine. She looked dubiously back at the secretary.

"Could you perhaps tell him who's calling?"

The secretary scowled at her, a thick vertical crease appearing between her brows.

"And just who *is* calling?" she asked, her voice acerbic. She slid a piece of notepaper underneath her pencil without dropping eye contact with Vivian.

"Vivian Witchell. That's *W-I-*"

The interior door swung open, and Charlie stepped into the small reception area. He was wearing his overcoat, but not his hat. Had she caught him on the way out? He glanced at Vivian, shooting her a slight smile, before turning to the receptionist. "It's okay, Maxine. Miss Witchell is an old friend."

Old friend, Vivian thought, narrowing her eyes at the detective. *Old indeed.*

He turned sideways, sweeping one arm toward the open door and ushering Vivian into his inner sanctum. She shot him a narrow look, but then found herself returning his smile. Damn it anyway, she found it impossible not to smile at the man.

She took off her winter coat and slung it across the coat-tree in the corner before realizing how cold it was in the room. Her eyes fell on the radiator under the window. It clanked and clunked but seemed to be producing precious little heat. She'd assumed she'd caught Charlie on the way out the door, but apparently he'd been wearing his winter coat in an effort not to freeze. The receptionist had been wearing her coat as well, and it hadn't been a fashion statement. Charlie followed Vivian's gaze to the radiator.

"I have someone coming to look at it this afternoon," he said.

There was one chair facing the desk, so she sat. Her eyes flicked over the room, not that there was much to see. The furnishings consisted of a large wooden desk that had seen better days and a secondhand filing cabinet that leaned to the right, all of the drawers offset in the frame and unable to close properly. Her eyes trained on an ominous rust-colored stain on the ceiling above Charlie's head. She cleared her throat.

He eyed her from behind the desk, unsmiling.

"I see your dreams have come true," she said, jerking her head toward the door and the voluptuous Maxine sitting at the ready in the reception area. Charlie raised his eyebrows, and Vivian elaborated. "A leggy brunette to answer your telephone."

After a moment, his initial confusion faded into a slight smile as he recognized the reference. They'd discussed leggy brunettes and his desire to have a secretary the first night they'd met. He leaned back in his chair and raked Vivian over with a long, hard look that made her skin tingle, but he said nothing.

Vivian glanced out the window, hoping that if she ignored it, the telltale flush on her cheeks would disappear. The view from Charlie's office consisted entirely of the grimy red brick of the building next door. She turned her attention back to Charlie, who was no longer smirking, but leaning back precariously on the two back legs of his rickety wooden chair, considering her.

She wanted to explain everything. About how she'd thought she would never see Charlie again, and that being the only reason she was "dating" Graham. About how she'd tried to contact him. About how distraught she was that he'd disappeared without any explanation. She could do it. There were no giggling girls to overhear. But that wasn't why she'd come today. She'd come for Charlie's help.

"I want to hire you," she said.

Charlie let the front legs of the chair fall to the floor with a thump. He tented his fingers underneath his chin and regarded her thoughtfully. "What for?" he asked.

There was a rap on the frosted glass of the closed door.

"Yes, Maxine?" Charlie said. "What is it?"

"Would you like me to hold your calls?" she asked.

Vivian placed a hand over her mouth, hiding a smile. She couldn't help but note that the phone hadn't rung once since she'd stepped into the office.

"That's not necessary," he said, glancing at Vivian. "Why don't you go ahead and take an early lunch? I can handle things around here."

"Sure," the secretary said, the disappointment evident in her voice.

Charlie waited until Maxine had gathered her things in the other room and shut the door on her exit before returning to the subject at hand. "So," he said. "I believe you were about to tell me why you require my services."

"I want you to find out what my father was up to," Vivian said. She thought for a moment and then added, "And I want you to prove that he wasn't a criminal."

Charlie's eyes widened before narrowing at her. "But we agreed that was the most likely scenario," he said slowly, as if talking to a child. "And, as I recall, we agreed that the safest thing for you to do would be to drop the whole thing."

"I know we did, and I've changed my mind."

"Why?"

"Because there's more to it now," she said. She wondered if Charlie gave the third degree to everyone who wanted to hire him or only her. Her money was as good as anyone's, wasn't it? By the looks of this place, he needed every job he could get. "That cash I told you about yesterday? It's gone missing."

Charlie arched one dark-blond eyebrow but said nothing.

"Actually, it's been missing since before I even told you about it."

Charlie continued to look at her, eyebrow frozen in place. Vivian shook her head in frustration. She was telling this all wrong.

"I mean, of course, that I found the money the night of the Christmas party, and when I went to look again on Christmas morning, it was gone… And then I looked again last night just to satisfy my curiosity, you see. The money was still gone, but now there is a note written on the bottom of the desk drawer."

Charlie blinked at her. After a long moment, he said, "What kind of a note?"

"It said 'Stop before you hurt everyone you love.'"

"Stop what?"

"Looking into my father's affairs, I assume," she said.

"So the first thing you did today was come to my office and tell me you want to hire me to do exactly that. You don't take your warnings very seriously, do you?"

Vivian exhaled in exasperation. She didn't want a lecture. Not today, and certainly not from Charlie. Of course he didn't see that the warning was the reason she needed to dig further. That warning meant there really was something to all of this.

"But I'm getting ahead of myself. I didn't tell you about the first note, did I?"

"The first note," he repeated.

"Yes, in the envelope with the cash was a note that said 'Talk and you lose everything.' Directed at my father most likely."

"So there was a threatening note with the secret wad of bills in your father's long-locked desk drawer, and you just forgot to mention it?"

"I didn't forget. I just didn't want to tell you unless you thought the money was important. And you didn't, remember? You told me my father was just a crook, and I should drop all of it… And it stands to reason that if he really was a crook, that was probably only one of many threats he received."

He looked at her without speaking, and she squirmed a little under his unrelenting gaze.

"Oh, and there's this," she said, holding the bronze key out to Charlie in the palm of her hand. "I found this taped to the back of the drawer on Christmas morning. I'm lucky that I took it. Otherwise it might have disappeared with the money and the note—the first one."

"What's it for?"

"I have no idea," she said. "That's why I need your help." She leaned over and dropped the key into Charlie's hand.

"Looks like it belongs to a safe-deposit box," he said, holding it up to the light. "Any idea which bank?"

Vivian shrugged.

"What else can you tell me?" he asked, leaning forward in his chair now, truly interested. Vivian hid a satisfied smile in the corner of her mouth.

"Not a lot. There was something written on the outside of the envelope. It said 'A. W. Racquet.' I dismissed it at the time, but now I realize the 'A. W.' stands for 'Arthur Witchell,' of course. But the 'Racquet' part has me stumped."

"*R-A-C-Q-U-E-T*? Like a tennis racquet?"

Vivian nodded. "Do you know what it means?"

"The Racquet Club in Cicero was a gaming palace for swells. Went belly up not long after Capone got sent to the clink—I assume from lack of qualified leadership," he added drily.

"A gaming palace? Like blackjack, roulette?"

"You got it."

The thousands of dollars in small bills flashed through Vivian's mind. "So maybe my father won big at blackjack?"

"Could be," Charlie said, drumming his fingers on the desktop in thought.

"But he didn't gamble."

Charlie shrugged. "Maybe you didn't know your father as well as you thought you did."

Vivian bit her lower lip. She was starting to suspect that she hadn't known him at all. "So you'll do it then? You'll take the case?" she asked.

Charlie drummed his fingers for a few seconds longer before answering.

"I'll do it," he said. Then he pointed at her. "But I want you to know that it may be an impossible task. I'm used to proving people *have* done things, not that they haven't."

She paused to lift her chin and gather her courage. "Then I want you to prove that he *was* a criminal." Her voice trembled a little, and she cleared her throat. "Either way, I want to know the truth."

"Are you sure that's what you want?"

She nodded. "I need to know."

Charlie regarded her for a long moment, his blue-green eyes betraying nothing. Then he smiled at her, and despite her reservations, Vivian felt the flip-flop in her stomach.

CHAPTER ELEVEN

❖

When they emerged from the dilapidated office building onto the street, Charlie had wanted to stay in the neighborhood and go to an unsavory nameless lunchroom. Happily, Vivian succeeded in steering him a little closer to civilization. The diner they stopped at wasn't the Ritz, but there also weren't any unwashed men staring hungrily at her from behind empty plates.

"More comfortable here with real china cups?" He lifted his own cup and set it down, deliberately clinking it noisily against the saucer.

She knew he was teasing her, but she nodded. Of course she was more comfortable here. Who wouldn't be?

"I think you secretly enjoy my part of town. It thrills you to see life on the other side of the tracks," he said.

She looked toward the door, unable to meet his eye and admit that yes, it did, a little. Marjorie Fox's murder investigation had been almost fun—if murder could ever be considered fun. Even believing her own life was in danger had almost been a thrill for Vivian. *Almost.*

"So where do we start?" she asked, glancing back toward him and leaning in over the Formica table.

"I'd like to say there's no *we*, but we both know how that conversation's likely to go," he said.

"Smart man," she said, smiling. "Besides, it was a trick question. I've already started."

"Of course you have."

"I went to see Uncle Freddy yesterday after I met you for coffee," she said.

"And Uncle Freddy is...?"

"Frederick Endicott. He and my father were law partners for about fifteen years—right up until my father's death. Uncle Freddy said hoarding cash wasn't that unusual for my father. That he was cautious because of the economic times. He'd been burned by the crash, and he always liked to have enough on hand in case of emergency."

"A reasonable enough explanation, I suppose."

"Reasonable for someone else's father. Something about it doesn't ring true with me. I was little more than a kid then, but I don't have any recollection of my father's finances taking a hit after the crash. Actually, he did well financially, as far as I know. You've seen where I live. You've seen how my mother dresses. She's got her own money, of course, but he also left a lot when he died." Vivian's mind flashed to the news about her unexpected inheritance, and she decided not to mention it. For some reason, she didn't want Charlie to know that she was, for all intents and purposes, about to become of those spoiled heiresses that she'd always abhorred. "And now that I know what the Racquet Club is... Well, Freddy's story *really* doesn't make sense."

"So you think Uncle Freddy lied to you?"

"I don't know." Vivian sighed. "Maybe he and my father weren't as close as I assumed. Maybe Freddy only knew the side of my father that my father wanted him to see."

"And you told Uncle Freddy about the cash you found?"

"Yes."

"And the threatening note?"

She shook her head. "But he said he'd be the first to know if my father had any enemies."

"Could he have taken the money?"

"I don't think so. It was gone before I told him I'd found it."

"What about the note, the second one directed at you? Could he have done that?"

Vivian hesitated for a second before nodding. "Freddy was over for dinner last night." And he had disappeared from the dinner table and stayed away for at least twenty minutes, presumably in the bathroom. But there had been plenty of time to scribble that note and come back to the table as if nothing had happened.

Charlie nodded. "Was anyone else over for dinner last night?"

"My father's old protégé, Martin; he's now an assistant state's attorney. My brother, Everett, and his girlfriend, Gloria. And my mother's new"—she stumbled, searching for the right word, before finally settling on—"friend, Oskar."

"Your mother's friend, Oskar?" Charlie arched an eyebrow. "What does your mother's friend Oskar do?"

"He's a financier of some sort," she said. Then she frowned, remembering the unsettling conversation she'd had with Oskar the evening before. "He told me that he knew my father—that he had been a client some years before my father died."

"Quite a coincidence."

She nodded. "That's exactly what I thought."

"Would he have known about the money?"

"It's possible, I suppose, but I didn't tell anyone but Uncle Freddy about it." She thought of Oskar, alone in the quiet house long after everyone had left.

"Not even your brother?"

Vivian cocked her head to one side. "It's obvious you don't have siblings."

Charlie had been adopted from the foundling home, likely by a couple that had tried for a long time to have a child of their own. Vivian wondered what his adoptive parents were like—well, his father. He'd told her his mother was dead.

"I love my brother, but I don't trust Everett as far as I can throw him." She frowned, smoothing the wrinkles in her skirt with her palms. That sounded terrible, even to her own ears. "He's immature, and I don't want him to blab the whole story to Mother. I don't want her to find out about any of this, not until I'm sure of what the truth is…and maybe not even then."

Now that Vivian thought about it, she wasn't sure that Everett *didn't* know about the money. She hadn't told him about it, that was true, but he'd come into Father's study right after she'd found it. Who's to say he hadn't seen something and simply didn't let on?

"And the others at dinner? Your brother's girlfriend, the hotshot assistant state's attorney?"

"Gloria's new to everything. I met her at the Christmas party. She wouldn't know about the money. Besides, Everett was practically glued to her side." But if Everett had known about the money, she thought, he may have told Gloria. Vivian shook the thought from her head. "And Martin, well, I haven't seen him in ages—not since my father died. I suppose if he'd known about that money and wanted it, he would have claimed it long ago."

Charlie frowned, then nodded decisively.

"Occam's razor," he said.

Vivian blinked. "Excuse me?"

"Occam's razor," he repeated. "The simplest explanation is likely the best one."

"Isn't that Sherlock Holmes?"

He smiled. "Not quite. I believe Mr. Holmes said, 'When you have eliminated the impossible, whatever remains, however improbable, must be the truth.' But if we're splitting hairs, I think both apply in this case."

"And that means?"

"That Everett is likely your man."

Vivian's stomach sank. She didn't want to believe that Everett had taken the money. But he'd been the only one with the opportunity.

Charlie pulled the brass key out of his pocket and tapped the end of it on the table, lost in thought for a moment.

"I'll find out which bank this key belongs to," he said.

"And I'll—"

"And you'll stay out of it…for now," Charlie said, tempering his harsh tone with a quick wink. "When I need your help, I'll let you know."

Vivian fumed. If this were any other man, she'd look up at him through her lashes and pout to get her way, but she already knew that act wouldn't fly with Charlie. She'd tried it several times during the Marjorie Fox affair, and it had gotten her nowhere.

"You know, this is like old times, Viv," Charlie said.

Vivian glanced up. It *was* like old times. She had to admit that the flutter in the pit of her stomach wasn't just from being in such close proximity to Charlie again after all this time. Some of it was from finding herself in the middle of a case, the thrill of detecting, of uncovering what someone wanted to remain hidden—even if that someone was her father. It was almost as if the last two months hadn't happened. Vivian swallowed, and the question that she had been carrying around with her for months popped out of her mouth before she could stop it.

"Why didn't you call me, Charlie?"

She watched the sardonic smile slip from his face as he set his jaw and glanced away from her. He shifted in his seat, then stared down at the table. He was silent for a long while, and Vivian thought he might not answer the question at all.

"I could ask the same question of you," he said finally.

Vivian shook her head. "I *did* call. I left a message with your answering service."

He glanced up at her. His brow furrowed, and then his eyes shifted from hers again as he shrugged. "I never got it."

She studied his face, but it was a careful blank. She wanted to believe that, even though she knew it probably wasn't the truth. Should she tell him that she'd gone to his office and found it empty? No, that sounded desperate. But she wanted him to know that she'd tried, that they hadn't lost touch because of her. She hadn't forgotten their deal. She'd needed him, and she'd called him. What had happened to make him change his mind about her? What had she done? What hadn't she done? It couldn't only be that he thought she was with Graham, could it? That hadn't stopped Charlie before.

"You moved your office," she said.

"About a week after I left the hospital. I was a mess after

what happened," he said. "I couldn't set foot in the radio station again, and I couldn't face anyone that reminded me of what had happened. I wasn't good company for anybody." He met her eyes again, and Vivian saw the flash of hurt in them.

"I'm sorry," she said.

Charlie glanced toward the window. "The truth is, I thought about calling."

Vivian's heart thumped in expectation.

"But then I kept seeing you pop up in the papers with Yarborough, and I didn't want to get in the middle of what seemed like a good thing."

Vivian felt her face flush. A good thing? With Graham? No, Charlie had gotten it all wrong. Everything was all wrong. She shook her head. "Listen, Charlie—"

He held up one hand to cut her off.

"It's okay, Viv," he said, his gaze narrowed. "What's past is past. I think we can work together on your father's case without all of *that* getting in the way."

Vivian's stomach clenched at the finality of his tone. He'd reduced everything they had to a snidely chosen one-syllable word tossed out of the side of his mouth. *That.* He wasn't going to let her explain, she realized, because there wasn't any explanation she could give him that would change his mind. He thought she was with Graham, and nothing she could tell him would convince him that she wasn't.

She could explain everything, she realized—the publicity,

the sham relationship—but it would make her seem vain and shallow, out for her little piece of glory. And wasn't she? It didn't matter that she'd called and he hadn't answered, because for all intents and purposes, she *was* with Graham. And she was with him because it was good for her career. Frustration welled up inside her.

We're not past, she wanted to say. *We can't be.* If Charlie would look at her, he could see it on her face. He'd understand. But he was studying the napkin on his lap, refusing to meet her gaze.

"My fee is twenty dollars a day plus expenses," he continued, his eyes finally flicking up to meet hers. He was back to business once again. "It's a little lower than my going rate, but I'll consider this job a favor for a friend."

She forced herself to nod. A friend. That was the second time he'd called her that in as many hours. Perhaps he was trying to convince himself as much as her, she thought. She forced a smile to her face and glanced at the oversized clock hanging behind the counter. She suddenly wanted to be anywhere but here.

"Well, I have to get going. I have—"

"A rehearsal to get to, yes." She watched Charlie's jaw clench before he smiled back at her. And if Vivian wasn't mistaken, his smile was as bright and forced as hers had been.

CHAPTER TWELVE

◆

There wasn't any fanfare surrounding Graham's adaptation of *The Scarlet Pimpernel*. He had a small cast, an even smaller crew, and a nonexistent budget. The time slot had been free—New Year's Day, when anyone with a pulse would be nursing a hangover from the night before and not likely to be paying much attention to anything on the radio. Graham had begged his way into the production through the good graces of Mr. Langley, who happened to have a hole in the schedule and wanted to indulge his station star. Well, his star now that Marjorie Fox was gone, that was. Anything to keep Graham happy. Mr. Langley and everyone with a brain knew that it was a real threat to lose someone like Graham to the pictures. But it was inevitable. Graham had a face made for the screen. And now that he had an ad campaign, Vivian imagined there would be no stopping him.

They'd been rehearsing for a solid week now, and things were still near a shambles. The script changed on a daily basis, and act 2 hadn't even seen a complete first draft.

The first person she saw in Studio D was the engineer, Morty Nickerson. Things had been strained between them since Marjorie's death—due to the fact that Vivian had not only suspected Morty of the deed and hinted as much to the police, but also spurned his clumsy romantic overtures. He didn't kill Marjorie, of course, and he claimed no hard feelings over having the police on his tail, but there was no getting over a broken heart. Unfortunately, they needed to be in the same room a lot. Morty worked the sound for almost everything Vivian had been involved in at WCHI, and *The Scarlet Pimpernel* was no exception.

His arms were full of records. Their eyes met briefly before his skittered away. When she greeted him, he jumped as if he hadn't expected her to speak to him, and the records slipped from his grasp to spill on the floor between them. They both bent down to gather them up.

"It's okay, Viv. I've got it," Morty said, his face flushed.

She handed a Bing Crosby disc to him. "I'm sorry," she said. "I didn't mean to startle you."

Morty said nothing and continued scooping the records into a neat little pile.

"What's with the dance records?" she asked, pointing to the disc resting on top, Benny Goodman's "Don't Be That Way." "Is *The Scarlet Pimpernel* getting a modern score?"

Morty glanced up, his blue eyes wide and sincere. "Oh no. I'm doing a little show," he said, ducking his head again. "A dance-music show."

Vivian glanced from the records to Morty's freckled face and back again.

"You mean you play records?"

He nodded. "It's called *Fantasy Ballroom*. I announce the records like it's a live remote. It was my idea, and Mr. Langley loves it. He thinks it's the wave of the future." He looked up at her as if he expected her to challenge him.

Vivian wrinkled her brow. That was one idea that was sure to fail. Who'd want to listen to recorded music over the radio? The audience wanted live content—something new every night.

"Well, congratulations," she said, smiling at him.

"Thank you." He stood and scurried off to the far side of the studio. Vivian sighed. She knew it would take time for some semblance of their old friendship to return, but it had already been two months and Morty didn't seem to be getting over his heartbreak. Maybe it was a lost cause.

Across the room, Graham's head was bent to listen to Frances Barrow, who whispered intently into his ear. Frances clutched a dog-eared copy of *Gone with the Wind* in one hand, marking a page about a quarter of the way through with her finger. She gestured to it once or twice, and Vivian could guess that Frances was speculating on who would play Scarlett O'Hara in the movie that was being cast right this minute. Vivian narrowed her eyes at her rival and frowned. She had to admit that Frances would make a great Scarlett O'Hara.

She had the looks—shiny black hair, dark-blue eyes—as well as the nasty temperament. Or so Vivian had heard. She hadn't read the novel herself.

Vivian moved to the other side of the rehearsal space and grabbed a copy of the latest version of the script off the table.

"Well, Viv, how was your Christmas?"

She turned to find Dave Chapman standing close to her. A little too close. She flinched away. He had a habit of coming on strong, despite being married. He wasn't drunk today, but it was difficult to work with the man. He was another person she'd suspected of having it in for Marjorie Fox.

"Splendid," she said. "You?"

"Banner year in the Chapman household. The oldest broke his arm running his sled into the tree, and the youngest has the flu."

"I'm sorry. That's terrible."

He shrugged. "I'm glad I get to leave the house and come here most of the day." He winked at her and turned toward the group.

Poor Mrs. Chapman, Vivian thought.

Graham clapped his hands from the center of the room.

"Okay, everybody, settle down. Let's take it from the top of act 2."

Vivian flipped the pages of her script. Act 2 started with a tense scene between Monsieur Chauvelin and Lady Blakeney. Chauvelin is trying to blackmail Lady Blakeney into revealing the identity of the Scarlet Pimpernel—who, unbeknownst to her, is the alter ego of her foppish husband. Vivian stepped to the nonfunctioning microphone with Dave. He looked at her, eyebrows raised, and she nodded. She was ready.

Dave leaned in. "Well, Lady Blakeney?"

"I've learned nothing yet," Vivian replied, her voice terse.

Dave tsked. "Come now, let's not be coy."

"I'm not being coy. I've learned nothing."

Dave eyed Vivian over the microphone, one eyebrow raised in silent menace. "If you don't tell me the Pimpernel's true identity, you know the alternative. The guillotine. Your brother's head will roll on the streets of Paris."

"Monsieur Chauvelin, you can't do this."

"My dear lady, the Pimpernel is under this roof. At this moment. Among your friends. Find him...or else."

After a dramatic pause, Morty dropped the needle onto the record on the phonograph in the corner. A thunderous swell of music crackled from the speaker. Vivian flinched at the volume and glanced over to Graham. She hoped it would sound better over the airwaves. Graham might not have much budget to work with, but this was amateur hour.

Graham held up one hand and Morty yanked the needle upward, stopping the music. Then Graham was silent for a long moment, chewing on the end of his pencil as he stared down at his script.

"Good," he said finally, glancing around the room. "Maybe

ease up on the accent, huh, Dave? Let's move on. Page 20 from the top, everyone."

Vivian flipped to page 20, relieved to find that Lady Blakeney did not appear in the scene. She sauntered over to the refreshment table, where Frances still stood scouring the dog-eared copy of *Gone with the Wind*.

"Hello, Frances."

She glanced up, noted who was speaking, and then looked back down at her book.

"Good book?" Vivian asked.

"Haven't you read it?"

Vivian shook her head. She had no time to read anything but scripts and her own press.

"You're the only one in the country who hasn't."

Vivian poured herself a glass of water and turned to view the rehearsal. Dave and Graham were heatedly discussing something. She watched Graham jab his finger at a line of dialog and then run his hand through his hair, making it stand on end.

"Did you see the photo in *Radio Guide*?" Frances asked.

"Mmm-hmm."

"Not the most flattering photo of me, but I suppose it'll do," she said.

Vivian glanced over her shoulder at Frances, but made no comment. Frances had looked ravishing in that photo, and she knew it. She was always fishing for compliments. Frances closed the thick book with a *thump*.

"Say, do you think this thing will come off?" Frances asked in a low voice close to Vivian's ear. Vivian followed Frances's pointed gaze toward the middle of the room. The cast had started rehearsing again, Dave and Graham playing awkwardly off each other.

"I hope so," Vivian said. "Graham's worked his tail off to get this thing going."

Frances frowned. "I'd like to say I have every confidence in the production, but I'm not so sure. Graham's a talented actor, but I think he may have bitten off more than he can chew with this one."

Vivian hated to admit it, but Frances might be right. It was five days before the live show, and things were still a mess.

"Of course I won't let that affect my performance," Frances added. "Or my wholehearted support of *anything* Graham does."

Vivian rolled her eyes. *Her wholehearted support of Graham, indeed.* But she wasn't going to take the bait, not today.

"That's nice," Vivian said.

"Speaking of Graham, do you two have any plans for New Year's?" Frances asked.

New Year's. That's right. She glanced over at Graham. The words *New Year's* hadn't so much as passed his lips. He didn't seem to be aware that it was happening on the same date again this year.

Vivian turned to Frances with a forced smile. "I think you

may be forgetting that we're in rehearsal for this performance all day on Saturday…"

"Oh, I'm not forgetting." A vertical line appeared between Frances's brows as she frowned. Even her frowns were annoyingly lovely, Vivian thought. "Surely, you don't mean that Graham will keep us past eleven o'clock?"

Vivian shrugged. "Who knows? I wouldn't make any plans if I were you, especially if you're serious in your *wholehearted support*."

Frances stuck out her lower lip in a pout. "Of course I am," she said.

Maybe Vivian should call Martin if the New Year's Eve rehearsal let out early. A party at the mayor's house would be something, she thought. And then Charlie popped to the front of her mind. What did he have planned for New Year's? Would he be working a case? Tailing a cheating husband? Enjoying a quiet night in? Or out with some mystery brunette—the leggy Maxine? Vivian bit her lip.

Across the room, they had started from the top of page 20 again.

"Blakeney?" Dave said with a haughty laugh. "That fool. Wake him up and ask him if he can have the decency to go home and sleep in his own bed."

"Yes, sir. Uh, Sir Percy? Sir Percy!" said the young man playing the servant. His voice shook with nerves. Vivian felt sorry for the boy, who she had never seen before. Heck of a production to have as your first big break. He shook Graham by the shoulder.

Graham rubbed his eyes, feigning being woken from a deep sleep. "Eh? What is it? Is there no peace for the weary? What ails you, man?"

"The French ambassador, Sir Percy. He would like to see you alone in the library."

"The French ambassador, you say? Ah, Monsieur Chauvelin." Graham paused, glanced through the page, and then held one hand up to keep Dave from continuing. There was a long, pregnant pause, then Graham looked up and smiled. "That's it!" he said, looking over toward Paul in the corner. Paul nodded, smiling, and gave a thumbs-up. "I think we have the beginning of act 2 licked, everyone!"

A smattering of applause broke out among those in the room, Vivian included.

"Thank God for small favors," Frances said a low voice.

CHAPTER THIRTEEN

◆

The First National Bank was on Dearborn and Monroe, a block from WCHI. Vivian didn't bank there, and as far as she knew, neither had her father. But she was quickly learning that "as far as she knew" about her father wasn't far at all.

She entered the vestibule of the imposing building and gazed upward at the twenty-foot vaulted ceilings and towering marble columns. *Banks always look like Grecian temples*, she thought. She stamped the slush off her shoes onto the mat inside the door and glanced around her. It was one enormous room. There was a black-and-white-tiled floor with wooden teller windows all down the far side. People scurried behind the windows, whispering to one another and passing little slips of paper. Typewriters clacked. A large clock occupied the upper portion of the far end of the room. It was 12:16 p.m. She was late, but a glance around the room told her that Uncle Freddy was even later.

Charlie had told her which bank the key belonged to and provided the unwelcome news that the law required the executor of her father's estate to help her open the box. That meant calling Freddy and explaining that she'd found the key and that her father held a safe-deposit box that no one had known about. She hadn't wanted to involve Freddy, but she had no choice. Freddy didn't seem to know about the safe-deposit box either. He hadn't said much on the telephone except that he would meet her today at noon to help her get it open.

She scanned the crowded lobby. Her eyes skipped over men and a few women and caught on a young man in a short jacket and flat cap standing near the windows on the far side, hands in his pockets. He was handsome in a boyish way, probably a delivery boy of some kind. He glanced away the instant her eyes met his. She'd never seen him before, but she'd recognized the quick smile, the sudden flash of his dark eyes. Vivian looked away, pretending she hadn't noticed. She studied her fingernails and readied herself for his approach. She knew his kind—he'd either want a date or an autograph. Possibly both.

"Vivian, there you are."

She turned around to find Freddy. He was out of breath though perfectly presented, as usual, tiny snowflakes glistening in his dark-blond mustache.

"I'm sorry. Delayed by a client. Couldn't be avoided."

Vivian grunted in reply. She'd almost forgotten how inconsiderate Freddy could be. There was always an appointment, a client, always something else more important than whoever he happened to be with at the time. He leaned forward, and she let him peck her cheek in greeting. Her eyes fluttered back toward the windows, but the young man was gone.

"I have half an hour," she said curtly, glancing at her wristwatch. "Then I have to get back to the station."

"Of course," Freddy said, already striding ahead of her to the manager's office at the far end of the large room, his heels clicking on the marble floor. "Mr. Hannigan is the manager at this bank, I believe. An old Yale pal of Leonard Halifax."

Vivian scowled at Freddy's back and tried to keep pace. *Who the devil is Leonard Halifax?* Freddy was trying to take over. Another of his not-so-endearing habits that she'd forgotten about after infrequent acquaintance. He could be a bit of a blowhard. The problem was that she didn't want him to take over. She didn't want him to know more about her father's affairs than he already did. If there was something embarrassing in that safe-deposit box, something that might damage her father's esteemed reputation, she didn't want Uncle Freddy to see it. She simply needed him, as the executor of her father's estate, to get her into that vault.

Freddy stopped abruptly, and Vivian ran headlong into his back.

"What the..." Freddy sputtered. He whirled around and put a strong hand on each of her shoulders, bending to look her square in the eye. "Viv, this whole thing has got you worked up, hasn't it?"

Exactly the opposite, she thought, looking into his widened blue eyes. He was the one who seemed worked up.

"I'm sorry," she said. "I guess it has."

He squeezed her shoulders and then let go. "Understandable, my dear. Perfectly understandable." He turned his back to her again and charged toward a harried-looking middle-aged woman sitting in front of a typewriter.

"Excuse me, ma'am. I'd like to speak with the manager."

"Regarding?" she murmured without looking up.

"The safe-deposit box of a deceased client of mine."

She glanced up, eyes wary above her half glasses. Vivian could almost hear the woman's exasperated sigh.

"And please mention that we have a common acquaintance—Leonard Halifax."

"One moment." The woman stood and disappeared behind one of the partitioned glass segments in the wall-long oak cubicles. They watched her speak to a short, mustachioed man. The man looked at Uncle Freddy, squinted, and then smiled before waving Freddy into the office.

"Wait here," Freddy said to Vivian. "I'll handle this."

Freddy spoke with the man for only a moment before he was back by Vivian's side.

"Spot of luck. He's agreed to waive all the official nonsense."

"Official nonsense?"

Freddy glanced around the cavernous room.

"I showed him the paperwork—proving that your father is

deceased and that I'm the executor of his estate. But technically, the box is supposed to be inspected by a tax man first to make sure that your father wasn't hiding scores of cash or anything of value—as a way to skirt death taxes and such. The tax man always wants his share. I told him we're short on time and promised to report anything out of the ordinary." He smiled at her, but the expression did not reach his eyes. "Finding any of that is highly unlikely, of course," he said.

Not according to recent discoveries, Vivian thought. She considered the stack of bills, now missing, and considered Freddy as well. He was not himself. Oh, he was putting on a good show, but there was nervousness underneath his confidence today. He had about as much idea of what was in that safe-deposit box as she did, she thought, and it worried him.

"Whatever we find in there," she said, nodding her head toward the open safe door. "It's all in confidence?"

"Of course," he said. "We'll call it attorney-client privilege."

"You won't say anything about this to Mother?"

Freddy narrowed his eyes. "Not if you don't want me to."

"Not just yet." Regardless of what they found, she didn't want her mother to catch wind of a mysterious safe-deposit box before Vivian could work everything out in her own head.

Freddy nodded curtly and held out his hand. Vivian stared at him.

"The key," he prompted.

She shook her head. "I'm coming in with you."

"It's not necessary," he said, frowning. "It probably just contains insurance papers."

Vivian stared impassively back at him. "I'm coming in with you."

"It's likely an empty box, Vivian," he said. "I don't want you to waste your time." His voice was tight. He'd expected her to roll over, to defer to his authority in this important matter. But Vivian was determined to see with her own eyes whatever was in that box. And Freddy seemed just as determined that she didn't.

"I'm already here. It's no trouble."

He looked down his nose at her, but turned without a word and headed into the vault area.

The huge, round metal safe door was open. The manager pulled a ring of keys from his pocket and stepped ahead of them to unlock the iron bars of the interior gate. The metal gate swung open silently, and Vivian stepped over the threshold and into the room. The air was stifling and close. She fought the sudden urge to turn and run.

"Mr. Hannigan, this is Vivian Witchell, the daughter of the deceased."

"Pleased to meet you, Miss Witchell."

Vivian nodded and scanned the rows of metal boxes, all identical except for the number stamped onto the small plaque in the front of each. Mr. Hannigan pulled a brass key out of his jacket pocket and put the key into one of the locks on a box about halfway up on the left wall: 242. There it was, she thought. It looked so harmless. She exhaled. It was now or never. She pulled the string from under the collar of her dress and up over her head. She handed the matching key to Freddy without a word.

Mr. Hannigan inserted Vivian's key in the second lock and turned, opened the door, and then pulled the flat metal box from the wall and handed it to Freddy.

"I'll leave you to it," he said with a curt little nod. He left them alone in the vault, glancing once over his shoulder as he stepped through the iron gate. Vivian shivered as he closed and locked it behind them.

She returned her attention to Freddy and the shallow metal drawer he'd set on the desk in the center of the room. He stood staring down at it, his lips pursed, his hands on his hips.

"What's in it?"

He stared into the box without answering. His expression hadn't changed. Vivian stepped forward and forced herself to look down. Her heart was pounding, her palms slick with sweat.

Inside the box lay a book—perhaps ten inches by twelve with a plain brown cardboard cover. A book? What could be so important about a book that it needed to be kept under lock and key inside a bank vault? She exhaled and reached out to pick it up. Freddy shifted toward her as if he was going to reach out and stop her, but in the end he remained unmoving, unspeaking.

Vivian slid her fingertips down the front cover. There was nothing remarkable about it so far. She scooped the book up and placed it on the desktop in front of her. She opened the front cover. On the inside in pencil it read: *July 1929—Racquet.*

Racquet—the same name as on the outside of the envelope in her father's drawer. She glanced at Freddy.

"What's Racquet mean?" she asked. She already knew the answer, of course. But she wanted to know if Freddy knew, and if he did, whether he would tell her.

Freddy didn't answer her, but she'd seen his lips purse at the mention of the gambling club.

"Racquet…" He looked up, eyes trained on the ceiling as if he were searching his memory for where he may have heard the term. "Ah yes, I believe that was some sort of illegal gambling concern in the suburbs. Gone now."

Vivian sighed an internal sigh of relief. He hadn't lied to her. She didn't mention that the same name had been written on the outside of the cash envelope. She wasn't sure why.

"Do you know what all of this means?" She passed a hand over the scribbled entries—a jumble of letters and numbers.

He flipped through the pages. "Receipts of the club, I suppose."

"Why would my father have had something like this?"

Freddy slapped the ledger shut and Vivian jumped, startled by the noise in the small suffocating room.

"Truthfully, I don't know." Freddy stared down at the

ledger for a moment longer and then up at her. "If I had to guess, I would say he'd been keeping it safe for a client."

"What kind of a client?"

"The kind that would deal intimately with illegal gambling concerns in the suburbs, Viv."

She shot a quick glance at Freddy's face. He was serious.

"My father had clients…like that?"

Freddy's expression didn't change, but the look in his eyes told her all she needed to know. The answer was yes; her father had clients like that. And now Freddy wanted her to stop asking questions.

"My father gambled, didn't he?"

Freddy stared at her for a moment, taken aback by the question. Then he sighed and looked up at the ceiling again. "Yes, Viv, he did. Sometimes."

"At the Racquet?"

His eyes stayed trained on the ceiling. "Sometimes."

"Did you gamble there?"

"Once or twice."

Where exactly had Freddy gone when he'd excused himself from dinner the other night? He had certainly been gone long enough to sneak up the back stairs to her father's study and write that note in the drawer. And if he'd written that note, then he'd also known about the envelope. Could he have taken it after all? That envelope had contained enough cash to cover any of Freddy's recently incurred debts.

"Do you still gamble?"

"Me?" His blue eyes were wide when they met hers. He seemed genuinely surprised by the question. "Sometimes I go to the track. Why?"

"Have you been there lately?"

"They don't run horses in the winter, Viv. What's this all about?"

Vivian felt herself blush. Of course they didn't run races in the winter. This was Chicago, not Hialeah. She felt ridiculous for pressing the subject. Freddy couldn't logistically have taken the money, and why would he have taken it if he knew Vivian was sure to find out?

"I'm sorry," she said. "Well, it was the way you were acting the other night, I suppose. It's got me worried about you."

Freddy exhaled through his nose. "I behaved boorishly, and I'm sorry for that. I should apologize to your mother, shouldn't I?"

Vivian nodded. Not that she would recommend voluntarily entering that sort of conversation with her mother, but he should.

"It's all this with Pauline. I was feeling terrible, so I had a few cocktails too many. That's all."

And what was with his attitude toward Oskar? The question was on the tip of her tongue, but she didn't ask it. Jealousy, the green monster, rearing its ugly head. Could that really be it—after all this time?

"I'm sorry about Pauline," she said, and was surprised to find that she meant it. She'd never liked Pauline, but she didn't enjoy seeing Freddy in pain.

He didn't say anything, but he reached over and squeezed her shoulder awkwardly. Then he reached for the ledger, and Vivian's hand shot out to grab it first.

"I'd like to take it," she said, shrugging as she clutched the book to her chest.

Freddy hesitated, his eyes lingering over the ledger in her arms. Then he smiled—a closed, tight-lipped smile. "Suit yourself," he said. "But if I were you, Viv, I'd let the whole matter lie. Your father was a fine man. I don't know why you insist on digging around, trying to find things to make you believe otherwise."

She didn't answer, and after a moment, he turned to return the box to its position in the wall. He shoved it in with a dull screech and closed the safe-deposit box door. She held her hand out for the key. As he dropped it into her open palm, another thought occurred to her. Freddy and her father had a safe in their office. Why not keep the ledger there? The answer, of course, had to be that her father hadn't trusted Freddy. And it occurred to her that maybe she shouldn't trust him either.

CHAPTER FOURTEEN

───────◆───────

*L*ove & Glory went live at two fifteen, and they did a run-through and rehearsal in the hour before they went on the air. Vivian had kept on as Donna in *Love & Glory*, despite her busy schedule with *The Darkness Knows*. She didn't need the show, but the show needed her, and she would play the part of the dutiful wife as long as they wanted her. These sappy fifteen-minute melodramas tended to have fluid plotlines, and it was only a matter of time until she was written out. It couldn't come soon enough, in Vivian's opinion.

All of this work was running her ragged. Two months ago, she had been bursting at the seams to take on as many parts as they could throw at her. Now, things were more complicated. She was more secure in her role as Lorna Lafferty in *The Darkness Knows*. She had two months' worth of Thursday night shows under her belt and whispers of a move to Hollywood in the works. No, she didn't need *Love & Glory* at all, but she kept on anyway. It was the professional thing to do. And if there was anything Vivian prided herself on, it was being professional.

She stopped by Imogene's desk on the twelfth floor on her way to rehearsal. Imogene was filing her nails, a script open in front of her on the desk.

"Genie, can I use your telephone?"

"Sure." She glanced at the ledger Vivian held and raised her eyebrows. Vivian ignored her, perching herself on the edge of Imogene's desk. She reached over and dialed Charlie's number. Maxine answered on the first ring with a breathy "Mr. Haverman's office."

"Hello, may I speak to Mr. Haverman please?"

She saw Imogene's eyebrows shoot up, and Vivian turned away.

"May I ask who's calling?"

"Vivian Witchell, Mr. Haverman's *old* friend."

"One moment, please." She heard the thunk as the receiver was placed not so delicately down on the desktop and the muffled click of Maxine's heels as she walked to Charlie's office door to announce her call. Another second later, there was the click of Charlie picking up his office extension.

"So what did you find?"

"A ledger from the Racquet Club dated July 1929," she said.

He was silent for a long moment. "Just the ledger?"

"Yes. We didn't get a chance to look through it."

"Do you have it?"

"Yes. It's right here." She patted it with her free hand.

"Can I come over and have a look?"

Vivian turned even farther away from Imogene and lowered her voice.

"Well, I'm at the station right now. I won't be home until this evening, but you can meet me there—say nine o'clock?"

"At your house?" She heard the hitch in his voice.

"You'd rather meet somewhere else?" She knew it was silly, but if she could get him alone, maybe he'd remember why he'd liked her in the first place.

"No, no, that's fine. Nine o'clock."

"Oh, and I've moved into the coach house out back. Go directly there, not to the main house."

"The coach house."

"See you then."

She hung up the receiver and looked at the ledger on her lap. She brushed her fingers over the cover. A ledger kept in a safe-deposit box and not the safe in her father's office. The ledger to a gambling house in notoriously lawless Cicero of 1929.

"Are you going to tell me what's going on?"

Vivian turned to find Imogene staring at her expectantly, a red pencil now clutched in her hand. "You've been holding out on me. I do believe I heard you invite one Charlie Haverman to your house this evening." She put on a breathy little-girl voice and said, "Meet me at the coach house... where I live *all alone*..."

"Stop," Vivian said, rolling her eyes. "Yes, well, he has to meet me so he can look at this ledger." She tapped the hard cover of the book on her lap.

Imogene smirked. "He could meet you just as well at the Tip Top Café."

He could, Vivian thought. He could theoretically meet her at any number of places. But it would be better to be alone.

"So what's this all about?" Imogene's eyebrows drew together at the bridge of her nose as she fixed Vivian with a determined stare. "Mysterious ledgers, detectives on call... This isn't a flimsy excuse to get back in touch with Charlie, is it? What have you gotten yourself into now?"

Vivian sighed. "My father's locked desk drawer," she whispered.

"The cash."

Vivian nodded. "And now this"—she tapped the cover of the ledger—"kept in a safe-deposit box at the First National."

"What does it mean?"

"I don't know. And that's why I'm having Charlie meet me. I've hired him to help me look into all of this—like you suggested."

Imogene smirked and raised a penciled brow. "And I thought the detective told you to let sleeping dogs lie."

"He did." Vivian said, frowning. "It's complicated."

"I'll say." Imogene put the end of the pencil in her mouth and chewed it. She removed it and pointed the unchewed end at Vivian. "Has he told you why he disappeared on you?"

Vivian looked up at the ceiling as the frustration of that conversation returned to her. "Graham," she said.

"Oh no."

"Oh yes," Vivian said. "Charlie seems to think I've chosen Graham over him—which is ridiculous. Well, not completely, I suppose. And I can't tell him otherwise, because—"

"Because it's the truth?"

"Yes. *No.*" Vivian shook her head. "I tried to explain, but Charlie won't hear it. He cuts me off and calls me his friend and tells me that's all in the past."

"Is it?"

"Not if I have anything to say about it."

Imogene raised her eyebrows. "You're planning a seduction scene."

Vivian blew air out of her nose at how ludicrous that sounded, but she didn't deny it. That *was* the plan, she supposed, if she had any sort of plan at all. A seduction scene. The very phrase was preposterous—something that Jean Harlow tried on Clark Gable in movies like *Red Dust*. Vivian had never had to seduce anyone before. Men had always come after her. Until now.

"This is a fine mess you're in," Imogene said, shaking her brown curls.

"You can say that again. Can you keep this in your desk while I'm at rehearsal?" She handed the ledger over to Imogene.

"I suppose."

"It's an important book. Don't let it out of your sight."

"Sure," Imogene repeated, regarding the unassuming brown ledger with a dubious expression.

Vivian watched Imogene slide it into her desk drawer. The book appeared unassuming, but Vivian suspected its looks were deceiving.

It was shy of four o'clock, but the light was already turning soft. Vivian knew that if she could see the western sky beyond the buildings, it would be filled with one of those beautiful winter sunsets the pastel of orange sherbet. Both frigid and lovely, like Chicago itself at this time of year. She craned her neck to see the pinky orange reflected in the upper windows of the department store. Her eyes ranged back down and fell on the evergreen wreath hung over the lamppost in front of her. The ends of the thick red bow were starting to fray from the wind, and the gold star in the middle of the wreath hung lopsided. It looked like she felt: bedraggled, worn out. She'd had a live show and two grueling rehearsals today: *The Darkness Knows* and *The Scarlet Pimpernel*. She couldn't keep this pace up for much longer. Around her, people clamored, rushing home with their packages.

She was beat, but she'd managed to make two trips before going home. She'd rushed off to Stop and Shop after rehearsals to pick up a box of the expensive Italian Majani candies that her father had loved, and then on to Carson Pirie Scott to buy herself a new dress. Not that Charlie would notice the dress. Not that he would care. It was senseless to pine for him when he'd told her in no uncertain terms that he wasn't interested. Still, she had to try. Because she'd never wanted anyone like she wanted Charlie Haverman. She'd been sleepwalking through the past two months, but she hadn't realized that until she'd seen him again. And perhaps, she thought, she wanted him so badly because she couldn't have him. She had to admit that was a novel concept for her, a man who was out of reach.

She stood on the sidewalk outside Carson's, her eyes ranging over the store's front window still decked out with its festive Christmas display of Shirley Temple dolls and toy trains while simultaneously proclaiming *Sale!* from banners hanging from the ceiling.

The scent of roasting chestnuts wafted on the air and her stomach growled, reminding Vivian that she hadn't eaten lunch. She reached into her bag and pulled out the box of candies. She popped one into her mouth and let the sugary, violet-flavored candy roll around on her tongue.

She wound the handle of the bag containing the ledger around her right wrist. She felt the weight, the realness of it. It was quite real, and it was evidently important. But why? She hadn't looked at it beyond what she'd seen inside the vault, and she'd decided not to look at it again until Charlie arrived.

Charlie. He'd be with her tonight. Alone. She smiled.

Someone bumped into Vivian from behind, jostling her. Her arms automatically pinwheeled forward to stop her from toppling over, but she felt her right arm pulled backward. She blinked, confused. Then she was yanked sideways. A gloved hand appeared in her view, clutching the strap of her bag. Someone was trying to pull it from her.

"Hey!" she said. She was more shocked than frightened, and the tiny sound of her protest was lost in the din of the crowd. The hand continued to grasp, pulling on the bag and rubbing the strap painfully against her wrist. "Hey!" she repeated. A few faces turned her way, but no one stopped to help.

Instinct and outrage kicked in. Vivian hitched in the biggest breath she could muster and screamed. It was the scream she saved for the live episodes of *The Darkness Knows*, the scream she was known for—shrill, high, and piercing. It echoed off the stone facades of State Street. Everyone, everything around her stopped. A dozen startled faces turned in her direction. "Thief!" she cried. Immediately, the hand loosened its grip and slipped away. Vivian's weight shifted in the opposite direction, and she stumbled, almost slipping to the icy pavement. Her eyes darted toward the movement of a dark figure rushing away from her through the crowd. She could make out nothing distinctive about the man except that he was young, dark, and wearing a flat cap—like the young man at the bank earlier today.

Vivian blinked and looked down at the bag, the strap still securely twisted around her wrist. It ached where the strap had slipped under her coat sleeve and rubbed against her skin. There would be a welt there. She rubbed it with her fingertips. When she looked up again, the man was long gone, replaced by a crowd of pale, worried faces. They swarmed around her.

"Are you okay, miss?" The question came from all sides.

She nodded numbly as snippets of conversation floated toward her. The outraged voice of an older woman rang in her ears.

"Filthy purse snatchers. At the holidays too. Don't people have any decency anymore?"

A purse snatcher. Panicked, she reached for the handbag slung over her left shoulder. It was still there. She patted it with her gloved hand, felt that the snap was still securely closed, and sighed with relief. A purse snatcher, she thought again. Not unheard of in a crowd already prone to confusion. But that snatcher hadn't gone for her purse, had he? No, he'd gone after the bag with the ledger.

Vivian plumped a pillow on the sofa and immediately felt silly for doing it. Charlie wouldn't care one bit if her pillows were plumped. But she had too much nervous energy to sit around just waiting. She put both hands on her hips and cast an eye over the interior of the tiny coach house, wondering what he would see when he entered. It was essentially one big room, with the front door opening directly into the living room. The stairway to the second floor made a division of sorts between that and the kitchen behind. The powder room was tucked into the nook behind the stairs. Her eyes skimmed over the furniture cribbed from the attic of the main house—the riotous checks of the overstuffed chair at war with the elaborate swirling vines of the sofa. The effect was cozy, cramped, and rather underwhelming, she decided.

She had no maid, and tonight was the only time she'd worried that it showed. She ran an index finger absently around the bottom edge of the lampshade and winced at the deep-gray smudge left on the pad of her finger when she pulled it away. She started toward the dust rag in the hall closet, and then a double knock sounded at the front door like a gunshot. Vivian put a hand to her throat as if clutching at imaginary pearls and glanced at the clock. *He was early*. She transferred the dust from her finger onto the back side of the chair and kicked a dust ball the size of a small tumbleweed under the sofa. Then she hurried to the mirror over the side table to check her reflection. She smoothed her eyebrows down with the wetted tips of her pinky fingers and smiled at herself to take the edge off her nerves.

He knocked again, and she forced herself to wait thirty seconds before opening the front door, timing it on her wristwatch. She didn't want to appear too eager. Charlie stood there, backlit by the porch light of the front house. His face was in shadow under the brim of his hat. She watched the breath leave his mouth in a puff of icy air as he opened his mouth to speak.

"So these are the new digs? You've come down in the world, Vivian Witchell." She narrowed her eyes at him, and he raised his hands to ward off her retort. "Kidding. This is a penthouse suite compared to my place."

He stepped slightly forward, his face becoming discernable in the yellow glow of her living room lamp. She followed his eyes as they darted over her shoulder and took in the interior of the coach house. But if he thought anything else of her tiny mismatched abode, he didn't say it. She wondered what his place was like—where he slept, where he brushed his teeth, shaved, hung his hat, among other things.

"So?"

"Oh, I'm sorry. Come in." She stepped backward and watched as he removed his coat and hat, which she took from him. They stood looking at each other for a long awkward moment.

"You found the place all right?"

He smirked. "It's right behind the old place."

"Oh. Yes. Would you like a tour?" She held her hand out, palm up. "Living room, powder room, kitchen." Her wrist ticked a few degrees to the right to indicate each separate space as she announced them. She walked toward the back of the room and threw her arm with his overcoat draped over it out to the side to indicate the stairway. "This way to the bedroom."

She stopped speaking, acutely aware in the silence that followed of how that had sounded. Her hand remained outstretched for another long moment before she lowered it to her side. She caught Charlie's eye for a split second, and then glanced away again to hide the blush creeping onto her cheeks. The best thing to do was to press on, she decided. Pretend that she hadn't said precisely what she was thinking. She started walking again and smiled at him over one shoulder. She opened the hall closet, set his hat on the shelf, and hung his coat.

"Well, that covers it. Nothing else to see, I'm afraid."

She turned and found he had stopped inches from her.

"Cozy little place," he said, looking down at her.

"I like it." She forced herself to maintain eye contact with him. "And it keeps Mother out of my hair."

He turned back toward the front of the coach house and walked over to the window. He drew the curtain back a bit with the tips of two fingers and looked out.

"I'm not so sure about that."

Vivian hurried over to the window. There was indeed a fuzzy-headed silhouette in the kitchen window that quickly slipped out of view. She frowned. Mrs. Graves.

"Is she about to scurry off and report that there's an unknown man in your house?"

"Probably," Vivian said, her frustration growing. How had she ever thought that living twenty yards away from her mother and under a different roof would exempt her from the woman's scrutiny? She exhaled and took a moment to calm her frazzled nerves.

"Who cares? I'm a grown woman. I can do as I please." She walked over to the small liquor cabinet and opened the door. "Speaking of… What I would like right now is a nice, stiff drink. Would you like one?"

Charlie looked at her for a moment, brow furrowed. Something flashed in his eyes. *Temptation*, she thought. She smiled at him and batted her eyelashes. *This is it*, she thought. *The moment he cracks. The moment he admits that he still feels something for me.*

Then Charlie's gaze slipped away. "How about we look at the ledger," he said.

"Oh, yes," she said. "Of course. The ledger."

She'd managed to forget entirely about that ledger. Charlie had commanded all of her attention. But apparently she hadn't had the same effect on him…because Charlie was all business. Again.

She pulled the ledger from the bag and set it on the side table. She watched Charlie approach and the frown deepen on his face. It was a frown of recognition.

"You know what it is?"

He didn't answer. He opened it, paused when he noticed

the date on the inside front cover, and started to page through, pausing every so often to take a more thorough look at one of the entries.

"Well?"

He held up one finger, silencing her. Vivian took the opportunity to mix herself that nice stiff drink. She sipped her gin and tried not to think about how her seduction scene was not playing out as she'd hoped. Not at all, in fact.

"Accounting. Collections. Payments," he said finally.

"I know that," she said in exasperation. "For the Racquet Club in Cicero. But why did my father have it? Why did he keep it in a secret safe-deposit box?"

"I imagine because it was important to him at some point in time."

Vivian grunted and finished off her drink. The liquor burned down to her stomach as she set the empty glass on the table. "It's not his."

"How do you know that?"

"Freddy said he was keeping it for a client. He said they did things like that."

"A client…"

"I know. I know. Save your lecture. The client was probably not a respectable citizen. But that doesn't mean my father wasn't respectable."

Charlie shook his head. "The Racquet was a high-end place, but it was still illegal." He looked off into the distance for a minute. Then he turned to look at her, his face serious. "Do you know anything about what sent Capone to jail?"

"Al Capone?" Vivian's stomach twisted.

Charlie narrowed his eyes at her. She was being naive, and they both knew it.

"Tax evasion, wasn't it?" she said. She looked away, not able to meet Charlie's gaze. She could still feel his eyes on her.

"Not murder, not bootlegging...tax evasion. He was convicted on the testimony of a bookmaker and a single dusty ledger that showed he'd earned money that he never reported to the federal government."

Charlie tapped an entry with his fingertip until Vivian turned back and looked down at it. "Two hundred dollars to Al," she read aloud. She glanced up at Charlie. *Al.* The word tasted sour in her mouth. "That could be Al anyone."

Charlie tilted his head at her. "But it isn't."

Vivian swallowed. Of course it wasn't any Al. It was *the* Al. Which is why someone had had her father hide this ledger. She glanced back at that line—so innocent and yet so incriminating.

"So this ledger is proof of Capone's income then. And my father was keeping this ledger until it could be used at trial?"

"Looks like it."

"For whom?"

He shrugged again. "The men who kept ledgers, the numbers men, tended to wind up in Lake Michigan wearing cement overshoes—disappeared along with the ledgers they kept. Which is why the feds could dig up only one solitary ledger with any reference to Capone's income, and that one had been sitting in a file cabinet for years collecting dust, acquired in a raid years before and forgotten."

Vivian swallowed. Cement overshoes. Dead. Like her father. She flipped through the remaining pages, then shut the book with a thump.

"And this was another," she said.

"The problem was that you couldn't just have the ledger… You also had to have the man who kept the ledger to testify that it was legit."

"So my father was keeping this for an accountant that was going to testify?"

"Looks like it."

"Capone's sitting in Alcatraz, and the man that this ledger belonged to is probably long gone. So this"—she tapped the cover with a fingernail—"is a dead end."

Charlie moved toward her, then hesitated. She stopped breathing for a moment as he gazed down at her. "You mind if I borrow it?"

She started breathing again.

"I thought it was worthless."

He glanced away again before answering. "It probably is, but I want to give it another look. Does anyone know you have this?"

"Just Uncle Freddy."

"And he knows what it is?"

"He knew what the Racquet Club was, and that the ledger is probably connected to one of my father's old clients." Vivian looked off into the distance, thinking. "There's one thing that bothers me. There was a safe in my father's office. Why didn't he keep it there?"

"Perhaps your father didn't trust his law partner."

That's exactly what Vivian had thought, but she hated hearing Charlie confirm her suspicions. "He and Father were best friends. They were law partners for almost fifteen years…"

"And yet your father kept secrets from him."

Charlie reached across her to snag the ledger. Vivian flinched backward and watched him slide it across the table and scoop it into his arms. She was treating him like a skittish animal, afraid that if she made any sudden movements, he'd run away. Unfortunately, Charlie wasn't a stray kitten. She couldn't give him a saucer of milk and a scratch behind the ears to win his affection.

He nodded and headed toward the closet. He pulled out his hat and coat and then stalked toward the front door without a word.

"You're going?"

"I have something to take care of."

At this time of night? The last time he'd said something like that, he'd disappeared for hours and had nearly been killed. The leggy Maxine jumped to the front of Vivian's mind, and she pushed her away. She frowned. She was hoping he'd stay. She was hoping they could talk, that she could explain things. Explain about Graham.

"You're sure you don't want a drink or anything?" She winced. That had sounded desperate. But she'd planned on getting him to have at least one drink. Loosen up a little. She was terrible at this. Seduction scenes were not her forte.

Charlie shook his head. She followed him to the door and considered telling him about how someone had tried to steal the ledger from her this afternoon. But she didn't have any proof that the thief wasn't just a purse snatcher, and she didn't want him to think she was making things up to guilt him into staying. Even though that's exactly what she wanted to do. Vivian Witchell was used to being the chasee, not the chaser, and she would not resort to desperate acts to get a man, she decided. Not even Charlie Haverman.

She watched him put on his coat and hat. Then he turned back right outside the door, as if a thought had just struck him. "Are you free tomorrow?"

Vivian shrugged. "That depends on what you have in mind." She caught his gaze and held it for an instant before he looked away.

"I think I know somebody who could fill in some blanks." He tapped the ledger with a forefinger.

"Oh."

"Swing by my office around noon," he said. "And bring a photo of your father."

"A photo?"

He nodded at her. "Noon."

She flipped through the day's agenda in her mind. "Okay, noon."

He hesitated on the doorstep, his eyes darting into the house once more as if he might change his mind and stay. But then he tipped the front of his hat toward her and turned to walk out into the night.

She closed and bolted the door behind him. Then she leaned against it and sighed. He was purposely making this difficult, she thought. She looked out the window, but Charlie had already disappeared into the darkness. Vivian's eyes drifted to the kitchen window, but Mrs. Graves was no longer watching. Her twenty-fifth birthday couldn't come soon enough, Vivian decided. When she inherited her money, she could move away from prying eyes and finally live her own life. She just hoped Charlie would be in it.

CHAPTER FIFTEEN

❖

Vivian had only been in the study a handful of times since her father died—most in the past week alone. But now that she knew what she knew, or suspected what she suspected, she saw everything with new eyes. Everything was a clue to who her father had truly been—even the most mundane things. She picked up the paperweight on his desk, tossing it from hand to hand to feel its heft. She peered at the real butterfly trapped inside—its orange-and-black wings outstretched as if it might fly away any second. She ran her fingertips along the leather spines of the law journals straight as soldiers on the bookshelves. She let her fingers drop to her side where the books ended and the framed photos began.

These were not family photos. These were photos relating to her father's professional life—the professional life fit for his family to see, anyway. She recognized none of the men her father stood so chummily with—shaking hands, arms over shoulders. All backslapping, glad-handing old men. Vivian paused in front of a large photo of her father and a large, buffoonish-looking man with a huge rounded nose, taken at a political rally. The sign on the podium behind them said *Mayor Thompson*—the glad-hander of all glad-handers. Her father looked young, happy, and healthy. He was smiling broadly for the cameras, cheeks flushed with pride and accomplishment.

She sighed. She didn't know what she was looking for. A signed confession? A secret diary explaining everything in terms she could understand—and his motivations for why in the hell he would ingratiate himself with such people, such criminals? Her eyes fell on his briefcase, still standing sentry at the foot of his desk. Yes, that's exactly what she was looking for. Why hadn't she thought of looking there before? She hauled it onto the desktop and flipped open the clasps with a hollow thunk. It was sure to be empty.

It wasn't.

Among the loose, meaningless sheaves of paper was a small, black leather book. Her father's appointment book.

Vivian snatched it up as if it might sprout wings and fly away. She flipped through the pages of the date book, her eyes scanning the words, the notations—most of it not making any sense to her. She knew she wouldn't find anything. There was nothing to find, she told herself. She flipped to the last page with writing and then beyond to where the pages went blank—heartrending proof of a full life cut short. Then she flipped back. No, she wasn't imagining it. The dates in the upper right-hand corner had jumped from 12 to 14. She flipped the pages—back and forth, back and forth a few times. Where was February 13?

Instinctively, she ran her fingertip along the inside seam of the book and found the rough edge of a page that had been cut out. She sat back in her chair and splayed the book apart until she heard the spine crack. She held it up to one eye and squinted. There it was, a tiny sliver of what had been the previous day's page still caught in the binding. Her heart began to thump.

She bit her lip and rubbed the pencil lead lightly over the entirety of the following page, obscuring the mundane tasks that her father had written there. The things he'd planned on being alive to do. Vivian swallowed the lump in her throat. It was something she'd seen Charlie do at Marjorie Fox's house—using pencil lead to reveal the written indentations of a page that was no longer there. She shaded over the blank page following the date of her father's untimely death: dinner with someone named Victor Hamer, reservations at Henrici's… Top-C. *What on earth does Top-C mean?* Then letters began to form in relief, a name appearing as if by magic—stark white in the leaden cloud of gray. Vivian blinked and leaned in closer.

She squinted at the name, printed in her father's large, blocky handwriting in a slant across the middle of the page. *W-son 1:00.* Vivian furrowed her brow, running through the imaginary list in her mind of all of her father's friends and acquaintances. Watson? Wilson? And was that a last name?

It could also be a first. The problem was that she hadn't known many of the people her father associated with when he'd died—even the perfectly legitimate ones. Her mind raced, clutching at fragments, at bits of old memories. She was certain that if she concentrated hard enough, the answer would come to her.

It didn't.

Vivian slumped back into the chair and glanced at the clock. She had to meet Graham at the Chicago Theater for an appearance on *The Gossip Club* in forty minutes. She shut the briefcase, returned it to the floor, and shoved the appointment book into her pocket. Her eyes swept over the photos again. No, she couldn't bring any of these to Charlie's office. That glad-handing ham-fisted man wasn't the father she knew.

Vivian stood on the corner of State and Lake. The day was bleak and cloudy, the sun a feeble white disk low in the sky. A Brown Line train screeched around the bend of the elevated tracks overhead. The wind stung, and Vivian sank her chin into the warm, soft fur of her coat's collar. *The Gossip Club* broadcast from a studio in the basement of the Chicago Theater, and she eyed the dancing lights of its marquee down the block with trepidation: *New Year's Eve Special: Paris Honeymoon Starring Bing Crosby!* and underneath, in a smaller font, *All-Girl Band The Melodears Live in Blazing New 1939 Revue.*

She knew the appearance on *The Gossip Club* was important, but the last thing she wanted to do right now was pretend all was right with the world on some silly radio chat show. So she dithered at the newsstand on the corner, her eyes skimming over today's headlines: SEND TROOPS TO CURB ITALY. She squinted at the small print under the headline. *Now it was Italy?* She was reaching forward to pull the newspaper from the stand when a gloved hand closed over her own. She started with a gasp and yanked her hand free.

"I'm sorry, did I frighten you?"

Vivian turned at the familiar voice. Martin stared back at her, his face a mixture of concern and bemusement under the brim of his gray homburg. She let her breath out in a relieved hiss. "Yes, you did a little."

"I'm terribly sorry," he with a grimace. "I assure you, that wasn't my intention."

Vivian waved his concern away. Martin just watched the traffic for a moment, worrying his lower lip, before meeting her eyes again. He inhaled sharply as if to speak, but then let the air out without making a sound, his brow furrowing. After a moment he tried once more.

"It's like this," he said. "I haven't laid eyes on you in years, Viv." He cocked his head to the side as he regarded her. "And well, I suppose seeing you for the third time in one week was an occurrence so unlikely that I had to touch you to make sure you were real."

Vivian's throat was suddenly dry under his intense blue stare. She noted the teasing lilt to his voice and the frank appreciation in his gaze. Then she felt the corner of her mouth curve up into a smile. "I do believe I remember you saying something along the lines of 'I couldn't keep you away now if I tried.'"

He smiled. "I did say that, didn't I?"

"Not that I'm trying," she said, placing a gloved hand lightly on his forearm. "To keep you away, that is. In fact, I find I rather like it when we meet unexpectedly on street corners."

His smile widened. She felt the force of that smile like the jab of an index finger to her chest. Oh, but he was handsome. She wasn't sure if it was the biting wind or her teasing that had added that delicate pinkness to his cheeks, but she liked it. It made him look mischievous—like a schoolboy about to place a tack on the headmaster's chair.

But then Martin's smile faded, and he shook his head. "I'm afraid that's no good."

"No good?"

"I like certainty, you see," he said, his voice low.

"Certainty."

"Yes," he said, leaning slightly forward. His warm breath mingled with hers in the frigid air. His eyes held hers, and after a moment, he lifted his eyebrows. "No more of this unexpected nonsense. Now that I've stumbled upon you again, I'm not letting you go."

Vivian swallowed.

"Tell me you don't have any pressing engagements," he said.

Vivian found herself pulled in by the unmitigated hope in his deep-blue eyes. Here was a man who wasn't looking for excuses to divest himself of her presence, she thought. Martin wanted to be with her. Now.

Alas, that could not be.

"I can't," she said with a sigh. "Because I do have a pressing engagement." She pointed over Martin's shoulder at the marquee.

He half turned and then looked back at her with incredulity. "They run pictures this early in the day?"

Vivian shook her head. "I'm appearing on *The Gossip Club* this morning. It's broadcast from the basement of the theater."

"What's *The Gossip Club*?"

"Oh, just a little show where they interview celebrities…or quasi celebrities, in my case."

"Well, well, Miss Witchell. Color me impressed." He held out his arm to her with a wink. "Then the least I can do is escort a star to her destination."

She took his arm, and they began walking the short distance to the theater, listening to the ambient honks and dings and rumblings of the city coming to life around them. Martin's uneven gate made a distinctive *click-thump*, *click-thump* on the pavement, but he had no trouble keeping up with her. Vivian was trying to think of something to breach the lull in conversation when they arrived under that dazzling marquee. They paused and looked at each other, Vivian's arm still looped through his.

"You couldn't have had an engagement just a little farther away?" he said.

She laughed. "I'm sorry I had an engagement at all. I would very much have liked to take you up on... Well, whatever you had in mind."

"I'm just glad I got a chance to see your lovely face this morning. It was the most pleasant of surprises." Then he shot her a look through half-lidded eyes that was so intense it made her toes tingle. "You haven't, by chance, changed your mind about the mayor's New Year's party, have you?"

She managed a coy smile as she removed her arm from his. He stepped forward and opened the front door of the theater for her. "Not quite yet," she said, stepping inside. "But by all means, please keep trying to persuade me."

Martin's throaty laugh rang out as the front door of the theater swung shut. She smiled and pressed a palm to her chest. Another one of Martin Gilfoy's smoldering looks might persuade her of a lot of things, she thought.

CHAPTER SIXTEEN

The Gossip Club was privy to famous guests by virtue of the fact that someone like Jack Benny had to change trains and stations—not to mention waste several hours in Chicago—in order to get from New York to Hollywood. Jack Benny had been there the week previous, as a matter of fact. He—along with his wife, Mary Livingstone—had stopped off in Waukegan, his hometown on the far-north suburban shores of Lake Michigan, to visit family for the holidays. Vivian had read all about it in the Tattler section of the *Radio Guide*. So it was quite an honor to have been asked to appear today along with Graham. She wished she could get her mind off her father and that appointment book thumping against her leg every time she took a step.

She opened the studio door and heard Graham before she saw him—as often happened with Graham. His deep baritone boomed through the small studio. Then the door clicked shut, and he turned and smiled at her. "Viv!"

"Good morning." She walked over and gave him a peck

on the cheek. Her smile faded when she saw who he'd been talking to. Wendell Banks, WCHI's head of publicity. What was he doing here?

"Hello, Viv," he said, smiling.

"Mr. Banks. An unexpected pleasure."

"Well, I thought I'd check in with the country's favorite crime-solving couple."

Vivian's smile stiffened. His emphasis on the word *couple* had been unmistakable. It seemed this morning's performance would be for a live, in-studio audience. They would perform their adoring couple act, not only for the hosts of the show and the listening public out in Radioland, but also for Mr. Banks.

"The Carringtons aren't quite ready for us," Graham said. "We were just chatting."

"I think I'll get myself some water," Vivian said, making her excuses to escape any pointers Mr. Banks might be waiting to give her about how to fawn over Graham.

They sat at an actual table set for breakfast—Graham and Vivian across from the show's hosts, Eddie and Franny Carrington. Two microphones were live in the middle of the table. It was supposed to sound like they'd stopped by and were chatting over their morning coffee, although they weren't allowed to touch anything on the table because shuffling china would interfere with the sound—not to mention that it would be terrible to talk through a mouthful of toast crumbs on the air. Mr. Banks leered over Franny's shoulder, ears open to everything that might come out of their mouths.

The interview itself was harmless enough, touching on their characters in *The Darkness Knows*. Vivian glanced at the clock throughout the ten-minute interview, willing the second hand to move faster before she put her foot in her mouth.

"That's a lovely pin," Franny exclaimed, leaning forward to get a better view of the golden bird on Vivian's lapel.

Vivian touched it and glanced at Graham. "Oh, thank you. It was a Christmas gift."

"Is that right?" Eddie said, looking significantly at Graham. "I've heard there might be another piece of jewelry headed your way soon."

Vivian stared blankly at him.

"*A little birdie* told us that there may be wedding bells in your future." Franny's eyes darted between Vivian and Graham. "Wouldn't that be lovely? Harvey and Lorna married in real life. Perhaps fiction will mirror reality as well?"

Vivian turned away from the microphones to mask the curse she uttered under her breath. *Married? Where on earth did they get that idea?* She glanced at Graham, but he was not looking in her direction.

"Who knows what may be in the cards for us," he said in his blustery, confident voice.

"Indeed. You heard it here first, folks. Who knows what may be in the cards? Well, best of luck to both of you. I'm afraid that's all the time we have this morning. Thank you for tuning in to…" Vivian had tuned out the rambling closer. *Wedding bells?* She looked at Mr. Banks, who shrugged his shoulders as if he hadn't known they'd bring the subject up. As if he hadn't planted the idea. She turned to Graham, but he was industriously examining his cuticles. He'd known too. He'd known this whole time that they were going to bring up marriage. And they'd blindsided her. Graham and the WCHI publicity machine were in on this together.

She stood and waited impatiently for the on-air light to blink off. Then she bent to Graham's ear and hissed, "A word, please," before stomping off to the far side of the room. He followed reluctantly.

She took a deep breath, calming herself.

"What was that all about?" she whispered, eyeing Mr. Banks over Graham's shoulder. He was chatting up Eddie across the room.

"Oh, it's nothing. Just a little something Wendell and Eddie cooked up to keep the fans interested."

"Nothing? You don't think I should have some say in whether I'm getting married or not?"

Graham looked alarmed. He held his hand up in front of him. "Hey, hey, nobody's getting married. It's a ploy."

"A ploy? I don't know how you can be so blasé about this, Graham."

He shrugged. "And I don't see why you're so upset. It's

show business, that's all. Give the people want they want."
He glanced at the clock and winced. "And we have rehearsal
in ten minutes."

A small crowd had formed on the sidewalk outside the theater
while they'd been on the air. Whenever Vivian and Graham
appeared in public together now, they attracted a fawning
group. Vivian suspected that today's particular crowd was all
Mr. Banks's doing. She had no doubt that he was tipping
people off to their whereabouts. Vivian was still angry, but she
forced a smile, her eyes flicking from person to person. All the
attention was flattering, and it was exactly what she'd always
wanted, she reminded herself. And these people were here,
in part at least, because they thought she and Graham were a
couple. *If that's what the people wanted, then that's what they'd get.*

Vivian clutched Graham's arm, shooting him adoring glances,
as he wove through the throng to the curb. Then someone
grabbed Vivian's sleeve and yanked her backward. Vivian held
fast to Graham's arm, and she felt him stop beside her. She
turned to find a young woman, eyes wide with hope. She held
a pen up in one hand and a piece of paper in the other.

"Sign this, please?" she asked.

Fawning and a bit intrusive, Vivian thought, taking the
woman's pen and paper. At least she said "please." *Smile,* she
told herself.

"When's the wedding?" the woman asked as Vivian scrawled
her name. Vivian's stomach somersaulted. She looked blankly

into the woman's excited face and found she had no idea how to reply. Thankfully, Graham pulled her forward then and gently pushed her toward the waiting cab.

"Come, darling," he said, projecting his voice over his shoulder at the crowd.

Darling, my foot, Vivian thought.

After rehearsal, Vivian took three streetcars and then a bus, doubling back to confuse anyone who might be following her. Not that that was likely. She fumed the whole way. About Graham. About Mr. Banks. About the Carringtons, of all people, thinking they could run her life like that. The idea that her relationship with Graham would end in marriage had always been like a joke. Now it was a frightening reality. Not that she thought they could make her marry against her will, but now all of Chicago would assume the match was inevitable and imminent. Mrs. Graham Yarborough. The thought made her shudder. The thought of being Mrs. Anyone made her shudder.

A dog scuttled down the street past Charlie's office building, the only source of movement except the icy wind whipping old newspapers down the empty pavement. Vivian glanced at her watch. 12:03 p.m. She climbed the steps and opened the door without knocking.

Maxine wasn't at her desk, and Vivian breathed a sigh of relief. She didn't know if she was up to the scrutiny today. Not after the morning she'd had. Charlie poked his head out of his office door and frowned at her. "You're late."

"By four minutes," she protested.

"Come in." He waved her into his office, and his head disappeared back behind the doorjamb. She took her coat off. Good to his word, Charlie had actually had someone come in to look at the radiator. Now it was sweltering in the cramped little space. She waved one hand in front of her face, but the warm, dry air it swirled in front of her nose did little to cool her.

A man was already there, seated in a chair behind Charlie's desk. He was in his mid to late sixties, dark hair peppered with gray and dark eyes—a rough but pleasant face. He cocked his head as she walked in, and the gesture reminded her of someone. Then Charlie walked to the opposite side of the desk. His head was cocked at her in exactly the same way.

He gestured to the man sitting next to him. "This is my father, Charlie Haverman Sr."

"Call me Cal," the man said, standing and thrusting out his hand for a shake.

Vivian took his hand, and he pumped hers forcefully several times. She tried to hide her surprise in her stilted smile. The person who might shed some light on her father's nefarious dealings was Charlie's father?

Mr. Haverman was darker than Charlie, shorter and stockier. She knew he was not Charlie's biological father, but there was something in the way he carried himself that reminded her of Charlie. Mr. Hart might have given Charlie his height and good looks, but this man had given Charlie his character.

"I must confess, I'm a little confused," she said, turning from Cal to Charlie and back again.

"Pops was a track detective at Hawthorne." Charlie turned to his father. "For how many years?"

"Twelve. And two at Lincoln Fields before that. I'm retired now. Well, semiretired."

Vivian glanced back and forth between the men again. That explained virtually nothing. She looked at Charlie, but it was Cal who continued.

"Hawthorne is right next to Sportsman's Park," he said. He registered her blank expression and continued the explanation. "They started running horses when the government ran Capone outta the dog-racing business in Illinois."

Vivian opened her mouth, and then closed it again.

"He's also familiar with the Racquet Club." Charlie tapped his index finger on the cover of the ledger sitting in front of him at the desk.

"I…" Vivian shook her head. It felt like she'd walked into a movie already in progress. "What's any of this got to do with my father?"

"Did you bring the photo?"

"Oh yes." Vivian pulled the frame from her bag and set it on the desk. Charlie's eyes focused on a young Vivian, and one corner of his mouth curved up in a smile. Then the smile faded and he pointed at her father, speaking to his own father out of the side of his mouth.

"Do you recognize that man?"

Cal squinted at the photo, leaned in, leaned back again, and then nodded. "Sure. That's Easy Artie."

Vivian narrowed her eyes at the man, unsure that she'd heard him correctly. "I'm sorry. Easy Artie?"

"Yeah, that's what they called him."

"Who?"

"Everybody," Cal said with a shrug. "He was at the track a lot. Last I saw him was sometime in the summer of…oh, that was probably 1930? The summer before Capone got in hot water."

He was at the track a lot. *Her father. Everyone called him Easy Artie. Capone.* This information was all coming too fast for her to process. And it couldn't be true. Charlie was pulling her leg. He had to be. She looked at him, but his expression was serious.

Cal leaned forward, smiled, and placed the tip of his index figure on the figure seated directly below her father. "And that cute little thing is you, isn't it?"

Vivian didn't answer. Her mind was numb.

When she'd gathered her thoughts, Vivian said, "So? He liked to go to the track, that's all."

Cal squinted at Vivian and thunked the tops of his fingers on the desktop twice. "As I recall, your father was pretty chummy with some important people."

"Chummy?" she said, her head swimming.

He nodded, looked at her for a long time, his finger tapping on the *$200 to Al* line in the open ledger. "Big Bill Thompson, for one. The crooked mayor himself. Capone had that fella in his pocket. Had 'em all in his pocket." The photo in her father's study flashed through her mind, and then the headline from the newspaper the night he'd died: CAPONE CITY HALL BOSS. "And the big man himself, of course—when he was still the big man. Your father knew him. Capone owned Sportsman's next door, but he used to come to Hawthorne from time to time. Better class of pony. I saw your father with Capone with my own two eyes. They were pals."

Vivian shook her head, her eyes on the fingers twisting in her lap.

"So, he met the man," she said, her voice flat. "Capone was a celebrity. My father couldn't resist."

"It was common knowledge that Easy Artie was under Capone's thumb. I don't know how far under, but—"

Vivian held up her hand. "That's not true." She settled her shoulders and took a breath. "I mean, this information is… unexpected. But where's your proof?" She looked from Cal to Charlie. Two men so unlike and alike at the same time.

Identical expressions of sympathy on their faces. That infuri-
ated her. There was nothing to sympathize with. Her father
could not be who they said he was.

"I figured you'd say that," Charlie said, leaning back in
his chair.

How dare Charlie think he knew her that well.

"Maybe you should take her to see Moochie," Cal said,
turning to his son.

Vivian returned her attention to the older man, one
eyebrow raised.

"Moochie," Charlie repeated, considering the idea. "Yeah,
maybe."

"I mean, there aren't many guys around from those
days anymore. But there's Moochie, and he might know
something. Give you this proof you're looking for."

She pulled at the buttons at the top of her dress. God, but it
was warm in this room. She felt light-headed.

"I'm sorry, doll. This is a lot to take in, isn't it? But it's the
God's honest truth."

All of this was a crazy fever dream, Vivian thought. She
blinked and looked out the window at the dirty brick of the
building next door. *Doll*, she thought. Had Charlie's father
just called her *doll*?

"Anyone for coffee?" Cal stood, his chair legs scraping
against the wooden floor. No one answered, but he left the
room anyway.

Charlie's eyebrows met over the bridge of his nose as he returned his attention to Vivian.

"Sorry, Pop's never been one for tact."

She couldn't focus on anything but the swirling fact that her father had been chums with Al Capone, and everyone on God's green earth but her seemed to have known about it.

"But Freddy said my father wasn't involved in anything illegal," she said. She looked back toward Charlie and was alarmed to see concern in his eyes. She must not have been taking this as well as she thought.

"Yeah? Well, I think it's pretty obvious that either Freddy is the world's most unobservant business partner, or he's been lying to you."

She shook her head. It was all hard to believe, but why would Charlie's father lie to her? He wouldn't, was the answer. He had no reason to.

She cleared her throat and pulled the appointment book from her pocket. "There's also this. I found it in my father's study when I went to get the photo this morning." She handed Charlie the book. "Someone tore out the page following his death."

Charlie opened the book, letting pages flip until he reached the one covered in leaden gray pencil. He studied it for a moment, passing his fingertips over it. His eyes flicked to hers, recognition there that she'd learned this trick from him. "Who or what is W-son?"

"I don't know, but my father never got a chance to meet him…or her."

She locked eyes with Charlie.

"And someone wanted to make sure that no one would find out they were going to meet?"

She nodded, her stomach churning at the idea. It could have been an innocent thing. Her father could have ripped that page out himself, but she knew he hadn't.

"And Top-C?" he said.

She looked down to where he was pointing on the page. In the upper right-hand corner, near the edge of the leaden-gray cloud where *Top-C* was written in her father's tight, precise hand.

She shrugged. She couldn't think clearly. "No idea."

"Maybe where they were going to meet? I'll look into that too."

He nodded and stood. He rested an index finger on her face in the photo, raising an eyebrow at sixteen-year-old Vivian, a childish bow in her neat bob. "Look at you, so sweet and innocent."

She snorted as he slid the framed photo back over the desk. She fumbled the photo into her bag with numb fingers as she stood to go. Charlie continued walking behind her toward the open door. Then she felt him lean down, his lips close to her ear. "I'll take experience over innocence any day of the week," he said, his breath warm on the nape of her neck.

CHAPTER SEVENTEEN

❖

Vivian glanced at the ornate clock that hung on the outside of the Fair department store at the corner of State and Madison. She should be headed to the studio. They had a live episode of *The Darkness Knows* tonight, and time was tight. Instead, she'd found herself walking the two extra blocks west past the Grayson-Cole Building to the Rookery.

"Vivian." Della seemed surprised. She hadn't expected her, which had been Vivian's plan.

"Hello, Della. Is Freddy in?"

"He is, but he's very busy. He's in conference."

Of course. Wasn't that convenient? All Vivian could think was *He lied to me. Freddy looked me in the eye and lied to me.* She eyed the half-closed door. "Might I come in?"

Della blinked. "Oh, of course." Della opened the door the rest of the way and stepped awkwardly to the side as Vivian entered. "Is there something I can do for you?"

Yes. Tell me the truth, she thought.

"I wanted to talk to Freddy, and I was hoping to get in out of the cold for a few minutes. It's terrible out there today." Vivian took off her gloves and rubbed her hands together.

Della glanced toward the window as if she didn't quite believe her. "Can I get you some tea?"

"That would be lovely. Thank you."

Vivian's eye fell on the windowsill next to the filing cabinets.

"You still have a green thumb, I see." She nodded toward the veritable jungle on the windowsill.

"Yes, they're my babies."

"What's this?" Vivian pointed at a glass dome over one of the plants.

Della smiled at her and then tapped the glass cloche with her fingernail. "It traps the heat," she explained. "Like a mini greenhouse. This poor plant would die in this climate without the heat and moisture."

Vivian followed Della's gaze out the window to the drab gray winter sky, still thinking about meeting Charlie's father...and what he'd told her about her own. She blinked the thoughts from her mind and smiled at Della. "I love that all these exotic plants are growing right here in dreary old Chicago."

"Me too. It gives one some sort of hope, doesn't it?" Della smiled down at the plant like a mother at her child.

"So what is that? The plant, I mean."

Freddy's door flew open and banged against the wall.

"Della, they've pushed the hearing up to—" He fell silent and glanced back and forth between Vivian and Della. Della had begun to raise the cloche from her prized plant to show Vivian, but automatically began to lower it again. "Della. I'm going to need your help immediately." His attention shifted to Vivian. "Hello, Viv."

"Hello, Freddy," Vivian said.

"A surprise to see you here again—so soon."

"I was hoping to talk to you."

"No time, I'm afraid," he said, glancing down at his watch. "I'm late as it is."

"Can we talk later then? It's important." She was unwilling to say more in front of his secretary.

"Of course," he said. Then he rushed from the office— without his coat and hat, Vivian noted.

Della and Vivian turned to each other. Della's brow furrowed in confusion.

"He did say he needed my help, didn't he?"

"I thought so," Vivian said. She shrugged.

"Mr. Endicott's been out of sorts lately," Della said, shaking her head. "Would you still like that tea?"

"I would, thank you."

Vivian sat in the chair in the small waiting area while Della went to the pantry in the back of the office. "You're in luck," she called back to Vivian. "I'd just put the kettle on to boil. Milk?"

"Yes, please."

Della returned in a moment and pressed a steaming mug of tea into Vivian's hand.

"You were about to tell me about your plant. What did you call it?"

"Oh yes, the odollam." Della walked over to the windowsill again and tapped her fingernails on the glass cloche. Then the telephone on her desk rang, startling them both. Della looked back and forth between the glass cloche and the ringing telephone a few times before she finally chose the telephone. "I'm sorry, I have to get this."

"Of course."

Della picked up the receiver. "Mr. Endicott's office. How may I help you?" She pressed her lips together. "Now? Okay, I'll be down in a minute." She hung up and blew the wisps of hair out of her face in exasperation. She turned to Vivian. "There's a package at the front desk in the lobby, and they refuse to deliver it. Told me I have to go down there and sign for it." She shrugged.

"Go ahead," Vivian said. "I was just leaving anyway."

"No, no, you stay right here and finish your tea. I won't be a minute."

And then Della was gone, the door of the office clicking shut behind her. Vivian sat with the tea warming her hands. Her eyes ranged over the plants, the drab square of Chicago sky in the window beyond, and then onto the filing cabinet behind Della's desk. *The filing cabinet.* Vivian put her cup down and shot a quick glance over her shoulder at the closed door. All was quiet in the hall.

Vivian pulled the drawer labeled *W* open with a grunt. She flipped through the files, mumbling each name under her breath as she passed. "Watson, Wilson," she repeated to herself until she reached the end of the files in the drawer. No Watson. No Wilson.

She started to return to her tea, but after one step reversed direction and went back to the filing cabinet. This time she headed for the H drawer. She flipped through the thickly packed file folders, not expecting to find anything in here either. But then she stopped and sucked in her breath. There it was. *Heigel, Oskar.* She glanced over her shoulder toward the door, then pulled the thin file out and opened it. She scanned the few papers it contained. It did indeed look like immigration paperwork—at least to her untrained eye. The date on most of the papers was March 1925.

She snapped the folder shut and lifted it to put it back in the file cabinet. She jumped to the chair and was sitting, legs crossed, serenely sipping her tea when Della returned with the package.

Vivian smiled close-mouthed as Della heaved the package onto the desk. One thought was in her mind: If Oskar and Freddy didn't know each other, why did Freddy have that file in his office?

The ad man was lurking in the control booth again for the eight o'clock show of *The Darkness Knows*. He stood chatting with Mr. Banks as he flicked ashes into the tray at his elbow. Vivian was watching them surreptitiously from behind her script when the studio door opened and Gloria appeared, a cheery smile dimpling her cheeks. Vivian had been hoping the girl wouldn't show—not without Everett—but there she was. Vivian glanced up at the clock. Yes, there she was with only five minutes to air.

Vivian glanced at Graham at the far side of the room, but he hadn't noticed Gloria's entrance, and there was no time to alert him now. Vivian sighed in exasperation. Graham had been the one to invite Gloria, and now he was so wrapped up in himself that he hadn't noticed she'd arrived. Vivian couldn't help but notice that Gloria's smile had dimmed somewhat when Vivian turned her attention back to her. Well, there was no help for it now. Vivian smiled brightly at the girl and headed toward the control room, motioning for Gloria to follow.

Strangers in the control room made Vivian nervous at the best of times, but the return of Mr. Marshfield, the Sultan's Gold Cigarettes ad man, had her sick with anxiety. All she could think about was impressing him enough that he would consider adding her to the nationwide magazine ad he had planned for Graham. And impressing him meant no slipups. Impressing him meant being the consummate professional—something Vivian had trouble with, despite her best intentions. She stopped in front of the men and smiled at each before half turning to include Gloria in the group.

"Hello, Mr. Langley, Mr. Marshfield," Vivian said. "We have a visitor for this evening's performance. May I present Miss Gloria…" Vivian faltered. She realized she'd forgotten the girl's last name.

"Mendel," Gloria supplied with a smile. She offered her hand to Mr. Langley, and he took it, giving it a firm shake.

"Nice to meet you, Gloria." He turned to Vivian while Gloria offered her hand to Mr. Marshfield. "I wasn't aware we were having guests for the performance."

"She's my brother's girlfriend. Graham invited her."

Mr. Langley's scowl lightened at the mention of Graham. *Ever the golden boy*, Vivian thought. She wondered what she'd have to do to gain the esteem Mr. Langley had for Graham. Promise her firstborn?

"Two minutes to air," Joe McGreevey announced into the microphone.

"Oh," Vivian said, glancing through the control-room glass into the studio. The actors had taken their places at the microphone in the center of the room. The organist's fingers hovered over the keys. "I'm sorry. I should get back."

"Yes," Mr. Langley said. "Don't worry about Miss Mendel. She's in good hands."

Vivian glanced at Gloria, who was in conversation with

Mr. Marshfield. She caught Vivian's eyes and gave her a jaunty thumbs-up.

Vivian rushed back into the studio and picked up her script. She had it memorized, but she couldn't stop herself from running through the first few lines again. And again.

"One minute to air," announced Joe's booming voice.

Vivian glanced up at Graham across the microphone, and one corner of his mouth quirked into a smile. Then he lowered his head and raked a hand through his wavy black hair and pushed the rolled cuffs of his shirtsleeves up past his elbows. Vivian's stomach fluttered with nerves. It always did before a performance, but she hadn't felt a churning in her guts like this since she'd first started on *The Darkness Knows* shortly before Halloween. She took a deep breath and let it out through her nose. Her eyes darted to the control room.

Gloria wasn't standing near the front with Mr. Langley and Mr. Marshfield as expected. No, now she hovered over Morty, smiling and fawning. The poor boy looked like there was a fox in his henhouse. His usually sure hands fluttered over the controls, and his freckled cheeks were pink. Vivian had no time to speculate what Gloria could be about, because the minute hand of the clock swept up to mark the hour and the on-air light blinked on. Bill Purdy stepped up to the microphone to start the show.

"And now it's—" Bill stopped speaking abruptly and

scowled into the control booth. His voice had come out flat, and Vivian realized she couldn't hear the telltale electrical hum. The microphone was dead.

Morty flushed and scurried over to the control panel. Bill took a breath and started all over again. Vivian glanced at the clock above the door, the second hand sweeping ever forward. The entire production was now approximately three seconds off. They'd have to make up that time somewhere.

She glanced at Graham, but his head was bowed. He hadn't noticed the loss of time, and that didn't bode well. Graham was usually on top of his game for Harvey Diamond and could be counted on to help cover any blips in the live show. Vivian took a sip of water and opened the script, her eyes focusing on her first line.

"And now it's time for another edition of that tantalizing tale of detective muscle, *The Darkness Knows*," Bill said, his voice rising with enthusiasm. "Sponsored by Sultan's Gold, the cigarette that's truly mellow. Today, we open on Harvey Diamond's downtown office. Diamond is at his desk when a well-dressed man of middle age bursts in, followed by Diamond's right-hand gal, Lorna Lafferty."

"Diamond, you've got to help me," Dave said, his eyes wide as he glanced up at Graham.

"I tried to stop him, Harvey," Vivian said. "He doesn't have an appointment."

Graham looked up from his script and held up one hand with

a smirk. "That's okay, doll," he said. Then the smirk faded as he looked to Dave. "Help you with what...uh, Mr....?"

"Gold."

"Mr. Gold. Have a seat and fill me in." Graham frowned down at his script, and Vivian hitched in a breath. Graham always held the character of Harvey Diamond, the gruff yet carelessly charming gumshoe, throughout every moment of the performance once they were live—even during the sponsor break. And now he'd dropped out of character, if only for a moment. He'd jump effortlessly back in, no doubt, but that lapse worried her. Of the two of them, Graham was usually the more reliable during a performance. Yet his concentration had just faltered. And if he went under, it would be up to her to drag him to the surface and keep them both afloat.

"It's my daughter, Diamond." Dave waited a beat. Then he leaned into the microphone, lowering his voice to a throaty whisper. "She's been kidnapped."

"Kidnapped? Oh, Harvey!" Vivian exclaimed, her free hand fluttering to her chest.

The organ came in with a dramatic stanza. Vivian glanced at Graham. He looked terrible. A fine sheen of sweat was visible near his hairline. He wasn't ready for this performance. *The Pimpernel* was eating him alive.

"Did you get a ransom note?" Graham asked.

"No, but I got this letter in today's mail."

"May I see it?" Dave handed Graham a sheet of paper close to the microphone so the audience would be able to hear the sound of shuffling. Graham read it, brow furrowed. "'They're holding me against my will. Please, help me. I'm at The Golden Lion. Myra.'"

"The Golden Lion? That's in Chinatown," Vivian announced.

The organ broke in with an ominous chord progression, followed quickly by a lighthearted jump into the Sultan's Gold jingle. The three girl singers stood in a tight half circle around another microphone in the corner of the room. They were sisters and so similar in appearance that Vivian couldn't tell them apart on a normal evening. Tonight they were dressed in matching gold sweaters and black skirts. They matched the Sultan's Gold box exactly, and that could be no coincidence, Vivian thought. "Sultan's Gold. You'll be sold on the cigarette that's truly mellow." They twitched their hips from side to side as they crooned in perfect harmony. Vivian's eyes strayed to Graham. He looked at her, and she winked. He forced a smile in return.

"And now back to our story. A mysterious Mr. Gold has asked for Detective Diamond's help in locating his missing daughter."

"Chinatown, you say?" Graham asked.

Vivian's eyes strayed again into the control booth. The ad man hadn't appeared to notice anything amiss. He caught her eye and smiled at her, raising his half-smoked Sultan's Gold in something of a salute. Maybe Vivian wouldn't be overlooked in this magazine advertisement after all. She smiled back. With all of her date dialog cut since the rehearsal, Vivian had a page with nothing to do before she was kidnapped by the white slavers, and then all she had to do was scream on cue. She could do that in her sleep.

The first live show went well, despite such an inauspicious beginning. Morty managed to shake Gloria's attentions and hit all of his cues.

When they finished the second live show for the West Coast, it was ten thirty, and it was almost eleven by the time she'd left the station and was on her way home. This workload was catching up with her. Vivian could barely keep her eyes open.

CHAPTER EIGHTEEN

❖

The streetcar was almost empty. Vivian entered from the back and made her way up the aisle to one of the wicker bench seats near the middle of the car. She slumped into it and rested her aching head against the window. The icy glass felt wonderful against her temple. She closed her eyes. She was so tired. Her last conscious thought was that this week would be the death of her.

"Excuse me, miss."

Vivian startled awake. She sat up with a start, blinking into the gloomy light of the streetcar interior. She could make out the shape of a man standing in the aisle at her seat. He was gesturing to something, his arm outstretched. She couldn't see his face in the dark, but he was wearing a flat cap. Just like the man who'd tried to steal her bag. Panic rose in her throat. But no, this man was shorter, stockier. The streetcar ambled down a darkened street. She glanced out the window, hoping to spot a familiar sign, a landmark, to help her orient herself. There was nothing. Every twenty feet or so, the streetcar passed from darkness into the yellowy-orange pool of a streetlamp.

"I didn't mean to startle you," the man said, his voice coming out of the darkness. "But I was walking past your seat and noticed that your bag had spilled."

Vivian jerked her attention to the bag resting beside her on the seat. The strap was still wrapped around her arm, and her hand was still in her pocket, but the bag itself was on its side, the top open and the contents spilled out onto the rough rattan of the seat. How on earth had that happened? Her mind was lazy. She was having trouble getting things back into focus. She blinked again.

"Oh," she said, scrambling to scoop the contents back into the open bag. "Thank you. I guess I fell asleep and knocked it over."

He nodded and made his way to a seat at the back of the car.

In the dim interior light of the car, Vivian scanned the things spread out in a clump on the seat. Everything appeared to be there. She hastily scooped it all into her bag and then closed the top. It hadn't been open, had it? But maybe it had. Maybe when she boarded the streetcar, she'd been in such a tired daze that she hadn't buttoned it properly, and then she'd dozed off, hadn't she? *Oh no...*

Her attention snapped back to the passing scene outside. Surely, she'd missed her stop. She reached up and pulled the cord. Her guts twisted. This was wrong. This was all wrong.

The streetcar clanged to a stop at the next corner, and Vivian hopped off. She watched the back of the red-and-cream car clamor up the street and glanced up at the street sign: Clark and Division—only a few blocks west of her usual stop. She sighed. The good news was that the distance was walkable. The bad news was that the icy wind was blowing in off the lake, and she'd have to walk an extra three blocks into it on this icy pavement.

It's amazing how much seedier the neighborhood becomes a scant distance from my house, she thought, glancing at the blinking neon signs of the bars and pawnshops that littered the avenue. Just south of here was Bughouse Square, a well-known gathering place for hobos and crackpots and left-leaning radicals lobbing opinions and abuse from their soapboxes. And just west of that was Death Corner, tucked among the Italian tenements near the north branch of the Chicago River where many a low-rent hood had lost his life to a bullet during Prohibition.

It wasn't the best area to be walking in just before midnight, to be sure. She scanned the passing traffic for a taxi, but saw none. Vivian pulled the woolen scarf tighter around her neck and wound it up over her head and around her ears. She shoved her gloved hands deep into her coat pockets and started walking east. There was no use for it. It was just a few blocks, she told herself. *Don't be a ninny, Vivian.*

She walked, head down. There were very few people on

the street on this bitingly cold December evening. She turned left onto a side street to use the buildings as a break from the unrelenting headwind. If the main thoroughfare was nearly empty, then this side street was decidedly so. Her heels echoed like gunshots on the pavement, and a chill that had nothing to do with the weather crawled up her spine. She passed under the electric glow of a streetlamp and breathed a little easier for those few seconds, but then was plunged back into darkness. She sucked in her breath. She couldn't feel the tip of her nose, and her toes were numb. Why hadn't she brought boots today? Why hadn't she stayed awake on the streetcar and gotten off where she was supposed to?

Then she heard them. Footsteps somewhere behind her. The cadence matched her own. She sped up, they sped up. She stopped walking and cocked her head to listen. The footsteps stopped as well. She hurried to the next pool of lamplight ten paces ahead. Then stopped and whirled around, feeling the Dutch courage of being in the light, even if no one else was around to hear her, to see her. She scanned the sidewalk, the street, and the snow-covered bushes, seeing nothing. Everything was an indistinct gray-black blur. She cocked her head and listened, but all she heard was the wind whining against her ears—like the sound of the ocean in a seashell. She glanced over her shoulder in the direction of home.

One more block to go. It was ridiculous to think anyone could be following her. Her mind fell on that man on the streetcar. He hadn't gotten off with her. Certainly she would have seen him. But what if someone had seen her get off alone and decided she was easy prey? Her coat was expensive, and it looked it. The same with her handbag, her shoes. She looked like she had money, even if she only had four dollars in her pocketbook at the moment. She took a deep breath, the icy-cold air searing her lungs. What could she do but hurry? She stepped out of the pool of lamplight into the darkness again. Walking quickly but carefully, she picked her way around the patches of ice. She didn't run. Not at first. And then she heard the footsteps again. Whoever it was, they were gaining on her.

She hitched her step and began to run, panic rising from her stomach to lodge in her throat. She could scream if she had to, but who would hear her? Her eyes swept over the homes she passed. All dark. Everyone asleep in their cozy, warm beds. She ran, and as she turned the corner onto her street, her heel caught an unseen patch of ice. Her right leg flew out from under her, and her weight shifted backward. Her right hand instinctively reached out behind her to break her fall. She felt the jolt of pain as her elbow buckled, then the searing heat as the ice scraped the fleshy part of her thumb as her hand slid out from under her.

Her head hit the pavement with a *thump*. She'd bitten her tongue, and she tasted blood. Her purse skidded away from her in the opposite direction, landing in a snowbank underneath some bushes. All she heard for the first few seconds was her own labored breathing. Then there they were—the footsteps behind her, coming closer, ever closer. She tucked her chin to her chest and threw her gloved hands up over her head.

The footsteps stopped, only a few feet away. Paused. Shuffled. Retreated. She lay there, hands over her head, until she couldn't hear anything anymore but the wind. It was only then that she started breathing again. As she opened her eyes, a searing pain shot through her right hand. Vivian pulled her hands down and saw that her leather glove had been torn clean through and there was blood seeping out around the wound. She sat up gingerly, glancing around her. Nothing moved. She felt underneath her coat for the sharp telltale outline of the keys she'd taken to wearing around her neck on a string. She rubbed them for a moment, and then pulled herself from the ground slowly, feeling every spot where her bones had hit the frozen sidewalk. She rubbed the back of her head and bent to retrieve her purse. She had to get home.

By the time she'd limped to the coach house, she'd almost convinced herself that it had just been a thug out to steal her purse who had chickened out at the last second. She let herself into the house and paused inside the front door, glancing around in the darkness. Nothing terrible had happened to her, she reminded herself. She was still in one piece. Yet her breath was short and her hands were shaking.

She unwound the scarf and turned to fling it over the

coatrack. The scarf fell onto the floor. She paused, her arms still outstretched. Had the coatrack moved? No, of course not. Her nerves were on edge. Carefully, she removed her coat and gloves and assessed the damage. Her shoes had been badly scuffed, her stockings ripped at the knee, and the scrape on her hand stung. She peeled the ruined glove from her hand and inspected the wound. It was painful, but the scrape wasn't too deep. She'd have to clean and bandage it to make sure it wouldn't get infected.

Vivian started toward the powder room but paused in the middle of the living room. She scanned the room in the darkness—the moonlight glinting off the snow lighting the room in shades of gray and black. There was nothing amiss, and yet the house felt odd. She sniffed. Was that cigar smoke? She paused to turn on a lamp, but the scrape on her hand demanded immediate attention. She rushed to the bathroom and opened the medicine cabinet, rummaging for the bandages and antiseptic. She closed the mirrored door, attended to her hand, and then straightened to replace the supplies.

She noticed in the reflection of the mirror that the linen closet door behind her was ajar. A chill went down her spine. Suddenly, she knew. Someone was in there, lurking, patiently waiting to jump out and clock her with a blackjack. Heart hammering, she whirled and flung the door all the way open. It hit the wall with a solid bang, exposing the contents of neatly folded sheets and towels. Nothing else.

She walked through the tiny coach house, turning on every light as she went. She stopped and studied the drawer of the side table. Had she left it ajar like that? She pulled it open and studied the contents. Nothing seemed missing, but her place was such a mess on an average day that she wouldn't even be able to tell if someone *had* been rifling through her things. She glanced around the room. She told herself that it was just her imagination and the adrenaline still pumping through her veins from being followed and slipping on the ice. But she couldn't shake the feeling that someone had been in her house tonight.

She realized she had no weapon that she could use to protect herself if that someone decided to come back. She searched the small house and, in the end, curled up in her bed, all the lights on, with a cast-iron skillet sitting on her nightstand. She'd have to swing it with both hands, but it could knock a grown man cold.

Vivian lay there wide awake, her right hand curled around the handle of the skillet. Then her eyes snagged on the Kewpie doll propped against the pillow on the opposite side of the bed. Impulsively, she reached for it with her left hand and pulled it close. Her father had won that cheap doll for her at a carnival game long ago—so long ago it seemed part of another life. She curled her arm and tucked the doll comfortingly under her arm.

She smoothed her fingers along the molded curve of the

curl over the doll's forehead as she stared at the ceiling. Who had followed her from the streetcar, and who had been in her house? And why? What were they looking for? Feeling the keys still on the string around her neck, she pressed them into her chest lightly with her fingertips. Then she finally admitted to herself that whatever she had unwittingly discovered went deeper than her father holding a ledger for a client. A lot deeper.

CHAPTER NINETEEN

❖

The day broke cloudless and bright. Vivian squinted out the dining room window at the sun-splashed snow. Looking out on the blindingly white morning, she found it hard to believe that her suspicions of last night hadn't been her overactive imagination.

"…Gloria?"

Vivian jerked her head toward her brother, little dots in her vision. "Hmm?"

"I knew you weren't listening. You had that faraway look on your face."

"I'm sorry. I didn't sleep well last night." She unfolded the napkin and placed it on her lap, careful to keep her bandaged hand under the table. She didn't want to answer any questions about it so early this morning. Not before she'd had a chance to think things through.

"Gloria said the show went swimmingly." Everett dipped one corner of his toast into the yolk of his fried egg.

Vivian shrugged, remembering Graham's queer mood. She

hadn't had to step in to save things, but he definitely hadn't been himself. "I don't know about swimmingly, but it went all right, I suppose."

"Well, if anything went wrong, she didn't notice it. She was thrilled to be there and see it in person. She went on and on about how exciting it was to see a live show." He smiled, happy for Gloria's happiness.

"I'm glad she enjoyed it," Vivian said. She gazed down at the eggs on her plate.

Everett studied her. "What's wrong?"

She sighed and glanced at Everett. She should just tell him. She should tell him she thought someone had been snooping around the coach house. She should tell him everything. He deserved to know, after all. Arthur Witchell was his father too. It would be a load off her mind, really, to have someone to share these confidences with. And who was to say he wouldn't be helpful? Everett was young, but he had matured. And God knows, she couldn't keep all of these secrets to herself much longer. "Nothing. It's stressful at the station these days. I don't think Graham's *Pimpernel* is going to go well."

"I'm sorry to hear that. He's put everything into this show, hasn't he?"

Vivian nodded and looked out the window, squinting again at the sun sparkling off the freshly fallen snow. The scrape on her hand ached, and she touched it gingerly.

"Do you have rehearsal all day?"

She nodded.

"You should probably eat something then."

She looked down at her plate again, but her stomach churned. She picked up a piece of dry toast and took a bite, chewing it slowly.

"Gloria and I are going out on the town this evening. Maybe you and Graham would like to join us."

"Thank you, but I doubt Graham will be in the mood. If we aren't rehearsing, he'll be holed up with Paul somewhere agonizing over the script."

She saw one of Everett's ruddy eyebrows rise.

"Maybe there's someone else you'd like to invite then. Martin, perhaps? He seems rather keen on you."

She narrowed her eyes at her brother. He certainly was observant. Maybe he'd make a good lawyer after all. She shook her head, but offered no further information. She took another bite of toast. "So you and Gloria are going out on the town, eh? You two are living it up."

"Why shouldn't we? We're young." Everett smiled and took a hearty bite of his toast.

"Where do you get the money, Ev?" Once she'd said it, the thought took shape in her head. She knew exactly where he could've gotten a sudden influx of cash.

"The money?"

"For such expensive gifts—the ice review tickets, nights out on the town."

"What does it matter to you?"

She swallowed, the dry bite of toast scratching all the way down her throat. She spoke slowly and carefully, because it had to be said. Now that someone was following her. Now that someone had been in her house without her knowledge.

"It matters to me if by trying to impress her and keep up appearances, you felt you had to take things that don't belong to you."

"What are you talking about?"

Vivian looked at her younger brother, cocking her head to the side.

"I'm talking about the money from Father's desk. You saw it the night of the Christmas party, didn't you?"

He stared at her, his face betraying nothing. "I saw you sitting at Father's desk looking at an ugly Saint Nicholas ornament."

"Come on, Ev. You can tell me."

"I can tell you that I have no idea what you're on about," he said.

She studied his expression. Everett had never been known for his poker face.

"Viv, what's going on?"

It was time that she told him what she suspected of their father. She still didn't trust Everett fully, but what choice did she have? Someone had taken that money, and if it wasn't Everett or Freddy, then who was it? Besides, she needed an ally in the family. And who would understand her position better than her own brother? She glanced over her shoulder at the closed door to the kitchen.

"It's about Father."

"Father? What about him?"

"I found something in his desk drawer that night I went looking for the Saint Nicholas ornament."

Everett leaned forward, resting his elbows on the table. "You found money?"

"A lot of money—almost $4,000 in an envelope marked 'A. W. Racquet.' Taped to the back of the drawer was a key to a safe-deposit box downtown."

Everett blinked and then shook his head. "And?"

"And our father, Ev…" She swallowed, unable to look her brother directly in the eye. "Our father was not who we thought he was." She fiddled with the edge of the bandage on her thumb. It was starting to come loose.

"I'm not sure what you mean."

"There was a ledger in that safe-deposit box," she said. "From the Racquet Club—a gaming palace in Cicero. Father knew the men involved with it…" She looked up and focused on Everett's deep-brown eyes. "Our father was chummy with Al Capone."

Despite her initial reaction to what Charlie's father had told her, she believed the story now. Now that she'd had time to think about it and let the idea settle into her consciousness. Now that someone had been in her house, snooping around.

Everett's brow furrowed. He didn't believe her. "Oh, come on. That's ridiculous."

"It's not. And Father was holding on to that ledger because inside was proof of Capone's income. One line that said '$200 to Al' from July 1929."

"So?"

"So what?"

"So what does all of this mean now? Capone's been in jail for years, and Father's been dead for even longer. Why are you dredging this up?"

Vivian looked at the rug, blurring her eyes against the intricate Persian weave. Why was she dredging this up? Why did they need to know—her, Everett, anyone?

"I don't know," she said with a shrug. "I started digging, and the hole got deeper and deeper." What she wished she could do was forget the whole thing. Go back in time and never retrieve that dumb ornament.

"Do you think Mother knows?"

Vivian shrugged again. "I don't know. If she does, then I'm not sure what to think. If she doesn't, then it might kill her to find out."

"Don't you think that's a little dramatic?"

"To find out that her whole married life was a lie—that her husband was good friends with someone who had people killed on a whim? That this whole house and everything in it was purchased with dirty money?" She looked around her, and her stomach turned. In her mind she continued, *That my inheritance, and yours, are tainted with that same filth?*

"Did you ask Uncle Freddy about it?"

"Yes, and he told me that the money was for a rainy day… that the ledger was being held for a client and that I should stop digging."

"Maybe you should stop."

I can't, she thought. *Not now.*

"So where did the money come for the gifts for Gloria? From Mother?"

Everett ducked his head as he shook it. "I got a job."

"A job? Doing what?"

"I'm an usher at the Varsity. That's where I was last night, working an extra shift. I've seen *Suez* ten times this week alone. I've had enough of Tyrone Power to last me a lifetime."

Vivian stared at her brother. She didn't quite know what to say. Her brother, future member of the bar, moonlighting as an usher in a movie theater. Wait until their mother heard about this!

"Well, that's…unexpected."

"I couldn't take money from Mother to buy gifts for my girlfriend. What would that make me?"

Under Mother's thumb, Vivian thought. Maybe she had underestimated Everett. Still, she held her tongue about his inheritance. He'd find out about that soon enough, assuming his would come to him at twenty-one. That was a year from now. Besides, it would do him a world of good to do some honest work for a change. It had certainly done her a world of good to be a secretary for a few years. Not everyone was born and raised in an ivory tower and would inherit a load of money. Not everyone had their path paved so easily for them in life. She smiled at him, and he smiled tentatively back.

"Look, I'm sorry I accused you of stealing. And I'm sorry that I didn't tell you about what I found right away," she said.

"I'm not a little kid anymore, Viv." He caught her eye, and she knew they both knew what he meant by that. "And I never told Father about what you were up to—no matter what you think."

She looked at him long and hard and found she believed him. He hadn't told Father about her sneaking out.

"I know you're not a little kid anymore. But still, all of this is between us, right? Not a word of this…" She jerked a thumb toward the closed door to the front hall.

"Of course. Wait, you accused me of stealing the money. That means it's gone?"

She nodded. "Someone took it."

"Who?"

She shrugged. "If I knew that, I wouldn't have accused you, would I?"

What she did know was that whoever had taken the money was the key to all of it, and that person had been present at dinner on Monday night. If it wasn't Everett or Freddy, that left Oskar and Martin, didn't it? Assuming that Gloria hadn't taken it—or Julia. At this point, Vivian couldn't rule anyone out, could she? After all, if her mother had known all this time about what her father had been up to, maybe she could have taken it. But why would she?

Speaking of her mother, Vivian wasn't looking forward to her certain look of triumph when Vivian asked to use her driver to take her to the station this morning. Her mother thought it was beneath her daughter to take public transport, not when there was a perfectly acceptable uniformed driver at the ready to take her wherever she wished to go. Vivian would tell her that she was trying to avoid the cold, all that standing on street corners waiting for the streetcar to show up, but in truth it was because she was terrified of a repeat of last night's events. Someone was most definitely following her. Why, she wasn't sure. The one consolation of eating crow and taking a driver was that someone following her car would be much more obvious. Well, that and the novelty of showing up at the station without frozen toes for once.

She ran back to the coach house to get her handbag and found a note stuck in the front door.

I'll pick you up at eight o'clock. Wear something nice. C

Vivian smiled. So she was wearing Charlie down after all.

CHAPTER TWENTY

❖

Vivian looked up at the blinking green and yellow bulbs of the sign, and her hopeful mood disappeared. The Green Mill. It was now a legitimate place for a cocktail, but it had been a speakeasy in those heady days when the Eighteenth Amendment reigned and Capone ruled the city. It had also been one of Vivian's preferred nightspots then. Not anymore.

She glanced around her, gazing longingly in the direction of the Aragon Ballroom a few blocks over, where Dick Jurgens and his orchestra were in residence. The elaborate gothic Uptown Theatre was next door. She could see the glowing marquee from here: *Angels with Dirty Faces*, starring James Cagney, was playing tonight. She'd worn the nicest dress she had—the dark-blue velvet backless number she'd been saving for a special occasion. But she knew this wasn't a date, as much as she would like it to be. She'd hired Charlie to dig into her father's past, and there was probably a good reason he'd taken her to the Green Mill tonight.

"Can't we go somewhere else?" she asked.

Charlie shook his head as he helped her from the passenger seat. "We're expected here."

Vivian felt Charlie's eyes on her.

She smoothed the fur lapels on her coat. The Green Mill's heyday had been years ago. But being there again was a strange coincidence. It seemed there were memories everywhere she turned these days. "I haven't been here in a long time. It reminds me of my father."

Charlie followed her eyes to that harmless blinking sign. *Green Mill Cocktail Lounge* was spelled out in scrolling green neon. The bulbs that surrounded those words in a field of yellow flashed as if to the syncopated beat of some soundless jazz tune.

"Your father? How so?"

Vivian sighed and watched her breath fog the air in front of her face. "I snuck out of the house one night a few months before he died and came here. He caught me."

Charlie's eyebrow arched. "Snuck out?"

Vivian nodded and could see Charlie making the calculations in his head. "Your father died in 1931."

"Yes, I believe that's been established."

Charlie studied her. "You were that kid in the photo with the big bow in her hair seven years ago."

Vivian rolled her eyes. "I was almost seventeen."

He stuck his lower lip out and blew air up toward his hairline.

He cocked his head as he appraised her. "'Almost seventeen' is a mere babe, in my opinion. What on earth were you doing at a place like this?"

"I wanted to have some fun. I… Well, I acted out a bit shortly before my father died." She shrugged, looked down at the sidewalk. And it had been fun, for a while—until she realized that the middle-aged shoe salesmen that had brought her was married with children and wanted to ply her with gin and press her into dark corners, snaking his greasy fingers up her skirt.

"I'll say."

Vivian sighed. "It wasn't anything that dramatic. I snuck out a few times, had a few drinks." *A lot of drinks on many occasions,* she amended to herself. Her head ached with the thought of all that horrendous bathtub gin.

"What happened?"

"My father found out and put the kibosh on it."

The smile slid slowly across Charlie's face. "He caught you shimmying down a drainpipe?"

Vivian couldn't help but smile in return. She'd told Charlie about that months ago, a lifetime ago—her one-time penchant for escaping from her own home via the drainpipe. She thought about that morning in his car. She'd been so furious at her mother, so grateful for Charlie's presence and his not-so-subtle interest in her. Had that been just two months ago?

"No. Actually, I'm not sure how he found out," she said. "But boy, was he ever steamed."

Her father had been waiting up for her in her bedroom, sitting in the dark, smoking a cigar. She'd stumbled in drunk and stinking of cigarettes. He hadn't yelled, hadn't even raised his voice. But he was disappointed in her, and that was far worse. And when she'd sobered up, she resolved to never do it again. And she hadn't—until her father died—and then she'd done even worse.

"Damn straight he was steamed, Viv. You were a kid. You had no business in a place like this, especially then."

She shivered, and not entirely from the stiff wind blowing in off the lake. The Green Mill had been a dangerous place in 1930, but it had also been glamorous. And that was precisely why Vivian had wanted to go there. It had been the only place on the North Side that sold liquor openly without any pretense of being a speakeasy, because Capone's men had bribed the cops to leave it alone.

Vivian had spent most of that evening in the ballroom-cabaret on the second floor. The notorious hostess Texas Guinan had been performing that night. Her trademark "Hello, sucker!" had boomed through the ballroom as she introduced her crew of fifty dancing girls to the hooting, well-heeled audience. The man Vivian had been meeting, whose name she could no longer recall, had tried to impress her by introducing her to the big shot who ran the place.

Vivian had been mildly impressed, though she hadn't even known who the man was at the time. She recalled that the tall, dapperly dressed man had repeated her name and patted her on the arm in a fatherly way before excusing himself. Vivian had recognized his photo on the front page of newspapers two years later. Ted Newberry, a known Capone associate, had been dumped by the side of a dirt road in Indiana with a bullet in the back of his head. That was Vivian's first lesson that there was a limit to a certain kind of ambition in this town.

Charlie moved toward the front door, and as he pulled it open, a group of laughing people spilled out onto the sidewalk. Vivian found herself face-to-face with none other than Frances Barrow. Her arm was hooked through that of a short, pudgy man, and she was whispering something into his ear. As she looked up, her eyes locked onto Vivian's.

"Viv!" she said, her eyes darting to Charlie and back to Vivian again. Her smile widened at the sight of the detective. "What a surprise!"

"That's a word for it," Vivian muttered. "Frances, imagine running into you here." She turned to the pudgy man and extended her hand. "I'm afraid we haven't met."

Frances's eyes narrowed. "Viv, this is Arnie Wolfowitz. He's my agent."

Agent? Since when did Frances have an agent? Vivian shook the man's hand.

"Arnie knows David O. Selznick and is getting me an audition for Scarlett O'Hara," she said, leaning toward Vivian, her eyes wide with genuine excitement.

Vivian held back a smile. "Well, isn't that interesting," she said. "Because I read that it's already down to Vivien Leigh and Paulette Goddard. They've done screen tests and everything."

"Simple gossip," Arnie answered, darting an anxious glance at Frances. But Frances was paying him no mind. She glared at Vivian for a moment longer, then smiled tightly.

"Where's Graham tonight?" she asked, her eyes lingering on Charlie.

"He's working on *The Pimpernel*, Frances. You know that as well as I do."

Frances's smile didn't falter. "While the cat's away…" she said in a singsong voice.

Arnie suddenly thrust his hand out to Charlie. "Arnie Wolfowitz."

Charlie shook it grudgingly. "Charlie Haverman."

"Say, Charlie Haverman?" Arnie rolled the name around in his mouth as he thought, then pointed a stubby finger at the detective. "You're that private detective that was consulting for *The Darkness Knows*, aren't you? I read about you in the papers." He peered more closely at Vivian. "I read about *both of you* in the papers."

Charlie glanced at Vivian with suspicion. She shrugged. The man didn't wait for Charlie's confirmation. He looked from Charlie to Vivian and back to Charlie. Then his eyes narrowed in calculation. "You have a real Nick and Nora Charles thing going here, don't you? Rich society dame and a private eye? You know, that's a popular idea right about now. I could do something with that…"

Vivian felt Charlie's arm tense under her hand at the backhanded compliment. Nick and Nora Charles were the main characters of the popular series of Thin Man books and the even more popular movie series of the same name. Nick, a somewhat washed-up, mildly alcoholic detective was wholly supported by his rich society wife while they stumbled onto crimes and solved them by happenstance. Vivian supposed the dynamics of the couple did bear some resemblance to Charlie and her on the surface, and she was positive that it wasn't meant as a jibe. But she also knew that the comparison to gadabout Nick Charles had Charlie's ire up. Vivian squeezed his arm in warning to check his temper.

The man focused his attention on Charlie. "Ever think of taking up acting?"

Vivian watched Frances's smile disappear as she tugged on the fat's man sleeve. "Sorry to dash, but we're off to the Aragon for some dancing," Frances said. Then she looked pointedly at Charlie, and her radiantly fake smile reappeared in a flash of perfect white teeth. "Lovely to see you again, Mr. Haverman. It was an unexpected treat."

Vivian watched the mismatched pair walk away, Frances's hips twitching under her too-tight skirt.

"If that man is a legit talent agent," she said, "I'll eat my hat."

Then she turned, took a deep breath, and yanked open the door to her past.

CHAPTER TWENTY-ONE

The cocktail lounge of the Green Mill was a cramped shoe box of a room. It looked roughly the same as the last time she'd seen it. Of course, the mob no longer owned the place, or at least not overtly. Capone had been sent to prison in 1931—eight months after Vivian's father died. Then Prohibition had ended, and most of the men involved had gone to the hoosegow or branched out into new lines of work. The establishment's luster had faded since alcohol became legal. Now it was just one of thousands of places to get a drink in Chicago—if more elegantly appointed than most. She eyed her reflection in the mirror behind the bar as Charlie checked their coats.

Her eyes swept to a green velvet booth to the west of the short end of the bar—where she'd been told Capone liked to sit so he could keep his eye on both the front and back doors. Tonight, it was occupied by an amorous couple, the man's nose nested in his companion's cleavage.

Charlie tugged on Vivian's sleeve and led her through the

crowd to the bar that ran along the left side near the entrance. "A drink?" he asked.

She shook her head.

Charlie signaled for the bartender's attention anyway. "Tell Caputto that Charlie Haverman's here, would ya?"

The bartender nodded. Vivian watched him motion a large man over and talk right into his ear. A box of party hats and noisemakers behind the bar reminded her that tomorrow was New Year's Eve. The end of 1938 already? How could that be?

"How do you know this man, this Caputto?" Vivian asked.

Charlie turned, taking her by the elbow, and led her to the far end of the bar, away from the band.

"Moochie—Caputto—is from my old neighborhood. I went to school with his younger brother."

Who didn't Charlie Haverman know? "Does he own this place?"

Charlie shook his head. "He's the manager."

She watched couples jostle for space on the tiny dance floor.

"And how exactly is he going to help me with my father?"

"Moochie's been around. He knows a lot of people, Viv. And he knew a lot of the same people I suspect your father knew. He might have even known your father personally."

Vivian opened her mouth to deny that her father ever would have associated with a man that went by the name of Moochie, but she held her tongue. She realized what Charlie was carefully not saying. Those people in question had not been the most upstanding members of the community—and neither had her father. And she and Charlie were here for corroboration of what his father had tried to tell her this afternoon. Moochie's assessment of her father's character was a foregone conclusion, and Charlie was subtly priming her for disappointment.

The band started up with "I'm in the Mood for Love."

Vivian could feel Charlie's stare, but she didn't turn to look at him. After a moment, he leaned down, his lips brushing her ear.

"We can't just stand here like cigar-store Indians," he said. "It draws attention."

He held his hand out to her and nodded his head toward the small dance floor.

"Oh no, I don't feel like dancing."

"C'mon," he said, grabbing her hand and leading her to the edge of the dance floor. "You're like a coiled spring. You can't meet Moochie like this. Who knows what'll come out of that mouth of yours?"

Vivian sighed. He was right. He raised her hand in his and paused.

"What's this?" Charlie held her right hand out, palm up to show the bandage on the fleshy part of her thumb.

Vivian yanked the hand back down and glanced at the floor, hiding her blush of embarrassment. "I slipped and fell on the ice last night."

He pulled her to him in response, his fingertips brushing across the bare skin of her lower back, and she sucked in her breath at his touch. "What have I told you about those heels?" he said into her hair. "You'll break your neck."

Vivian's head was still bowed, but she could feel the heat of his breath on her bare flesh. His fingertips traced tight little circles on her back as their feet began to move to the music.

Charlie pulled her right hand back up into the hold. She looked up, forcing her gaze to meet his, the air thick between them. The hairs of her forearms stood on end. Electricity crackled in the air. She loved dancing with him. She'd thought she might never have the chance again. He smiled at her and she smiled back, the tension loosening—not disappearing entirely, but loosening. What was all that talk about the past being past? She didn't ask. She didn't want to know. Because the way he was looking at her in this moment was everything, and she didn't want to spoil it.

She let her cheek fall onto his chest. It fit so perfectly there, she thought. Everything about them fit so perfectly.

"Pop likes you," Charlie said. His voice rumbled up from under his breastbone and vibrated against her cheek.

"Yeah?" Vivian said without lifting her cheek.

"Yeah. He said you've got spunk."

She closed her eyes and smiled into Charlie's chest as their feet moved in time to the music.

I'm in the mood for love, simply because you're near me.

After one circuit of the floor, Vivian was contemplating telling Charlie to forget the whole thing. Forget Moochie. Call it off. She didn't need to hear from another stranger about what a terrible person her father had been. She could forget the whole thing, and they could stay on the dance floor like this forever. That would suit her fine.

Then a large man stopped their forward progress with a beefy forearm to tell them Mr. Caputto was ready for them. However much Vivian might wish otherwise, it seemed already too late to call it off.

The man led them up a back staircase to the upper floor and the manager's office. He knocked on the door and waited for a voice from the inside saying "Enter!" before opening it. The room was dark, most of it in shadow. One lamp on the corner of the desk cast a weak, greenish light. The man behind the desk stood as they entered, making his way around to the front, his face going from light to shade to light again.

He was dark, definitely Italian. Not attractive, but imposing. His hair was longish and slicked back behind his ears. When he smiled, his teeth glowed a muted white in the darkness of the room. Altogether wolfish, Vivian thought. Like he might lunge forward and take a bite out of her.

"Charlie, it's been a long time," he said.

"It has," Charlie agreed, clapping the man on the back. He pulled away and held an arm out toward Vivian. "Vivian, this is my old friend Vincent Caputto."

The man eyed Vivian up and down. And he took his time about it. Charlie shot him a warning glare, but he said nothing. Caputto just shrugged before taking a seat behind the large wooden desk. A man used to getting what he wanted, Vivian thought. He opened an Epoca box and removed two cigars, offering one to Charlie. Charlie waved him off.

"What can I do for you, Charlie?" Caputto asked. He made a quick hand signal to the beast of a man standing in the doorway, and the man retreated slightly to stand outside the open office door.

"I was hoping I could jog your memory."

"My memory ain't so good no more." The tone was joking, but Caputto's jovial smile had vanished.

"Not even for an old friend? Hey, remember that time Old Man Stiglitz caught you stealing penny candy and chased you all the way down Rose Street, and somebody tripped him right before he could nab you and give you the whupping of your life?" Charlie coughed lightly. "Seems like old friends tend to help one another out."

Caputto smiled a slow, greasy sort of smile. He held his hands up in an "I surrender" gesture. He took a puff on his cigar to light it, then regarded Charlie through the haze of smoke. "What do you want to know?"

"Tell me about the Racquet Club."

Caputto eyed Charlie warily. "What about it?"

"Did you know a lawyer named Arthur Witchell?" Charlie asked.

The man smiled slightly, but his dark eyes were hard. "Easy Artie, sure. He's dead. Been dead a while."

Vivian's stomach clenched at hearing that nickname again unprompted. A confirmation. Easy Artie. Her father.

"What was his connection to the Racquet Club?"

Caputto exhaled in a steady stream and watched the smoke plume toward the ceiling.

"He sort of worked out of the back a couple of times a week."

"Worked?" Vivian asked.

Caputto leaned back in his chair, threading his fingers over his midsection. He glanced from Vivian to Charlie.

"Who is she again?"

Charlie glanced to Vivian, his eyes narrowed, signaling for her to keep quiet. "Viv's my assistant. I'm working a case."

Caputto smirked, eyeing Vivian all over again. "Assistant, huh? Any more like you at home, honey?"

"What about Witchell?" Charlie said gruffly. Caputto's eyes lingered on Vivian for another long moment before he turned his attention back to Charlie.

"What kinda case you workin' anyway?"

"Divorce case," Charlie answered. "Things have gone… sour…between the couple since—a custody thing. Witchell was the wife's attorney before he died. I'm just checking all avenues."

Caputto's dark eyes narrowed with interest. "How sour? Like *dead* sour?"

Charlie nodded, and Vivian felt the side of his foot press against hers, signaling her to keep quiet.

"Divorce, huh? That guy handled everything, I guess." Caputto shook his head and tapped his ash into the cut-crystal receptacle on his desk. "Artie sort of held court in the back room of the Racquet—had regular office hours, like. Anyone with a problem went back and got it taken care of."

Vivian swallowed the lump in her throat. No problem with keeping quiet now. She couldn't speak right now if she wanted to. Her father "took care" of problems in the back of a gambling house? How could that possibly be true? Why would he have done such a thing? This just got worse and worse.

"Anyone with a problem," Charlie said, leaning forward, elbows on his knees. "Like who?"

Caputto fixed Charlie with a level stare. "Anyone who got in trouble," he said.

"What kind of trouble are you talking about? Big trouble? Jail kind of trouble?"

Caputto didn't answer right away, but the corner of his mouth twitched as if in amusement. "Didn't matter. Whatever size your trouble, Artie could fix it."

Vivian glanced at Charlie. She could see the frustration flash over his features. Moochie was giving him the runaround, and he knew it.

"Was Witchell involved in the workings of the place?"

Caputto shrugged and glanced at his watch. "He was involved in all of it. He owned it."

"Owned it?" Vivian asked.

"Well, he owned a share of it—along with a couple of other big shots. I don't remember who."

Vivian and Charlie exchanged a quick glance. *Other big shots*, she thought. She had a feeling that if they looked a little more closely at that ledger, they'd likely find her father's name or some variant of it listed there—maybe underneath Al Capone's. Vivian bit her lower lip to keep it from trembling.

"I think you do remember who," Charlie prodded.

"Nah, my memory's gotten real bad in the past few years," Caputto said, puffing on his cigar. "Real bad."

Charlie returned the frank stare. "You owe me, Moochie."

"I can't help you with this, Charlie," Caputto said, his dark eyes cold.

"What about Freddy Endicott?" Vivian blurted out.

"Endicott?" Caputto stared at her for a long moment before cocking his head to one side. "Doesn't ring a bell."

Maybe Freddy had used some sort of nickname, Vivian thought. Her mind scanned through anything he might have used as an alias, but she came up blank.

"How about Oskar Heigel then?" Vivian asked instead,

her voice strangely high-pitched sounding to her own ears. Charlie's hard-soled wingtip was insistently and painfully pressing down on her toes, but she refused to acknowledge him. He was right, of course. Asking a man connected to the mob impetuous questions was a dangerous gambit, no matter how badly she wanted the information. She squeezed the edges of the chair and tried to keep her breathing steady.

Caputto turned to her, his brow wrinkled in thought. Then his face cleared as a memory came to him, and he smiled at her. He mimed a belly with his hands out in front of him. "Short guy, big, gray mustache?"

She nodded, feeling her stomach drop to the floor.

"Yeah, he was in the club a lot. He and Artie were pals." His brow wrinkled. "He got something to do with this divorce case too?"

"Maybe," Charlie said quickly. He glanced at Vivian, his brow furrowed.

Pals, Vivian thought, eyes trained on the floor. Oskar and her father had been in on the Racquet Club together. Oskar knew about the money hidden in the desk. She was sure of it. He'd taken it to keep her nose out of it, to make her lose interest, to keep Vivian from finding out about his past misdeeds. To keep her from souring her mother on him.

"When was the Racquet raided again?" Charlie asked.

Caputto's expression didn't change, but a warning flickered behind his dark eyes.

"I don't know nothin' more about it," he said again in a low voice, pointing an index finger at Charlie. "What I will tell you is that I know Easy Artie was the keeper of a lot of confidences, and there were people that wanted to make sure he didn't spill those confidences."

"What are you saying?"

"I'm saying there was talk that Artie was flappin' his gums— that the big man wanted him out of the way."

"Flappin' his gums about what? To whom?"

"I'm saying that it's a good thing he went and had that… What was it again? A heart attack?" He smiled, but his eyes were cold.

"Meaning?"

"Not a bad way to go in this game. I've seen a lot worse."

Vivian's stomach clenched. She looked at Charlie. He glowered back at her, warning her to keep her mouth shut.

There was a knock on the door, and a slim, blond woman sauntered into the room and made a beeline for Caputto, garnering every bit of his attention.

"What—" Vivian began.

But Charlie pressed his heel down hard on the toe of her shoe, and she squeaked before shutting her mouth again. The problem was, she didn't need to ask. She knew exactly what Caputto had meant. Charlie shook his head slightly, but he didn't look at her.

Vivian's mind was reeling with the revelations—they'd come

so rapid-fire, one after the other. But when she finally looked at the blond whispering in Caputto's ear, she sucked in her breath sharply, and all of his revelations went out of her mind. She'd met the woman only once, when they'd gone sailing on Freddy's boat months before, but she could have sworn that the young woman sidling up to Vincent Caputto right now was Pauline Endicott, Uncle Freddy's lately estranged wife. Vivian held her breath as the woman's eyes slid over Charlie. Then she ducked her head before Pauline could see her face.

Caputto smirked at something Pauline said and put a palm familiarly on her hip.

"Now, if you'll excuse me, I got a club to run," he said. Then he stood up and swiftly left the room with Pauline, leaving Vivian and Charlie alone with the hulking bodyguard.

"Do you think—"

"Not here," Charlie said in a low voice with a pointed glance at the bodyguard.

Charlie took her hand and pulled her from the chair. He led her wordlessly from the room, down the narrow set of stairs, and back to the boisterous main room of the club. Vivian watched as Caputto made his way across the crowded dance floor to the bar on the far side of the room. She didn't know what to say, where to start. A man like that had known her father, she thought in disbelief. A man like that had known her father…and had called him Easy Artie. She shook her head. "Do you think it's true?"

"Which part?"

"Any of it."

Charlie nodded, the corners of his mouth turned down. "Moochie's a hood, but he's not a liar. And he's not going to say another word—not if he wants to keep breathing. He may be close to straight now, but he'll always be mixed up in something. I didn't expect him to give us any real information, Viv. But at least you heard from the horse's mouth, *another* horse's mouth, about what your father was up to…"

No good, she thought. Vivian let a breath out slowly through her nose in an effort to calm her racing pulse.

Her eyes fell on the green velvet booth at the end of the bar—now empty. She knew something else then too. Of course her father had known that Vivian had been at the Green Mill that night when she'd been not quite seventeen. He'd known because Ted Newberry, the dapper, tuxedoed, soon-to-be-dead associate of Al Capone, had smiled at her and patted her arm and then gone off to place a telephone call. Newberry had told her father that he'd been introduced to his daughter out with a much older man—and three sheets to the wind on a school night. A gangster had known her father well enough to call him at home in the middle of the night to tell him to rein in his daughter. She remembered again how icily angry her father had been. How sure he'd been about what she'd been up to, even when she'd denied everything. Her palms were clammy.

"And what he said…at the end—that it was a good thing that my father went and had a heart attack?" Her voice faltered. She felt numb. Every bit of emotion had drained from her body.

Charlie put his hands on her shoulders and flexed his fingers. He crouched down to look directly into her eyes and opened his mouth to speak. But she shook her head and held up one hand to stop him. He didn't need to answer. It was written all over his face—the verification of what Vivian already knew. Her father hadn't had a heart attack eight years ago. He'd been murdered.

CHAPTER TWENTY-TWO

❖

They drove in silence. Vivian looked out the window and watched her breath fog up the glass.

Murdered. Her father had been murdered. The idea swirled around and around in her mind, trying to find purchase. How could that be true? He'd had a heart attack. The doctor had said so. She'd been there when he died. No. That's not right. She *hadn't* been there when he'd died. She'd gone to meet that boy, and when she'd come back, Father was dead in his favorite chair by the radio. What exactly had happened after she'd left? Why hadn't she stayed? She glanced over at Charlie. He hadn't spoken on the ride either.

Her father had known too much, and someone had killed him for it. What had he known? And did that even matter anymore? And then there was Oskar. Caputto had known exactly who he was. He and her father were pals. And what about Pauline? What on earth was she doing at the Green Mill with someone like Vincent Caputto—and what did that mean about Uncle Freddy? Vivian had a sick feeling in her stomach.

There were too many questions and no proof, only suspicion. All of this was too much.

Charlie turned onto her street, which was dark and quiet at this time of night.

"You know, Sister Bernadine speaks highly of you," he said, breaking the silence.

Vivian glanced at Charlie before pretending to be absorbed in the twinkling lights of the Christmas displays outside the passenger-side window. She blinked and forced her mind to slow down, to switch gears. She knew that's what Charlie had intended the question to do—to slow the swirling thoughts in her head.

"When did you speak to Sister Bernadine?"

"I dropped by the foundling home on Christmas Day," he said. "I usually do. She said you were there last week handing out presents to the children. She said you even brought an authentic-looking Kris Kringle with you." She could hear the smile in his voice, even if she wouldn't turn to look at him.

"I... Yes..." She was suddenly tongue-tied and embarrassed that Charlie knew what she'd done. She wasn't sure why, except that she'd meant it to be private. The foundling home seemed like such an intimate thing between them. After all, he'd confided in her about being left at that foundling home as a child. That confidence had opened her eyes to the plight of those poor children. Without Charlie, she wouldn't have given more than a passing thought to those parentless children at Christmas. What's more, he seemed to know that too.

"I never thought I'd see the day when Vivian Witchell did something nice without an agenda." He steered the car to the curb in front of her house and put it in Park with a jerk and a rumbled screech of the engine.

Finally turning to face him, she said, "I do nice things all the time," though her protest sounded feeble even to her ears.

"I'm teasing you, Viv," he said, his face taking on a more somber expression. "I think it's great. Those kids deserve all the happiness they can get."

"Thank you, Charlie," she said. "I think so too." She glanced away, her throat closing off with pent-up emotion. Tears sprang to her eyes, and she balled her hands into fists on her lap.

"You okay?"

She gazed down at the floor and shook her head without looking at him. She took a deep breath and let everything out in her exhale. "This whole time I was hoping we'd find nothing, Charlie. All this time I was hoping I'd have to accept that lame story Uncle Freddy gave me about why my father had that cash. But now I know for sure. He was a crook. My father was a crook. All this time I'd believed he was a good man, a respectable man. And he wasn't." She hitched in her breath again sharply, refusing to cry.

"I'm sorry, Viv, but you did say you wanted to know one way or the other." His voice was soft in the silence of the car.

"And I'm sorry I ever said that," she said. "Because I don't want to know any of it." She sighed, closing her eyes. "They called him Easy Artie, for God's sake. I didn't know him at all... And somebody...and somebody..." Her voice cracked despite her resolve to put on a brave face, and she couldn't continue. She couldn't say what she knew was true—that somebody had killed him to keep him quiet. She looked at Charlie, narrowing her eyes, almost unable to see him through the welling tears. "You knew, didn't you? You knew about my father this whole time. Easy Artie. All of it."

"Ah..." His eyes strayed over her head, and he seemed to be searching for words that he couldn't find. He gave up and glanced away from her. And she knew it was true. He paused for a moment and then continued without looking at her. "I didn't know all of it, but I knew who your father was. I'd even seen him at the racetrack once. Pop pointed him out with Capone—told me he was some big-shot attorney. But that was years ago. I'd forgotten all about it until I met you. And then it didn't make much difference to me one way or the other— who your father was, I mean, or what he'd done." He glanced at her, his brow furrowed. He cleared his throat. "So I knew who Arthur Witchell was all right, but then I realized a few days ago in the Tip Top Café that *you* didn't know who your father was, not really. And I also knew it wasn't up to me to tell you."

"But if you'd told me, it would have saved us all this trouble…"

He shrugged and glanced away again. "You wouldn't have believed me."

She looked at him, at his strong profile backlit by the streetlamp outside. He was right. She wouldn't have. She had wanted proof, hadn't she? What would she have thought if he'd told her the truth that day in the Tip Top Café? She'd have fought it tooth and nail.

"But the problem was that I *did* know who he was and who he was involved with, and even though I couldn't tell you, I could stop you from digging any further and getting yourself hurt."

Vivian swallowed. He hadn't wanted her to get hurt. That meant something. But he also hadn't wanted her to stick around, had he?

"But, of course, that didn't work. Because then you came to me to tell me the cash was missing. And that got me worried that more was at stake than your father's memory. So I let you hire me."

"*Let* me hire you?" She stared at him in incredulity. The corner of Charlie's mouth twitched, and she realized it was a joke. She sat back in her seat again, biting down the smile that had sprung to her face.

"Then you found that ledger, and things got serious. So I brought Pop to tell you who your father was, hoping that would end your digging. But you didn't believe him either," Charlie said. He looked at her, a slight smile on his lips. "You're a tough nut, Vivian Witchell."

A tough nut or a fool?

"You *do* believe it now, don't you?"

She looked out the window at her house, her father's house. The house that his lies had built. She swallowed. There were needles in her throat, and she couldn't answer.

"Viv?"

Vivian shook her head. A tear spilled over her lower lid, and she wiped it away with her balled fist. She sniffed, and out of the corner of her eye, she saw Charlie watching her with concern. "Why do I have this damned habit of bursting into tears around you?"

He smiled and handed her his handkerchief. "Maybe because you know I'm a sucker for a damsel in distress."

Vivian snorted and jerked her head toward the passenger-side window.

"Look, Viv, I know this is upsetting. I know you admired your father."

"I used to," she said. She was surprised at the anger in her voice. She stared at the house, at her breath making icy tendrils on the glass. She hiccupped once, pathetically, and bowed her head. She was tired suddenly. So tired.

Then she felt Charlie's large hand on the back of her neck, his warm fingers slipping under the fur collar of her coat. She inhaled sharply at his unexpected touch, but she didn't move or turn her head to look at him. She was afraid that if she acknowledged it, he would pull away from her, and she didn't know if she could ever recover if he pulled away from her now. His thumb started to trail lightly up and down the nape of her neck. Vivian closed her eyes and let her head drop back onto it. Neither of them spoke.

Vivian felt the gooseflesh break out on her arms. Then Charlie's hand slid up the back of her head, and he cupped her head with his palm, turning her toward him and pulling her forward. He pressed her cheek into his shoulder as he enveloped her in his arms. Her arms slid around him, and she inhaled deeply with her eyes still closed, breathing in the comforting scent of Brylcreem and aftershave. The wool of his overcoat scratched her cheek, but it felt so good to be in his arms again, to feel protected. His fingers moved down to stroke her back as they embraced, and Vivian felt the shiver of anticipation travel up her spine even through the heavy wool coat. Finally, she lifted her head. When she opened her eyes, she found him gazing down at her. He trailed the tip of his index finger down the side of her face and cupped her chin with his fingers.

"I should've called you, Viv," he said. His eyes traveled down to her mouth and back up—a slow, lazy circuit.

She let out a ragged breath.

"I thought you said what was past was past."

He tilted her chin up with the tips of his fingers and leaned down halfway. Then he paused, his warm breath mingling with hers.

"I lied," he whispered.

And then his lips were on hers. She responded automatically, her lips parting, tasting him. Reveling in him. Then his lips were on her neck, her cheeks, her nose, her eyelids. Her hands moved to his hair, sliding through the thick waves. They moved down to slide up and down over his chest. His hands were everywhere, roaming over the thick wool of her coat, then under it and down across the velvet of the dress drawn taut over her hip. His fingertips slid underneath to tease against the lacy edge of her garter, then continued up to brush the sensitive skin on the inside of her thigh.

Finally, he tore his lips from hers, and she opened her eyes slowly with a dreamy, ragged sigh. More. She wanted more. He leaned back against the driver's-side door, and they looked at each other for a long moment in perfect silence. Her eyes flicked from his lips, stained red with her lipstick, to the windshield, and she noted that the insides of all of the car windows were now encased in looping curlicues of frost.

"I should go," he said as she whispered, "Stay."

His brow creased as he looked at her. Then before he could refuse, or worse, before he could say something about staying purely out of a sense of duty, sleeping on her sofa or some such nonsense to watch over her in her time of need, she wanted to make her intentions perfectly clear. She nodded toward the opaquely white windshield and smiled, her face the picture of innocence.

"I'm afraid you can't drive anywhere like this, Detective. You'll get into an accident."

He glanced at the windows, then back to her. He smiled— the smile that turned her insides outside. Then he reached out to smooth a strand of hair behind her ear, his thumb trailing down her jaw to brush over her lips. "Mmm," he said, his eyes again trained on her mouth. "And that's some thick ice. I'm afraid it may not clear until morning."

Vivian slid over on the bench seat and ran her gloved hand up his leg to rest lightly on the inside of his thigh.

"What a shame," she said. Then she tilted her head up to his for another kiss.

CHAPTER TWENTY-THREE

❖

Vivian stretched lazily and reached across Charlie's sleeping form to register the time on the alarm clock. She was late. Incredibly late. It was almost ten o'clock, and she was supposed to be at the station by ten thirty for the first of several dress rehearsals for *The Pimpernel* today. She bolted from the bed with a mumbled curse, inadvertently dragging the tangled bedsheets with her.

"Hey," Charlie said, his voice thick with sleep. "What's the big idea?" He yanked the sheets back without opening his eyes. She stood at the side of the bed and looked at him for a long moment, seriously considering chucking stupid Percy Blakely and his alter ego the Scarlet Pimpernel to spend the day lounging blissfully in bed. But then sense prevailed. She couldn't do that. An entire crew of people were depending on her. Graham was depending on her. She sighed. *Graham.*

She turned, spying one of Charlie's socks flung haphazardly over the radiator. Lord, they'd been in a hurry last night. She smiled at the memory as Charlie's arm snaked around her waist from behind. He pulled her back down to a seated position and planted an affectionate kiss on her naked shoulder.

"Good morning," he said. She half turned to him and swatted at the hand that had started to find its way up her midsection.

"I have to go," she said. "I'm very, very late." She started to rise, but Charlie tightened his grip around her waist, preventing her.

"Go?" He pulled her back onto the bed with surprisingly little effort. Before she could explain, he had pinned her hands above her head and straddled her hips with his knees. "You're not going anywhere, Miss Witchell," he said with a smirk. He leaned down and nuzzled deliciously into her neck, and Vivian closed her eyes with a sigh. No, she didn't *want* to go anywhere, she thought. Then the guilt returned. *The Pimpernel*. An entire crew of people. Her reputation. Graham.

She struggled to free her hands, scowling. "Charlie," she pleaded. "I have to go."

He released her hands and rolled to the side with a grunt of disapproval.

She rushed to get dressed, struggling with her stockings. Charlie didn't say anything, but she could feel him watching her and could sense his mildly amused disappointment. She brushed her hair furiously, trying her damnedest to get it to lie down. Finally, in desperation, she placed a clip on either side, drawing her hair back from her face. It still looked messy, but there was nothing to be done for it. She automatically reached for the enamel bird pin in the tray on the top of her jewelry box, and then drew her hand back.

She turned and found Charlie watching her, one arm lackadaisically placed behind his head. God help her, he looked wonderful: dark-blond hair tousled, cheeks unshaven. He smiled at her. "Should I wait here for you?" he asked, patting the bed beside him. She knew he would stay if she asked him to, and she was tempted. Boy, was she tempted.

She smiled. "I'm afraid it's going to be a long day," she said. "*The Pimpernel* is in terrible shape, and we're live tomorrow night."

"Can I offer you a ride to the station then?"

"No," she said. Too quickly, she realized, and she covered the gaffe with a smile. She moved to the side of the bed, kicking something sticking out from under the frame. She absently picked up the Kewpie doll that had been knocked to the floor the night before and sat down next to Charlie on the side of the bed. "I mean, no reason for you to rush. Stay here. Take your time." She smoothed the doll's frilly dress back down and propped the doll up next to Charlie. "Here, Topsy will keep you company."

Charlie eyed the doll and raised one eyebrow.

"Oh, stop. It's sentimental. My father won that for me at a carnival game. He must have spent twenty dollars to win this fifty-cent doll." Her voice faltered, and she reached over to trace the molded curves of the doll's forehead curl. He'd taken her to Riverview Park one sticky July afternoon when she'd been about ten. He'd won the doll and then let her ride the thrilling new coaster, the Bobs, as he white-knuckled by association from the walkway below. She smiled at the memory.

And when her father hadn't been playing happy families, he'd been mixing with Capone and his cronies. Her smile faded, and she shook the memory from her head. No time to wallow in thoughts of her father or what any of the revelations of the night before meant. She looked into the Kewpie doll's face, frozen into an image of childish happiness with its insipid toothy grin. It stirred a memory. Something she'd recently seen somewhere? Heard somewhere? She shook her head. It was no use. Her mind was a rattletrap of thoughts, and this particular one was gone as quickly as it had appeared.

"Have some breakfast. I think there are eggs in the icebox," she said. "You'll have to take your chances on how fresh they are."

"I could go to the big house for some breakfast," he said.

Vivian's eyes widened in alarm, and she smacked him not so playfully on the chest. "Don't you dare!" The elderly housekeeper's scandalized face sprang to mind at the thought of a disheveled and half-dressed Charlie showing up at her breakfast table, sheets clutched around his waist. And her mother. Oh, Vivian couldn't even think of what her mother would do.

"Your mother loves me," Charlie said as if he'd been reading her mind.

"Not enough to have you chat her up over her morning toast, she doesn't."

Charlie laughed. "Don't worry about me. I make my living by skulking around and alluding detection. No one will be the wiser. Besides, I can't afford to lounge in bed all day. I have that Watson…or Wilson…or Whatever-son fellow to find today."

Vivian's stomach twisted. "You're not still looking into that?"

"I think there's more to it."

She did too, and that was the problem. She sat on the edge of the bed, her back to Charlie. "I don't know. I don't think I want to know any more about what my father was up to. He was involved with gangsters…" The thought of those footsteps on the icy sidewalk speeding up in the dark echoed through her mind suddenly, and she shivered. Someone else was on to them as well, on to her. She thought about telling Charlie, but she had no proof, and all he would do was lock her in a gilded cage to try to protect her. He'd try to stop her from going to the station, from leaving the house at all. And then she'd be no good to anyone. She had obligations. Not only *The Pimpernel*, but she had to end things with Graham. The playacting had to stop. Today.

"Maybe it's time to let sleeping dogs lie," she said. "Maybe I should've dropped all of this when you told me to at the Tip Top Café."

"I'm glad you didn't." She felt his hand on her waist, warm and comforting.

Vivian smiled and leaned over to kiss him good-bye.

"I'm serious, Charlie. Promise that you won't tell me if you find anything worse than what we've already found?" His eyebrows rose, but he nodded at her.

"Promise," he said, pulling her down for another longer, more thorough kiss.

Still, something gnawed at her—the idea that her father being murdered was only the tip of the iceberg.

CHAPTER TWENTY-FOUR

❖

V ivian took a taxi to the station. She couldn't bear the idea of facing her mother to ask if she could borrow her driver, pretending that she didn't know what she knew about her father in order to spare her mother's feelings. During the whole drive to the station, her mind kept returning to her father and what had been alleged. Not only that he'd been murdered, but—even worse, in Vivian's mind—that he'd been part of Capone's criminal empire. Arthur Witchell had held court in the back of an illegal gambling house, and if Moochie was to be believed, her father had owned part of that illegal gambling house.

Her mind scrambled to find memories that might fit this new image of her father, and she came up empty. He'd been home at the same time every evening—almost always making it for dinner with the family. He had rarely gone out at night without her mother. He'd never acted suspicious. There had been no visits from strange men, no phone calls that seemed ominous, no hushed conversations behind closed doors. Then again, she'd been young and her attention had been almost solely focused on herself and her own petty concerns. Maybe she just hadn't noticed any evidence of a double life.

The truth was, Vivian didn't want to believe it. Her father had been her champion, her sole support in living a life that was truly her own. He'd nixed the idea of sending Vivian to boarding school. Instead, he'd let her go to a public high school. He'd encouraged her free thinking, her free spirit. He'd been in the back of her mind when she'd decided to become an actress, certain that if he'd been around, he'd have given his wholehearted support and encouragement—despite her mother's feelings on the subject—as he did with most things that his daughter wanted.

But the proof was impossible to deny. Her father hadn't been who she'd thought he was, not entirely. And now the one thing that could set her free—the inheritance he'd left her—was likely tainted money. Would she accept it? Could she? And if she didn't, how on earth would she ever manage to get out and fully live her own life?

And then there was the other large issue looming. She needed to end it with Graham—their fake relationship. How, she didn't know. But she knew things couldn't continue the way they were. Charlie wouldn't be willing to play second fiddle to Graham, even if it was just for the newspapers. And she didn't want him to.

Angelo tipped his hat to Vivian as she entered the elevator. "Miss Witchell," he said. "You're looking well."

"Thank you." That's the way their exchange always started, she mused. Like a script. Angelo always told her that she was "looking well," regardless of whether it was the truth. She smoothed the front of her coat and tried not to think about how well she might be looking after last night with Charlie. Beyond well, she suspected. "Twelfth floor, please."

Angelo shut the doors and pulled the lever on the floor to set the car in motion. The elevator lurched upward, and Vivian watched the bronze arrow above the doors move slowly to the right as it indicated their rise to the top floor.

"Mr. Yarborough taking you out for New Year's tonight?" Angelo glanced back at her.

No, she wanted to say. *No, of course he isn't. He hasn't asked, and I wouldn't accept if he did. It's all a sham, and it has to stop.*

"No, I'm afraid we'll be working too hard on *The Scarlet Pimpernel* to celebrate New Year's," she said instead, hands balled into fists at her sides.

Angelo shook his head. "Working too hard to take a lovely girl like you out on the town?"

Vivian forced a smile. "I'm afraid so."

"You two are… How do you say it? Peas in a pod." He looked at her, eyebrows raised.

She swallowed. "That's how you say it," she said, hoping to avoid commenting on the implication that she and Graham were a match made in heaven. She watched the arrow, willing it to slide to twelve already.

"I hear that you'll be married soon," he said, a smile spreading over his face.

Vivian sighed and closed her eyes for a moment. No doubt Angelo thought that was something that pleased her. She took a deep breath and then another. Angelo was just an innocent bystander, she reminded herself. He didn't deserve her misplaced hostility.

"Oh, I don't know about that," she said, forcing a lightness to her tone that she didn't feel.

"No?" He put one hand to his chest, seeming to be genuinely hurt by the news. "But I heard—"

Vivian put a hand up. "Don't believe everything you hear, Angelo."

Angelo said nothing until the elevator reached the twelfth floor and he pulled the door open. As she stepped forward, he put a hand on her arm. She turned and looked into his kind, sincere face. "It's just that I want you to be happy, miss."

"Me too, Angelo," she said. "Me too."

Vivian passed by Imogene's desk on the way to the studio. Her friend was absorbed in a copy of the *Patriot* and didn't look up as Vivian stopped in front of her.

"May I?" Vivian asked as she snatched the newspaper out of her friend's hands.

She flipped to the gossip section, page 6, and scanned it quickly. Nothing about her and Charlie at the Green Mill. Not that she had expected anything. She hadn't seen any photographers, and why would they have been there? Graham hadn't been there to call them.

Vivian also half expected to see an exposé about her father. She felt as if the world should know, that the world should care what she'd found out. Her world had imploded in the span of twenty-four hours, and yet the earth kept spinning. No one seemed to notice her inner turmoil—nor would they. She had a job that was in no way related to her father and what he may or may not have done, and she would do it.

She dropped the newspaper unceremoniously on the desk, lost in thought.

"So?" Imogene asked.

"So what?"

"Spill," Imogene said and cocked her head ever so slightly toward the closed door of Mr. Langley's office. "What happened last night?"

"A lot happened last night," Vivian said. "Why do you ask?" Imogene was her best friend, but Vivian was on guard.

The main thing she'd learned over the past week, with all of the revelations about her father, was that not everyone was as they seemed.

"I ask because Mr. Banks is in heated discussion with Mr. Langley. On a Saturday."

Vivian's eyes darted to the closed door.

"And they wanted to see you as soon as you came in today," Imogene continued.

Vivian swallowed.

"Just me?" Vivian asked.

"Just you."

It could be about anything. It could be about the new magazine ad campaign for Sultan's Gold. Yes, that had to be it. Didn't it? Vivian looked into Imogene's worried face and suddenly felt like there was a brick in her stomach. No, that wasn't it. Frances. She'd seen Vivian and Charlie outside the Green Mill. Vivian had been lulled into a false sense of security where Frances was concerned over the past few months, but now Frances had seen her chance to undermine Vivian. So Frances had told Langley what she'd seen and likely embellished it quite a bit—even though the reality needed no embellishment, Vivian thought. Imogene cocked her head to the side, staring daggers at Vivian.

"What else aren't you telling me?" Imogene asked. Frankly, Vivian was surprised Imogene didn't know already. Imogene knew everything there was to know around the station.

"Charlie," Vivian whispered.

Imogene smiled and raised one eyebrow. "What about him?"

"We went to the Green Mill last night."

"Oh?"

"Part of the investigation into my father, you see."

"And?"

Vivian decided that now was not the time to drop the bombshell about her father.

"And we ran into Frances there."

"Aha. That explains it." Imogene sat back in her chair. "Frances scurried up here not thirty minutes ago, breezing right past me and straight into Langley's office. I tried to listen at the door, but I couldn't hear anything. So Frances told Langley that you've been seen with a man who was not Graham."

"That's not all of it. I... Well, last night we..."

Imogene's eyes went wide. "Your plan worked."

"I suppose."

"Would Frances have told him that?" Imogene jerked a thumb toward the closed door.

"Of course not," Vivian said. "How on earth would she know?"

"I've been rooting for you two. That's great, Viv." Then her eyes flicked to the closed door. Voices were barely audible, an insistent rolling burr. "But also not great."

Vivian sighed. "Exactly."

"What are you going to do?"

Vivian shrugged. "I suppose that all depends on what Mr. Langley has to say."

"What if he says 'Drop Charlie, or we'll drop you?'"

Vivian shrugged. What would she say in that situation? Would Mr. Langley do something like that to her? Force her to choose between Charlie and the show? She'd considered that before, but that was when everything was just starting for her. Now she had traction, momentum. It would be harder to toss her career aside for him. But she would do it if she had to. She could only hope it wouldn't come to that.

The door swung open, outlining a thunderously unhappy Mr. Langley in the frame. His eyes trained directly on Vivian, and he pointed a finger at her.

"You. In here. Now."

It hadn't been as terrible a dressing-down as Vivian had expected. It had been much worse. A talking-to by a disapproving father—two disapproving fathers. Of course they knew she and Graham weren't a couple. Of course she might have feelings for men other than Graham. However, there was more at stake here than her romantic feelings. The show was at stake, ratings were at stake, ad revenue was at stake. The station's profile was at stake. Essentially, she thought, the entirety of WCHI was riding on her shoulders and her ability to pretend that Graham Yarborough was truly the man of her dreams.

They didn't explicitly say she *couldn't* see Charlie. But they did say that it could never get into the papers. Mr. Langley had soberly reminded Vivian of the morals clause in her contract. She could not be publicly ensnared in any sort of morally questionable behavior—like being linked romantically to Charlie while she was "seeing" Graham—or the station would have perfectly legal cause to throw her out on her ear. And it was implied that she would continue this ruse with Graham in perpetuity, or she could kiss Lorna Lafferty, as well as any future roles at WCHI, good-bye.

Things could be worse, Vivian thought, but not much worse. Charlie would not think highly of this arrangement, if he agreed to it at all. He wouldn't like having to share her. Langley's various veiled and not-so-veiled threats rang through her mind. Biggest of all was his implication that *The Darkness Knows* was close to moving to Hollywood. They were "in discussions" right now, as a matter of fact, he'd said. So she couldn't lose Lorna now. Not now. Not when there was the imminent promise of Hollywood on the horizon, and everything she'd always dreamed of—at least professionally— was at her fingertips.

She needed to talk to Graham. Really talk to him. Lay everything out on the table. Maybe they could work something out, something where they could both see who they wanted and still perpetuate this ruse. There certainly had to be someone else in his life, judging by the scant interest he'd shown in her. Yes, she needed to find Graham.

"Viv."

She glanced up, biting her thumbnail, to find Gloria bearing down on her. Gloria?

"What are you doing here?"

"Graham invited me to see a rehearsal of *The Pimpernel*."

"When did he do that?"

"After Thursday's *Darkness Knows* broadcast."

"Oh." The girl didn't waste any time ingratiating herself, Vivian thought.

"Say, can I talk to you about something?"

"I have to get to rehearsal." Vivian started walking again, but Gloria stepped in front of her.

"It's rather important, I think."

Vivian held out her wrist and pointed to her watch with an exaggerated shrug.

"It won't take long, I promise."

Vivian sighed. The girl ingratiated herself, and she didn't take no for an answer. *Future reporter all right*, she thought.

Gloria headed toward the actor's lounge, tugging Vivian along by her sleeve.

She pulled her into the empty room and closed the door. Vivian got a flash of a time not too long ago when another girl had pulled her into an empty room at the station. That time it had been Peggy Hart, and she'd been planning to kill Vivian. She shivered at the memory.

Gloria's choice of a place to have a tête-à-tête couldn't have been worse, in Vivian's opinion. She didn't willingly enter the actor's lounge on the twelve floor. Not since Marjorie Fox's murder two months ago. This is where Vivian had found the body, and being in here made the hair on the back of her neck stand on end. She couldn't believe people still had coffee and ate their lunches in this room. Here, where the life had leaked out of a human being onto the linoleum.

"So what's this about? Everett?"

Gloria shook her head. "Graham."

"Graham?"

Gloria nodded. "And his secret."

Vivian wrinkled her brow, distracted. Her eyes swept over the spot where Marjorie's dead body had lain: her hair matted with blood, her eyes open and unseeing. Vivian shook her head and blinked at Gloria, trying to refocus on the conversation at hand. Secret? Her mind latched on to what she imagined Graham's secret might be. "Oh, Graham's not a communist," she said. "Don't worry. That was bluster, and it's all blown over now."

Gloria's blue eyes widened as she considered the idea. Then she leaned in toward Vivian and pitched her voice low, even though there was no one else to overhear. "I'm not talking about communism, Viv," she said.

Vivian's mind was still spinning around and around over

what Mr. Langley had told her. She had to keep up this pretense with Graham. But how could she, now that there was Charlie? Her face flushed at the memory of him lying in her bed, sheets rumpled. She realized the Gloria was looking at her with expectation.

"Then what are you talking about?" Vivian said impatiently.

Gloria's voice became a soothing whisper. "You know about Paul, don't you?"

"Paul? Of course. He's Graham's collaborator."

Gloria snorted. "I'll say."

Vivian studied the girl. There was something in her face that Vivian didn't like: calculation.

"I honestly have no idea what you're talking about, Gloria." She had lost patience with this game, whatever it was. She started toward the door. "I need to get going."

Gloria grabbed her arm. Vivian looked down at it, and the girl let go.

"Look, I heard all about you and this other man. It's all over the station."

Vivian's stomach sank. "So?"

"Well, I think there's something you should know...a bargaining chip for you perhaps. The real reason the brass at WCHI are so keen on keeping your relationship with Graham in the papers."

Vivian stared at the girl studying her so earnestly with big, blue eyes. "The *real* reason? What do you mean?"

"I hate to have to put it so bluntly," she said. She puffed out her cheeks and flicked her eyes toward the ceiling. Then she let the air out and fixed her eyes on Vivian. "Graham prefers the company of other men."

Vivian blinked. "He what?"

Gloria nodded. Everything came back to Vivian then, flashes of times she'd tried to kiss him. Times when they'd actually kissed, and it had left her cold. He was attractive, he was charming, but there was no chemistry between them. His persona, everything she'd known about him, everything she thought she'd known, was an act.

She was shocked, but not quite to the marrow of her bones. She feigned incredulity, but she felt her heart fall like a brick into her stomach. And yet, a part of her, a large part of her, felt an immense relief. So that was it, she thought. Her way out.

"How do you know?" Vivian asked, trying to keep her voice steady.

"I followed him," Gloria said. "Well, not *me*. I've met Graham. He'd recognize me. One of my friends from school followed him."

"Followed," Vivian repeated. Gloria didn't even have the grace to look ashamed of herself.

Then the realization hit Vivian like a punch to the stomach. That man she saw everywhere. The man who had been scaring her half to death all week. The man she'd thought was working for a shady underworld crime figure and out to kill her. The man who'd chased her down the icy street before she'd fallen. He was one of Gloria's school chums. He had to be. Vivian glanced down at her still-bandaged hand.

"You had me followed too?"

Gloria's eyes widened. "Of course not. What do you think I am?"

"I think you're a journalism student, and you'd probably do anything to get your name above the fold." How could she believe anything Gloria told her, now that she knew this? She thought of that snake Mack Rippert and wondered if Gloria had known all along—if they were in cahoots.

"I'm hurt that you'd think that of me. I had Graham followed out of curiosity. That's all. I'm not proud of it, but I'd been talking to Mr. Banks about the station's publicity campaign—about the two of you. There's something lacking there… I'm not the only one who's noticed."

Vivian grimaced. Was she the last person to know about Graham's secret? She felt like such a fool.

"Maybe there was a mistake. Maybe you misunderstood."

"Viv, I *saw* them together." There was no mistaking the girl's expression. Revulsion over barely disguised glee.

"So why exactly are you telling me this?"

"I thought you should know. It's not fair that you don't."

Fair? Vivian cocked her head and studied this chit of a girl. Was this truly about what was fair? No, of course it wasn't.

"What do you want?"

"A job," Gloria said, crossing her arms. "Here."

Oh God, Vivian thought. *Another scheming wannabe actress.* She sighed. "I can get you a bit part on *The Darkness Knows*."

"No. I don't want to be on air. I want to work in publicity."

"Well, then talk to Mr. Banks."

"He said he doesn't hire kids with no experience."

Vivian rolled her eyes. "Then I don't know what you expect *me* to do."

"Grease the wheels a little."

"Why not go to Graham?"

Gloria shrugged. "Maybe I will. But I feel sorry for you. Being played for a fool. You deserved to know either way. Besides, you're Everett's sister. And this way I scratch your back, you scratch mine."

"And if I do this for you—talk to Mr. Banks, get you a job—you'll keep what you know to yourself?"

"Of course."

Vivian looked at Gloria. Her little brother's innocent-looking girlfriend. It was like making a deal with the devil, she thought. Graham's situation wasn't unusual. A lot of men in the entertainment business were of that ilk. Vivian had run into several who she suspected of leaning that way, but none of them had ever admitted it. It was always a secret, whispered behind backs. Rumor, innuendo. But rumor and innuendo could ruin careers. She would keep this secret—she owed Graham, after all. He'd single-handedly kept her on

The Darkness Knows. And if his career was ruined, then hers might be as well.

Graham and Paul stood on the opposite side of the studio, heads bent together in heated discussion. Paul pointed to something in the script and shook his head. Graham threw his head back in exasperation, his eyes rolling toward the ceiling. Nothing about them suggested they were anything other than writing partners. Now it was time to find out if there was any fire to that smoke, Vivian thought. She marched right up to them.

"Graham, we need to talk."

She felt, rather than saw, all heads in the room swivel in their direction. Forget *The Pimpernel*. This was today's real show.

Graham ducked his head, avoiding the eyes on him. "Not here," he said. He shot Paul a look, then took Vivian by the arm and marched her right out of the studio and into the hallway, his fingers digging painfully into her flesh. He shoved her into an empty studio and turned to her, his arms crossed.

"So it's you and Chick then? This whole time?"

"Not this whole time, no." She was taken aback by the vehemence in his voice, the betrayal.

"Do you know how this makes me look, Viv? Like a fool."

That's rich, she thought. He thinks *he* looks the fool.

"Graham, you and I both know this has never been a real relationship. Maybe it's time we end it."

"We can't just end it, Viv."

He was right, of course. She knew he was right, but she had to hear him say why. He had to admit everything Gloria had told her.

"Are you going to tell me then?"

"Tell you what?"

"The real reason we can't end it."

He stared hard at her. She couldn't read his expression.

"The real reason is that Langley and Banks have us by the short hairs. You and me both."

Vivian stared at him. It was on the tip of her tongue, so close to spilling out. So he wasn't going to admit to what Gloria had said. She narrowed her eyes and looked at him. Maybe it wasn't true after all. Maybe Gloria had misread everything. But, then again, she'd been so certain. She'd said she seen Graham and Paul together. Still…there were doubts. Graham had to be the one to tell her, not the other way around. She wouldn't accuse him. This was too big to be wrong about.

"We'll discuss this later, Viv. Frankly, I don't have time to think about it right now. This is terrible timing. Terrible. Until tomorrow night, we're going to pretend nothing's wrong."

"Graham, we can't—"

"We can, and we will."

He stormed from the room, all fiery temper and flare, and

for a moment that fire reminded her of why she'd found him attractive in the first place. But any feelings of admiration soon faded into confusion and then into frustration. How did things get so complicated? He couldn't put her off forever. One way or another, they would have their talk, and then everything would be out in the open.

CHAPTER TWENTY-FIVE

❖

When they broke for lunch, Vivian headed across the street to the Tip Top Café to meet Imogene. She needed to talk through all of this with someone who might understand. Her father, Graham, Charlie, all of it. She needed an impartial ear. But as she hopped up onto the curb on the south side of Madison, someone called Vivian's name.

Vivian spotted a familiar blond in a bright-red coat among the crowd waiting at the corner of Madison and LaSalle for the eastbound streetcar. Della. She was waving. Vivian returned the wave. If there was any guilt in Della, she hid it perfectly, Vivian thought.

She hurried toward Della, her heels clicking on the pavement. As she approached, so did the red-and-cream State Street streetcar, dinging madly to alert everyone to back up and get out of the way of the tracks. Vivian caught Della's eye again and smiled. Della was looking not at the streetcar but at Vivian. Vivian was steps away as the streetcar bore down on the stop on the corner. Suddenly, Della lunged forward, her eyes wide with surprise, and stumbled onto the tracks directly in front of the approaching streetcar.

Vivian dashed the final two steps, shoved through the crowd, and reached desperately for the flash of red of Della's coat sleeve that she could barely see through the throng of people. She reached blindly, grabbing hold of something—what she hoped was Della—and then yanked backward, throwing all of her body weight into it. Vivian fell roughly to the pavement, a female body tumbling on top of her. They landed in a heap on the sidewalk. Vivian's hip slammed against the pavement with a bright burst of pain. The streetcar stopped with a screech of the brakes, and a murmur went up among the crowd. But there was no scream, no sound of impact.

Vivian groaned.

The crowd around them parted like the Red Sea, and Vivian looked up into a dozen confused faces.

"You okay, miss?"

Vivian blinked the stars in her vision away, but the faces still swam in front of her. She couldn't speak. All the wind had been knocked out of her.

"I'm okay, I think," said the other woman. She finally rolled off Vivian and looked down at her. It was Della after all. If Vivian could breathe, it would have been to let out a sigh of relief.

"Viv," Della said. "Viv. Oh God, Viv, don't—"

And then the world faded and went black around her.

Vivian woke a few seconds later to that sea of confused faces, a smaller pool now that the streetcar had loaded and departed eastbound down Madison toward State. Her eyes caught on a familiar face—the young man with the flat cap. She blinked to clear her vision, but when she focused on that spot again, he was gone. Someone helped her to her feet, and she rubbed her left hip. The bruise there would be enormous. She could already feel the lump. Her breath had come back in short little gasps. She stood wheezing in front of Della and assorted strangers, her mind a jumble at what had just happened. She looked at Della's pale face, her eyes wide with shock. Della had almost been killed. That's what had just happened.

Vivian glanced around at the faces, but none of those remaining were familiar, and none of them registered anything but surprise, concern, or mild disinterest.

"Oh, Viv, let's get you somewhere to sit down," Della said, grabbing Vivian's arm. "Can you walk?"

Vivian stepped forward with her injured leg and gingerly tested whether it would hold her weight. It did, barely. She nodded to Della. They waved off a few Good Samaritans and their assistance, and she and Della headed the fifty feet or so down LaSalle to the Rookery Building.

Once they were in Freddy's office, Della settled Vivian in a comfortable chair, clucking like a hen over her. "I'll get you some tea." She rushed off before Vivian could protest.

Della took three steps, then stopped dead in her tracks. She shrieked, an ear-piercing and unexpectedly loud sound in the silence of the office on a Saturday afternoon. Vivian jumped and rose halfway in her chair. But the pain in her hip made her gasp herself, and she sat swiftly back down.

"What is it?" Her heart thrummed against her rib cage. Was someone lying in wait for Della in the pantry—ready to finish the job botched when Vivian pulled her away from the street-car tracks? Or was it Freddy, lying prostrate in a pool of blood on the floor, his head bashed in? She braced herself against the chair for certain tragedy, wondering what she would do if she needed to run to save herself.

"My plants!" Della sobbed, turning back toward Vivian. There was true anguish in her voice and on her face. "They're smashed all over the floor."

Vivian's eyes moved to the window behind Della's desk where days before the veritable jungle had stood in assorted pots of all sizes. They were all gone now. Nothing remained except a few shards of pottery and a large, ragged piece of the glass cloche.

"Oh," Vivian sighed. Just the plants.

"Who could have… Why…?" Della struggled for words, and then she turned back to Vivian with decision. Her face was set. "The cleaners. This has happened before. They're so careless with that cord—sweeping it across the sill like that when they vacuum." She looked helplessly at Vivian.

"I'm sorry, Della."

Della shook her head sorrowfully. She crouched down and came back up with a limp green plant cupped in her hands, with two nutlike brown objects attached. "This one was my baby. And now there's no saving it. I've tried to grow this one for years."

"What is it?"

"Odollam. It's called the ping-pong plant because of these." She lifted one of the brown nutlike objects. "It's a tropical plant. Terribly hard to grow in this climate."

Vivian watched Della sadly and reverently place the remains of her prized plant on the now-empty windowsill. She stared at it a moment longer and shook her head.

"I suppose it's an easy enough mistake." She pointed to the outlet next to the window. "That's the one outlet in this room. If they want to vacuum, they'd have to unplug my lamp to use it." Vivian noticed that although the cleaners had destroyed an entire windowsill of plants that they hadn't bothered to clean up, they'd plugged the lamp back into the socket afterward.

Then Della went on her way to the small pantry at the back of the office, still shaking her head. She came back a moment later with two cups on saucers, steam rising in tendrils from the hot drinks. She handed one to Vivian.

"Are you sure you're okay?" Della asked for what seemed the umpteenth time, her brow wrinkled in concern.

Vivian nodded, rubbing her hip. "I'll survive. But what about you?"

Della nodded. "Shaken up, but I'll be fine."

"What happened out there?"

Della shook her head and shrugged. "I was standing there waiting for the streetcar. I called to you. We waved to each other, and then suddenly I was stumbling into the street and onto the tracks."

"You were pushed?"

Della's hazel eyes went wide. "Pushed? Heavens no. There were a lot of people out there on the street, and you know how people jockey for position when the streetcar approaches...people out for the after-Christmas sales, juggling all those packages. I slipped on the ice, that's all."

Vivian thought of the man with the flat cap. Had she really seen him? Her vision had been blurred from the fall to the pavement. Maybe her mind had inserted his face where it hadn't really been. Her imagination had been working overtime lately.

They sat in silence, each lost in her own thoughts as they sipped their tea.

"Della..." Vivian said, her eyes straying again toward the plant carnage under the window. "Did you know what my father was up to before he died?" She left the question deliberately vague.

"Up to? What do you mean?" Della's tone was innocent, but her eyes had narrowed.

"I know what he was doing. With the Racquet Club.

Capone." Vivian reached out and patted the secretary's hand. "You don't have to protect me anymore." She glanced significantly toward Freddy's closed office door.

Della followed her eyes and glanced quickly away. Vivian took a sip of her tea and let the woman gather herself.

"I'm sorry, Viv. About your father. About all of it. I feel like it was my fault," she said, her voice breaking. "And I didn't come to Arthur's funeral—any of it—because I couldn't bear to face you, to face your mother."

Vivian's mouth went dry. She took a sip of tea, but didn't taste it. "What do you mean, your fault?"

"I could have stopped it. I think about it all the time, about how I could have saved him."

Vivian swallowed. Her heart started to hammer in her chest. She was right. Della had known everything. She said nothing, waiting for Della to explain herself.

Della hitched in a great gulp of air and straightened in her chair. "I knew Arthur was having chest pains that day. I should have made him see a doctor. But I didn't."

Vivian took a deep breath. She didn't realize until that second that part of her had been expecting a confession. That she'd been expecting Della to admit outright that she knew exactly what Vivian's father had been mixed up in—that he'd been murdered—maybe even that she'd helped murder him. Vivian searched Della's face, but the woman seemed to be telling the truth.

"He'd been having chest pains?"

"Yes, that afternoon. I'd seen him grimace a few times and touch his chest, but I didn't say anything. I didn't even ask if he was feeling well. I was so busy that day, but that's no excuse. Your father was so good to me. I'm sorry, Vivian."

"It's not your fault," she said automatically.

Vivian thought of meeting Della at the kitchen door as she left that night to meet her boyfriend at the time. "Is that why you came over to the house later that evening? To check on him?"

Della's brow furrowed, and she touched her temple with her fingertips as if it physically pained her to think about it. She'd been the one to find Arthur Witchell dead in his favorite chair. Vivian could sympathize. She'd never forget the moment she stumbled upon Marjorie Fox's body.

"Oh, no. Mr. Witchell had taken a brief that Mr. Gilfoy needed the following day for court."

"Why didn't Martin come by himself?"

"I volunteered to go. Martin was working late on an important case. He was due in court first thing the next morning with Mr. Endicott. Martin was flustered, and I wanted to help him out." Della blushed. She'd had a crush on Martin from the first. Of course she'd wanted to help him out. Vivian sympathized. She would have done the same. "He was out of sorts because Mr. Endicott and your father weren't here. They'd left the office early to have a drink and hadn't returned."

Freddy had had an important court date the next day and

had left early to have a drink? She remembered her father sitting in the chair the night he'd died as she sat at his feet. He'd smelled of tobacco and stale beer.

"Is that something they did often, Freddy and my father?"

Della shook her head. "I can't say they did."

"Any special reason for it this particular time? Were they celebrating something, perhaps?"

"I was busy filing when they left. I wasn't paying much attention, I'm afraid."

Vivian decided to try a different tack. "My father had been under a lot of stress before his death. Do you know what he'd been working on?"

Della looked down at the desk and rubbed her temple. "No. I mean, it was so long ago that I don't recall. I'm sorry." She didn't look up. Vivian knew she was lying. The *sorry* wasn't an apology for her faulty memory. It was an apology for not telling the truth. There was fear behind her eyes. Della knew something. But if that something was her father being mixed up with Capone and his ilk, Vivian didn't blame her for not recalling things clearly. She probably wouldn't either. The stigma of Al Capone still hung heavy over Chicago.

"I'm sorry, Della. I don't mean to give you the third degree." Vivian reached over and patted the secretary's hand resting on the desktop. Della pulled it away and then looked stricken that she'd done so.

"No, I'm sorry, Viv. I'm out of sorts."

She stood suddenly and slid the remnants of her now-dead prized plant from the windowsill into the trash can. She looked sadly down at it, her lower lip shaking. "So senseless." She shook her head.

"I think you need to fire those cleaners."

That got a weak smile out of Della. She clapped her hands together to get rid of the excess dirt.

"Do you want me to see you home?" Vivian asked.

"No, I'll take a taxi. I don't think I can face the streetcar. Not today."

"I don't blame you."

"Any plans for the New Year?" Della asked casually.

That's right, Vivian thought, rubbing her hip. *Tonight is New Year's Eve.*

Then she noticed Della's pinched expression and suddenly understood that she was asking if Vivian had plans with Martin. Vivian had been a witness to their flirtations earlier in the week, and she knew that what to Martin was a casual monthly flirtation was Della's whole life. Then she realized that Della had heard Vivian invite Martin to dinner earlier in the week, and she felt a sudden stab of pity for the woman. Vivian knew that she had no intentions toward Martin now that Charlie was firmly back in the picture, but she hadn't informed Martin of that yet, had she?

"Just rehearsal," she said with a sigh. "We have a live show tomorrow, and I'm sorry to say that it's a shambles at the moment. I doubt I'll ring in the new year from anywhere other than a stuffy, windowless studio down the street. You?"

Della shrugged. "I think, under the circumstances, that I should stick close to home," she said. She looked meaningfully at Vivian, and Vivian knew Della understood more than she was letting on.

◆

CHAPTER TWENTY-SIX

The afternoon rehearsal for *The Pimpernel* went poorly. Missed cues, fumbled lines—everything that could go wrong went wrong. The cast was so frustrated that they ended early. Graham's face was a dangerous shade of vermillion, and his hair stood up in corkscrews all over his head. Vivian wanted to finish their conversation from earlier, but this was not the time. He was in no mood for rationality.

Vivian was already on her way to Imogene's desk to call Charlie when Imogene caught up to her in the hallway.

"Well, that was terrible," she said. Imogene had been helping out with the rehearsal and had witnessed the worst of the debacle. "I don't have high hopes for the performance tomorrow."

Vivian grunted in reply as she hobbled down the hallway, a hand pressed to her left hip.

"Say, what happened to you? You didn't show up at the Tip Top Café for lunch. And…you're limping? A lot. Gosh, are you okay?"

Vivian heaved a great sigh. Her hip had grown stiff during

rehearsal, and it ached like the dickens. "Oh, Genie. So much has happened today."

"Do tell."

Where to begin? Imogene already knew about Charlie. Should she tell her what Gloria had told her about Graham—the other piece of this convoluted puzzle? She'd have to, but not before she talked to Graham himself. She shook her head.

"I saved Della, my father's secretary, from being run over by a streetcar at lunchtime. I pulled her away, and she landed on top of me on the pavement. I'm sure I have a great big goose egg on my hip. I'm afraid to look."

"What? She fell?"

"That's what she says."

"Wow, no wonder you stood me up at the Tip Top. What was it that you wanted to talk about?"

Vivian's mind raced as she looked at Imogene's earnestly concerned face. She was too tired to explain all of it now—that is, if she could explain it at all.

"Never mind, Genie. It can wait."

"Well, I don't think you should be alone tonight, Viv."

Vivian had no plans to be alone. She looked over at the telephone. She was longing to call Charlie, but Imogene clearly had ideas of her own.

"I think we all deserve to let off some steam. What do you think of having a little party?"

"A party? I don't know, Genie…" She thought of Charlie

and how much she'd like to see him—if to not explain all that had happened, then just to escape *The Pimpernel*, Graham, everything. Then to lean on his shoulder and shut her mind off.

"Well, I think it's a great idea, and I think you should host."

"Oh no, you don't."

"You have the biggest house... Well, your mother does. Everyone's in. I already took a poll."

"Genie..."

"Come on, Viv. You host and we'll bring everything else, including the noisemakers." She smiled at her.

"You're not asking me, are you? You're informing me that it's going to happen."

"Aha! Now you've got it."

Vivian sighed. "Give me an hour to clear it with management," she said. Hopefully, her mother would be out on the town. That way, she could ask for forgiveness in the morning rather than permission tonight.

CHAPTER TWENTY-SEVEN

V ivian picked up the note from beside the telephone in
the entryway.

*Vivian—Martin phoned to ask if you'd changed
your mind about the party tonight.*

She frowned and dialed the number left on the message.
There was no answer. It was just as well, because she was
calling to turn him down. Whatever lingering teenage feelings
she'd had for Martin Gilfoy were nearly extinguished now that
Charlie was back in her life. Teenage infatuation could not
compare to grown-up love. And that's what it was, she thought
with some amazement. She loved Charlie. She smiled to herself
as she looked down at the telephone. She would call him now.

Vivian placed her hand on the receiver, then noticed the
mumbling sounds of the radio in the den. Someone was here
after all. Everett, perhaps? No, he should be out with Gloria
by now. Gloria… Vivian sighed. What was that girl after? She

pondered that while she walked toward the den. Was Gloria so transparent that all she wanted was to clue Vivian in on Graham's motives in exchange for a leg up at the station? Maybe she wanted Vivian's good opinion—that is, if she was serious about Everett. Vivian had the sneaking suspicion that Gloria was. And then there was Graham. She doubted he would show at the party. Then again, if he didn't, tongues would wag even harder than they already were. She sighed and stepped through the doorway from the front hall to the den.

Oskar sat in the chair in front of the radio. He didn't hear Vivian enter, and she stood regarding him for a moment. She hadn't seen him since the revelation at the Green Mill, and she didn't know what to make of the man. What was his game? Did he have a game? Now was as good a time as any to find out, she thought. She walked toward him, her footsteps muffled by the thick carpet.

"Is there news from Europe?" she asked.

His shoulders jerked as she startled him. He shook his head. "Nothing new."

She looked toward the blazing fireplace and the shimmering, tinsel-covered Christmas tree beside it.

"I thought you and Mother would be cutting a rug right about now," she said.

"Oh, we plan on it. Your mother wanted to stop here to freshen up a bit after dinner. She will be down shortly."

Vivian glanced toward the doorway and the staircase. She

listened for a moment to the muffled voices from the radio. All was quiet in Europe, the announcer said. Hitler was probably busy celebrating the new year too. Oskar reached over and turned the dial.

"Enough of that morbidity. Tonight is for celebrating, yes?" He stopped the dial on an upbeat dance number—a live remote from some ballroom in the city where Vivian wished she could be right now. She would love to just close her eyes and pop into that other place, that other time, turn her mind off and dance like everyone else seemed to be doing tonight. But when she closed her eyes, she saw her father dead in the chair in which Oskar now sat.

"Something is bothering you?" Oskar said.

Vivian opened her eyes to find him studying her. "Yes, actually. My father... Something you said the other day..." She paused to find the right phrasing, words that wouldn't put Oskar off before she could get anything out of him. "He didn't just do immigration paperwork for you, did he?"

"I'm not sure what you mean." But she could tell from his closed expression that he knew exactly what she meant.

"I know how chummy you were with Easy Artie."

Oskar's eyes widened. He sighed heavily and looked up at her.

"No," he said. "He did not just do immigration paperwork for me. And he never liked that nickname, Easy Artie. It was deplorable."

Vivian waited for him to continue, but he only stared outside for a long moment in silence. Fat, wet snowflakes splatted against the window, making soft plinking noises on the glass. The radio played softly, gaily.

Oskar turned to her and studied her, his expression unreadable. "I care for your mother," he said. "I want you to know that, Vivian."

Vivian didn't respond. He was evading the question, and she would wait him out.

"I wanted to preface my next statement with that…in case it leads you to question my involvement with your mother."

Vivian kept quiet. Oskar looked hard at her and then sighed again.

"I have not lived an exemplary life, my dear." He shook his head sorrowfully, looking down at his hands. "I have done things I regret with individuals I regret having known." He glanced up at Vivian, but she worked hard to keep her face blank. He shrugged and looked down again.

Vivian glared at him. She couldn't stay silent any longer. "You mean you did things you regret *with my father*," she said.

He narrowed his eyes at her. "What do you mean?"

"I mean the Racquet Club," she said, trying and not succeeding to keep the anger out of her voice. She clenched her fists once, tightly, and then released them.

Oskar stared at her for a moment longer and then leaned back in his chair, eyes on the floor.

"How, might I ask, do you know about the Racquet Club?"

"I found the envelope in my father's desk." She stared at him, registering his reaction. There wasn't a reaction though. "And I know you took it."

He blinked slowly. "Envelope?"

"Let's not do this," Vivian said, sighing. "I know you took it so I wouldn't find out about my father—about you and my father. But now I do know."

Oskar shook his head, his bushy gray brows drawn together over his nose.

"I won't lie to you. I had been to the Racquet Club. I had been there with your father. In those days, I liked to consort with people I had no business consorting with." He looked off into the distance as if trying to remember. "But I didn't steal any envelope."

Vivian stared into his gray eyes. Could he be telling her the truth? She had been so sure of his guilt. But if Oskar didn't take it, who did?

Oskar rubbed his palms on his trousers. "I think I owe you the truth, Vivian."

Vivian's heart pounded. She thought of the money, the ledger, *$200 to Al.* Oskar's voice rang in her head—*I have done things I regret with individuals I regret having known.*

"I, myself, didn't do anything illegal. But I had the habit of consorting with unsavory characters. Stupid, but it was a hobby of mine at the time. I was new to the country, and there was so much glamour in it." He looked pointedly at her, and she found that part of her understood that allure. That's what had made her shimmy down drainpipes and risk her father's disappointment—glamour and a bit of danger. But she made sure none of that was betrayed in her expression. "Your father was, indeed, my lawyer. He did do immigration paperwork for me."

"And?"

"We became friends. And, well, I introduced your father to some unsavory people. At that time, they happened to be in the business of kidnapping wealthy men for ransom. A snatch racket. A dangerous game. One day, they took the wrong man, who turned out to be a friend of Capone's." He raised his bushy eyebrows at her. "Talk about a dangerous business. Your father smoothed things over between all parties concerned, and no one lost their head. Capone liked that. Capone liked Arthur."

Vivian felt sick. "And that's when my father started working for him."

"In a manner of speaking."

"What did he do exactly?"

"He solved problems."

That was a familiar vague statement—exactly what Caputto had told Vivian her father had done. He'd fixed things. For Oskar, apparently. For a lot of people.

"Look, Vivian, your father was a good man who got himself

involved with the wrong people. That's all you have to know. You might say we had that in common—for a time. But that's all in the past now. I got out of the whole thing after the Saint Valentine's Day mess," he said.

St. Valentine's Day. Vivian felt her hands grow cold. Seven men had been lined up against a garage wall and gunned down on Saint Valentine's Day in 1929. The papers had called it a massacre. She could still see the images from the front page of every paper—the twisted bodies lying in a spreading dark pool. It had never been proven, but had always been assumed that Capone had ordered the hit to keep Bugs Moran of the North Side from infringing on his liquor-running territory. She took a step back and swallowed the lump in her throat. "You were involved with that?"

Oskar's eyes widened with alarm.

"Heavens no. But one of those men killed was an optometrist…someone like me, a regular man that liked to hang around bad men because it gave him a thrill. That scared me, reading about that in the papers. So I stopped all of the nonsense after that. I distanced myself. I didn't want to end up full of bullet holes."

"But my father didn't distance himself."

Oskar shook his head. She considered the man in front of her—whether he might be the type to push someone in front of a streetcar. What was that adage? Keep your friends close and your enemies closer?

"Why are you with my mother?"

"For the reason I told you. I met her at the charity function. I hadn't known her before. Your father kept his business life and his private life quite separate, as I think you are now finding out."

"Does she know about you and my father?"

He shook his head.

Vivian's eyes darted toward the door. *Where was her mother?* "Well, you need to tell her or I'm going to."

"Vivian..." He held his hand out to her and then lowered it. "I have, as you say in English, turned over a new leaf."

"Yes, you do charity work, you said. For whom?"

"The European Aid Society. There are people in Germany—and Europe, in general—that need help right now." He looked pointedly at her.

"Like your family."

"And those like my family," he said solemnly. "Something horrible is going to happen, Vivian. The Nazis have plans. Kristallnacht was just the beginning, and I cannot sit by and watch if there's something I might be able to do to help those people. My people."

He was right. She admittedly knew little about the situation, but the papers were full of stories about restrictions against the Jews, new ones seemingly being reported every day. The noose was tightening. Things were coming to a head. Her throat was suddenly dry. She felt it hard to form the words to her next question, partly because she didn't know if she wanted to hear the answer after everything he'd already told her.

"Did you know Freddy before you met him at dinner the other evening, Oskar?"

"I told you—" he began, but Vivian held up one hand to cut him off.

"I know what you told me. Now I want the truth."

He smiled sadly at her. "I don't know much about Freddy, but I believe Arthur thought of him as sort of a younger brother—or at least he treated him that way. He kept him away from all of that." Oskar waved his hand in front of his face. "The only time I ever saw Freddy was at your father's office... and I hadn't seen him since your father's death until dinner the other night. I don't know why he harbors such ill will toward me, except that he probably knows what I got your father involved with...who I got your father involved with. Part of it, I suspect, is that he also has an interest in your mother. And it was simple jealousy at seeing her with another man."

Vivian stared at Oskar and looked into his steely gray eyes. She had no idea if he was telling the truth about any of this. What—who—could she believe? Everyone she knew seemed be lying or dancing around half-truths.

"I also think these are matters that a sweet young woman like you should not concern herself with." He looked down at his hands. "And Vivian, what we discussed here—about my past, about what your father may or may not have been involved with—that's between us, eh? I suppose it's not a secret, not to a certain set of people. But it's not exactly common knowledge among my new set of friends and acquaintances. And I feel my role in my charitable interests would be comprised if it got out among them."

His new set of friends—her mother included, Vivian assumed. She could keep a secret, but why should she? Why shouldn't her mother know exactly who Oskar was, who he had been, what he'd gotten her husband involved with that, indirectly, had gotten him killed?

"People are depending on me, Vivian," Oskar said solemnly. "Innocent people who need my help, who need my contacts. Time is running out for them." His voice faded away as he looked off into the space beyond her. "I did some bad things in the past. I won't deny it. But I'd like to think this is my small way of making amends."

"Oskar, darling, are you ready to go?" Julia swept into the room, her black Persian lamb coat already slung around her shoulders. Her eyebrows rose as she saw Vivian standing by the fireplace. "Viv, what are you doing here? I thought you'd be in rehearsals all night."

Vivian exchanged a quick glance with Oskar. There was fear in his eyes, genuine fear that she would tell her mother everything right now, and the jig would be up. Vivian bit her lip. She looked at her mother. Why shouldn't she tell her? Didn't her mother deserve to know? But that one small truth would snowball into others, and Vivian wasn't ready to tell her mother that her husband had been murdered. She didn't think she'd ever be ready.

So she wouldn't say anything. Not for Oskar's sake, she decided, but for her mother's, and for the sakes of all of those people in Europe he claimed to be helping. She couldn't expose Oskar and have those lives on her conscience—not if he could actually help them somehow by keeping his past hidden.

"Rehearsal ended early. Do you mind if a few of the cast and crew come over here? We need to blow off a little steam."

"The play's not going well?"

The play? Her mother would never get the lingo right—purposely, Vivian thought. She sighed and shook her head. "I'm afraid tomorrow's live show is going to be rough."

Her mother tsked and had the good sense to at least look disappointed for her, Vivian thought. Even though inside she was likely secretly rejoicing, celebrating what could be another setback in Vivian's acting career.

"Can't you use the coach house?"

"Not enough room. I'm afraid we'd be packed in like sardines." Vivian smiled without mirth. "I'd have people toasting to the new year in the bathtub."

Her mother looked at her for a long moment, but then she returned Vivian's smile. She must have had a few cocktails with dinner, Vivian thought.

"That's fine, I suppose. As long as it's not too many people," her mother said. "But be mindful of the rugs. I've just had them cleaned."

Vivian nodded and looked at Oskar. He smiled at her and stood from the chair, snapping the radio off.

"Happy New Year, Vivian," he said. Then he leaned in and gave her a kiss on the cheek. His moustache was scratchy, and she fought the urge to recoil at his touch. She stared after them as they left, trying to parse together what Oskar had told her. He'd known all about her father. He'd introduced her father to the criminals that led him to Al Capone, and he didn't exactly apologize for it, did he? No, he'd turned it around on her so she was the one who felt guilty about uncovering the secret, about wanting to tell her mother that her current paramour was a liar. Oskar had successfully talked his way out of trouble, she thought, and it probably wasn't the first time he had done so.

———————————◆———————————

CHAPTER TWENTY-EIGHT

V ivian looked out the back kitchen window at the coach house. She could see everything from here—all the comings and goings.

"Oh, Vivian. I wasn't expecting you to be here."

Vivian turned to find Mrs. Graves. "Sorry to startle you," she said.

"Why aren't you out for the New Year?"

"I'm having some people over, a little party. We'll be quiet. I don't want to disturb you."

"Oh, no. Don't worry about me, dear. It is a night for celebrations."

Vivian wondered if Mrs. Graves had indeed been spying on her and reporting on the goings-on in the coach house to her mother. And what would it matter if she had? Soon Vivian would inherit enough money to move out from under her mother's roof forever. And she'd decided she would take it, even if it was tainted.

"I was thinking of mixing up a pitcher of Bloody Marys,"

Vivian said. "You know, hair of the dog for the morning." She motioned to the bottle of vodka on the counter in front of her.

"Your father's favorite. No one drinks those around here anymore with him gone."

Vivian thought of handing him that drink the night he died, and her stomach twisted. The housekeeper put one hand on Vivian's forearm.

"You've been thinking about your father a lot, haven't you?"

"I have with the holidays." She glanced at the housekeeper as she went about gathering the ingredients. Mrs. Graves disappeared into the pantry and then reappeared, her arms laden with a can of tomato juice, Worcestershire sauce, and black pepper.

"I've always felt guilty that I wasn't here when he died. Maybe I could have done something." Vivian felt her throat constrict. She did feel guilty, she realized. She always had.

"Oh, you couldn't have done a thing. When it's someone's time to go, it's their time to go."

Mrs. Graves face was grim, the corners of her mouth pulled down as she punched a triangular hole in the lid of the tomato juice can with the can opener and then dumped the blood-red liquid into the pitcher. She didn't meet Vivian's eye.

"I know," Vivian said. "But it bothers me that I don't actually know what happened."

Mrs. Graves said nothing in reply as she measured out and added the Worcestershire sauce.

"Could you tell me what happened? What his last moments were like?"

Mrs. Graves turned and looked at Vivian for a long moment, her forehead creased with worry. She wiped her hands thoroughly on her apron. "What do you want to know?"

"Tell me what happened after I left that night."

Mrs. Graves nodded. "Well, I took him his Bloody Mary, as usual."

Vivian shook her head. "I took him his Bloody Mary that night…before I left."

"You did?" The old housekeeper's brow furrowed in thought.

"Yes, and then you called me to the telephone a few minutes later."

The housekeeper looked confused. Vivian realized that Mrs. Graves's memory had faded and anything she might remember should be taken with a grain of salt.

"Yes, then I left, and I saw Della at the kitchen door on the way out," Vivian said. She remembered Della at the back door, wiping the slush from the treads of her shoes onto the mat.

"That's right. Della came over to retrieve some paperwork. We talked in the kitchen for a few minutes after you left, and then she went in…and found him…"

"He was already dead?"

"Yes. Della screamed." Mrs. Graves grimaced and shook her head at the memory. "Then she called for my help, and

I hurried in. He was gone. Slumped over in his chair." She shook her head.

"What did he look like?"

Mrs. Graves blinked. "Pale...himself, but not. His hand was on his chest." She shook her head again. She either couldn't or didn't want to remember anything more. "I'm sorry, but it happens, Vivian. People have heart attacks all the time—even the ones who seem to be the picture of health." She put her hand lightly on Vivian's arm. Then she turned back to her task. She was silent for a long moment before adding, "Though your father hadn't been feeling at all well that day."

"He hadn't?" She thought of him that night—pale, drawn, wincing with a hand on his chest.

"He came home in the early afternoon for some bicarbonate of soda. He'd had lunch somewhere with a client, had eaten something he shouldn't have. You know how touchy your father's stomach was. I don't know why he insisted on Bloody Marys every evening. They gave him terrible heartburn."

"He was a stubborn man," Vivian said absently. She remembered going to the icebox that evening after he'd died, looking to nip some of the Bloody Mary, but the pitcher had been gone. She assumed someone else had beaten her to it. Her mother? Della? Mrs. Graves herself?

"Was he alone when he came home that afternoon?"

So far, this was the same story that Della had told, Vivian

thought. Her father had been having chest pains—a sure sign of a heart problem.

Mrs. Graves's brow furrowed. "I don't recall, but I imagine that Herbert had driven him. He usually did." She looked off over Vivian's shoulder.

"And what about the car accident afterward?" It was only after she registered Mrs. Graves's pinched expression that Vivian realized she'd spoken aloud.

The older woman shrugged. "Herbert was driving Mr. Gilfoy back from a late night at the office. They hit some ice."

The office, Vivian thought. She shook her head.

"Martin said it happened on Ogden. Yes, he said Ogden was a solid sheet of ice that night." And Ogden Avenue was nowhere near the route they'd have taken back from the office. She was sure he'd said Ogden—and what was on the other end of Ogden Avenue? Cicero, that's what. The Racquet Club was in Cicero.

Mrs. Graves didn't answer. She wasn't going to answer. She'd turned away, the subject still too painful to discuss.

Vivian didn't know what to believe anymore. Either Mrs. Graves was mistaken or Martin was. And what did it matter anymore? All signs did, indeed, point to a heart attack. Maybe Moochie had only been trying to stir up trouble—spreading rumors with no truth behind them. Maybe Vivian was looking for a pattern that didn't exist.

CHAPTER TWENTY-NINE

G raham had shown up to the party at eleven forty, looking his old dapper self and bearing a bottle of champagne. Vivian had been so surprised when she met him at the door that she didn't know what to say.

"Here's to a good performance," he'd said, handing her the bottle. She knew that he meant the performance between the two of them. They had to pretend their quarrel was all made up, didn't they? She was angry with him for perpetuating this lie, for not letting her explain, and for not trusting her enough to tell her the truth.

She'd stared at him and watched him walk into the den. Vivian had followed as far as the doorway, the bottle of champagne clutched in her hands. She watched everyone clustered around the piano. Morty played "A-Tisket, A-Tasket" while Frances sang. Vivian was pleased to note that Frances's singing voice was nothing special. Then her eyes trained on Graham. He was smiling and singing along as if he hadn't a care in the world. Maybe he hadn't, she thought. There was still the possibility that Gloria had misunderstood the situation. But how could Vivian go on pretending that she didn't suspect? And even if it wasn't true, how could she go on pretending that Graham was her one and only? No, this had to end. Tonight.

There was a knock on the door behind her. She jumped, her nerves on edge. Who could be knocking at almost midnight on New Year's Eve? Everyone she'd invited to the party was already here—Graham, Imogene, Morty Nickerson, Dave Chapman, Bill Purdy, Joe McGreevey, Frances. Even though Vivian knew that the man following her had been one of Gloria's undergraduate friends, she was still tense. She tiptoed over to the window at the side, intending to take a peek, when the top of a man's head popped into view from the opposite side of the glass. She jumped again, heart hammering, and then realized it was Charlie.

She threw open the door.

"Oh, Charlie…" She had to stop herself from flinging herself into his arms.

"What's wrong?"

"It's nothing," she lied. "It's been a rough night." She was glad to see him, but she was overwhelmed with everything that had happened. She wanted to see him alone, not with a house full of people lurking around. She glanced over her shoulder toward the singing in the den. Then she turned and walked farther into the dark foyer. He followed.

"Where have you been? I've been calling all day."

"Rehearsing."

A raucous shout went up from the group in the den as Morty launched into a jaunty rendition of "You Must Have Been a Beautiful Baby." Charlie's eyes moved to the bottle of champagne she still held.

"And working hard, from the sound of it."

"Oh, posh," she said, rolling her eyes. *Of all the times for Charlie to get jealous*, she thought. She set the bottle on the hall table. "We've been rehearsing all day. I invited everyone over to let off a little steam. So you came to check up on me?"

"Of course not."

She sighed in frustration. She was irritated—not at Charlie, but she knew it sounded like she was. Her mood had nothing to do with him and everything to do with him, and she couldn't tell him one thing about it, not yet.

"I'm sorry. I'm under a lot of pressure to help pull this *Pimpernel* show off tomorrow night, and from all indications today, it isn't going to go well."

"Sorry to hear that."

They stood awkwardly in the foyer for a moment. Vivian knew he was expecting her to invite him in, but she couldn't do that. She was supposed to have told Graham about them today. It should be all settled, not still up in the air as it was. So for the interim, Graham couldn't see Charlie, and Charlie couldn't see Graham. She didn't want Charlie to leave, but he had to. If he didn't, there was sure to be a scene.

"I came by because you weren't answering the telephone and I have something to tell you. Something important about your father."

"I don't want to hear any more about my father," she said in a low voice. She half turned, intending to leave him and the subject in the foyer, but he grabbed her arm and whirled her around to face him. She grimaced at the pain in her injured hip.

"I know who your father was supposed to meet the day after his death," Charlie said.

"So," she said impatiently, "what does it matter now?"

"It matters a lot, actually."

Vivian wrenched herself from Charlie's grasp. "Well?"

Charlie glanced over her shoulder toward the ruckus in the den. He frowned. "Isn't there somewhere more private we can talk?"

Vivian's stomach clenched. "I thought you promised not to tell me if what you found out was worse than what we already knew."

"I know," he said. "It's not worse."

Confused, Vivian limped up the stairs, Charlie trailing behind. She rushed into her father's study and shut the door. She leaned back against it, hands on the knob.

"So what is it?"

"Maybe you should sit."

"I don't want to sit. You said it wasn't worse."

He paced in front of the desk for a moment, his eyes

roaming over the shelves, the framed photos showcasing her father's storied career. He paused and studied her father arm in arm with Big Bill Thompson for a long moment and then turned to her, his hat in his hands.

"The name in the appointment book was Wilson," he said.

"Wilson?"

"Frank Wilson, the Treasury agent who made the case against Capone."

Vivian shook her head slightly. Capone. The name was like a smack in the face. More evidence of her father's relationship with the mob boss.

"I spoke to Frank Wilson this afternoon by telephone. Your father called him a few days before he died, Viv. Set up that appointment personally. Said he had something big."

Vivian stared at him. "The ledger?"

He nodded. "Wilson said that all your father told him was that he had something big for him. And that the ledger was one part of it."

She suddenly remembered her father's intense look of unease at the front page of the *Tribune* the night of his death. The headline screaming in all caps CAPONE CITY HALL BOSS. He was going to give what he had, what he knew, to a federal agent the next day. No wonder he'd been nervous, not himself.

"I don't know what to say," she said, her voice a croak.

"You don't have to say anything. I think it's enough that

you know. I wanted you to know that no matter what your father may have done before, he was on the right side at the end. Or trying to be on the right side."

"At the end…" Vivian said numbly. They looked at each other in tense silence.

Charlie stepped forward and put his hands lightly on her hips. Vivian gasped and jumped at the intense pain that shot up from her most recent injury.

Charlie jerked backward. "What is it?"

"I fell."

"Slipped on the ice again?"

"Not exactly."

Charlie's brow furrowed in concern. "You're hurt."

Vivian rubbed her hip. "Not too badly."

He put his hand lightly over hers. "You're taking a beating this week." He pulled her other hand up into his and pressed it to his chest.

"I'll survive."

She considered telling Charlie about being followed, but she didn't have any proof that the young man in the cap was anything more than an innocent journalism student. She didn't have any proof that someone had pushed Della in front of that streetcar, or that the cleaners hadn't knocked the plants off the windowsill with the vacuum cleaner cord. She also had no proof that her father hadn't had a heart attack, or that Oskar knew more about all of this than he'd let on.

Everything was a jumble in her head. If she could sit and think for a minute, she might come to understand how it all fit together. Or more likely she would come to the conclusion that none of it fit together at all, that her imagination had been running away with her.

Charlie pulled her injured hand toward him and kissed it lightly. Then he pulled her even closer, pressing her cheek to his chest. She couldn't think right now. She didn't want to. Right now, it felt good to be wrapped in Charlie's arms.

She tilted her chin up. His lips were on hers, and everything else faded away. Vivian didn't hear the telltale creak of the step. She did hear the gasp though, like the air from a deflating balloon.

She pulled back and turned toward the source of the interruption: Graham, in the doorway, holding two glasses of champagne, his mouth dropped open into an almost comical O of surprise. Then the countdown started from the group downstairs: *10, 9, 8, 7…*

They all stared at one another in suspended animation until the countdown reached its zenith. A tremendous racket erupted on the floor below from party horns and ratchet noisemakers. The year 1939 was starting with a bang in more ways than one, Vivian thought. The racket finally broke Graham's paralysis. He blinked, closed his mouth, and opened it again.

"I demand an explanation." His eyes darted from Vivian to Charlie and back again.

"Graham, this isn't—" she said, trying to pull away from the circle of Charlie's arms.

But Charlie pulled her even more tightly to him. "No, actually, it's *exactly* what it looks like," he said.

"I…" Graham began. Then he stopped, looking down at the champagne glasses in his hands. Then his brown eyes flicked up to meet Vivian's. By all rights, he should be outraged, but he didn't seem able to muster the enthusiasm for it. There was something in Graham's dark eyes that Vivian couldn't quite place.

"I'm sorry," she said. "I wanted to tell you everything today, but you wouldn't let me."

Graham frowned at her. "Yes." He glanced backward toward the raucousness of the party below. He didn't turn back immediately but stood lost in thought. "Let's not ruin the party for everyone with a big nasty scene, eh? We'll talk this over tomorrow."

Vivian watched as Graham stepped forward and placed one of the champagne flutes on the desk in front of her and then turned on his heel and left the room without another word. She glanced at Charlie, registering the confusion on his face and certain it was mirrored, to a lesser extent, in her own.

"Well, he certainly took that in stride," Charlie said, glancing back toward the now-empty doorway.

The crowd downstairs had burst into a rather off-key rendition of "Auld Lang Syne." Vivian gazed at the bubbles rising to pop at the surface of the champagne Graham had left for her. Then she placed the emotion she'd seen flit behind Graham's dark eyes at seeing Vivian and Charlie together. It hadn't been jealousy or even anger. No, it had been fear.

CHAPTER THIRTY

V ivian's head thrummed. Somewhere in the cotton wool of her mind, there was a ringing telephone. She felt the pillow beside her. Empty. That's right. Charlie had left. After Graham had caught them kissing...

Graham. Her mind spun in circles around the name. Graham had disappeared by the time she'd finally gone downstairs to explain. Then she'd drunk glass after glass of champagne, and now her mind wasn't working correctly. She rubbed her temples.

She glanced at the alarm clock—12:14 p.m. Had she slept the morning away? What day was it? New Year's Day. That's right. She'd had a party, and quite a lot to drink after Charlie and Graham had gone. She pulled herself from the warm bed and padded into the front room. She picked up the receiver to quiet the insistent ring.

"Hello?" Her throat was scratchy, thick.

"Viv. It's Freddy."

"Oh, Freddy." She slumped against the table. "I'll have to

call you back. I'm not feeling so well." She noticed the note next to the telephone.

Spent the night on your couch. Went out for a bit. Stay here. C

She smiled. Charlie hadn't left her after all. She should have known.

"I'm afraid not, Viv. There are some things we need to discuss."

"Like what?"

"Well, in the spirit of the new year, I want to apologize. For not telling you the truth about your father from the beginning."

"The truth…"

Vivian's stomach dropped. It was too early in the day for more unwelcome revelations. She suddenly wanted to retch. Her eyes scanned the room for a suitable spot. "Can't this wait?"

"No. I'm sorry. If I don't tell you this now, I may never do it."

She didn't especially feel like being Freddy's confessional—not this morning, afternoon, whatever it was. Why should she be the one to ease Freddy's conscience? And what exactly did he want to get off his chest? She felt nauseous, and not just because of her monstrous hangover. She decided to cut him off at the pass.

"Well, if it's any consolation, I already know what you're going to tell me," she said, wincing at the volume of her own voice. "You knew what my father had been up to, didn't you? His involvement with the Racquet Club? What he was doing with that ledger? All of it."

"All of it?"

"You're a terrible liar, Freddy."

Freddy sighed heavily into the receiver. "I was a coward, Viv, and I didn't think things would get this far," he answered. "I thought you would give up long before you came upon the truth. And, truth be told, I wanted you to go on believing your father was the upstanding man you always thought he was."

There was a twinge in Vivian's stomach. She almost wished that too. Freddy had tried to warn her, to his credit. He'd tried to get her to leave it when they'd found that ledger. Why hadn't he told her the truth? Sat her down and told her everything? Why had he let her twist in the wind? Maybe he was a coward, or maybe he wanted to tell her a carefully curated version of the truth to get her to stop asking questions.

"So you knew what the ledger was from the second we laid eyes on it, and you knew who he was going to give it to?" she asked.

There was a long silence on the other end of the line.

"Yes," Freddy finally said. He sounded defeated. "Your father had been subpoenaed, Vivian."

"Subpoenaed?"

"By the prosecutor leveling the tax case against Capone."

Wilson, she thought absently. A thought niggled at her. Hadn't Charlie said last night that her father had called Wilson and volunteered the information? He hadn't said anything about a subpoena, had he? She placed the flat of her hand against her throbbing temple.

"You ripped that page out of his appointment book," she said. "The one dated the day after his death. The one with 'W-son' written on it."

There was a long pause. She'd surprised him.

"Yes," he said finally.

"Why?"

"Because I worried that one day you or your mother or Everett would start to piece things together, figure things out. Then you'd realize what Arthur had been up to all those years, and your memory of a wonderful man would be tarnished by a few bad decisions he made."

"Well, I did figure it out, Freddy," she said bitterly.

"Yes, well, you were the one I was the most worried about. You've always been the sharpest knife in the drawer."

Vivian laughed, her throat like sandpaper. That laugh abruptly turned to a dry, coughing sob.

"I'm worried about you, Viv," Freddy said finally, his voice weary.

She hitched in her breath and steadied herself. She sounded hysterical. She *was* hysterical. *I'm worried about myself*, she wanted to answer.

"Don't be," she said. "Now that I know what Father was up to, what kind of a man he was, I'll let sleeping dogs lie." *That may or may not be the truth*, she thought. She hadn't decided, but she was certainly leaning toward not disturbing them now. She wouldn't be doing any more digging today anyway—not with this throbbing head and the sure-to-be disastrous *Pimpernel* to prepare for.

"Good. Have you spoken to your mother about any of this?"

"No."

"Don't," he said. "She doesn't know anything about it. Any of it, Viv. It would only hurt her to find out now."

Vivian nodded, swallowing the lump in her throat. There was a long pause, and she thought maybe the connection had been dropped, but then Freddy spoke again.

"Look, Viv, I feel like I can't leave it this way—a discussion over the telephone. Can we meet to talk it through?"

"I can't now."

"Later, then?"

"Maybe. I have to go. Good-bye, Freddy."

"Wait. I want you to know that your father was my best friend, Viv," He paused and then said, his voice raw with emotion, "I want you to understand that what I did... I did it to protect you and your mother and Everett."

"Good-bye," she said.

She set the receiver gently down in its cradle. *What he did*, she thought. He lied. But perhaps he'd meant something else as well. What else had Freddy done? Her mind refused to take that thought any further. Then she hurried across the room and was abruptly sick into the wastepaper bin.

Vivian poured herself a tall glass of Bloody Mary and stood at the kitchen counter staring down at the red liquid. It seemed so ominous, the color of blood. Still, she sorely needed it this afternoon if she was going to make it in to do *The Pimpernel* in a few hours. She took a long gulp and winced as the liquid sloshed in her empty stomach.

"Drinking already?" Everett had come into the room.

"Hair of the dog," she said without turning.

"Rough night?"

"You could say that. How was your New Year's?"

"Great. Gloria and I went to the Aragon and danced the soles of our shoes off."

Gloria, she thought sourly. Just the thought of the girl turned her stomach. Everett poured himself a glass and took a sip. He made a "not bad" expression and then leaned down, his voice a whisper. "Anything new about Father? Who took that money from his desk?"

A lot, but none of it substantiated, she thought. She shook her head. "I'm starting to think all of this is for nothing," she said. "Father's gone. And nothing I dig up will bring him back."

Everett nodded.

"I think that's best, Viv," he said. Then he patted her shoulder. He took his glass and headed out of the kitchen. "Oh, and Mother was looking for you," he tossed over his shoulder.

Vivian gazed at the family photo on the mantel. It was the one she'd taken to Charlie's office. She glanced from her younger self to the others in the circle of faces: her mother, her father, Everett. They all seemed so happy. She looked again at her own face, leaned in. She was smiling, but she knew she'd been anything but happy then.

"Oh, hello, Vivian. How was your party?" her mother said as she entered the room.

"It was fine."

"Just fine?"

"Yes." She thought of the embarrassing scene with Graham and shuddered. She'd have to face him today. They'd have to finally get everything out on the table. It was past time. She continued down the line of framed photos on the mantel. She stopped at the photo of her mother's sister and her family.

"Why didn't Aunt Adaline come to the Christmas party?"

"Oh, you know she never comes, so I don't even invite her anymore."

"She only lives ten miles away, and you never see her."

Her mother shrugged.

"Did something happen between you two?"

Her mother pursed her lips. "Not as such. Adaline is older than me, and ten years can make a big difference between siblings. I didn't know her growing up. She was married and out of the house by the time I was eight years old. We were never close."

She didn't sound especially sorry about it, Vivian thought. Adaline had married a man from another Chicago industrial family, and her husband had taken over the running of the family meatpacking business. Vivian's eyes strayed to the next photo—of her mother's eldest sister and her family. A pasty older husband and two pasty boys who would now be pasty men of the gentry. They lived on an estate in the English countryside. She'd met all of them once when the family took an abbreviated grand tour of Europe when Vivian was twelve. She didn't think of it much, but her mother's eldest sister had a title—an actual title.

Both of her mother's older sisters had made much better marriages than her mother had. Her sisters had married men with storied families. Vivian's father had no family, no wealth. What he had made of himself, he'd made exactly that way—by himself. He'd inherited nothing except his intelligence and charm.

"You know, you never told me how you met Father," Vivian said.

Her mother glanced at her, not hiding her suspicion at Vivian's reasons for asking such a question out of the blue.

"My father brought him to dinner."

"And?"

"And I liked him."

"Ah, the romance," Vivian said, sarcasm dripping from her voice. This was like pulling teeth.

"He was my father's attorney—one of his attorneys. He was fresh out of law school then." Her mother leaned toward Vivian slightly and smiled. "And he was so handsome."

"And just like that, you got married?"

Her mother laughed. "Not quite. I held him off for a long time."

"Why?"

Her mother tipped her chin down and studied Vivian for a long moment. "Well, Arthur was charming, and I was quite taken with him, but my heart was still mending when we met."

"Mending?"

"I'd been promised to another man. He died quite suddenly of pneumonia two months before we were to be married. I was nineteen."

Vivian didn't know what to say. She'd never known that about her mother. She thought of that apple-cheeked girl in the photo from her mother's study. Her mother hadn't been far removed from that and was already dealing with heartbreak.

"I'm sorry," Vivian said. "That must have been terrible."

"It was, I didn't know what to do with myself. I considered entering a convent. My mother quickly put an end to that idea. And then I met your father, and he pursued me until I accepted him."

Her mother fussed over the tinsel on the tree, picking up a strand from one branch and placing it on another.

"I've set that meeting with the attorney over your inheritance for January 12. Will that be all right?"

Vivian turned and looked over her shoulder at her mother. "I suppose."

"A Mr. Henrick—his office is on Monroe and LaSalle."

"Uncle Freddy's not handling it?"

"Your father arranged it through Mr. Henrick. That's all I know."

"I've been thinking a lot about Father this past week... since you told me about the inheritance. And I was wondering... Did you know anything about Father's business? About his clients?"

Her mother shook her head. "I stayed out of your father's business."

"Of course you did."

"Your father was a defense attorney for a long time, criminal cases... I know enough to know that everyone he represented couldn't possibly have been innocent of what they were accused of."

"So you decided to look the other way."

"Oh, Vivian."

"Don't 'Oh, Vivian' me. Father was involved with some bad people."

Her mother stared at her. "Why on earth would you think such a thing of your father, Vivian?"

Vivian swallowed and looked down at the floor.

Her mother didn't know after all. It was obvious in her expression—the outrage at the idea that her father had knowingly done anything beyond the pale. Vivian found herself both relieved and disappointed. Relieved that her mother hadn't been lying to her this whole time, and disappointed that Julia could be so obtuse. Her mother saw what she wanted to see, and she certainly hadn't wanted to see what her husband had been up to, and where the money to support her cushy lifestyle had come from.

"I don't know why I said that," Vivian said, feeling chastised. "I'm sorry. I've been under a lot of pressure lately at the station with *The Pimpernel* and *The Darkness Knows*." She wondered how long she could keep using work as an excuse.

Her mother harrumphed. "I think maybe with this inheritance, it's time to finally quit all that nonsense."

Vivian looked into the crackling fire and pretended she hadn't heard.

CHAPTER THIRTY-ONE

❖

The front door of the coach house opened under Vivian's fingertips. Hadn't she locked it when she left? She pushed the door the rest of the way open and braced herself for confrontation. What she wouldn't give for that cast-iron pan right now! The front room was dim, but she could make out the outline of someone sitting on the sofa.

"Where have you been?" a voice boomed from the darkness.

Charlie.

Vivian let the breath she'd been holding out in a whoosh. "You scared the life out of me. What are you doing sitting here in the dark?"

"I asked you first. Where have you been?" He reached over, and the table lamp sprang to life, illuminating the scowl on his handsome face.

"Arguing with Mother."

"I told you to stay here." He held the note up in the yellow glow of the lamplight and pointed to those very words. "I underlined it."

Vivian stuck her lower lip out and exhaled so that her bangs ruffled. "Posh. I didn't even leave the property."

She flopped down next to him on the sofa. She rested her aching head against his shoulder and closed her eyes. His hand cupped the back of her head, fingers threading through her hair to massage her scalp. She sighed with pleasure.

"You came back last night," she said.

"I was worried about you. I didn't like the idea of you being here all alone. Especially after what I'd told you last night—and what you told me. And how Yarborough reacted to seeing us together. So I let myself in." She felt him shrug. Let himself in was his way of saying he picked the lock—if she'd even remembered to lock the door in her drunken state.

"And when you let yourself in, I was..."

"Sleeping like a kitten."

She grunted in reply. It wasn't terribly comforting that someone, even someone as benign as Charlie, had gained entry to her house while she was sleeping and she'd been none the wiser.

He pulled away, and Vivian opened her eyes briefly to watch him plop two Alka-Seltzers in a glass of water. He nudged the fizzing glass toward her on the coffee table, but Vivian didn't reach for it. She didn't want to move from this spot—ever. She wanted to curl up in Charlie's lap and ignore the world.

"You talk in your sleep, you know," he said.

"Do I? What do I say?" She resettled herself on his broad shoulder and closed her eyes again, almost instantly on the edge of drifting off to sleep.

He laughed. It sounded wonderful, she thought, Charlie's laugh. She didn't hear it often enough.

"Something about lambs. Odd lambs."

"Odd lambs?" she said lazily.

"You kept repeating it. Those odd lambs had you in a lather."

Vivian opened her eyes and lifted her head. It rewarded her with a painful thump. She stared out the window, lost in thought. Odd lambs. Odd lambs. The connection was so close to clicking into place. Then it did.

"Not odd lambs, Charlie," she said, her pulse quickening. "Odollam."

"Odollam? What's that?"

"A plant Della grows—grew—in the office. The cleaners knocked it off the sill and destroyed it yesterday."

"Why are you dreaming about one of Della's plants?"

She wasn't exactly sure, but maybe her brain had kept working on things even while she'd been sleeping last night. She tried to remember what the dream had been about, but it was gone except for the feeling of unease it had left in its wake.

"I don't know. But she was terribly proud of that plant and very upset that it was ruined. She kept it in a glass cloche because it was tropical and hard to grow in this climate."

Charlie pulled back to look at her. His smile was gone. "Destroyed yesterday, you said?"

"Pulverized."

Charlie reached out to smooth a strand of hair behind her ear. He thought for a moment. "Dreams are strange things, Viv. I had one the other night that I was having a Gin Rickey with Sherlock Holmes. Probably because of all the Occam's razor talk. Dreams don't mean anything at all."

They looked at each other for a moment. Then Charlie smiled at her, and his hand slid from her temple to the back of her neck, and he rubbed up and down her vertebrae with his strong fingers. Vivian took a long sip of the Alka-Seltzer and put her head back down on his shoulder.

She fell asleep like that and woke an hour later stretched out on the sofa. Charlie was still there, reading the newspaper at the table, the ledger at his elbow. He'd brought it back, Vivian thought, the sight of the book churning her guts. She didn't want that thing in her house. That ledger was like an albatross around her neck.

And the odollam still flitted in the back of her mind. She didn't agree that all dreams were nonsense. Her headache was gone, and she decided that she'd like to sit in her father's study for a few minutes before Charlie drove her to the station. Being there might give her some peace of mind. Being there might help things fall into place once and for all.

The house was quiet. Her mother and Everett were both out. Vivian sat in the leather desk chair, staring off into space. She wasn't purposely thinking of anything. Her mind seemed to work better when she didn't focus. When she didn't force connections to be made. Unfortunately, that method wasn't working this time.

The board creaked in the hall, and Vivian turned her head expectantly toward the open door. The housekeeper came into view.

"Hello, Mrs. Graves. Happy New Year."

The older woman smiled. She paused at the edge of the desk, one hand pressed to something in the pocket of her apron. "I find you in here a lot lately."

"Yes." Vivian cocked her head and considered the housekeeper. There was something odd about her. Her stance, her expression. She wouldn't look Vivian directly in the eye.

"There's something I need to tell you," Mrs. Graves said. Her voice was low, almost a whisper.

Vivian's stomach twisted. *More confessions. More secrets.* She held a hand up to stop the woman, not wanting to hear any more.

Mrs. Graves pulled something from her pocket and held it in front of Vivian. An envelope. *The* envelope, still fat with cash. Vivian glanced quickly up at the housekeeper in confusion.

"*You* took it? Why?"

The elderly woman shrugged. Funny that Vivian had never noticed how old she was until right now. Her hair was no longer just steely gray; it was also starting to thin— getting that cobwebby look that an old woman's hair has. Her eyes were tiny behind her spectacles and sagging upper lids. "I was trying to dissuade you from digging into your father's business."

"You knew about…his business?"

She nodded. "Herbert was his valet, his right-hand man. He knew everything."

"And he told you *everything*?"

The housekeeper looked off toward the framed photos on the bookcase. "Not all of it, but enough."

Herbert Graves. Her father's valet. The valet that had died a month after her father. He'd known everything. Too much, like her father.

She blinked and followed the housekeeper's gaze to the framed photos on the wall.

Mrs. Graves turned back to her. She reached out suddenly and squeezed Vivian's hand. Then her brow furrowed.

"Oh, my dear," she said. "I'm so sorry for stirring all of this up. I was trying to help you, but I ended up making things worse, didn't I?"

Yes, she had made things worse, Vivian thought. Infinitely worse. If she hadn't taken that money, Vivian might have gone on with the rest of her life, never truly knowing what her father had been up to all that time. All the time he pretended to be the model husband and father. But Vivian shook her head and patted the elderly woman's hand.

Then she gazed down at the envelope of money sitting on the desktop. She was going to lock it back in the drawer and put the keys back where she found them and try to never think of this again. Yes, that's exactly what she would do.

Mrs. Graves had turned to go, but then she paused and turned back.

"And please tell Mr. Gilfoy when you see him next that I'm sorry for the way I acted the other night. He's a nice boy. And he's not responsible for what happened to my Herbert. I suppose I was startled to see him after all this time. It stirred up a lot of memories, and I behaved badly."

Vivian nodded. Martin had said he'd suspected they'd been forced off the road, hadn't he? Had someone purposely tried to kill Mrs. Graves and Martin too? Mr. Graves was gone, but what did Martin know? More than she'd originally suspected. He'd been so close to her father. Was Martin in danger too? From whom? No, it was over, she thought. She'd decided this was over, and it had to be.

Vivian's head throbbed. Her headache had come back with a vengeance.

"Oh dear," Mrs. Graves said, looking at the clock on the

bookshelf. "Is it four o'clock already? I need to get some dinner started."

Vivian glanced at the clock. Four o'clock? She was due at the station in half an hour.

The telephone on the desk rang, startling them both, and Mrs. Graves reached over to answer it. Vivian's mind immediately replayed the conversation they'd just had. It seemed that she, her mother, and Everett were the only ones that *hadn't* known what Arthur Witchell been up to.

Mrs. Graves held the receiver out under Vivian's nose.

"Mr. Gilfoy for you," she said.

Speak of the devil. She took a deep breath and grabbed the receiver. She forced a smile to her face and into her voice.

"Hello, Martin. Did you say hello to the mayor for me?"

He laughed. "Yes, yes, he sends his regards."

"How was the party?"

"As much of a bore as I thought it would be—especially without you."

Vivian glanced down at the desk. She'd have to tell him sooner or later about Charlie, and now was as good a time as any. She sucked in her breath.

"Had a bit of excitement on the way home though…an accident," he continued.

Her head jerked up in alarm, and she let her breath out in a whoosh. Bad news was coming at a rapid clip today.

"An accident?"

"I'm fine. Nothing to worry about."

"What happened?"

"Well, the brakes went out on the old Cadillac, and I slid into a ditch."

Her heart lurched and then started to hammer in her chest. "Your brakes went out? My God, Martin."

"I'm fine." He sighed. "I'm sorry. I've worried you. That's the last thing I wanted to do."

"What happened?"

"Don't know. I pressed the brakes, and they didn't respond. Luckily, the street was deserted at that time of night, and I skidded into a little ditch. I'm not going to lie. I was frightened out of my wits, flashbacks to my previous accident and all that, but I wasn't hurt in the slightest. No other cars involved. Had to get a tow truck to pull it out—took forever on New Year's Eve, mind you. And for that, and that reason alone, I was glad to not have you with me last night."

"Oh…" She couldn't say anything else. He was blasé about it, but suddenly she was certain. This had been no accident. Someone had pushed Della in front of a streetcar, and that someone had also cut Martin's brake lines. Who could have done such a thing except the person who had killed her father? Martin and Della knew too much. That was apparent. But *what* exactly did they know?

"Is it on? I'll tune in."

"I'm…I'm sorry?"

"Your show, *The Pimpernel*. When's it on tonight?"

Yes. Yes, The Pimpernel. She still had that to do. She glanced at the mantel clock. It was already four ten. She needed to get to the station soon.

"It's at seven tonight."

"I'll be listening."

"Martin," she said, the whole story on the tip of her tongue. She needed to warn him, but how could she? There wasn't time, and if she couldn't explain everything now, she didn't want to worry him unnecessarily.

"Yes?"

"I think someone may be trying to hurt you. Promise me you'll be careful."

"Of course," he said. She could hear the amusement in his voice. He wasn't taking her warning seriously. Why would he? "Don't worry about me, Viv. I'm used to attempts on my life. I make a lot of people unhappy in my line of work."

"That's not funny."

"Sorry. A little gallows humor, I guess." He paused, and when he spoke again, his voice was more serious. "I assure you, Viv. No one's out to get me. Life isn't like the movies. Brakes wear down, go out all the time. It was happenstance that it occurred to me last night. Car's in the garage getting fixed up as we speak. And if it makes you feel any better, the entirety of my plans for the day are to stick by the radio with bated breath, waiting to hear your beautiful voice. Hey, I've got an idea. What would you say if I pick you up at the station after the show and we have a celebratory late supper?" He paused and then added, "Pick you up with a different car, of course. Brake lines intact."

She smiled in spite of the guilt roiling her stomach. It was a shame. Finally something she and her mother agreed on: Martin would be perfect for her—perfect if Charlie didn't exist, that was.

"I'd love to…" Her voice trailed off regretfully.

"But you can't."

"I'm not sure how the evening's going to go. If things turn out badly, I'm sure I won't be fit company for any sort of celebratory supper. If it goes well, then I'll be celebrating with the cast and crew, I suppose."

"A late night for you either way," he said. She could hear the disappointment in his voice, and she felt terrible for leading him on—even if it was unavoidable.

"I'm sorry," she said. "I'll call you tomorrow, okay?"

"I look forward to it."

If he only knew what she would to tell him, she thought. Not just about Charlie. All of it. He might not look so forward to the conversation.

"Break a leg," he said.

"Thanks. Good-bye, Martin."

"Bye, Viv."

She hung up the receiver. *Break a leg* was an ironic thing for Martin to say, she thought, especially considering what that accident had done to his own leg. Especially after what had happened to him last night.

CHAPTER THIRTY-TWO

❖

Vivian watched Charlie's profile in the flash of city lights as he drove her to the station.

"Mrs. Graves took the money? Why?"

Vivian shrugged and twisted her gloved hands in her lap. "She wanted to shield me from the truth about my father," she said.

"Well, I'd say that attempt failed spectacularly."

Vivian let out a shaky laugh. "I would have dropped the whole thing if she'd left that cash where it was. And I may have been the one person in Chicago that hadn't known all along what my father was up to. Well, me, Everett, and Mother." She looked out the window as they made their way over the Chicago River. "I mean, even your father knew, Charlie." It was still odd, she thought. Having met Charlie's father in that way. She glanced at him, feeling the smile creep onto her face despite everything. "He really liked me?" she asked.

"Of course he did," Charlie said. "Why wouldn't he?"

He winked at her, and she felt the warmth in the pit of her stomach.

She wanted to ask what Charlie had told his father about her, about them, but she wouldn't. She didn't want to jinx anything now that she had him back. Well, had him back for the moment. There was still the small issue of Graham.

"Do you think Martin's okay?"

Charlie shrugged. "Hard to say. Probably if he stays at home like he said he would, he'll be fine."

"I hope so."

Charlie looked sharply at her as he pulled up in front of the Grayson–Cole Building, but he said nothing. He put the car in Park and they sat there for a long moment, the engine idling roughly. Vivian watched snowflakes drift down in the yellow arc of the streetlights.

"Come in with me," she said. "You can watch the train wreck from the control room. Front-row seat…"

"I *would* like a word with Yarborough."

Vivian's heart thumped as she studied Charlie's expression. She was so close now. She couldn't risk Charlie ruining everything, knocking the whole delicate house of cards down around her before she could dismantle it herself.

"Charlie…I said I'd handle it with Graham. Maybe it's best if you don't come in."

Charlie sighed, eyeing the building. "I can't anyway. Not yet."

She stroked his arm and leaned in to peck him on the cheek. He accepted it, but as she drew away, he caught her by the waist and drew her back for a proper kiss. Then she pulled away again, laughing breathlessly as she dodged his searching hand.

"I'll meet you right here afterward," he said.

She slid to the passenger side door and opened it. She leaned down before closing the door to smile at him.

"Right here," he said sternly.

"Yes, sir." Then she saluted and turned to walk through the front doors of WCHI.

Someone grabbed her arm as soon as she came off the elevator. Vivian started and pulled her arm away. It was Graham.

"You owe me an explanation," he hissed.

"*You're* the one who owes *me* an explanation."

His eyebrows rose, but he said nothing.

"Honestly, Graham, I didn't think you would care," she said.

"Wouldn't care?" he asked, incredulous. His eyes darted up and down the empty hallway. "My girl is out kissing other men, and doing God knows what else. Why in hell wouldn't I care?" His face was flushed.

"Not other *men*, plural," Vivian said. "Just Charlie."

He waved a hand at her dismissively. He nodded his head

toward the alcove near the elevator, and they stepped into it for the modicum of privacy it provided.

"You told me you hadn't heard from him, and this whole time—"

"This whole time, nothing," she said, her anger rising. "Cut the jealous act, Graham. You know I'm not your girl, and you don't want me to be."

"What are you talking about, Viv?" There was wariness in his voice now.

"Graham. I know," she said.

"Know what?"

"I *know*," Vivian said again. He was going to make her say it, wasn't he? Graham looked at her, his face a careful blank. "I know your secret..." she whispered. "The one that would ruin you if it got out."

Graham's face turned from deep pink to white in an instant. "I don't have any secrets," he said.

He was still denying it, and if she dropped it now, he would deny it forever.

"I know about Paul," she said, and it was like she'd slapped him in the face.

Graham's mouth dropped open, but he snapped it shut quickly, coming to his senses. "You don't know anything," he retorted. He turned his back to her.

"I *know*, Graham," she repeated slowly. There could be no mistaking her tone. Did he want her to say it outright? That she knew he preferred men? That she was a front to keep anyone from suspecting, to keep him from ruining his hopes for a Hollywood career?

"What are you going to do about it?" Graham asked, his back still to her. His voice was tight.

Do? She hadn't thought there was anything for her to do. She hadn't thought past confronting him with the knowledge.

He turned to face her, pleading in his eyes. "What do you want?"

"Want?"

"You already have a starring role," he said, his voice panicked, the words running together. "I'll get you in on those Sultan's Gold ads…"

Vivian shook her head, her face growing hot with indignation. "This isn't a black-hand scheme, Graham."

His eyes narrowed. "Then what is it?"

Vivian shrugged. "You lied to me," she said, surprised at the tremolo in her voice. Surprised at how much it mattered to her. The anger bubbled to the surface. She'd been taken advantage of—by Graham, by Banks, by Langley, by those idiots at *The Gossip Club*.

He shook his head. "I never lied to you."

That was technically correct, she supposed. He hadn't lied. He'd just never told her the truth.

"Then you used me. Why didn't you tell me?" Vivian knew

he'd been using her. She'd been using him too. But he hadn't told her why, and that's what irritated her.

"I was going to… I swear. I had to be sure I could trust you. How did you find out?" Graham asked quietly.

"Gloria," she said.

"Everett's little girlfriend?" Graham's eyes were wide with astonishment. "How did she—"

"She had you followed." It sounded ludicrous coming out of her mouth, but there it was.

"Followed?"

Vivian nodded. "Bored on Christmas break and following misguided journalistic instincts, I guess. She suspected something was up between us. She got bored, and she had you followed—and she got more than she bargained for, I'd say."

"What…what is she planning on doing about it?"

"Nothing. She said she wouldn't tell anyone."

Graham let his breath out in a whoosh of air that ruffled her bangs.

"She told *you*."

Vivian nodded. "She thought it was only fair that I know. I think it's only fair too."

"Viv, I'm sorry. I should've told you, and I was working up the courage to tell you the truth. You deserve the truth." There was such a look of naked sincerity in his eyes that it made her heart hurt to look at him. She'd never seen him like that before—without his public persona, his shield of confidence and swagger. He seemed older. He seemed tired.

He was right. He couldn't have told her something like that, at least not until he was sure he could trust her to keep his secret. But hadn't she proven herself trustworthy over the past two months? Hadn't she been a friend to him? Hadn't they shared confidences? Surely none anywhere near as big as this one, but they'd kept each other's little secrets. Then something occurred to her.

"Marjorie Fox knew, didn't she?" Vivian asked with sudden clarity. "That's what made you so jittery about her murder and the blackmail. She knew about you, and you were afraid someone would figure it out after her death?"

Graham nodded.

Vivian laughed suddenly. "You know, for a while, I thought you were being so secretive because you'd killed her."

"Me? Kill Marjorie?" The shock on Graham's face was almost laughable. "How could you believe such a thing?"

Vivian shrugged. "What was I supposed to believe? I wouldn't, in a million years, have suspected this," she said, holding her hands out to encompass everything they'd been talking about.

"Well, that's a relief," he said. "That even you hadn't suspected."

That wasn't entirely true. Some part of her had always suspected; she just hadn't wanted to believe it.

"This is one fine predicament. I assume Banks and Langley know the truth?"

He nodded.

"And they're obviously 110 percent behind this whole Harvey-and-Lorna-in-real-life thing…"

He nodded again.

"How far are you willing to go for your career, Graham? Marriage? Children?"

"Would that be so horrible? To be married to me?" She knew he was half joking and would marry her this minute if he thought that would secure his future as a matinee idol.

"I don't love you, and you don't love me."

"Successful marriages have been built on far less than mutual affection." Graham put his hands in his pockets and stared at the floor.

Vivian thought of the lavender marriages that were whispered about in Hollywood circles—including, she had been shocked to find out, her beloved Rudolph Valentino. It would be a marriage of convenience to hide the sexuality of one or both of the people involved so that they could continue their show-business career. Graham would never be accepted as a romantic lead if it got out that he had no interest in romancing women in his private life. Marriage would divert attention from him—especially a marriage to a costar whose career was also on the rise. She should have seen the signs all along. How could she have been so naive?

She sighed. "Well, you can forget it. Find another sucker."

She watched his face fall and immediately felt sorry for being so blunt.

"I'm sorry, Graham. I'm not marrying anyone. Least of all you."

He was quiet for a long moment. "What about Chick?"

"What about him?" She ignored the implied question. Would she consider marrying Charlie—in theory, if they were anywhere near that—if he asked her? Would she? She suddenly felt angry, frustrated, trapped. Vivian bit her lip. All of this had been an elaborate, unnecessary, utterly confusing sham. She had known she was being used, but she didn't realize why. She didn't like being played for a fool. By all rights, she should be angry with Graham, but she couldn't force herself to be. Graham was in a bind. A huge bind, and she couldn't leave him in the lurch. What would she do about Charlie? She couldn't tell him about Graham, surely? Would he even understand? She shook her head.

Vivian sat for a moment, considering the situation. Then she turned to him. What had Charlie said—that Vivian Witchell never did anything out of the goodness of her heart?

"So I guess it's status quo then. I play the role of dutiful girlfriend as long as necessary," she said quietly. "At least until we can figure something out that won't ruin either of us."

"You'd do that for me?"

"Of course I would," she said, her stomach twisting at the

thought of what it might mean. But what choice did she have? If Graham went down, so did the show. She could kiss Lorna Lafferty good-bye just when she was gaining momentum. She wasn't simply doing it for Graham; she was doing it for herself too. She was doing it for everyone that worked on any show she was involved with. She was doing it for everyone at WCHI. And it felt like she had the weight of the world on her shoulders.

CHAPTER THIRTY-THREE

◆

Dave leaned in to the microphone. "Well, Lady Blakeney?"
Vivian opened her mouth and hastily closed it again.
She felt the belch slowly making its way up her windpipe.
Good lord, to belch on the air would be career suicide. She
forced it down, turned to the microphone, and delivered
her line.

"I've learned nothing yet," Vivian said. She turned to the
side and covered her mouth—and met Frances's eye across the
room. Frances smiled slightly, acknowledging Vivian's misfortune. Vivian pressed a hand to her stomach. It was pitching and
roiling. Something she'd eaten? Something she'd had to drink?
Had Frances had a hand in this? She wasn't content to ruin her
personal life, but she had to give her indigestion too?

She shook her head. Of course it hadn't been Frances. Stress-
induced indigestion. And after what Graham had confessed,
there was no doubt that the news could induce vomiting.

"Come now, let's not be coy," Dave cooed.

"I'm not being coy," Vivian said. "I've learned nothing."

"If you don't tell me the Pimpernel's true identity, you know the alternative. The guillotine. Your brother's head will roll on the streets of Paris."

"Monsieur Chauvelin," Vivian pleaded, stifling another belch. "You can't do this."

"My dear lady, the Pimpernel is under this roof. At this moment. Among your friends. Find him...or else."

The music swelled from the phonograph in the control room.

Someone pressed a glass into her hand. Vivian looked up into Frances's startlingly blue eyes. "Bicarbonate of soda," she mouthed. Then she mimed a drinking motion and patted her stomach. Vivian eyed the milky liquid with trepidation. Could Frances really be trying to help her? She brought the glass to her lips and tasted the tiniest of sips. It was chalky, slightly salty, bitter. Bicarbonate of soda all right. Vivian downed the glass and handed it back to Frances with a grateful smile. Perhaps she wasn't all bad.

The Pimpernel was going well. Surprisingly well. They'd reached the end of the play without mishap. Vivian couldn't help but think she was jinxing things by having the audacity to think of how well they were going.

"The firing squad is waiting, monsieur," Dave said.

"You will come to see me die?"

"Ah, no, I will picture the scene."

"Be sure to make it as horrible as possible."

"Oh, have no doubt."

The head soundman opened and closed a metal door on its special stand. It clanged ominously.

Another soundman stood far off in the corner, covering his mouth with his hand to muffle the sound. "Ready!"

The head soundman and his assistant picked the prop muskets off the table and locked them.

"Aim!"

A pause. All was silence in the studio. Vivian looked at Graham, his eyes trained on his script, waiting for the blast. Her eyes flicked to the control room. All were rapt with attention, mouths agape, including the ad man practically on his toes in anticipation.

"Fire!"

Then the thunderous sound of rifles firing filled the studio. Vivian flinched, even though they'd been through this scene ad nauseam in the past week.

"And so it is done," Dave said with barely disguised glee. "That infernal Pimpernel is no more."

There was a long pause. Silence. Long enough to think it might be over and that the Pimpernel had not escaped justice after all.

The soundman wrenched the metal prop door open and let it clang against the frame.

"Excuse me, monsieur," Graham said. "I seem to have forgotten my hat."

"Blakeney! What the deuce!"

"Perhaps you should sit down, Chauvelin. You look as though you've seen a ghost!"

The soundman opened a wooden door with an exaggerated creaking groan. Then Dave screamed, crouching down toward the floor to mimic falling into a pit.

"*Bonsoir, monsieur! Vive la France!*" Graham turned to Morty in the control room with a flourish of his arm.

Morty dropped the needle onto the record, and "La Marseillaise" rang out loud and clear. After one stanza, Morty lowered the volume, and Vivian stepped up to the microphone.

"Oh, Percy darling, you're here."

"Yes, Marguerite, and we're safely on our way to England."

"We're free now? Really free?"

"Yes, darling. Both of us."

The music swelled again, and Vivian looked up, catching Graham's eye. He smiled brilliantly. The smile of the Graham of old. The first time he'd smiled in days. They'd done it. They'd pulled it off. Graham had pulled it off against all the odds. They all stood stiff as statues until the announcer had finished his spiel and the music had died out dramatically. The on-air light blinked off at eight o'clock, and a spontaneous cheer erupted from everyone in the room. They'd done it. They'd actually done it.

Graham held up his hands in the middle of the room to hush the celebrations.

"Congratulations, everyone! Fantastic. Just fantastic." Vivian thought she saw a tear or two sparkle in his deep-brown eyes. He smiled, his gaze sweeping over the crowd of people assembled in the studio space. She watched as his eyes caught and lingered on Paul's. A smile passed between them, but it was brief and his eyes swept on. Her stomach twisted. She hoped she was the only one who had noticed, would ever notice.

Affairs of this sort were not tolerated anywhere, but especially not in a rising star. Graham would have to pretend for the rest of his career, for the rest of his life. He'd lead a double life—one for the public and one for himself. And maybe the one for himself would eventually fade away to be replaced by the hollow comfort of a sham marriage, and maybe even some sham children. She glanced away. The bicarbonate of soda was no longer helping her stomach.

"Viv!" Graham waved her over to the far side of the room. He was flanked by both Mr. Langley and Mr. Banks, as well as the ad man. Both men were slapping Graham's back and smiling ear to ear. Oh yes, things had gone well—better than either she or Graham could have dreamed.

She approached the group and shook the men's proffered hands.

"Wonderful program!" the ad man intoned.

"Top-notch!" Mr. Langley said.

Both men nodded their heads at her.

"Yes, Graham's done a magnificent job." She smiled at Graham, patting his arm.

"We were saying that this would be a capital idea as a series—dramatic presentations of the great works of literature, helmed by our young genius Graham here."

Vivian's mouth dropped open slightly. "A regular series? Wow." Her eyes flicked to Graham's, but she only saw pride and accomplishment there. But what would this mean? For *The Darkness Knows*? Certainly he couldn't keep this sort of pace, deal with this sort of stress, in the long term.

"And we were talking of the Sultan's Gold spot and how much we think you would add. The public loves both of you and especially loves you together. I think an ad with both of you would be terrific."

"Wow. I don't know what to say." Her mind flashed on that previous image she'd had of Graham, illustrated in three-quarter profile, but now she joined him. A national magazine ad. She could hardly believe it.

"Say yes."

"Yes," she said, laughing. "Yes."

"That's great. We'll start working on the particulars tomorrow."

"I can't wait. But I'm afraid right now I must be going."

She shook their hands again and headed toward her coat and bag on the opposite side of the room. Graham grabbed her arm, stopping her progress. He moved close to her, his mouth next to her ear. "Thank you, Viv. For everything this past week...and for being so understanding. I owe you a huge debt of gratitude."

She looked at him, meeting his eyes briefly before looking away again. Her eyes lit on the ad man, Banks, and Langley, all watching her and Graham. "You're my friend, Graham. Friends help each other, don't they?"

The Packard was not waiting at the curb in front of the building. Vivian stood on the sidewalk, slightly bewildered. It had kept snowing while they were doing the show, and there was another half an inch covering everything. Vivian waited for five minutes. Charlie had said "right here," hadn't he? She looked up and down the street, but there was no sign of him. She looked at her watch again. Had something happened?

She pulled her coat tightly around her and looked back into the building, then scanned the street once more. She looked across the street into the lighted windows of the Tip Top Café. Charlie's blond head was not visible anywhere. Surely, she should go back inside. If he came and she wasn't waiting, he'd go inside and find her. That's what she should do, yes.

Instead, she started walking toward the street corner. Maybe she'd heard him wrong. Maybe he was waiting around the block. Maybe he'd gotten caught up somewhere. Maybe she should meet him at home. She turned the corner—no black Packard. She sighed, pressed the flat of her hand against her stomach. She scanned the street, looking for a taxi. She was being silly. She would take a taxi. This was no reason to panic.

She hailed a cab, and it pulled up on the other side of the street. She glanced both ways and then stepped off the curb, her right foot hovering in the air.

From the left came the revving of an engine, then the squealing of tires. Her head jerked to the left, but all she could see were blinding headlights coming straight for her. Adrenaline flooded her veins. She tried to hop back onto the curb but lost her balance on the freshly fallen snow, arms flailing frantically. She fell back hard on her heel as the car came to a screeching stop on the street in front of her. The passenger-side door flew open.

"Vivian, Jesus! What in the hell are you doing?"

She pressed one hand to her chest, feeling the outline of the keys against her palm. *Charlie.* Her breath came fast.

"What the hell am I doing? What the hell are *you* doing? You nearly ran me down!"

Charlie scowled at her. "Don't be so melodramatic. I told you to wait where I'd dropped you—right in front of the building."

"I did wait there. I waited there for ten minutes."

"Get in."

They drove in silence until they were almost back to Vivian's house. She stared out the window, silently fuming. Her heart had slowed to a reasonable pace. She'd thought her time was up for a moment there. She'd been convinced in that second that her father had been murdered and that person who had killed her father, pushed Della in front of that streetcar, and cut Martin's brake lines had finally come for her.

"I'm sorry, Viv." Charlie's voice was soft. Vivian turned to him, eyes narrowed. He took his eyes from the road to meet hers. "I didn't mean to scare you. But I pulled up in front of the building and you weren't there, and then I saw you hurrying away from me up the street and I...panicked." Viv's mood softened slightly.

"It's all right." She sighed. She wasn't about to admit that she'd panicked a bit too. She couldn't wait for all of this to be over. All of this excitement had long since worn out its welcome. There was no glamour in danger, despite what she'd thought a few days ago.

"Rough show?"

"No. Actually, it went much better than expected. An almost-perfect performance."

"Congratulations."

"Congratulations go to Graham. It was his baby." Vivian glanced out the window again. "You should have seen it. It was something."

Charlie grunted. "I hear congratulations are in order for something else too."

"What's that?"

"Your engagement."

Oh no, she thought. Her head snapped back toward him. "Where on earth did you hear that?"

"So it's true?"

"Of course it's not true. Wherever did you hear such a thing?"

"I hear it was on the radio. Some gossip-show hosts announcing it and offering both you and Graham their felicitations."

He wasn't looking at her. His tone was light, but she watched his jaw work. It hadn't occurred to her that Charlie would hear that stupid rumor—or that he might take it seriously.

"Oh, Charlie. Don't be ridiculous," she said. "It's just a publicity thing. I don't know a thing about it. I'm as surprised about my engagement as you are." She laughed, but Charlie didn't.

"So there *is* an engagement?"

"No…" She flapped her hands in front of her, flustered. "Charlie, of course there isn't."

She'd forgotten that he didn't know that Graham wasn't and had never been a threat for her affections. Seen in this light, it was a bit endearing, this jealousy.

"Charlie…" She reached out and ran her fingertip lightly around his ear. He flinched away from her. She sat up straighter, suddenly alarmed. He was serious about this. "You believe me, don't you?"

He shrugged and looked away. After a few tense moments of silence, he cleared his throat.

"I was late picking you up because I went to see a chemist about that plant. The odollam."

The odollam. She hadn't asked him to do that. She swallowed the lump in her throat. She wanted to tell him to stop, that she didn't want to hear it, but nothing came out of her mouth. Charlie continued.

"It's not something to be trifled with. It's an extremely poisonous plant that grows mainly in India. They call it the suicide plant. Mash it up and slip it into something spicy, and you wouldn't know it's there. Looks like a heart attack, I'm told."

Her hands had grown cold inside her expensive fur-lined gloves.

Something spicy. "Looks like a heart attack," she whispered.

"Yes, I was told it's a good thing it's virtually unavailable outside of Asia."

But it's not completely unavailable, is it?

Della had had that terrible plant growing in Freddy's office, her father's office, all along. That terrible plant that someone could mash up into something spicy and someone else would never know it was there. Spicy, like what? Her father avoided spicy foods because of his indigestion. Then it hit her. *Oh God.* Spicy, like a Bloody Mary. Vivian had handed her father the Bloody Mary that night. She'd handed him the poison that had killed him. She hadn't known and she knew it wasn't her fault, but her stomach twisted painfully with guilt all the same.

She bit her lip against the tears that threatened. It was no use thinking this now, and crying certainly wouldn't help. If her father had been poisoned, it had happened eight years ago. What could they do about it now? Nothing, that's what. They certainly couldn't prove it. And if they couldn't even prove he'd been poisoned, how would they ever find who'd poisoned him? The frustration welled up in her. She clenched her fists in her lap.

"And I'm afraid there can never be any proof, no matter what we may suspect," he said softly.

Charlie pulled the car to the curb in front of her house, then reached over and squeezed her leg in sympathy.

"Let's drop it, Charlie," she said, sliding over to him on the bench seat. "Please. All of it."

She looked up at him, pleading with her eyes. He nodded slightly. Then she pressed her lips to his. He returned her kiss with enthusiasm, and the hand on her thigh slid up under her skirt. She pulled away, breathing heavily. All she wanted was Charlie. She wanted him to make her forget everything about her father, everything about Graham, everything in the world.

"Come on." She pulled him by the lapels as she jerked her head toward the coach house.

Charlie's brow furrowed.

"You told Yarborough it was over," he said. It wasn't a question.

"I…" Vivian sat back on the bench seat, glancing out her

window. She didn't want to lie to Charlie, but she hadn't told Graham it was over, had she? No, she'd done the opposite.

Vivian looked at Charlie, his strong profile backlit by the streetlights. This was absurd. She wanted to tell him the truth, but how could she? She'd promised to continue the ruse, so she'd couldn't renege on it now. It could mean Graham's career—even his life, in the worst-case scenario—if any hint of this got out. But surely, if she could tell anyone it would be Charlie.

"It's strictly for the show," she said, speaking slowly so there could be no mistaking her meaning. "It's a fake relationship for publicity. It's always been fake."

He gripped the steering wheel.

"Present tense," he said. "It *is* a fake relationship."

Vivian sighed. She didn't want to talk about this. She didn't want to talk at all.

"Maybe this was a mistake, Viv."

"What?"

"All of this. Us. I don't want to play this game." He turned to look pointedly at her, a vertical line between his brows.

"It's no game," she said. "And it's not a mistake."

"I don't want to be your second choice. The secret you hide from the respectable crowd."

"Oh, Charlie, you've got it all wrong." But her mind immediately moved to the evening before. Charlie had happened upon a party she was throwing without him. A roomful of people, her friends, coworkers—none of which she would introduce him to. He *was* a secret, Vivian thought, but only temporarily. She needed time to work all of this out. He needed to give her time.

"Have I got it all wrong? Are you still seeing Yarborough?"

"I'm not *seeing* him. It's…well, it's complicated."

"Complicated how?" Charlie asked slowly, his voice carefully controlled.

"Well, I can't just throw Graham over," she said. She thought of Banks and Langley. Their stern, reasonable lecture. "What would the papers say?"

She regretted the words the second they came out of her mouth. She watched Charlie's fingers grip the steering wheel once, hard, then relax.

He turned to fix her with a long, hard stare before saying in such a low voice that Vivian almost couldn't hear him, "I don't want you for what you can do for me, Viv. I want you for you, and I think that should be worth something."

Vivian swallowed, unable to speak for a long moment. "It is worth something, Charlie," she whispered. "It's worth everything."

She held his blue-green gaze, feeling her resolve give way little by little. After all, she'd been willing to chuck her career two months ago when the whole fake relationship with Graham had been proposed. Before she'd agreed to make that deal. Then again, things were different now. She was a star. People recognized her on the street and wanted her autograph. She would go with the show to Hollywood. Then surely a screen test. The pictures. Everything she'd ever dreamed of. Surely, she could have both that and Charlie. Yes, she would tell him. She had to. She was certain she could trust Charlie.

"There are some things you don't understand," she said. And she knew immediately that it was precisely the wrong way to begin.

Charlie snorted. "Oh yes, how could I ever understand your complicated world of show business intrigue and backstabbing?"

"Charlie—"

"Think about what you want, Viv."

You, she thought. *I want you*. But the words wouldn't come out, and something told her that he wouldn't understand if they did. He wouldn't compromise. It was all or nothing with him. And if she told him that she had to continue the public ruse with Graham, even for another minute, then he would choose the nothing.

"I want you to come in with me, Charlie," she said. Her voice was little more than a whisper.

He didn't answer. He continued to stare icily out the windshield as if he hadn't heard.

So she opened the car door and paused, completely at a loss for what to do. She glanced up and saw that Everett's bedroom light was on. She walked up the wide limestone steps to the main house and pulled open the door. Charlie didn't pull immediately away, but she forced herself to keep looking forward, not to turn back. Then she heard the engine rev, and the car pulled away from the curb.

Her mind was already formulating a plan. Everything would be fine. She'd call Charlie tomorrow and explain everything. All of it. She'd grovel if she had to. She wasn't letting Charlie Haverman disappear from her life again. He would understand. He had to. Everything would be fine, she told herself. But as soon as she closed the front door behind her, she burst into tears.

———◆———

CHAPTER THIRTY-FOUR

T he doorbell rang, and Vivian's pulse quickened. It had to be Charlie. He'd come back after all. She turned and swung the front door wide. "I'm sorry!" tumbled from her lips. Damn her pride.

But it wasn't Charlie standing on the threshold. It was Uncle Freddy. The short hairs immediately rose on the back of her neck. She glanced away, unable to meet his gaze.

"Viv, are you all right?"

"I'm fine." She sniffed, wiping at her eyes.

"Can I come in?" he asked.

"No," she said, pushing the door closed automatically. "I mean, this isn't the best time."

He stopped the door with his palm and slid inside before she could react. Her hands had gone cold.

"It's going to have to be the right time. We need to finish our talk."

"I don't want to talk."

Freddy ignored her and walked straight to the liquor cabinet in the den. He said nothing as he mixed two drinks. Vivian watched him with trepidation. All she wanted to do was bury her head in a pillow. She certainly didn't want to talk to Freddy about her father. She wasn't in the mood to ease his conscience about anything.

"Here," he said, handing her the drink. "It looks like you need it. Bad night?"

Vivian sighed, looking down into the amber liquid. "You could say that."

"Want to talk about it?"

"Not especially."

"I'm sorry you had to find out about any of this. I tried my damnedest to keep you away from it. That's what your father would have wanted."

"Is that why you and Oskar pretended not to know each other?"

He glanced quickly at her, then walked over toward the fireplace and looked into the darkened hearth for a moment.

"Oskar," he said with a snort. "What's he playing at with Julia?"

"He says he cares for her."

Freddy's eyes rolled to the ceiling. "That and a nickel will get you a cup of coffee."

Vivian watched as he looked over the Christmas cards displayed on the mantel. He paused on the one signed *Freddy and Pauline*. He reached out and touched the front with his fingertips, then drew his hand back.

Freddy looked at her for a long moment, and then his face softened. "He did all of this for you, you know."

"Me?"

"For you, Everett, your mother…for this…" He held his hands out to either side to indicate the lavish den. The house in general.

To give Mother the life she'd been accustomed to, Vivian thought.

"He would've done anything for you, for his family."

"And it got him killed."

Freddy's eyes widened, and then he shook his head. "It was a heart attack. A long-overdue heart attack."

"I don't believe that."

She waited for the silence to weigh on him, on his conscience. After a moment, he lifted his head. He sighed heavily.

"Arthur was going to the feds of his own free will. And once he did it that…" He held up his hands, and then his gaze shifted to the floor.

Vivian didn't say anything. *Killed, murdered*, she thought. Those harsh words ran a loop in her head. The syndicate was violent. Capone was violent. She thought of the crime-scene photos on the front of the newspaper and shivered—the pools of blood under the bullet-mangled corpses. What had Caputto said—that it had been a good way to end the game and that he'd seen much worse?

Poison, on the other hand, was intimate. Inheritance powder, they called it in the papers. Poison was usually used within the family. She stared into the amber liquid in the glass Freddy had given her. Her stomach turned, and she set it on the side table with a *thunk*.

Freddy glanced up at the sound.

"I'll tell you the truth..." he said. "And this *is* the truth. A man came to me shortly after I found out about Arthur's intentions. Some punk I'd never seen before came to see me. Told me that the whole family—your whole family—was caput if I didn't take care of Arthur before he talked to the feds."

"What?"

"Said they'd make it look like a gas line exploded in the middle of the night. The whole house...this house...up in smoke, with all of you sleeping peacefully inside."

Vivian's mouth went dry.

"Don't you see? Arthur needed to go. They knew he was in contact with the feds. They also needed it to look like an accident... It needed to arouse no suspicion. Arthur was too high-profile to gun down in the street like a dog."

Vivian winced.

"So...you're telling me you killed him quietly as a favor to us?" She started to back away, hands protectively held up in front of her chest as if to ward off a blow.

He shook his head.

"No, Viv. God, no. I told the man that Arthur was like a brother to me, and I couldn't kill him. I said I'd talk Arthur out of going to the feds. If I kept him quiet, there was no need to kill anyone."

Vivian stared at him in incredulity.

"I swear." He crossed his index finger over his heart.

"And you talked to my father?"

"I tried. I took him out for a drink the night he died. There was no reasoning with him. He wanted to be a better man, Viv. He was ashamed of what he'd done, the way he'd behaved, the type of people he'd associated with. You were becoming a lovely young woman, he said. He said you were acting out, and it was all his fault for not being the kind of man you could look up to. And it would start to matter soon what kind of man your father was."

She thought of the coming-out discussion they'd had. Tears sprang to her eyes.

"Please don't say you did it for me, Freddy. Please."

"I didn't do it at all, Viv. I'm a spineless coward. I couldn't talk him out of it, and I couldn't kill him to save his family or myself."

"So what happened?"

"I don't know. I was petrified. I thought I'd get a phone call in the middle of the night telling me you were all dead. And then I'd be next."

Vivian stared at him.

"And then when your father died like that at precisely the right moment to save everyone, to save himself—his reputation, at least... Well, I decided to chalk it up to divine intervention, I suppose."

Vivian's mouth worked silently. Her father's death had been divine intervention. An exquisitely timed heart attack. "I don't believe that," she said. "I can't believe that."

Occam's razor, she thought. That's what Charlie had said, hadn't he? *Uncle Freddy's your man.* He may not have taken the money from the drawer, but he had killed her father. She was certain.

"So my father dies and saves the day for everyone—including you. You get to go on with your life without a blemish on you. You get to continue your successful career. You get to be a judge." Her voice was rising in pitch, becoming shrill.

"Now, Viv, calm down. I think you've got the wrong end of the stick here..."

"And Della knows what you did, even if she doesn't realize it. That plant... It wasn't the cleaners that destroyed it. And then you tried to kill her for it... Oh, you didn't do it yourself, but you hired someone to push her in front of that streetcar."

"What... Viv, what are you talking about? I did no such thing."

"And you cut the brake lines on Martin's car."

"Brake lines?"

"You're a terrible liar, Freddy."

He shook his head, blue eyes wide. He stepped toward her, his arms straight out in front of him like he were dealing with a rabid animal. Vivian raised her arm, and he lunged suddenly at her, grabbing her arm as she lowered it to strike.

"Vivian," he pleaded, his voice a gasp. "Stop." He grabbed her roughly around the waist, pinning one arm to her side. She flailed out blindly with the other, her fingers snagging something from the mantel. She held it above her head and then let down with as much force as she could muster, watching her mother's favorite china Pekingese shatter with a satisfying crash against the back of Freddy's head. Then she watched his eyes roll back as he slumped to the floor unconscious.

The front door flew open with a bang, and Charlie strode into the room, revolver in hand. "What the hell is going on in here?"

Vivian's mouth opened, but nothing came out. Her hands covered her thudding heart.

"I think I killed Freddy," she said finally, her eyes fixed on the motionless form on the parlor rug.

Holstering his gun, Charlie crouched by the unconscious man. He put his hand in front of Uncle Freddy's mouth and paused. "He's still breathing," he said. "But we need to call an ambulance."

Charlie jumped up and ran to the hall telephone. He ordered an ambulance from the operator in a staccato voice and returned to Vivian's side. She hadn't taken her eyes off Uncle Freddy, still motionless, his chest barely rising and falling.

"I think he killed Father." She shivered. "And he didn't

want anyone to know, so he attacked me. He tried to…" She broke off in a sob.

Charlie followed Vivian's glance toward the remains of the china Pekingese on the living room rug. Uncle Freddy groaned, and Vivian turned away from the horrible sight, burying her face in Charlie's chest. He wrapped his arms around her and held her in silence until she said, her voice muffled against his overcoat, "I thought you left."

"I did," he said gruffly. "I got a block away before I turned back. I was coming up the front stairs when I heard the crash."

Vivian sniffed, and Charlie nudged her with a clean handkerchief. She took it and wiped her eyes. He'd come back for her after all. And thank God he had.

There was a rumbling on the stairs, and soon Everett burst through the doorway. He stopped short, his eyes wide upon seeing Freddy laid out on the rug. His eyes darted back and forth between Vivian and Uncle Freddy's motionless form.

"Jesus. What happened?" Before Vivian could answer, Everett's eyes shifted to Charlie. "And who the hell are you?"

Vivian buried her face in Charlie's chest and closed her eyes. Where on earth did she begin?

CHAPTER THIRTY-FIVE

———————— ◆ ————————

Vivian left Charlie and Everett to watch over Freddy and wait for the ambulance while she hurried out the back door to retrieve the ledger. She hoped Freddy hadn't already taken it. Without it, she and Charlie couldn't prove anything. Without it, he might walk free of her father's murder. She pulled the house key from her pocket and went to use it, but the front door was already ajar. She swallowed. So Freddy had already been here. Her stomach sank. She pushed the door open with her fingertips, unease crawling up her spine.

All was dark. She stood in the open doorway for a moment. There was a sound. Footsteps. Upstairs. The sound of a drawer being opened and closed. Vivian's breath caught in her throat. She should turn and run, go back to the front house. Tell Charlie. But she couldn't move.

Something shifted on the landing at the top of the stairs. A form came into view. A man. In her house. Still, she was rooted to the spot. She glanced over her shoulder at the main house, the homey light of the kitchen window a few yards away. She could scream, she decided. Yes, of course. She turned back to the landing, hitched in her breath, and then let it out in a rush.

"What are you doing here?" she said.

The man's face had come into view as he made his way down the stairs. It was Martin.

Then before he could answer, she saw what he was holding, and the truth hit her like a punch to the stomach. She wasn't crazy. Someone had been following her, and someone had been here before looking for that ledger. The night she'd scraped her hand. The night she noticed the coat-tree was out of place. The man in the flat cap had been following her. He'd pushed Della in front of that streetcar. All for Martin. It had been Martin all along.

"Where is the statement?" he whispered as he limped toward her. His eyes were wild in the dim room.

"Statement?"

"Viv, please. I tried to stop it from ever coming to this, but I need that statement your father wrote out—the one he was going to give to the feds."

"I don't have any statement."

"I think you do, and it's important that you give it to me. It's not in this ledger. It has to be somewhere. Is it in the safe-deposit box?"

He limped closer, and she instinctively backed up and

raised her hands in front of her as if he'd been about to strike her. Then it all became clear.

"You killed him," she whispered.

Martin's mouth opened. He shook his head. "You don't understand."

"Oh, I understand everything." Everything she'd just accused Freddy of had been done by Martin. Freddy had been telling her the truth. After those men had gone to Freddy, they'd gone to Martin, asking him to do the same thing. Martin was a kid then. He wasn't as strong as Freddy. He couldn't have stood up to anyone. Her legs gave out, and she sat heavily in the chair next to the radio.

He hadn't even had the guts to do it himself, or be there when it happened. He'd let Vivian give the drink with the poison in it to Father and then sent Della to make sure the deed had been done. Martin had used her and Della. He'd had the temerity to flirt with both of them. He'd played with their emotions, knowing all the time what he'd done. How far would he have let things go? And had that been the point—keep your enemies close? How close would he have kept both of them to prevent anyone from finding out? He'd been having lunch with Freddy every month, keeping Della on a string so that he could get information. That's how he knew Vivian was asking questions.

"You had that man follow me. He told you about that ledger, and you had him try to take it from me on the street that day. He told you about everything I was doing. He chased me down the street. He pushed Della in front of that streetcar."

Martin shook his head, but he didn't seem surprised by the accusation. He'd done it, Vivian thought. He'd done all of it.

He held one hand out to her, and she flinched away. Vivian saw hurt in his eyes. He opened his mouth to say something else, but the sound of sirens broke in the air. Martin's head jerked to the front window. He stood perfectly still for a moment, listening. Then he turned abruptly, still clutching the ledger, and rushed off through the front door, leaving it standing open.

Vivian didn't follow him. She hadn't the energy to stand up from the chair. *Statement*, she thought. What on earth was he talking about?

There was scuffling outside in the courtyard. A muffled curse, then shouting—sounds of a fistfight. Vivian finally found her strength and moved to peek out the front window. In the dim light of the courtyard, she could two men wrestling. Then Martin was restrained on the ground, his face pushed into the dirty snow. The hair of the man lying on top of him flashed a muted orange in the moonlight. Everett.

Vivian stumbled backward and sat back down in the chair.

Statement. What statement could he mean? Her mind worked as the sound of the sirens grew closer. When the sirens stopped with a screech of the brakes in front of the house, the piece clicked into place without effort. She didn't know what the statement was, but she knew *where* it was.

Vivian flipped on the bedside lamp. She stood for a moment, stunned at the scene. Martin had destroyed her room. He'd pulled the drawers out of the dresser and strewn her clothes about so that they littered every visible surface. Her eyes fell on the contents of her intimates drawer dumped unceremoniously near the radiator. She was repulsed that Martin had been anywhere near her underthings. He'd shredded her pillows, making ugly gashes across the covers with a pocketknife. Tiny white feathers floated up toward her as she pressed down on them. The bed had been stripped, the mattress flipped up and set half off the frame on a diagonal.

For a moment, she thought the statement might be gone. Maybe Martin had found it and taken it, not realizing what he had. If he had, it would be over. Then she crouched and looked under the bed. She exhaled as she pulled the doll out by its rigid composite legs. She held it for a moment in her cupped palms, feeling the weight of its little body in her hands. She stared down into that insipid, gap-toothed smile as her fingertips traced the molded curl springing from its forehead.

Topsy, the Kewpie doll her father had won for her so many years ago at the ring toss. Topsy that she'd slept with every night since. Topsy that had calmed her hammering heart the other night when she'd been convinced that someone had been waiting to do her in the second she closed her eyes. And Topsy, the Top-C from the missing page of her father's appointment book.

She exhaled and yanked the frilly dress over the doll's head and tossed it onto the mattress. She flipped the doll over and considered its molded celluloid body for a moment, tilting her head to the side and bringing the doll close her nose, examining it from every possible angle. She slid her fingertips over the smooth surface. Nothing. It was unblemished. She slumped onto the bed, staring into the doll's wide, unblinking eyes. She picked up the frilly, pink polka-dotted dress, and it crunched under her fingers. She paused and squeezed it in her palm again. Yes, it crunched. There was something inside the doll's dress. She flipped the dress inside out and gasped at the tiny square of fabric that had been sewn inside with ragged, uneven stitches. It was obviously done by someone not adept at the task. She lunged for the sewing kit Martin had tossed to the floor and pulled the tiny silver scissors from the box. Then she inserted the tip of the scissors into threads and tore the patch away. A tiny folded square of paper fell into her open palm.

She stared at it for a long moment, the mutilated remains of Topsy's dress in one hand, the square of cream stationery in the other. She could hear a commotion now at the main house, men's voices raised in excitement. Charlie would come to see about her soon.

She tossed the dress onto the bed and opened the sheet of paper. Her eyes scanned down the lines in father's precise hand, each word hitting her like a fresh punch to the solar plexus. She read it twice through before comprehension dawned on her. It was a confession, and it was worse than anything she could have ever imagined.

CHAPTER THIRTY-SIX

◆

Vivian was sitting at the kitchen table in the coach house, staring into a cup of coffee gone cold when there was a knock on the door. She glanced at the clock— 8:14 a.m. She and Everett had spent the night explaining things to their mother. That had been a horribly tough conversation. Her marriage to her beloved husband had been a lie. Oskar, Freddy, Martin, Mrs. Graves…all lying to her for years. Vivian had just left Julia to think things over, but she couldn't sleep herself. She'd jumped at every noise, terrified that Martin had somehow escaped police custody and come to finish her off. It was irrational. She'd seen the look in his eyes before he'd run off. He was mortified by what he'd done. Maybe he hadn't done what she suspected after all? Maybe he'd had nothing to do with her father's death. Her stomach constricted at the idea.

She stood, tightened the tie on her pink chenille robe, and headed to the front door. There was no time to change, and frankly, she didn't have the energy.

Charlie stood on the doorstep, his brow wrinkled in concern under his gray fedora.

"Sorry to call so early. Did I wake you?" He eyed her warily. She knew she looked a fright in her robe. She watched him take in her unkempt hair, her smeared mascara.

"No." She sighed. "I haven't slept. Come in." She turned her back on him and started toward the living room where she slumped onto the sofa.

"Gilfoy confessed."

Vivian sighed again, her eyes trained on the ceiling. She suddenly felt like crying. She'd tried to trick herself into believing otherwise, but she'd known the second she'd seen that look of exquisite guilt on his face the evening before. "Of all people... Why, Charlie? Why did he do it?" But she already knew the answer. He did it because he had to. He did it because he'd had no choice.

Charlie moved toward her, his hat held awkwardly in his hands, but he didn't sit next to her.

"Threats, intimidation. They'd told him if he didn't kill Arthur, then Arthur's whole family, *your* whole family, would go." Charlie's hand flipped up toward the ceiling, miming an explosion. "And on top of that, they'd ruin Gilfoy's promising career."

"They tried that with Freddy too. He told me last night. That's why I thought... Well, that's why he's in the hospital with a concussion. I guess I put two and two together and got five."

"It's not your fault."

"I know that." Vivian fussed with fringe on the pillow next to her. "I guess Freddy told me the truth after all. He refused them. So they hedged their bets and went to Martin, and he was weak enough to do it."

Charlie nodded, frowning.

"Mrs. Graves told me that my father came home that day after lunch for some bicarbonate of soda. He wasn't feeling well. My father was notorious for indigestion. Likely Martin had convinced him to eat something he shouldn't to make it seem like he was having chest pains. Della told me she'd noticed that afternoon. She'd seen my father clutching at his chest."

"Setting the scene for a sudden, devastating heart attack."

"Anyway, my father stopped here after lunch, and though Mrs. Graves didn't remember seeing Martin, he must have been here. Mrs. Graves had just made the pitcher of Bloody Marys. My father was a creature of habit, and if anyone knew that, it was Martin. He slipped the odollam into the pitcher…and then all he had to do was leave and wait for me to hand the drink to my father when he came home from work…" Her throat constricted suddenly, and she couldn't say any more.

Vivian finally looked up, catching Charlie's eye. She noticed then that he wasn't looking great either. Red-rimmed eyes, a day's growth of dark stubble. He'd been up all night. For her.

"And what doctor in Chicago, Illinois, would ever think to look for a tropical poison in someone's system—especially someone under a lot of stress and a prime target for a heart attack?" he said. "Do you think Della was in on it?"

Vivian thought of Della at the kitchen door that night. Della's horror-stricken face on remembering her father's death. Hearing that her prized plant killed her boss and that her beloved Martin had used her that way might finish her off.

"No. I think Martin used her though. He knew Della thought he was the bee's knees. He charmed his way into getting knowledge of that poison. He set her up as a secondary witness to my father's chest pains all that day. And then he sent her over that evening to make sure the deed had been done."

Charlie shook his head. "That rat."

"What about Mr. Graves? Was the accident truly an accident?"

"Gilfoy claims it was. He said Mr. Graves knew what he'd done and they were arguing about it, and then the car skidded on the curve, and they were headed for the lamppost, and *wham*."

Vivian shook her head. "I don't know if I believe that. I don't know what to believe anymore." After all, she'd believed Martin when he'd told her that story about his brake lines. Why wouldn't she? She hadn't suspected him of anything. And all that interest he'd paid her, asking her when her shows were, subtly marking her whereabouts… It was only to make sure she'd be out of the house so he could search her things.

"Had you suspected Gilfoy?"

Vivian shook her head. She felt so stupid. She had fallen for it.

"Surely he knew that. Then why didn't he just let things go? There wasn't anything to tie him to your father's death."

"There was the odollam. And there was Della—whether or not she realized she knew something she shouldn't. And there was something else to tie him to more than my father's death. That's why he was here ransacking my place last night." Vivian's eyes flicked around the room. It was still in disarray.

"The ledger?"

She shook her head. "Topsy." She watched the confusion wash over Charlie's face. "My Kewpie doll. Except he didn't know that's what he was looking for, and that's why he didn't find it."

"Your Kewpie doll?"

Vivian nodded. "Topsy, or 'Top-C' as my father had written in on the missing page of his appointment book."

"Top-C," Charlie repeated, his eyebrows raised.

Vivian stood and retrieved the paper that had been hidden in the doll's dress. She handed it to Charlie.

"This is what Martin was after."

She watched Charlie's eyes scan the paper as he read. "Jesus, Viv."

"It was so much worse than I could have imagined." Tears sprang to her eyes. That statement was a coldhearted depiction of the meeting her father had hosted for Capone and his most trusted lieutenants at the family cabin at Cranberry Lake in October 1928. Where they'd planned in great detail how they were going to kill his archenemy, Bugs Moran. Of course, their best-laid plans had gone wrong and turned into what the papers had called the Saint Valentine's Day Massacre. There it was in black and white. Signed in her father's hand. Witnessed by Martin Gilfoy.

He'd known all along what her father had been doing. He'd been part of it—the confession at least. And he'd known her father was going to turn and confess everything he knew to the feds. And then Martin had been approached by the same men that had approached Freddy, and he couldn't refuse. He'd killed her father, but he couldn't close the loop. He could never find this last bit that would have tied him to everything. If this piece of paper had gotten out, even now, the stigma of Martin having been involved in such a notorious event would stop his political ambitions dead in their tracks.

"That's what my father was going to hand that over to the feds."

"Why? What good would it have done? The massacre was a local matter, not a federal one. And the Chicago police were in Capone's pocket."

"It wasn't meant to get Capone convicted of anything. It was a way of gaining their trust—proving he was for real, proving that he was in it all the way. That they could trust him to supply information."

"Why would he do such a thing? Take such a terrible chance?"

"For me…for Everett…for Mother…" Vivian thought of her father that night, resting his fingertip on the picture of Barbara Hutton. It will matter who you associate with. *And who your father associates with*, she amended.

Charlie's eyes flicked from the paper to Vivian. "Your mother doesn't know about this?"

She shook her head. Her mother would never see this statement. Her mother could never know this. She took the paper from Charlie's hands and set it on the side table. She should burn it, she thought. Get rid of the evidence of her father's terrible criminal past for good. Then again, it was evidence that might put Martin away where he belonged. For now, she'd let it sit there. Maybe she'd take it down to the safe-deposit box.

"How's Uncle Freddy?"

"He'll have one hell of a bump on his head, but he'll pull through."

Vivian grimaced, thinking of how she'd knocked him unconscious. He hadn't done anything except lie to her to try to spare her feelings. How could she ever make that up to him?

"And how are *you* feeling, Viv?"

She swallowed. "I'm not sure," she said. "I was up all night turning things over and over in my head. I still can't believe Martin killed—" She broke off as the words stuck in her throat.

"He'd said my father was like a father to him—and he was." She felt the ire rising in her, and she tamped it down. Anger would do her no good now. What was done was done.

She stood, pulled the tie on her robe tighter, and headed toward the kitchen.

"Would you like some coffee? I was about to start a fresh pot."

Charlie shook his head. "I only stopped by to put your mind at rest. Gilfoy's behind bars. It's over. Try to get some sleep, Viv." He turned toward the door, but Vivian rushed forward and grabbed his hand, yanking him backward.

"Wait."

She tugged him over to sit next to her on the sofa. He sat willingly, but he looked at her without expression. She took a deep breath.

"Can you keep a secret?" she asked.

He narrowed his eyes at her. "Secrets are my business, remember?"

"Right," she said. "Well, the thing is…" She looked into his eyes and lost her nerve. How on earth could she tell Charlie something like that about Graham? It was embarrassing to *her*, quite honestly. The man he thought—the man they had *both* thought—had come between them had never been a threat in that way. They'd wasted so much time. She shook her head at the thought. They had wasted time, yes, but there was no reason to waste any more. She took another deep breath and said it before she lost her nerve again.

"The thing is…I want to be with *you*, Charlie. I've always wanted to be with you." She smiled at him then and half stood from her seat on the sofa to lean over and impetuously plant a kiss on his slightly parted lips. He responded immediately, grabbing her waist with both hands and pulling her down roughly onto his lap.

After a long moment, his lips moved to her ear and he whispered, "No offense, Viv, but that wasn't much of a secret." She laughed, eyes closed, her cheek resting against his.

"Wasn't it?" She sighed. Then his lips moved to her neck, and she found that she was rapidly losing interest in what the real secret had been. She'd have to tell him about Graham, of course, but not now. For the first time in hours, her mind was no longer going round and round about her father or Martin. Now she could think of nothing but how Charlie's lips roamed down her throat and over her collarbone, and where else they might roam if she let them. He lifted his head again and pulled slightly back, regarding her with half-closed eyes.

"And Yarborough?"

"That very fake relationship is over," she said. Not technically true, she thought, but she *would* end it. Soon.

"What about the papers?"

"Oh, hang the papers."

He smoothed her hair back from her face with his hand before kissing her forehead. "Hang the papers? Now those are words I never thought I'd hear Vivian Witchell say."

Something important tried to work its way to the front of her mind as she watched Charlie's lips curl into a smile. An event? An appointment? Something to do with the ad man? Something momentous happening today. Then Vivian slid her hand around to the back of Charlie's neck and pulled his lips to hers again. *Nothing as momentous as this,* she thought.

READING GROUP GUIDE

❖

1. How do you think Vivian's father's death during her teenage years affected her? How have you been affected by the loss of a loved one, either during your adolescence or later in life?

2. Radio performances became less popular once TVs became affordable enough for people to have at home, but today podcasts have surged in popularity and brought back some of the enthusiasm for storytelling in an audio format. Do you listen to podcasts? If so, what are some of your favorites, and how does the experience of listening to a story differ from watching it on TV or in a movie?

3. Was the revelation about Graham's personal life surprising to you? Do you blame him for not telling Vivian and encouraging their faux romance? What kind of challenges might he face as an openly gay man in show business in the 1930s?

4. *The Darkness Knows* is sponsored by Sultan's Gold cigarettes, and they play commercials during the broadcast. How do old advertisements compare to today's TV and radio commercials? Do you have any favorite commercial jingles?

5. Vivian finds herself attracted to both Charlie and Martin. What are the similarities and differences between the two men? What do you think Vivian finds attractive about each?

6. How is Vivian able to reconcile the memory of the father she loved with the fact that he worked for Al Capone? Have you ever discovered a damaging secret about someone you were close to? How did it affect your relationship with that person?

7. Did you suspect who the murderer was at any point before the revelation? What were the clues that pointed you toward one suspect over another?

8. What do you think Vivian and Graham's relationship will be like now that their staged romance is over?

A CONVERSATION
WITH THE AUTHOR

❖

Homicide for the Holidays **is the second book in the Viv
& Charlie mystery series. What were some of the
challenges of writing the second book as opposed
to the first? Were there elements of the storytelling
process that were easier this time around?**

I've never written a series, so that was the major challenge.
In a series, you not only need to keep the individual plot of that
particular book going but also keep all the balls in the air from
the previous book while planting seeds for all future books.

Homicide for the Holidays was half-written when I signed
the contract for the series, so I had most of the research done
about radio, the time period, and Chicago. That made it easier
to focus on the story itself.

**Why did you decide to include Al Capone as a
character in** *Homicide for the Holidays***? Did you learn
anything surprising about him as you were doing
research for the book?**

How could I write a series set in 1930s Chicago without mentioning Al Capone? Capone was actually in Alcatraz in December 1938, so it's really more the shadow of Capone and his era in this book. I based Vivian's father, Arthur Witchell, on a real life associate of Capone's named Eddie O'Hare (the father of the war hero Butch O'Hare and where O'Hare Airport got its name). I found Eddie's story first and then worked Capone into Arthur's story backward.

I think it's surprising how quickly Capone rose to the top and how short his reign in Chicago actually was. He took control of the organization in 1925 and was convicted of tax evasion in October 1931. In only six years he created such an international reputation that people still mention him today when I tell them I live in Chicago (along with Michael Jordan, of course).

What are some of your favorite films and radio shows from the 1930s?

Radio shows: *Jack Benny*, *Lights Out*, *Big Town*, *Burns and Allen*, *Lux Radio Theatre*, *Mercury Theatre on the Air*. My absolute favorite radio show, *Suspense*, didn't come on the air until 1942.

Films: *The Thin Man*, *My Man Godfrey*, *Bringing Up Baby*, *It Happened One Night*, *Top Hat*, *Swing Time*, *Red Dust*. (There are too many to mention, but I love anything screwball comedy, musical, or pre-code.)

Who are some of your favorite authors? Do you think any of them have inspired your writing style?

I was directly inspired to try my hand at historical mystery (with a dash of romance) by Deanna Raybourn and Tasha Alexander. I think everything I've read influences my writing style. I think what most directly influenced it, though, was writing notes to my friends in high school. I learned to inflect drama and excitement into the events of an otherwise boring fifth period study hall.

What do you think Vivian would be like if she had lived in the twenty-first century? Would she have a career or a family, or both? How would her relationship with Charlie change?

A woman in the 1930s usually chose one or the other—career or marriage and family (if she had the luxury to be able to choose). You don't see many women from that period that were successful as actresses and also had happy home lives. (Think Joan Crawford, Bette Davis, etc....) One or the other usually suffered. I'm sure there were women who made it work, but the gender roles were so much more rigidly defined then.

You see Vivian struggle with the idea of marriage in this book (and even more so in the next book in the series). I think it might still be a struggle for her in the twenty-first century, but her options wouldn't be nearly as limited. After all, I have a career and family (though I'm not entirely sure of my level of success with either...kidding), but at least I have the option.

I think her relationship with Charlie would probably be a little more relaxed in the twenty-first century. He's supportive of her acting career in the 1930s, but is a little threatened by her independence. I don't think that would be such a threat to him in the twenty-first century. I'd like to think Charlie would support Vivian's career ambitions—and also gladly cook dinner and do the laundry.

ACKNOWLEDGMENTS

Thanks to my agent, Elizabeth Trupin-Pulli, for being my champion. Thanks to my editor, Anna Michels, for loving my characters as much as I do and being the master of constructive feedback. Thanks to Barak and Kate, of course, for giving me the time and space to create. Thanks to my beta readers—Jessica Crawford, Marla Kelsey, and Julie Shaner Jones—who let me know if I was on the right track (or not) with my first few drafts of this book.

And finally, thanks to the readers who have reached out to me to express their own love of old-time radio. You're kindred spirits, all of you.

ABOUT THE AUTHOR

Cheryl Honigford is the author of *The Darkness Knows*, the Daphne Award–winning first installment in the Viv and Charlie Mystery series. She lives in the suburbs of Chicago where she enjoys listening to old-time radio, watching classic movies, tumbling down historical research rabbit holes, and living vicariously through her writing.